# The Buffalo
# Soldier

## Book 3 in the Clarence Duval Series

# Also by Rob Bauer

## Fiction

*My Australian Adventure*

*The World Traveler*

*Darkness in Dixie*

*The Long Way Home*

## Nonfiction

*Outside the Lines of Gilded Age Baseball: Alcohol, Fitness, and Cheating in 1880s Baseball*

*Outside the Lines of Gilded Age Baseball: Gambling, Umpires, and Racism in 1880s Baseball*

*Outside the Lines of Gilded Age Baseball: The Origins of the 1890 Players League*

*Outside the Lines of Gilded Age Baseball: The Finances of 1880s Baseball*

# The Buffalo Soldier

## Book 3 in the Clarence Duval Series

# Rob Bauer

Although some of the people who participated in the story of the Cree Deportation Act of 1896 described in this book were real people, this is a work of fiction. My portrayal of each character is fictional, and so are the events I've written about. This story should not be interpreted as an accurate description of the Cree Deportation Act or its participants.

This is a work of historical fiction. Names, characters, places, and incidents are the product of the author's imagination or are used fictitiously. Use of actual historical events, authentic texts, and names is of public access and public domain.

For any inquiries regarding this book, please contact Rob at robbauerbooks@gmail.com.

No part of this book may be reproduced in any form or by any electronic or mechanical means, including information storage and retrieval systems, without written permission from the author, except for the use of brief quotations in a book review.

For the Montana Métis and all those forced from their homes for the sake of someone else's profit and ambition.

The world needs to hear your stories.

# Author's Note on Language

One of the difficult things about writing historical fiction featuring African Americans is the use of racist language. Words that are painfully demeaning today were, sadly, commonplace usage in the era when this story is set. I've chosen to keep these words for the sake of historical accuracy. I mean no offense to any of my readers.

# Contents

# Chapter 1

## The Road East Is Closed

"Are you all settled, Mary?" Clarence says to young, brown-skinned Mary Healy while straightening the red ribbon atop her shoulder-length dark hair.

"Yes, Clarence. I'm so excited! This is the first time I've ever been on a train. Did you ever ride on one when you lived in Chicago?"

"Yeah, I got to ride them all the time when I was the mascot for the White Stockings. Maybe when we get to St. Louis to see your Uncle John, we can go watch a professional baseball game. You've never seen one, have you?"

"No, but I've wanted to ever since you told me about baseball. Sometimes, I see kids playing in the park with a ball, but they won't let me join them. They just yell at me to go away. I'm not sure why they won't let me play with them."

Clarence knows, all too well, why most of the children of Butte won't allow Mary to join them in their ball games. It's the same reason he rarely had any friends in Chicago growing up.

Instead of telling Mary, however, Clarence says instead, "Well, maybe we can see a game of baseball someday in St. Louis. We can go see the St. Louis Browns when they are in town. Or, we could just go watch your Uncle John at his games, even though he isn't a professional anymore. We'll have plenty of time to decide on our way there, Mary. It's a long trip to St. Louis, so you just get comfortable."

While Clarence and Mary talk, the train whistle blows for the final time, and it lurches into motion, laboring to pick up speed. Fleeting wisps of black smoke from the train's engine drift past the window as the noise from the moving train drowns out the muttering from the passengers nearby. There's also a light mist falling, just enough to darken the wooden train platform and leave tiny specks of moisture on the train's window. For a moment, Mary looks out the window, her eyes wide with excitement. Then she turns back to Clarence, young eyes sparkling while her small legs dangle from her seat, not quite touching the floor of the train car. Clarence can just see her worn, scuffed, leather shoes sticking out below the line of her cream-colored dress.

"Will we get there today, Clarence? I want to see my Uncle John very much. I've never met him before."

"No, Mary. Like I said a minute ago, St. Louis is a very long way from Montana. It's going to take us about two days to get there, I think. That's why we bought tickets for a train with a sleeper car, so we can rest on the way."

"When we get to St. Louis, will you and Uncle John try to free Ireland again?"

Clarence smiles at the memories this comment brings up. Not so much the memories from Nice, on the French Mediterranean, where he and John Healy, Mary's uncle, had formed a plot to kill the Prince of Wales and liberate Ireland from British rule. Those memories still frighten him, even today. Nor does Clarence smile at recalling the anarchist plot he nearly found himself embroiled in when he visited Paris a short time later. Instead, the happy memories come from two days spent in rural Ireland with John Healy a little more than six years ago, and a dance with a red-haired young girl who was just about Mary Healy's age.

2

Thinking back, the unlikelihood of it all astounds him, even today. He'd been a twelve-year-old boy then, orphaned and homeless. Yet, there he'd been, visiting the family of an Irish anarchist, parading around a bonfire while Irish music played and people danced, enjoying one of the best times of his life.

That day had been magical in so many ways. The dancing, music, laughing, food, and everything else. The most magical part, however, had been that for once, Clarence's dark skin hadn't seemed to matter to the people around him.

After musing over these things quickly, Clarence says, with a little laugh and a smile, "No, Mary, I don't think so. I don't know that we'll ever get another chance to free Ireland."

"Well, if you do, I want to help."

"I'll be sure to tell your Uncle John that you're with us," Clarence tells Mary as he tousles her hair playfully. This, of course, upsets the bright red ribbon, so he adjusts it again. "You might only be ten years old, but I was only twelve when I tried to help your uncle, so I guess that's close enough."

While Clarence tells Mary this, he smiles again to reassure her. Clarence doesn't know if she paid attention to all the angry glances and hostile whispers that occasionally were a little louder than whispers he overheard on the train platform while they boarded and took their places, but he hopes not. Clarence supposes the good citizens at Butte's Great Northern rail depot do not expect to see a colored person and a young Métis girl on a train in the sleeper section. She's still young, innocent, and hopeful; Clarence hopes that she can hold on to that innocence a bit longer before the adults of the world spoil it for her.

When the Great Northern train pulls out of Butte and steams northeastward toward the cities of Helena and Great Falls, Mary returns to gazing out the window. She just stares with a distant smile on her face, blissfully unaware of anything else. The train car they occupy features deep red carpets and plush, cushioned seats set inside a walnut frame. Clarence smells, if only dimly, the acrid odor of cigar

3

smoke as a handful of passengers move from his car to the smoking car next door.

The Rocky Mountains loom up on the left, so tall, solid, and immovable that Clarence has no doubt they'll still be there at the end of time. Their peaks are invisible today, however, because of the low-hanging clouds draping the city of Butte in a gray mist. Clarence guesses he isn't missing much. Old-timers in Butte told him that the mountainsides used to have trees, but now they barely have any because the mining companies cut them all down to feed their smelters, and the rest died, poisoned by the air of Butte. A few scraggily junipers are all one can see now on a clear day.

At least the clouds are natural for once. Clarence still remembers back six years, shortly after he came to Butte, in 1889, when the air itself sometimes killed people. The worst was in December of 1891 when the Boston and Montana Consolidated Mining Company built a copper smelting heap right in the middle of the city. The company laid down a layer of timber, then a layer of rock containing copper ore, then more layers of each, until the pile was several feet tall and covered an entire city block. Then the company set the heap on fire. It burned for three weeks. The fires burned, but the wind didn't blow, and so gray, irritating, choking smoke engulfed the city the entire time. The street trolleys put out lights and rang their bells all day and night to avoid collisions with people on foot who couldn't see anything through the smoke. Clarence later read that a local doctor named Heber Robarts attributed 200 deaths in Butte that year to smoke poisoning, mostly from people inhaling arsenic and sulphur dioxide. *No wonder some people call Butte "The Smoky City of Sin,"* he thought.

Looking over at Mary again, he's glad she's distracted by what passes by outside the window because as a few other passengers walk by, they scowl and mumble to each other, and this way, she won't have to see their hard eyes, the deep, angry frowns, the arms crossed over chests, or the shaking heads and wonder why they're so angry.

Still, Clarence thinks, the train is moving, and we're on our way. The car is almost full; he sees people sitting in nearly every seat when they depart, although a few leave their seats and go into the smoking car next door once the train is underway. *They can grumble all they want*, Clarence thinks to himself, *but Mary and I are going to St. Louis and leaving Montana.* He doesn't know if it will be for good, but it seems likely.

Nothing happens for the first few hours, and Clarence starts to think this will be a relaxing journey leading to a new start in life for both him and Mary. So far, 1895 has been a disastrous year for Mary's family, the Healys of Butte, which means it's been a rough year for Clarence, too. Now, in early September, he's hoping that the move to St. Louis will be good for them both. Things can't get much worse, at least.

They steam through Helena, Montana's state capital. Then Great Falls, on the Missouri River. Eventually, the train reaches Pacific Junction, where this branch of the Great Northern joins the railroad's main line and heads east toward Minneapolis. At the station, Mary and Clarence get off to stretch their legs and get some fresh air while passengers get on and the train adds some new cars.

The platform is all bustle and activity. Porters load baggage. Clarence sees sweaty, dirty men with blackened hands hauling coal to the train's engine and shoveling some into its supply bins. Women in white dresses fold their parasols and step aboard, their arms interlaced with those of their husbands. Some of the men flick cigar ashes to the platform before boarding, settling their derby hats and smiling through bushy mustaches. Others hug friends or family members goodbye, waving white-gloved hands as they step aboard the Great Northern train.

Although things seem immensely busy and chaotic, Clarence knows the train will resume shortly, so after a few minutes he gestures to Mary that it's time they return to their seats. They walk toward their car. Mary sees it first.

"Clarence, is that our suitcase on the train platform?"

He looks at the battered old container, its light-brown leather cracking and peeling from age and use, the brass coverings protecting its corners now dulled and smoothed with wear. It is one of the few possessions Mary's family had left to leave her after Mary's mother died. "I think so," Clarence says to Mary.

"Why isn't it in our room where we left it, Clarence?"

"I'll go find out. You stay here and watch it. I'll be right back. I promise, Mary."

Clarence boards the train in search of someone who can explain. Before long, he finds a conductor helping a man wearing a black suit jacket and black derby hat and his wife settle into the sleeping car he paid for.

"What's going on here? This is our room!" he shouts at the conductor.

"No, it isn't," he replies with a light Southern drawl. From Missouri, perhaps?

"What do you mean? Here's my ticket." Clarence pulls the ticket out of his coat pocket and brandishes it in the conductor's face. His lying, plump, red-cheeked, white-whiskered face just smiles back from beneath his black conductor's hat.

The conductor says, "I have a ticket for this couple right here, clearly marked for this sleeping car. You must have forged yours. Now, I suggest you leave, boy. I'm sure the paying customers find your presence here objectionable."

When he says this, both he and the man stealing Clarence's sleeping car draw back their vests just enough that Clarence can see their pistols.

"This way, boy," the conductor says as he grabs Clarence by the collar of his leather jacket, turns him around, and gives him a sharp shove in the back. Not satisfied with merely stealing Clarence's money, when they get to the door of the train, he kicks Clarence in the backside. Clarence tumbles down the steps of the train car and rolls onto the wooden station platform, cursing all the while. The platform is nearly empty by now, so the scene doesn't cause much commotion.

From the train, the conductor growls, "Get out of here, you nigger. And take your half-breed squaw with you."

While Clarence looks down at his skinned, bleeding hands, the train's whistle blows, and a few instants later, the metal behemoth staggers into motion, slowly at first, but gaining speed inexorably until it's out of sight. He's left sitting with Mary on the platform, bruised, bleeding, and pricked with a dozen wooden splinters that somehow penetrated his patched trousers. A faint whiff of burning coal remains in the air, settling over the platform. Clarence coughs. The one suitcase he and Mary share sits beside them. He looks at his hands again; little trickles of blood form. A few drops fall to the train platform, where they mix in with the small puddles from the light rain that seems to be falling everywhere in central Montana today.

"They stole our sleeping car, Mary. Just stole it from us."

"Now what do we do, Clarence?" Mary asks, her young brown eyes already glistening with tears. "Now how are we ever going to get to St. Louis to see Uncle John?"

"I don't know, Mary. Let me think for a moment."

Clarence, still seated, puts his head down, laces his hands over the back of his head, bleeding be damned, and closes his eyes. He's furious, of course, but with no sympathetic people around, it doesn't do much good. Shouting won't get their train berth back. Clarence doesn't want to lose his composure in front of Mary, either, because he doesn't want her to panic.

"Do you think that man in the uniform over there behind the window might help us?" Mary asks him after a few moments.

Clarence raises his head and looks to see at whom she's pointing. The man in the office window wears the uniform of the Great Northern Railroad. He won't help, Clarence thinks. He's probably the one who resold Clarence's ticket, just to make some extra money from the bribe he received in exchange. Briefly, Clarence hoped Mary might be pointing at a policeman. But then again, even if there were a policeman on the platform, he'd likely be in on the scheme, too, so no matter what, they're out of luck.

Clarence decides he'd better tell Mary the truth. "No, Mary, I don't think so. I think that man helped the man who stole our sleeping car."

"But how do you know, Clarence?" she sobs as the tears start rolling down. Her shoulders slouch while she sits on top of their suitcase. Mary puts her head in her hands while her elbows rest on her thighs.

"I rode the railroads a lot when I lived in Chicago, Mary. I just know it." It's a half-truth. Besides all the times Clarence rode the train traveling with the White Stockings, he often hitched rides on the railroads in Chicago when the conductors weren't looking. More than once, he overheard them talking about the ways they got rid of passengers they didn't like.

Clarence hates to admit to Mary that they have no options, but even as he gets ready to say so, the memories of Chicago trigger an idea. He sees another train in the yard and starts forming his plan.

"Mary, here's what we're gonna do. Follow me," Clarence says, a spark of hope returning to his voice.

They step down from the station platform and make their way onto the dirty, unpaved street. Clarence carries their battered suitcase while Mary trots behind. They both take care to dodge the horse droppings in the street as they step from one wagon rut to another. Even though it's misting today, it looks like the last serious rain here at the train depot was a day or two ago, so the mud isn't that bad, and the footing isn't too treacherous.

"Why are we going this way, Clarence?"

"Shh, Mary, just follow me and don't say anything," he says to her as quietly as he can without breaking stride.

Pacific Junction isn't a large town with lots of homes, but the railyard has a few extra buildings beside the stationhouse where the Great Northern keeps supplies for its trains, which is just what Clarence needs for cover. After he's passed several of the flat-roofed, whitewashed but dust-caked wooden frame buildings near the train tracks, he ducks into the space between two of them and motions Mary to follow. They crouch down for a quiet conversation.

"We're in luck, Mary. See those train cars over there? That's a freight train, and it looks like a couple of the cars are empty right now. What we've gotta do is sneak over there and jump inside one of the cars. We'll hitch a ride east that way and just hope that no one sees us. It's a train for freight, not passengers, so our chances are pretty good. We need to time it just right, though. When I tell you to, start running for that car there," Clarence points to show Mary which one, and she nods, "and I'll be right behind you."

Clarence thinks they're in luck. Someone even left the door to one of the freight cars slightly ajar. He thinks they can squeeze aboard, then shut it so no one sees them while they get away.

He waits for about fifteen minutes until he hears the first whistle and the locomotive's engine starts belching its trademark black smoke. Clarence looks at Mary; her tears are dry now, her eyes intent and focused. He's about to tell her it's time, when suddenly he hears heavy, booted footsteps scraping the soft dirt behind them.

"Hey, you there, what are you two doing?"

It's a policeman. The man is large and heavy, and although he's not excessively fat, Clarence thinks he can probably outrun him if things come to that. He doesn't know if Mary can, though, even if the officer didn't have a Colt at his waist, which he does. The man puffs smoke from a cigar clenched between his teeth and slaps his meaty left palm with a leather blackjack. Clarence's eyes follow a small flurry of cigar ashes that land on the officer's right shoulder thanks to a gentle breeze. Instantly, he decides their best chance is to play dumb. While Mary looks at him with questions in her eyes, Clarence rises from his crouch and steps forward.

"I'se sorry, suh, I'se dun gon an tunned de rong way. I thunk dis war de train platform, suh," he says, faking a Southern accent as best he can.

"Well, ya thought wrong, ya stupid coon. Platform's that way." The officer uses his blackjack to point back to where they just were. "Tell me," he continues, eying Mary, "what's a coon and an Injun squaw doin' looking for the train platform, anyway?"

*We must get out of this, quick*, Clarence thinks to himself. The train will leave soon, and then they'll be out of luck and stuck here. He doesn't see any other trains in the yard right now.

"We's goin' to meet mah paps. He comin' to take us home to Mis'ippi, suh." Clarence doesn't have a Southern accent at all because he grew up in Chicago, but he hopes this man won't know the difference if he doesn't say the words quite right. The tactic usually worked on the police back in Chicago, at least.

"Well, that's a good place for the two of ya, if ya ask me. Get back South where your kind belongs. We don't need no Negros here in Montana, no thank you, and the more squaws ya take with ya, the better we'll be. Well, ya gots some time before the next train arrives, I figure, but don't ya be causin' no trouble. I got my eye on ya both." The policeman emphasizes this last statement with another loud slap of his palm with the blackjack. Then he inhales deeply and blows a puffy cloud of white cigar smoke in their direction.

"Thank you, suh. You'se raht, suh, we jus' wants ta leave heah an go home. We gets to the platform soon. Thanks fo' showin' us de way, massa offisa."

The man just shakes his head while he moves off down the row of storage buildings and around the corner, mumbling something to himself. *It's probably best we can't hear whatever he's saying. We don't have time to listen, anyway*, Clarence thinks to himself. As soon as the officer is out of sight, he looks at Mary.

"Why were you talking funny like that, Clarence?"

"I'll tell you later. Go! Now!"

They sprint across the open space to their target freight car, Mary moving just as fast as her little legs can run while Clarence struggles to lug their suitcase alongside. The train's already begun edging forward. Because Clarence needs new shoes just as much as Mary does, the dark gray and black gravel of the railroad yard bites into his feet as he runs, bruising them. Then Clarence hears a shout.

Trying to look over his shoulder without slackening his pace too badly, he sees the overweight officer running after them. Well, he's not really running; a lumbering trot better describes the man's movement as he puffs after them, cheeks already flushing from the effort. That's not as important, however, as the fact that the man unholsters his Colt while chasing them.

Luckily, Clarence has almost reached the train when it starts moving. He gets to the door of the car just before Mary does, but just when he thinks they might make it safely, the officer fires his weapon. No!

Looking over his shoulder once again, Clarence looks to see if the policeman hit anything. He and Mary are in luck when the officer's aim is poor. When Clarence doesn't hear the bullet strike anything, he assumes the policeman must've fired too high.

Not waiting to give the man a chance to correct his aim, Clarence heaves their suitcase upward and forward and breathes a sigh of relief when he hears it thump into place inside the car. Just one sigh, however, because even as he grabs the floor of the moving freight car and hoists himself aboard, he turns to see Mary struggling to reach the train. Her young arms flail wildly, and she gasps for breath, her long dress trailing out behind her while she runs. Clarence squats down at the edge of the car and extends his arms for her as far as he dares. "Reach, Mary! You can make it!"

Another shot. Mary screams when it hits right behind her and splinters of a railroad tie burst everywhere.

Clarence knows that if they wait any longer, Mary won't get aboard, and she'll be at the mercy of the angry policeman. He shouts to Mary once again, "Reach!"

With a final effort, she does, and Clarence grabs her tiny, trembling hands. Success!

Before he can pull Mary up, however, she trips on a railroad tie, and her legs go out from under her. Clarence isn't expecting this and doesn't have a chance to brace himself. He loses his balance and starts falling forward off the train.

Just as Clarence feels the downward pull of gravity mixed with Mary's weight start to topple him from the freight car, a strong hand grabs the collar of his leather jacket and yanks him up! The hand's strength is enough to pull Mary off the ground and onto the train, too.

A moment later, standing safely inside the train car and momentarily lost for words, Clarence turns around to see his savior. He appears to be an Indian man, maybe thirty-five years old, and bears a pink scar diagonally across his forehead.

"Welcome aboard," the man says with a crooked smile. "Whose company will I be sharing this ride with?"

"Thank you," Clarence manages to pant as he puts his hands on his knees, still struggling to take in everything that just happened. "Where did you come from?"

"And I might ask the same of you, my friend," the Indian man says. "Louis Berger," he says, extending a hand for Clarence to shake. Not the kind of name Clarence expected. Louis pronounces his name with a strange accent. It's like French, but not exactly, so his last name comes out sounding bur-gee.

Mary exclaims, "Hey, you're Michif, just like me!"

The men both look at her.

"I can see your sash," she says by way of explanation, proudly pointing at the man's waistband. "I used to have one, too, back when my dad and granddad were still alive."

Louis Berger smiles at her. "You two are in luck. If you hadn't of almost crushed me when you tossed your suitcase on board and it landed right by my ear, I might never have woken up in time to see you try to jump aboard, and then I couldn't have saved you. Lucky for you that I left the door ajar on accident when I climbed in myself. Speaking of your suitcase, let's close the freight car door and then sit down while we finish our introductions. Formerly, this was a car for shipping cattle, I'm afraid, so it's not going to be a very comfortable ride when it comes to smell, but the price is agreeable, I'm sure."

Only now does Clarence notice that stray pieces of straw cake Louis's tan, creased, leather vest, as well as the animal smell in the train car. He hadn't noticed either in all the excitement.

Louis looks like a man who's spent his share of time outdoors. Although not old, lines crease his face, his clothes are well-worn, and his boots are a dark brown leather. Louis looks like he could be a cowboy but has no hat over his dark hair. Clarence and Mary follow his suggestion, and soon they're watching the Milk River Valley pass by through the slits in the side of the car while the train chugs east.

When the conversation resumes, Louis addresses Mary first. "You said you were Michif, young one. Who were your parents, my *nitanis*?"

"What does that mean, *nitanis*?" Mary asks him.

"It's a term of affection, my little dear."

Mary smiles, then tells Louis about the Healys of Butte and about who her mother's parents were. She talks about how her mother's parents, her Irish grandfather and Chippewa grandmother, met and came to Butte, and how they, along with her mother and father, were all dead now. He nods, and then Clarence describes to him why they ended up stealing a ride on this train. Only after Clarence finishes the story does he realize how tired he is after all the day's drama. When he finishes, he gives a big yawn.

Louis sees it, too. "Well, the two of you have had a busy day, to say the least. Why don't you sleep a bit? I'll keep watch and wake you should anything important happen."

Clarence agrees and sits down, his head against one wall of the empty freight car. It isn't easy getting comfortable enough to sleep on a noisy, rocking, clattering freight train that still smells of animal waste, but he manages it. Mary sits down beside him, and soon, they've both dozed off. Clarence goes to sleep thinking they might make it to St. Louis after all.

# Chapter 2

## Left in Havre

Louis startles Clarence and Mary awake, frantically tugging at their shoulders. Clarence feels like he's barely even closed his eyes. "Clarence, Mary, wake up! Quickly!" he says to them in a harsh whisper.

"What is it?" Mary asks, her eyes slowly refocusing to the reality that's she's lying in a cattle car.

"An inspector is coming around. We've got to run for it!" Louis says in the same whispering voice.

While Clarence gathers himself, Mary, and their suitcase, he asks Louis, "Where are we? I don't feel like I slept more than a minute or two."

"That's because you were only out for about fifteen minutes. We've only made it as far as Havre."

After Clarence helps Mary to her feet, he looks through the slats in the side of the freight car. The track bends a bit in the Havre railyard, so he can see forward to the front of the train. Sure enough, a man in a uniform walks slowly toward them. "He's got a rifle."

"Run when he stops to look in the next car," Louis says to them.

"Yeah, that's what I was thinking, too," Clarence replies. To Louis's raised eyebrows, he responds, "This isn't the first ride I've hitched on a train, either." Louis gives Clarence a mischievous grin.

Clarence turns and whispers to Mary. "Now, when it's time, Louis will open the door. You jump down and run over there," he points, and she nods. "We'll be right behind you. I don't know if the inspector will try to fire or just scare us away, but try to keep the train cars between you and him just in case, okay?"

Mary, her mouth set and eyes focused on Clarence, gives a determined nod.

"That's my girl," Clarence says while removing a stray piece of straw from her hair.

"Get ready," Louis whispers to everyone. "Go!"

Louis tries to slide open the door slowly and smoothly, so it won't make any noise, but it squeaks a bit despite his efforts. Just when the trio leaps down and starts toward the edge of the train depot's railyard, the inspector jumps down from the car he'd been looking inside, and he spots them.

"You there! What're you doing?" he yells. "I'll teach you to steal a ride on my train, you damn Indians," the inspector shouts next while he grabs the rifle he'd set on the edge of the freight car before jumping down.

Clarence is colored, not Indian, but he doesn't wait around for that nuance to register with the inspector. Instead, everyone ducks under the metal bar coupling their freight car to the one behind it and runs.

After a short distance Clarence hears a loud click. He glances back to see what the inspector's doing. The man takes aim at them. The click must've been him levering a bullet into the chamber of his rifle. Clarence tries to get between his aim and Mary just as the rifle fires, the report as loud as a thunderclap.

At the sound, Clarence's body shivers in anticipation, and he braces for the worst. The inspector doesn't hit him, however. Instead, he hears a loud "thunk" sound when the bullet goes right through his suitcase.

"Don't run in a straight line!" Louis shouts to Mary and Clarence. They can see he's moving first to his left, now back to his right, while he runs away.

Another loud click. Clarence tries to run diagonally, but the weight of the suitcase in his right hand unbalances him, and he stumbles and falls to his right. He glances back again, just in time to see the inspector take aim and pull the trigger for the second time.

Another shot rings out, but this one passes between Mary and Clarence and hits nothing. It might well have hit Clarence, had he not fallen. Clarence thinks his heart is about to explode from the tension. It beats so hard in his chest he can hear it in his ears. He gives a quick look at Mary while he stumbles back to his feet. She's crying again but running her best zig-zag all the same, her hair and dirty, cream-colored dress trailing out behind her. Clarence doesn't know why he notices now, but the red ribbon is gone.

They reach the edge of the railyard, running north toward the Milk River. *If we can just get to the river, we should be able to disappear into the trees along the riverbank*, Clarence thinks to himself. He can see the tops of some of them from where he is, their green and gold leaves fluttering in the light breeze.

They're just about to clear the crest of a low hill and drop down toward the river's edge when the inspector fires for the third time, and Clarence sees Louis go down off to his right, clutching his left shoulder. Louis cries out.

"Mary, keep going to the river!" Clarence shouts to her. "We'll catch up to you in a minute."

He veers right to help Louis to his feet. Louis's eyes show great pain when he looks up at Clarence, but he simply grits his teeth and says, "I'm all right. Keep going." Blood drips down the left side of his leather vest and white cotton shirt, staining both a dark crimson.

Clarence pulls Louis up by his right arm, looking back at their assailant at the same time. Clarence can just see him from here over the edge of the hill. The inspector stares at them now, barrel of his rifle pointing skyward, as if satisfied that he's shot enough Indians for one day. Louis and Clarence run down the far side of the hill, out of his sight, into the trees and underbrush near the Milk River's edge. Louis's left arm dangles at his side.

They run along the river for a short distance and find a stand of aspens where they can take cover and hide in the undergrowth. Most of the small, circular aspen leaves are still green, but a few have turned golden with fall on its way. They wait for several minutes to see if the inspector decides to pursue them after all, but it appears he figures he's done his duty. Once their heartrates slow down a bit, they can hear the beautiful sound of the aspen leaves rustling in the breeze just over the constant gurgle of the river.

"Now what do we do?" Mary says in a panicky voice.

"I'm sorry," Clarence says to Louis. "How badly are you hit?"

"Not as badly as I thought. The bullet just scratched me, that's all. Look."

Louis removes his right hand from his left shoulder, so Clarence can see his injury. There's some blood there, quite a bit of it, but he's right. The bullet merely grazed him, and the wound isn't deep. The bleeding has slowed already.

"I think I just fell down from the shock of getting hit. I've been shot worse than this before," Louis announces to everyone.

Then he looks Clarence in the face. "Don't worry; it's not your fault. That inspector would have found me whether you were along for the ride or not." The question Clarence has been thinking in his mind must have shown in his face.

"But what should we do?" Mary asks again, pleading in her little voice. "Now how will we ever get to see my Uncle John in St. Louis?"

"We'll think of something, Mary," Clarence says to calm her down, even though he has no idea what they should do.

Louis says, "Follow me. I know where we can go."

# Chapter 3

## Remembering Old Friends

Clarence sits on the nearly-frozen ground outside the shack built from coulee logs and plaster that leans badly to one side. He thinks about how he got here, sitting in a draw in northern Montana, trying to take shelter from the chill of the night. It's only late September in the year 1895, but cool night air and the fierce, unrelenting wind make this a cold evening, indeed. Another shiver wracks his body as the wind blows over his short, fuzzy hair. The moonlight is bright enough that Clarence would be able to see his breath puffing out in front of him, but the searing wind drives the vapors away too quickly. What the temperature feels like out on the high plains, away from the shelter of the draw, Clarence can only imagine. He pulls the dark brown buffalo robe closer to his chest, trying to seal in a little warmth, and thinks to himself again, *It's only September. It can't be this cold and windy already.*

But, it is. Although Clarence doesn't mean to stay too long, he's come outside for a breath of fresh air. A few dozen paces away, the fiddle music plays on inside the cabin. It's a merry tune, almost like Irish jig, but not quite. The fiddler, a Métis man named Pierre

Ouellette, referred to the style as *une gigue métisse* when Clarence asked him what he called the music. Clarence feels a bit too much sadness for a jig tonight, however. Melancholy. Old Newton MacMillan taught him that word to describe these feelings, back when Clarence took lessons from MacMillan and Nellie Williamson on reading. Those lessons seem like a very long time ago now, even though it's only been six years.

Clarence knows he should probably go back inside the cabin and rejoin Mary before she comes outside in the cold to look for him, but he doesn't. He's not ready yet. The cabin isn't all that much warmer than it is outside, anyway. Between the gaps in the plastered log walls and the fact that they're saving most of what firewood they have for the real Montana winter, warmth is hard to come by anywhere this evening. Instead, Clarence pulls out his wallet from his pants pocket under his buffalo robe, his almost-numb fingers struggling to unfold an old newspaper article.

Creases from years of folding and unfolding crisscross the yellowing paper. It's an obituary from a Philadelphia newspaper, the *Philadelphia Public Ledger*, dated May 21, 1891. Although it's too dark outside to read the paper, Clarence memorized it a long time ago. The title of the obituary simply reads, "Sporting News: Fogarty Dead."

Jimmy Fogarty had the best sense of humor of any man Clarence ever met, and for a few weeks back in 1889, Fogarty was his friend while he traveled the world. Clarence saved Fogarty's life once, when they tried to climb Mount Vesuvius in Italy and the volcano almost erupted, but nothing could have saved his life in May four years ago. According to the newspaper, Fogarty arrived in Philadelphia from his home in California in late February to try to earn a spot playing baseball for the Phillies but checked into a hospital instead, believing he had pneumonia. In fact, it was tuberculosis, and Fogarty died on May 20, just a few months after turning twenty-seven years old.

The obituary isn't very long because Jimmy never married, and he left no family behind, but Clarence keeps it with him more than four years later because of what it reads a few lines down the column. At the end of his life, Jimmy insisted that if he died, his friends had to bury him wearing a dark blue bandleader's hat he always kept with him. That was once Clarence's hat. He still remembers the day when he gave it to Jimmy, more than six years ago in Chicago. When Clarence said goodbye to him, and Clarence's other best friend from his travels, John Healy, that day, he never imagined it would be the last time he'd see Jimmy. Clarence gave his hat to Fogarty and his marching baton to Healy, so they would have something to remember him by.

At the memory, Clarence sniffles a bit and blinks back a tear. He was only twelve then and had a little bit more youthful optimism in those days. How could Jimmy be dead at such a young age? When Clarence knew him, Fogarty had this glow around him, almost, as if life could throw anything at him and he'd never get a scratch. *Maybe he just ran out of luck without me*, Clarence thinks to himself. "Awooo," he howls softly out loud, the way Jimmy taught him to do.

Clarence wonders if Healy keeps his old baton in his house in St. Louis. If everything had gone according to plan with Mary and the trip east, he'd know the answer by now, but it didn't. Healy told Clarence he would keep his baton, but Clarence hasn't heard from him for some time. After he wrote Healy to say he was coming to St. Louis with Healy's niece Mary, Clarence had to leave before he could get a reply. It's been three years now since Healy last pitched a major league baseball game, Clarence thinks, but more importantly, two years since Clarence last saw Healy's brother, Thomas, in Butte.

When Clarence parted ways with Healy and Fogarty, he told them he'd decided to head west, and so John suggested he stay with Thomas in Butte until he settled in. Clarence did, and he and Thomas became good friends, especially after Thomas learned of all the adventures Clarence had had with John when they traveled around the world together. Thomas thought their plans to free Ireland from the British were nuts, of course, but he said he admired their spirit. Looking back, Clarence is pretty sure Thomas was right about the plan's wisdom.

It's been two years since Clarence last saw Thomas's gravestone, he corrects himself. Thomas died in a mining accident in the summer of '93; a cave-in trapped him and a few other men in their tunnel for days. By the time anyone could reach the trapped miners, they were dead. From the state of things, it appeared that falling rock crushed Thomas's ribs and left leg; he probably died right away. *Better than starving to death or asphyxiating*, Clarence thinks to himself, *but still, what a frightening way to go out, with a mineshaft falling all around you and knowing you have no way to escape.*

Thomas's death started Clarence on the path to this patched-up, tarpaper-and-plaster winter shanty in Montana's Milk River Valley. Of course, the copper mine where Thomas worked, the Anaconda, gave no compensation to his widow. The families of the dead miners sued Anaconda for taking improper safety precautions in its mine, but Anaconda claimed that a cave-in was part of the risk that Thomas accepted when he took the job. The Montana courts found in the mine owners' favor. They always did. That's how the courts work in Montana. Anaconda buys the judge, and the judge clears the company of wrongdoing while workers die. The copper keeps flowing out of the mines, and the profits pile up. The profits pile up for everyone but the miners, that is. Too late, the Healys and Clarence learned that the angry Australian miners Clarence met long ago in Ballarat had it right all along. Yes, they had it right, even if they almost killed him.

A sound breaks Clarence's reverie for a moment. Just an owl, he thinks, or maybe a hawk landing somewhere nearby. Soon, it's quiet again, except for the ceaseless whistle of the wind. Clarence tries to control another shiver but fails. He smells just a whiff of smoke from a fire in another cabin nearby, but in a moment, it's gone.

When Thomas died, the rough times began for the Healys in Butte. Thomas's widow, Mary's mother Louise, had no way to support herself without him. Clarence chipped in what he could from doing odd jobs around town. He swept floors in saloons, delivered groceries to society women, unloaded freight for the dry goods merchants, washed windows in hotels—you name it, he probably did it. Except for one job. Louise forbade Clarence to go into the mines after what happened to her husband. Copper mining was one of the few jobs in Butte he never tried, and he's happy that he never did. Sometimes he gets claustrophobic underground anyway, so he didn't mind it when Louise said she wouldn't let him do that.

Louise Healy never got over her loss. She took to drinking—morning, noon, and night, when she could get it. Then, in March of this year, she shot herself in the head. Poverty wasn't what made her despair enough to take her own life, though, Clarence believes. He thinks it was the way Butte treated her. Because her father was Irish and her mother Chippewa, Louise was Métis, but the people of Butte referred to her as a half-breed, or worse. Louise's parents married and came to Montana back in the buffalo days of the late 1870s and settled in Butte once the hide hunters killed off the buffalo for good. Louise was her family's third child, but the first to live past infancy. She ended up being an only child after her mother got pregnant for a fourth time and then died in childbirth, along with the baby. A few months later, a drunken timber cutter shot Louise's father dead in an argument over a gambling debt.

Thomas Healy was a large, burly, barrel-chested man who wasn't afraid to use his fists. He always stood up for his wife and defended her honor. There were a few times when he stuck up for Clarence, too, when Clarence first came to Butte as a youth. Without Thomas to watch out for her, however, the abuse and the insults grew too great for Louise, and she finally gave in. Clarence thinks she was drunk the night she put the Colt revolver in her mouth and pulled the trigger.

After Louise died, that left just Mary and Clarence, and because Mary was only nine years old at the time, Clarence tried to take care of her the best he could. Before long, however, he realized he couldn't do it himself and that Mary needed her family. So, Clarence used the last money he had to buy the two of them train tickets to St. Louis, so Mary could live with her Uncle John, and Clarence could look for another new start in life. His thoughts drift back to that fateful day when they boarded the train, the corrupt railroad station employees who stole their car from them, trying to hitch a ride on the freight train, and then that train inspector who nearly shot them for all their trouble. Clarence's spare set of clothes still has a hole in it from where the bullet passed through their suitcase.

After that, Louis Berger led them from Havre to this cabin in the Milk River Valley. Several other Métis families live here with them. Or perhaps Clarence should say that they live with the Métis, since he and Mary are the homeless ones. Back when the buffalo still roamed free across Montana, the Métis used these shacks as winter shelters while they hunted. Now that no more buffalo remain, however, they are the only homes that many Métis people have.

"Clarence?" It's Mary's voice. He hadn't heard her come outside and sneak up on him. It was hard to hear anything because the frigid wind blew the sounds away. She says to him, "What are you doing out here in the cold? The fiddle music is so nice inside. I want to dance with you."

"Okay, Mary, we can dance for a while," he tells her. "Remember Jimmy Fogarty, my friend I told you about before? I was just thinking about him, and my adventures with your Uncle John, and how we got here, that's all."

"Are we still going to go to St. Louis in the spring and see Uncle John?" she asks him.

"I hope so, little dear. Louis tells me that a group is going to travel to the Turtle Mountains in the spring. He thinks we can get to St. Louis from there."

While Clarence tells Mary this, he thinks again about how Mary is a very bright young girl. She has the tan complexion of her mother, the same dark, straight hair, and most of her delicate features appear Indian despite her mixed background. She isn't very tall yet, but Clarence thinks she will be someday because both her parents were. He also thinks she'll be a very beautiful woman in time. *What a shame*, he thinks to himself, *that white society will never accept her*.

His mind switching back to their immediate situation and need to get to St. Louis somehow, Clarence also thinks about what Louis said about how some people he knew had participated in something called a Wild West Show earlier this year. Louis believed they might be able to travel with some of the Métis to get to St. Louis if someone tried producing a similar show again next spring. He's skeptical of this plan because he doesn't think anyone will let a colored person like him join the show, and he's vowed not to lead any more parades. The Wild West shows are supposed to feature Indians, not colored people, anyway. Louis also said how the men who hired people to be in the last show were frauds but that Clarence might still use them to travel as far eastward as he needed to go.

Once again, Mary brings him back to the present. "Can't we go sooner, Clarence? It's really cold here."

"I know it is, Mary. I know it is. I'm scared, though. After how you almost died last time we caught a ride on a train, I'm scared to try to do it again. And we have no money left to buy a ticket."

"I'm sorry, Clarence. I promise I won't trip and fall next time."

"I know you didn't do it on purpose," he tells her. "But by next spring, you'll be older and more prepared. By that time, you're gonna be big and strong, like a bear, or a buffalo, and then you'll be ready."

While Clarence tells her this, he picks her up, spins her around twice as her little legs kick the air, and then sets her down and takes her hand as they walk back toward the cabin. Mary giggles, then curtsies and waits for him to enter at the door of their shack. She follows him inside and then drags the door shut.

As they dance, Clarence tries to put off thinking about how they are going to survive until the spring. He doubts if even the buffalo robes Louis gave them will be enough against the Montana winter.

# Chapter 4

## Charles Hartman

Montana's sole member of the United States House of Representatives, Charles Hartman, sits at a polished oak desk in his Washington, D.C., office, looking at a stack of letters and newspaper articles that has been building up for some time. *I've finally done it*, Hartman thinks. Just to make sure, he looks through the stack one more time, starting with the oldest documents, and replays the sequence of events in his mind.

First, there's the article from the *Anaconda Standard*, dated January 11, 1895. It's titled "Those Pesky Crees: Cascade County Wants to See Them Deported." True to what he'd told Hartman he would do late in 1894 when they last met, Montana governor John Rickards gave a speech calling for the deportation of Montana's Cree Indians to Canada. The Montana legislature signaled its approval immediately thereafter. Hartman focuses on the key lines of the article, which he's underlined in careful pen strokes: "That portion of the governor's message which recommends that the legislature take some action looking toward the deportation of the Cree Indians struck a responsive chord in this section, where these marauders for the past 10 years have been troublesome." Hartman also had underlined the reason they'd been troublesome: "These unpatriotic feelings are prompted by the fact that the Crees are renegade Indians, who hastened to this country after the collapse of the Riel rebellion, in which they are understood to have played a part, in order to escape the wrath of the Dominion authorities."

Deep down, Hartman knows the actual amount of marauding the Cree have done in ten years is minimal, if any, but the *Standard*'s white readers would believe just about anything when it came to Indians, and the tone of the piece hit the nail on the head. *Besides*, thought Hartman, *it was high time to do something about the renegades, marauders or not*.

Within a week of receiving this news clipping in January, Hartman had convinced his friend in the Office of Indian Affairs, Daniel Browning, to petition the Canadian authorities for the deportation of the Cree. The next day, Browning shared the letter he planned to send to the Canadian Indian commissioners in Regina, which Hartman found quite satisfactory. It stated that, among other depredations, bands of lawless Cree were hunting in Montana's Flathead Valley out of season and that large bands of more than 100 Indians would steal from Montana settlers and ranchers and then escape north of the international boundary before United States authorities could catch and punish them.

Hartman picks up the next news clipping and frowns. No, not frowns. Scowls. He feels his pulse pick up a bit and his cheeks flush as he reads. After this promising start, the Montana legislature had then made a mistake. In late February, it petitioned Governor Rickards, in a joint memorial, to ask the U.S. Congress to consider a solution to the Cree problem. Hartman blocked this from ever taking place. Far too many softhearted congressmen still remembered Wounded Knee. In their weakness and misplaced compassion, they might cry out, "Lo! The poor Indian," should things ever come to a debate in Congress. These so-called "friends of the Indian" just might succeed in attaching an obscure rider or amendment to a bill, creating a reservation for the Cree in Montana, or, more likely, putting them on an already-existing reservation. It is unthinkable. Hartman, and the state of Montana, can accept no solution short of deportation. Immediately on receipt of this information, Hartman had telegraphed governor Rickards, telling him that he must reject the memorial and laying out the reasons why.

Rickards rose to the occasion in his rejection of the joint memorial, stating that Montana could never approve accepting the Cree as wards. For one thing, the governor said, their unlawful conduct would have a destabilizing effect on the partly-civilized Indians already dwelling on Montana's reservations. Furthermore, offering sanctuary to some bands of Cree would only encourage the migration of more Canadian Indians claiming to be Cree into Montana, thus taxing Montana's resources. Finally, how could the state of Montana continue its plans to open more of the existing reservations to white settlement if more savages settled there? The governor closed with another call for the complete removal of the Cree from Montana, for good and forever.

*It was a quality performance by Rickards*, Hartman thought. Rickards had been wise enough to use Hartman's rationale almost word for word, and the vote to override the governor's rejection, mustered mainly by opposition Democrats, failed. Hartman's friends in the press did their part in sustaining the governor, too, with the *Anaconda Standard* opining,

Apparently, Governor Rickards has the right grip on the Cree Indian business. The bill he has vetoed is in the nature of a compromise under the terms of which these pests who belong on the other side of the border might remain in Montana. Thus far, the effort of the state to rid Montana of these invaders has not met with success—it is reasonable to assume, however, that, in time, if the question is pressed, the federal authorities will take it up and do what manifestly ought to be done.

Yes. Do what manifestly ought to be done. Hartman knew no better way to put the matter than that.

After all, Hartman reasoned, how could Montana, which had been a state only since 1889, tolerate these miscreant Indians wandering about within its borders? They must go, for the safety and security it would afford good, productive, God-fearing white settlers. The good, or lives, of a few small bands of heathen red men carried no weight in comparison. No one in Montana would miss them; most would be happy to see them go. Hartman was already doing his utmost to promote a homestead boom in his state. If word got out of Indian problems, the boom might never materialize, Montana's population would stagnate, and Hartman might remain the lone Montana representative indefinitely.

Putting such an unacceptable thought aside, he read on. Reading the next article, from the *Fergus County Argus*, Hartman curls his lip in distaste. He would have spat in disgust, too, had he kept a spittoon in his office. He almost spat anyway. A Helena dreamer, Don Davenport, had organized a "Wild West Show" in the spring of 1895 and hired these vicious Cree to travel east in the show and perform. Hartman shakes his head vigorously and slaps his desk in frustration. Ever since Bill Cody had started touring the U.S. and Europe with his show back in '83, small-timers and hucksters throughout the West had tried imitating him just to make a dollar, putting together shoestring, rag-tag outfits and wild schemes to play on people's Old West nostalgia.

Hartman scowls angrily and clenches his fist tighter the more he thinks about people like Davenport. Didn't these amateurs and con men understand how much damage they did? It was 1895! The frontier era was over. For good. The Bureau of the Census had said as much in 1890. It is time to get on with development, agriculture, and manufacturing. Montana's future is copper mining, short horns, homesteading, and railroads, not Indians. Yet, here were these small-town imitators trying to beguile modern people with Indians, teepees, and who knew what else?

Starting to seethe, Hartman clenches his right fist again, knuckles whitening and fingernails denting his palm. Davenport had even hired a half-breed as interpreter, the damn fool, selecting a multilingual Métis Big Timber rancher named Robert Jackson for the job. Trouble was, Jackson was legitimate. He'd scouted for generals Miles and Custer during the Great Sioux War in 1876-1877, he was smart, and he knew his work. Back in the early days of Lewistown, when an outlaw known only as "Rattlesnake Jake" had tried to take over the town, Jackson had been among the posse who shot the ruffian dead in the street. Jackson had plugged the outlaw four times with his Winchester if the stories were true. A risk existed that someone like Jackson might provide the actors in the show with enough guidance that they'd seem legitimate to the hayseeds in St. Louis, Chicago, and Cincinnati who still thought that everyone in Montana traveled by covered wagon and cooked meals over an open campfire. Hartman's clenched fist pounds the table, his silver cufflink making a clicking sound as he does so.

It didn't matter that Davenport's show had been, by all accounts, a failure that didn't pay and that by June, the show's organizers were already in arrears in their promised payments to the relatives of those Cree who had gone east. These shows helped shape the public image of Indians and, for the sake of entertainment, portrayed these thieves and vagabonds more as noble savage than murderous savage. Take, for instance, the reception that Davenport's miserable crew received in Joliet, Illinois, in May. Some unnamed scoundrel for the *Chicago Daily Inter-Ocean* wrote of the Cree: "A tribe without a country! A people without a home! A nation of absolutely homeless wanderers upon the face of the earth—not one of them with a resting place they can call their own. A race willing and anxious to work for themselves, their wives and their children, but no one that could or would give them employment." Later in the news article, the nonsense and rot continued when describing the return of the renegades to Montana after the treacherous Riel Rebellion of 1885:

They were made the scapegoats of all the criminals in the territory. If there were any horses or cattle stolen, the crime would be laid to the Crees. If they attempted to settle upon a piece of land and work it, about the time the first good crop would be ready for the harvest some white man would come along and take up the land and drive them off with the crops still in the ground, and the Cree could get no redress. That they were peaceable and industrious, they have dozens of letters from army officers and other authorities to show.

Before the unnamed author finished, he also heaped praise on Little Bear, the so-called chief of the Cree, for his nobility and grace. It was an outrage! Hartman pounds the table a second time and curses aloud.

The cursing brings the sound of scurrying feet and a soft knock at his door. "Is everything okay, Mr. Hartman?" calls the soft, submissive voice of Hartman's secretary. She pokes her head through the heavy wooden door.

"Yes, I'm fine. This paperwork is just dreadfully dull stuff, I'm afraid, especially when it's the Gold Bugs of your own party who are the problem," he answers.

Just then, Hartman realizes how much he's begun to sweat in the heat of Washington, D.C. It is almost October, but every now and again, the weather reminds one of July and August, and today is one of those days. His windows stand wide open, but there isn't much breeze outside, so it isn't enough.

"Can I bring you another cup of coffee, or today's newspaper, Mr. Hartman?" she asks. "Or some water, maybe?" she adds, noticing his perspiring face.

"No, I'm fine for now, thank you. Keep that newspaper handy, however. I'll need it eventually, my dear."

If he really needs a drink, Hartman always has something good stashed in the liquor cabinet against the opposite wall. He finds it's always a good idea to keep some quality Kentucky bourbon on hand.

Hartman might need some before today is over, too, because the gold standard Republicans have been beating the Democrats with the currency issue too often lately.

His secretary hesitates in the doorway for a moment, adjusting her glasses. "What's a 'Gold Bug,' if I may ask, Mr. Hartman? I hear people say that term often, but no one has ever explained it to me so that I can understand."

"Most Republicans want to circulate money solely based on the gold standard," he replies. "Many of the Democrats want to print money based on both gold and silver. The people who want just gold are the Gold Bugs."

"But you are a Republican. Why aren't you a Gold Bug?"

"Yes, I am a Republican. I'm not a Gold Bug because I represent Montana and Montana has many silver miners. I'm standing up for the interests of my constituents like a congressman is supposed to, even though most of my own party is against me in this case."

"Is that why you've been talking to Senator Carter so often lately?"

This is too much inquisitiveness for Hartman. He has indeed had many conversations lately with Thomas Carter, a fellow Montanan, the former Chair of the Republican National Committee, and now a U.S. senator, but he has no desire to explain things any further. Defining what Gold Bug means for a confused woman, he can handle, but a congressman does not explain his actions to a secretary. "That's a conversation for another day, I'm afraid. That will be all for now. Just keep track of any correspondence coming in like I've asked you to."

"Whatever you'd like, Mr. Hartman," she answers as she softly closes the door to his office.

Why did he even have a female secretary? Hartman's colleagues ask him this question sometimes when drinking after a day of work. Most assume it is for the occasional bit of sexual gratification, although he thinks the woman rather plain. For many men that doesn't matter, but not Hartman. He is a married man with two children who loves his wife, for one thing, and for another he can't afford for his opponents to tar him with scandal while taking part in a minor revolt within his own party over the silver issue. In addition, the woman is good at her job, never complains, and doesn't ask too many questions. Other than today, at least.

Hartman pauses for a moment to consider the irony of the situation. It was the Republican Gold Bugs who had applied the greatest pressure to repeal the Sherman Silver Purchase Act back in 1893. They claimed repeal and a strict adherence to the gold standard would put the nation on a sounder economic footing, when in fact the United States economy nearly collapsed during the depression that began that year. It is now late in 1895, and the depression still hasn't gone away, but his party continues pinning its political hopes on gold. In truth, Hartman doesn't know if coining silver will help or hurt the nation's economy. He doubts whether any of his colleagues know for certain, either. Hartman understands, however, that people in Montana want to resume coining silver, so he must favor coining silver, too. That will give him enough credibility and support among the voters to pursue his real goal, getting rid of all the Cree Indians in Montana.

Recovering from the distraction, he eyes the next news clipping in his stack. Another piece, dated April 10, from the *Anaconda Standard* bid the Cree "Au Revoir" as they left with Davenport's show. Hartman particularly enjoys one section of the article, which reads, "The governor should not let the present opportunity slip to tender to the departing Crees some slight token of the peculiar esteem in which the people of Montana have held them. A fitting testimonial might take the form of a carload of chloride of lime, or some other good and powerful disinfectant." That brings a smile to Hartman's face. The article concludes, "We may never see these Crees again. The chances are we will, but a benign and inscrutable providence may intervene. Farewell, O Crees, farewell, and if forever still farewell, and please send back for the rest of the tribe at your earliest convenience." A week later, the same paper announced the departure of the show to Illinois from Havre. It was fine sentiment, but of course, the failure of the tour meant that Montana would see these miserable people again.

In addition, having 100 or so Cree leave for Illinois left plenty of scum behind in Montana. By the end of May, the *Anaconda Standard* reported ten teepees of Cree camping near Anaconda, scavenging from the Anaconda dump and slaughterhouse while trying to sell trinkets to the locals. Some of the locals, it appears, had sold them alcohol in return, which Hartman approves of. The drunker the Cree became, the more depredations they'd commit, and that meant people's attitude toward them would grow more hostile. Why didn't the *Chicago Daily Inter-Ocean* report *that* to its Eastern readership?

Then Hartman thinks about that yearly abomination, the Sun Dance, with which the Cree defile Montana each year. This past July they'd chosen to curse the growing town of Havre with their four-day bacchanalia of pagan idolatry. Hartman's stomach churns at this new thought. Once again, nearly a thousand savages gathered in hedonism, performing self-mutilation and other worthless rites to appease their heathen gods and generally making life miserable for the good Christians of northern Montana. Then, they'd troupe off to some other destination in the state, Great Falls or Helena, perhaps, and raid the garbage dumps there for a while.

Hartman is nearly at the end of his stack of news clippings now but pauses a moment to look over one of his favorites. It is another piece from the *Anaconda Standard*, this one titled "Didn't Pay." Not only had the organizers of Davenport's Wild West Show abandoned the Cree whom they'd hired, but they'd also abandoned them without pay. In addition, Davenport left them in Cincinnati in July with no funds to get home. What brilliance! Sadly, however, the article also reported that the Cree had found a way around their problem. They hired themselves out as an attraction in the Cincinnati Zoo, spending several weeks alongside the giraffes and other creatures, to raise the funds needed to return to Montana, and by mid-July, they were back. These people are just like cockroaches; you can never quite get rid of them, no matter how hard you try. Even when caged in a zoo, they still find a way to escape.

This brings Hartman to the final article in his file, dated just about two months ago, in August. Apparently, some ranchers and stockmen in the Great Falls area had managed to concoct evidence that the Cree were guilty of cattle rustling. The evidence, as described by the *Anaconda Standard*, would certainly not stand up in a court of law, completely circumstantial as it was. This bothers Hartman a bit. He is a member of the United States Congress, after all, and supposedly he should concern himself with upholding the laws he's voted for as a member of that body. However, it only bothers him a little bit when people take matters into their own hands where Indians are concerned. The article reported that a local group of about 400 whites was preparing to drive the Cree into Canada or kill them, should any further evidence of rustling appear. The same group of men also pledged to drive the miserable thieves from Montana after the beef roundup if the Cree didn't heed the proper warnings and depart voluntarily by that time.

While Hartman replaces the file folder with these news clippings in his filing cabinet, his secretary knocks again and pokes her head into his office. "Mr. Hartman, Senator Carter is here to see you. Oh, and sir, I think you'll want to see what happened according to the Montana newspapers that arrived by post today. They all have something to say about those Cree Indians you always talk about."

# Chapter 5

## Gabriel Ouellette's Story

The mid-October dawn blossoms slowly and majestically over the broken plains of Choteau County, Montana. The concentrated clouds on the eastern horizon are a deep pink, blending to red, almost as if nature was blushing over how badly it had treated the Milk River Valley the previous few weeks with its unseasonable cold. Today, however, the temperature is considerably higher, with the wind in the south, and it promises to be the first warm day in quite some time. Clarence has a fishing pole while he and Gabriel Ouellette trudge over the crunchy, half-thawed blue grama grass toward the Milk River in search of trout.

"Clarence, how come you didn't go on the deer hunt with the rest of the men?" Gabriel asks him.

"I didn't learn much about hunting game growing up on the streets of Chicago. I decided I'd leave the hunting to the professionals."

"I know you don't have much practice at it, but don't you think you'd better learn before winter sets in? You can't ever predict these Montana winters, Clarence; you just never know when you'll need to bring down some game just to feed yourself and Mary."

"How come you aren't hunting, then?"

"Because I'm no good at it, either," Gabriel says with a big grin and a quick laugh. "My daddy, Pierre, is a crack shot, but he says I need more practice before I can go. I don't think I'm as bad as he says I am, but I guess his standards are pretty high."

"How old are you, Gabriel?"

"I'm gonna turn twenty-two pretty soon. How about you?"

"Eighteen. I've lived in Montana for six years. Did I ever tell you about what I did when I was twelve?"

"Someone told me you got to sail on a ship on the ocean."

"I did, all the way around the world. Those were some of the best days of my life, sometimes, but at other times they were some of the worst."

"You really got to play baseball in other countries?"

"Well, not exactly, Gabriel. I was the mascot for the teams. The mascot doesn't get to play in the games."

"What does the mascot do? I've never heard of a mascot before."

"The mascot is supposed to bring good luck to the players. The players thought I was lucky, so they brought me along." Clarence doesn't tell Gabriel that he also danced and marched in parades. He doesn't want to relive those memories with Gabriel, at least not yet.

Gabriel goes on. "You got to travel all the way around the world just because you were lucky?"

"Baseball players are a very superstitious group. I've known players who have lucky mustaches or lucky numbers. One player only ate chicken before games and refused to eat anything else, so everyone just called him 'Chicken,' even though his real name is William."

"Do they believe in bad luck, too, Clarence?"

"Sure. Of course, they do. If you are bad luck to someone else, they call you a 'Jonah.'"

"Where does that name come from?"

"I think it has something to do with the Bible, but I've never read the Bible, so I can't say for sure."

"You can read, though, can't you, Clarence?"

"I can."

"Will you show me how someday? I want to learn to read and learn to play baseball. It sounds like a fun game."

By this time, they've reached the river and are setting up to cast in their lines. The air is so still this morning, save for an occasional light breeze, that hardly a ripple breaks the perfection of the water as it rolls by.

Clarence looks over at Gabriel after his last question. Gabriel is a little short for his age, but so is Clarence, and they're about the same weight, too. Clarence stands five-foot four-inches, which is three or four inches shorter than most men, and Gabriel is about the same. Gabriel is thin and wiry, as well, but he's tougher than he appears. Clarence has seen how much work he does in a day. Gabriel's face looks boyish, so one wouldn't guess he was nearly twenty-two, and his dark hair reaches almost to his shoulders. Clarence isn't sure if he'd make much of a baseball player but doesn't say that to him.

Instead, he tells Gabriel, "I'd like to teach you to play. It *is* a fun game. I'm not sure where we'll ever get a real ball to play with around here, though. It takes some money to buy them, if they're even available in this part of Montana, and we don't have much of that. Maybe we can make a ball out of something and give it a try someday." *If I had any spare money, I'd use it to buy another train ticket for Mary and me and get us out of here*, Clarence thinks to himself.

The conversation pauses while both young men bait their hooks with worms and cast them into the river. For a moment, they can enjoy the growing warmth of the sun and the beauty of the prairie, its golden tallgrasses wavering ever so slightly, with no one else in sight. Except for a pheasant that decides to break cover and fly away, the silence lasts ten minutes or so while they sit breathing in the brisk, clear, invigorating air and wait for a bite. When nothing happens for a while, Gabriel resumes speaking.

"Did I ever tell you about what I did when I was twelve, Clarence?"

"I heard your dad was part of the Northwest Rebellion in Canada. Were you in it, too?"

"The Northwest Resistance," Gabriel corrects Clarence. "I didn't fight in the Battle of Batoche like my father, but I scouted for Louis Riel all up and down the Saskatchewan River Valley. Father made me get out of there when the fighting started, though. Told me to ride hard and gallop south on my horse, to get back to Montana. He said he wasn't afraid to hang if he was captured, but I was too young for that."

Clarence smiles. "Yes, the Northwest Resistance. Thanks. Did you know I met one of your opponents that day, General Strange, when I was on my way around the world?"

"Butcher Strange," Gabriel corrects again. "Daddy told me all about how many women and children that man killed on his way to the battle. It was as though Satan possessed him. He was that cruel."

"He lost his military commission because of his cruelty, if that makes you feel any better."

"It doesn't, but I'm glad to hear you say it, all the same. How on earth did you end up in his company, anyway, Clarence?"

"He was traveling as a civilian to London, hoping to clear his name and get his rank back. I never heard whether his efforts were successful. In any case, he was aboard our steamer and one day he decided to tell the ballplayers the story of the army he led against the Resistance. They all sided with him, naturally. Well, most of them did. I imagine Mary's uncle John Healy did not, although I was unaware of his political loyalties at the time."

"His army," Gabriel says indignantly. "You mean his vigilantes. Murder women and children and loot their homes. That's all his men did, the damned villain."

"What did you do after the battle?" Clarence returns to where their conversation began, still waiting for a fish to bite. He doesn't have much experience at fishing, any more than he does at hunting, so he watches while Gabriel jerks his line now and then. That teases the fish into biting, Clarence supposes, and he does his best to copy Gabriel.

"My father told me to leave before the battle began, and I did. He got away, too, and we made our way back to Montana, where we lived before the Resistance began. We didn't have much to come back to, however. The buffalo were all but gone by that time, so the hunting wasn't enough to support our people like it used to be."

"Hearing about people killing all those buffalo makes me sad," Clarence interrupts. "I've only seen photographs of them. Have you ever seen a real one?"

"Yeah. Sure. I saw plenty of them when I was little."

"Are they as tremendous a beast as they look?"

"I'm not sure what you mean by tremendous, but they were fast, powerful, beautiful animals. That's why we Michif developed Red River carts, you know, so that when we killed buffalo, we could take the meat and hides back to our camp. The Michif invented the Red River cart, and no one else had them unless we shared how to make them. I know they don't look as impressive today, when white people have railroads to move things around, but at one time, they were the best thing going out here on the plains."

After lowering his head in thought for a moment, Clarence says, "I hope I'll get to see a buffalo someday. Do you think some might still be alive, maybe down South somewhere?"

"I don't know. I hope so, but these whites want to kill everything that moves, so I doubt it. Maybe now, all you can do is read about them in schools."

"That's a shame."

Now it's Gabriel's turn to pause a moment. "I did go to school a little bit when I was younger. For about a year or so, I was at the school at St. Peter's Mission over near the Sun River. I didn't like it there, though, so I decided to come back and live with my father again. They didn't want me to leave, but I sneaked out one evening. I was lonely there."

"I know what you mean," Clarence says, remembering his own brief stay in an orphanage and all the nights spent by himself on the Chicago streets after the Chicago police killed his best friend Tommy.

Gabriel continues. "After that, I thought about going back to school once or twice, but because we moved around a lot, traveling to the Turtle Mountains and back, I never had too much time for learning. After what happened this summer, though, I think I'd better try again."

"You were with the group that was in the Wild West Show, weren't you?"

"I was, yeah."

"What happened to you on the trip, exactly, Gabriel?"

"A bunch of us hired on to be part of 'Beveridge's Montana Wild West Show' earlier this year. Our main chief, Imasees, who the whites call Little Bear, even joined the show. I know it hurt his pride to be a show attraction and have to fool around to amuse the whites, but the promoters said we were going to play Washington, D.C., so he agreed to go."

"What kinds of things do you do in a Wild West Show?" Clarence wonders.

"Stupid things that white people find amusing and will pay to see. The actors fight pretend battles, but the Indians and Michif always must fight with bows, arrows, and tomahawks, never with rifles like real people use, and then after the pretend fighting the performers do what the promoters call 'Indian Dancing.' All that means is that we put on beadwork and feathers and stomp around for a while. We'd never show our real sacred dances just for the entertainment of the whites, but most of them are too stupid to know the difference. They think it's the real thing. Then you try to sell them some trinkets at the end of the show to make some extra money. It's all cheap junk, of course, but most of them never realize they've been taken in."

"Why was going to Washington so important to Imasees?"

"Imasees wanted to make our people's case to the government. His goal was, and still is, to get recognition from the national government in Washington for the rights of our people, and hopefully a reservation so that we have a place to live now that the whites have killed all the buffalo. We never made it that far, though, Clarence. We left Helena in April, and we performed in Joliet and Chicago in Illinois, plus New

Orleans and St. Louis. But, when we got to Cincinnati, the tour ran out of money, and the promoters just skipped town and left us there. I think the men who organized the tour realized it wasn't making as much money as they had hoped, so they just took the cash on hand and got out of town one night. We were stuck in Cincinnati with no way to get home and no money because the promoters hadn't paid us in some time."

Gabriel spits in disgust while recounting his treatment. Clarence slowly shakes his head in sympathy. Then Clarence says, "You might not believe it, but that is sorta how I ended up going around the world. I was part of a company of actors back in 1888, and we were touring the country, but when we got to Omaha, in Nebraska, our tour leader just decided she didn't want me no more and let me go. The baseball players I toured the world with found me the same day. I take it your story doesn't have such a happy ending though, does it?"

"No, it doesn't. We were stuck in Cincinnati with no money, so we had to do something to get home. With no other options, we hired ourselves to the Cincinnati Zoo."

"You were in a *zoo*?" Clarence asks incredulously, his voice rising just a little on the last word. "Like, in the cages with wild animals?"

"Sometimes, yes. There were four cages. We were in one, surrounded by elephants, giraffes, and tigers. We stayed there six weeks, in a cage at a zoo. Here, look at this."

Gabriel hands Clarence a folded handbill printed on brown paper that he extracts from one of his pockets. He tells Clarence, "My father said to keep this and remember the humiliation, so I'd never trust white people again. Read what it says at the top."

Clarence looks down at the creased paper and begins reading. "The exhibition of wild people is in line with zoology, and so, when we exhibit Indians, or any wild or strange people now in existence, we are simply keeping within our province as a zoological institution. Securing a village of wild people for the remaining season will not only be of vast educational value, it will be a profitable investment."

Clarence hands the paper back to Gabriel, whistling in surprise as he does so. Gabriel folds it again and places it back into his pocket. "Even Miss Jarbeau never treated me that badly," Clarence tells him. "How did you finally get back here?

"After six weeks we'd earned enough money to ride the railroad back to Havre. We danced for the white people who came to the zoo, sold our horses, and got a few sympathetic donations from the whites who pitied the 'poor savages in their desperate plight,' or whatever nonsense they told themselves." Gabriel spits again for emphasis. "A railroad strike in Chicago delayed our trip home, too, but we finally made it back to northern Montana. Now that we're back, though, I don't know what we're going to do. We're still broke, the whites still hate us, and we don't have a real home."

"What about your mother, Gabriel? You've never said anything about her. Did she go with you in the Wild West show?"

"No, she died when I was born. I never got to meet her or talk to her."

Clarence is just about to say something else when, just on the edge of hearing, he notices a faint horn blow and then popping noises, louder than the horn. They sound like gunfire. He looks at Gabriel. "I hear it, too," Gabriel says as they both drop their fishing poles and sprint back toward the cabins.

# Chapter 6

## The Milk River Pogrom

It doesn't take Clarence and Gabriel long to run back to their homes, but by the time they get there, chaos reigns. They see the smoke from the fires first, gray-black and angry-looking as it rises into the morning sky. A posse of rough-looking, grizzled white men gallop about on horses, passing this way and that through the little cluster of shacks. It looks like thirty or forty men in all. Clarence notices some of the shacks burning already—the source of the smoke.

Gabriel and Clarence pull up just on the edge of the draw and drop to their bellies to get a look at what's happening, peering through the bunchgrass that's turned brown as summer gives way to fall. It doesn't seem that any of the riders have noticed them yet. "What do we do?" Clarence asks, his chest rising and falling as he heaves for air. "Has this ever happened before?"

"Yeah," Gabriel gasps out a response while catching his own breath. His eyes dart about frantically, like Clarence's, taking in the frenzied scene, so Gabriel can judge what to do. "We've got to get a horse and get out of here," he tells Clarence after a moment. "Follow me, and I'll show you the way." Still skirting the edge of the ravine,

Gabriel runs toward the small corral where the horses neigh and dart about in their fright at all the gunshots and commotion. He runs hunched over, trying to stay low and out of sight while circling the edge of the draw, darting between large rocks whenever possible.

Clarence starts out following Gabriel, but then he remembers. He needs to find Mary and get her to safety! By chance, he's near to their cabin, and he still doesn't think any of the riders has seen him yet. A short distance away, he watches several of them enter the Ducharme cabin. It looks like they are looting what few possessions are in it because random household items fly through the open doorway in rapid succession. Clarence also hears the repeated screams of Clemence Ducharme coming from inside her cabin. He doesn't know much French, but he knows enough to understand when he hears Clemence scream "No!" and "Stop!" between her cries.

He hears another gunshot, and another scream. Francois Laverdure's wife, Marie, kneels at the entrance to the horse corral. She is trying to unfasten the rope holding the gate closed, but now she bleeds profusely from her left shoulder, clutching it in pain where one of the ruffians shot her. Marie's right hand covers the entry wound in her shoulder, but blood spurts from the exit wound in the back, staining her pretty, sky-blue linen shirt and pooling on the ground behind her. She screams something through her pain, but it's in Michif, so Clarence can't make out the words. Just as Marie looks up, toward her attacker, right hand extending in a plea for mercy, another vigilante comes up behind and shoots her directly in the center of her back. She drops to the dusty ground, twitches once, and then lies still, a pool of blood slowly staining the earth around her a dark crimson.

Just then, the door to Clarence's cabin bursts open, and Mary runs out. "Clarence!" she yells. "Clarence, help me!" She must have been watching for him through the cracks in the cabin walls, Clarence decides.

He can't blame her for it because she is only ten and frightened out of her young mind, but her shout draws attention, and a handful of the riders finally notice Clarence's presence.

"Look! Over there! Shoot the girl, and the nigger, too!" one of them, a man with a bushy brown beard and several missing teeth beneath his slouch hat, yells while he spurs his horse in their direction.

Another vigilante, also mounted and closer than the first, levels his rifle at Mary. Even as Clarence moves to protect her, throwing himself between Mary and the gunman, he can see the shooter curl his finger and pull the trigger. Just as he does so, Clarence launches himself through the air, jumping in front of Mary to shield her.

At the same instant, Clarence hears the loud, sharp crack of the rifle firing, and the bullet strikes him. He hits the dirt with a light thud, spinning around and landing on his stomach.

Seconds later, a third member of the posse also shoots at Mary, but his aim is poor, and he misses, even as Mary screams again and kneels next to Clarence. "Clarence, are you dead?" the young girl sobs hysterically as she tugs at his left arm.

Rising to one elbow, Clarence looks down at his left leg where the bullet struck him, trying to suck in some breath. From the pain and shock, he expects that a big chunk of his leg is missing. It turns out the bullet only grazed him, and the wound isn't deep. Painful as hell, but the bullet shattered no bones, and the bleeding is moderate.

"Quick, get inside the cabin!" he gasps to Mary while pushing her in that direction. Clarence can hear their attackers cock their rifles for another shot.

Fortunately, the door is only a few feet away, and Mary left it open when she ran out. Mary jumps through it. Clarence limps inside after her, left leg trailing, losing blood as he does, and then grabs the door and pulls it shut, just as several more bullets strike the front of the cabin. He hears wood and plaster splinter. Some shards hit him in his chest.

Clarence looks down at Mary. She's on the floor, whimpering and crying, arms cradling her head.

Frantically, Clarence looks around, trying to figure out what to do. The white ruffians have trapped them here, and he has no guns to fire back. He hears the horses of their attackers circling the shack. They can't even lock the door to protect themselves because the door has no lock.

"What do we do, Clarence?" Mary asks him in a pathetic, panicky voice. "Why are the men shooting at us?" Her tears continue flowing freely. "You aren't going to die, are you Clarence?"

Before he can answer, Clarence hears one of the men outside shout, "Hey, let's set the cabin on fire and smoke 'em out! It'll be just like a turkey shoot!" The others shout their agreement.

Moments later, Clarence and Mary hear a thud, and something lands on the roof. Instantly, the bone-dry prairie grass used to fill in some of the cracks in the log-and-plaster walls goes up in flames with a whooshing sound. The coulee logs that roof the shack are very dry, too, so in moments, they burn as well.

Clarence has no time to make a plan, so he shouts to Mary, "Here's what I want you to do, Mary. I'm gonna burst out the door and try to draw their attention. We can't stay here. When I do, you run for the edge of the draw, get as far from here as you can, and don't look back, okay? Try to find a good hiding spot and wait for me there."

"But what about you, Clarence? You can't leave me!" Mary grabs Clarence's shirt and shakes his arm, the fear palpable in her shaking arms.

It hurts Clarence to lie to her, even now, as the end of his short, miserable life approaches, but seeing that neither of them are likely to live anyway, he tells her, "You just run, and I'll find you as soon as I can. You remember our fishing spot? The one down at the river? I'll meet you there as soon as I can get away."

"You're lying!" she screams hysterically. "Don't leave me all alone, Clarence!" Her small hands, with their skinny fingers, latch onto his arm again, frantically tugging at the coarse fabric.

Then, they both take note when their attackers toss a couple more pieces of wood onto the roof of the shack. They hear a series of dull thuds, and shortly, the mud plaster starts falling around them. In another few moments, the coulee logs that serve as the roof start to shift and crack. It's getting smoky and hard to breathe inside the cabin.

Clarence and Mary both cough after inhaling the acrid smoke. Even though they are both crouched down, as far from the burning ceiling as possible, Clarence's eyes water. Another piece of mud plaster falls from the ceiling and hits his right arm.

Clarence looks over at Mary and nods. It's time to face the end. She's still crying a bit, but sets her mouth in grim determination, an angry look in her gaze. "When you see your Uncle John in St. Louis, tell him I was brave, okay?" Clarence says to her.

He limps over to the door, hopping on his good right leg because his blood thoroughly soaks the left leg of his blue trousers, and leans up against it, blinking his eyes to hold back the pain and keep the smoke from irritating them. "You run just like I told you to, Mary, you hear me?"

She nods and walks to Clarence's side. He takes a hop back and lowers his right shoulder, so he can ram the door as hard as he can and force it wide open. From somewhere deep inside, Clarence lets out a roar and launches himself toward the door.

Just as he does so, the walls of the shack shift slightly, the doorframe included, and when he strikes the door, Clarence bounces back. It's jammed! Not prepared for the impact, Clarence falls backward to the packed earth floor of the cabin, screaming in pain. They're stuck inside a burning house.

Through his curses, Clarence can hear the men outside taunting them. "Come on out, nigger, and get what's comin' to you!"

"What's the matter, boy? You can't even open a door? I knowed your kind was dumb, but I thought even a nigger could open a door."

Another crack! One of the ceiling beams lurches, and mud plaster rains down on them. A hot, burning coal lands on Mary's right shoulder. She screams and brushes it away.

Mary looks at Clarence, terrified, mutely pleading with her eyes for him to do something, but he's still lying on the floor of the cabin, coughing from the smoke and gritting his teeth against the pain in his leg. There's nothing else to do except try again, however. Clarence is about to say so when a bullet strikes the side of the house, sending more splinters flying.

He hears one of the men say, "I'm tired a waitin'. Let's make it hot fer 'um."

"You got it, Jed! Come on out, boy! Whoo-ha!"

Another rifle blast rips through the noise of the burning shanty. This time the bullet passes all the way through one wall before striking solid wood on the opposite side.

"Come on Mary, we've got to try again," Clarence says in despair. His eyes burning and watering from the smoke, he pushes up to one knee. He braces for another lunge to try to force open the door.

Just as he does, Clarence hears another barrage of rifle fire, except that this time, it seems to be coming from farther away. One of the voices outside yells out, "Are you hit, Tommy?"

Another voice answers, presumably Tommy, "Those Injuns up there on the ridge is firing at us. Get 'em, boys!"

The hunters must have come back! Clarence turns to Mary and manages to cough out a few words through the choking smoke. "Now's our chance, but we've gotta be quick. Come on!"

Again, he hurls his body at the door. Smack! It wedges open a few inches. Clarence draws back and tries again. Success! They're free. "Come on, Mary! Come . . ."

Before he can finish speaking, a roof beam cracks in two, with one half descending in a fiery arc. It collides with Mary's head just as she gets up to follow Clarence. She cries out, falls back to floor, and lies there, silent and motionless.

"No!" Clarence shouts, limping to her and kneeling on the floor, pushing the smoldering beam off Mary's legs. "No, Mary . . ."

Cursing again, he cradles Mary in his arms, lifting her frail body up before her clothes or hair catch on fire, and then drapes her over his right shoulder. Clarence staggers, burdened by Mary's extra weight and his injured leg, out into the sunlight. For a moment, he stops to take in the scene while he gets his bearings and breathes in some clear air at last.

Almost every log shanty in the small village burns. A couple of them have already collapsed. Clarence sees several bodies; almost all appear dead. Young Jean Latreille, a seven-year-old boy, tries to drag himself on his knees and elbows to the rim of the draw a short distance away, but his wound is severe. One member of the white posse shot him in the back. It doesn't appear he's going to survive. Jean limply falls into the dirt, face down. A little swirl of dust curls outward from his mouth as he takes his last breath.

Clarence looks up to the rim of the draw opposite from his location. The party of hunters starts falling back. The ruffians outnumber them badly, and the hunters no longer have the element of surprise. They'll scatter across the prairie and regroup, but Clarence knows that means he must move quickly if he's going to make it because the murdering band won't stay distracted much longer.

No, wait. If *we're* going to make it. He won't accept that young Mary is dead. Clarence limps and staggers in the other direction, away from the action. When he turns to flee, he looks to the horse corral to see if any horses remain. Almost all of them are there, and the gate's tied shut. Then the reason hits him. The white gang plans to steal the horses, too, so they are keeping them penned in one place. Clarence notices the man guarding the corral. Fortunately, he has his back to Clarence while he watches the action between the hunters and his friends. Still, Clarence can't get a horse to escape with while he's standing there.

It seems like it takes forever, but Clarence reaches the edge of the draw and starts to climb out. Mary is too much weight, though. With his injured leg, he can't get up the steep slope and carry her on his back, too. He bends over and gently sets her on the ground. When he does, her brown eyes perk open. "Clar . . ." she starts to say, but he puts his hand gently over her mouth and shushes her.

"We're trying to get away," he says quietly. "Quick, now. Can you walk?"

She stands up, a bit wobbly at first, but then regains her balance and nods.

49

In another minute or so, they've climbed out of the ravine and turn to look back. Just as they do, they see their former shanty collapse on itself with a dull roar, sparks leaping high into the air. Just a few more minutes, and they'd still have been inside.

Clarence motions to Mary. "This way." He's trying to run, but the pain in his left leg has increased and he's dragging it behind him. His right calf burns from the extra effort of hopping as quickly as he can, but Clarence knows he can't stop here. He doesn't how they'll get far enough away to avoid capture or death if the vigilantes come after them. They won't be hard to find if the posse tries, considering the trail of dust and blood Clarence leaves while he staggers along.

Then he hears a whistle from off to their right. It's Gabriel, and he has a horse! From how cut up he is, it appears he had to fight to get it, but Clarence decides now is not the time to ask Gabriel about that. Gabriel gallops over, and soon they are putting all the distance they can between their attackers and themselves. They have no food, Clarence is wounded, and Mary has a tremendous headache, but they're alive. For now.

# Chapter 7

## The Camp

The night of their escape, Gabriel, Mary, and Clarence sit around a campfire, trying to figure out what to do next. Each stares off into the lightless expanse of the northern Montana prairie. The stars are out, shining in thousands of tiny bursts of light.

"We have to go back in the morning, don't we?" Gabriel offers. "We have to see how many were killed and if we can salvage any supplies. The survivors will scatter and regroup. That's always been our strategy whenever the whites attack and destroy our homes like this."

"This isn't the first time this has happened to you?" Mary asks him in surprise, her voice rising on the last few words.

"No, it's the third time just for me. My father has survived several more attacks just like this."

"But what are we going to do now?" Mary asks plaintively while she massages her bruised head. "Our homes are gone, and now we're on our own. And I'm cold."

Clarence puts his arm around her, even though he knows it won't help much, and then says, "I'll put a bit more wood and dried grass on the fire. Probably, we're far enough away from anyone that no one will notice our fire, sheltered here in this ravine like we are. However, I think Gabriel is right. We need to find out if the vigilantes left anything useful at our camp. We won't last very long without some food or somewhere to live."

"At the very least, we can get our fishing poles back," Gabriel says, "and maybe catch something to eat. I don't know if the murderers will come back again, but now that they've destroyed our homes and taken most of our horses, I doubt it."

"Why did the awful men do that?" Mary asks her companions, her young eyes glistening with reflected firelight and forlorn tears.

Clarence looks toward Gabriel, who looks down at the ground where the wispy, skeletal shadows of the buffalo grass dance in the breeze and the shifting firelight. After a few moments, Gabriel looks up at Mary and tries to explain. "Mary, the white people hate us because we're different from them. You know how your mother's parents were part Indian and part white and how a lot of people in Butte hated her because of it?"

Mary nods.

"Well, having a mix of parents is what makes us Michif. Our ancestors are a mix of Indians and Europeans. Except the whites, they call us half-breeds. When they even bother to notice we aren't full Indians."

"But why do they hate us so much? Why did they shoot Clarence?"

"Because we don't look like them. The whites think that all Indians should live on reservations and that all the whites should be farmers or ranchers or live in towns. They don't think that we should live the free life, hunting the buffalo like Michif people have always done. So, they killed all the buffalo with their rifles and began moving in to occupy our lands. Now, if you ride south of the Missouri River, where the buffalo used to roam, all you'll see are ranches with cattle instead."

"How come you don't have a reservation to live on?" Mary asks him.

"Because of our mixed bloodline the United States government doesn't think we are real Indians. So, we don't live on a reservation like real Indians do. Some people also call us Cree Indians, even though we aren't."

"How come?"

"According to my father, the U.S. government calls us Cree because the Cree are supposed to live in Canada. If people believe that we are Cree, then we are trespassing here in the United States, and people believe that justifies trying to get rid of us. That's what the men today were trying to do, I think. Get rid of us by destroying everything we have or killing us so that we'll move away."

"Why are people so mean and angry?" Mary asks sadly, her bright eyes hoping for an answer she can make sense of.

"Mostly, I think they want more land, so they can make money from it," Gabriel tells her. "Whoever is in their way, the whites just ignore them or push them away, so they can run more cattle or plant wheat."

"How come you don't go to Canada, then, and get away from the bad men?" Mary questions.

"The Canadians don't want us, either. And it's dangerous for us to go there because of some things that happened about ten years ago."

"What are we going to do, then?"

"Like I said, Mary, I think we should go back to our camp in the morning and see what we can find. How is your leg, Clarence?"

"Not as bad as I feared. It hurts a lot, and it's stiff, but the bullet didn't hit anything important. I've lost some blood, for sure, and it'll be a while before I can walk normally again, but I think I'll live."

The three homeless companions huddle close around the fire the rest of the night, with nothing but hard-packed, dry earth for a bed. Sleep comes eventually for Clarence, but his nightmares return. Ever since he was a young boy living on the streets of Chicago on his own, he's had nightmares, especially after something bad or stressful happens. In this one, he's back in the burning cabin with Mary, but in the dream, he's fast enough to stop the falling log from the ceiling, and it doesn't hit her on the head. However, when he goes to force open the door, it opens just before his shoulder strikes it, and he stumbles, face down, to the ground. When he looks up, men with guns stand all around. Their eyes are coal-black. All of them.

Clarence wakes with a start and jolts upright. The fire is dead, and it's very cool in the open air, but he's sweating under his leather jacket anyway. He tries to move his wounded left leg a bit. It flexes slowly, painfully, and stiffly. Clarence feels the wound throb a bit still, but it's tolerable. Blood stains the bandage he applied by tearing off part of his shirt, but all the blood is dried, so the bandage did its job. Flexing his leg hasn't caused any new blood to seep through the bandage, so perhaps the wound is as superficial as Clarence hopes.

He rubs his hair, a gentle film of dust settling over his shoulders when he does. Another gentle film of dust, he should say. It cakes Clarence's clothes. He looks over at their horse, its reins tied to a lone tree a few feet away. It perked its head up when it saw Clarence sit upright, but now, seeing nothing important is about to happen, the horse lowers its head again.

Clarence tries to sleep a bit more, but the temperature is too cool, and the pain and stiffness in his leg are too much, so instead he stands and limps around a bit. It's nearly dawn. He can see the eastern horizon as the first traces of light appear. He's not sure what to do. Perhaps, when they return to the camp, some of the other Métis people will be there, and they can plan something, but with no homes to return to, he has no idea what that plan should be.

While Clarence stands and watches the horizon grow lighter, gold and yellow slowly brightening the eastern sky, he tries to understand what happened yesterday and remember everything he saw. Some things stand out in his mind. He can picture the rough men who destroyed the camp, of course. What engraves their faces indelibly in his memory, though, is the fact that not only did they destroy the village but also that they looked so *happy* when they did it. Clarence remembers the pleasure in the eyes of the man who shot him after he saw Clarence bleeding and the way the men surrounding the burning cabin compared killing them to hunting turkeys. Then, he thinks of the look of triumph on the face of the man who shot Marie Laverdure, an unarmed and elderly woman, in the back from five feet away. In his mind, he still hears the screams of Clemence Ducharme and remembers how the ruffians looted her cabin even as some of them raped her.

Back when he was a kid on the streets of Chicago, Clarence saw people fight sometimes, of course. When people live on the street and have nothing to eat, sometimes they get desperate. Those people had the look of beasts fighting for survival. However, not once did Clarence see people fight and hurt others just for sheer pleasure, unless it was the police roughing up a beggar and telling the person to clear out and move along. That was what he saw yesterday, however. People killing, looting, and destroying and taking pride and enjoyment from it as if they believed God himself had blessed their actions.

He wonders to himself where he can go, and where he can take Mary to protect her from people like this. There must be a place, somewhere. But where? And how can he find out how to get there? While Clarence muses over the situation, he hears Mary stir behind him.

"Good morning, Clarence," she says in a quiet, sleepy voice. "Is your leg still hurt?"

"Yes, a bit," he replies truthfully. "It will get better, though. It isn't bleeding anymore, at least. How is your head, little one?" Clarence asks her as she rises slowly from the hard ground and walks over beside him, their one blanket that they removed from their horse's saddle still pulled tightly around her.

"It hurts a good deal, and I have a lump where the beam hit me, but it's much better this morning. My headache is gone. Mostly. Do you still mean to go back to the camp today?"

"Yes, and I suppose now is as good a time as any. Let's wake Gabriel and start. The sooner we check things out, the sooner we can get our fishing poles and maybe catch some food. Are you hungry like I am?"

"Yes, Clarence, I'm very hungry. And cold, too."

"Well, let's get going, then."

About an hour later, with the sun just rising into the sky, they stand at the edge of the draw, looking down to where the camp used to be. Not a single cabin still stands. The smell of charred wood wafts up to them, but there's something else in the air Clarence has never smelled before. The scent of burned human flesh. Mary covers her nose with her sleeve when she smells it.

Leaving Mary to watch the horse and serve as lookout for anyone who might approach, Gabriel and Clarence search through the ruins. Clarence's shoulders slump while he limps through the village. Gabriel walks with his head down, shirt pulled up over his nose, raising his head only to call out when he comes across something important. While they shuffle slowly about, they come across more murdered people. Gabriel finds Louis Turcotte, a man almost eighty-five years old, slumped over a rock. Next to him, on the ground, he finds Louis's great-grandson, Antoine, in a dried pool of his own blood. Antoine's dead body still holds his great-grandfather's hand.

Clarence comes across two more bodies, burned almost beyond recognition, in the remains of one of the smoldering shacks. He steps through what used to be the doorway, tears running down his cheeks, and asks Gabriel, "Do you know who this is?" Clarence can't yet bring himself to speak of these people, who had been kind enough to take in him and Mary and share their few possessions with them, in the past tense.

"I think it's Pierre Belhumeur and his wife, Elisa. Look, remember how bright the beadwork on their sashes was?" Gabriel holds up what remains of one of the sashes, shaking his head and shivering at the horror. "They were almost sixty years old. Pierre made such beautiful music on his fiddle, and Elisa had a marvelous singing voice."

"Yeah, I think that's a good guess," Clarence says while pulling a burned-out shell of a fiddle from the ashes. Reverently, he sets it next to the burned remnants of Pierre's body.

As they stride through the wreckage, blackened logs and smoldering ashes strewn everywhere, Clarence and Gabriel count twenty-one bodies in all. They are all old people, women, and children.

"What are we going to do, Gabriel?" Clarence asks his companion. "We can't just leave the bodies here and let the wolves and coyotes eat them. They deserve proper burial. Where are all the hunters who showed up at the end of the attack yesterday? Why haven't they come back?"

"I don't know where they are," Gabriel answers. Then, "Hey, look at this. A little luck at last."

Gabriel points to an ancient, brown leather steamer trunk that, somehow, did not burn up inside one of the cabins. They go over and open its lid, lifting the brass latch carefully. Inside they see spare buffalo robes, four of them, along with sundry other pieces of clothing. There is no food or money, but it's something useful, at least.

"This was Jean Baptiste Larocque's cabin, wasn't it?" Clarence asks Gabriel.

"Yeah, I think so. He was a great hunter back in the days of the buffalo, so I'm not surprised he'd have some extra robes left over. Do you think we should take them?"

"I think he would understand, don't you?"

"Probably. Well, hopefully, we'll meet him again soon, and we can ask him ourselves, right, Clarence? I don't see his body here."

"Yeah, I think so. Gabriel, is this really all that's left from our whole village?"

Wiping the last of his own tears from his cheek, Gabriel responds, anger mixed with defeat and despair seeping into his voice, "It looks like it, doesn't it? Those robbers took everything else we had or burned it to the ground. I say we go catch some fish, so we can at least eat a little bit. We can figure out what to do next while we wait for a bite. Maybe the hunting party will come back in the meantime."

"Wait just a minute. I need to go back and check out my cabin before we do," Clarence states before hustling to where his cabin used to stand.

He walks back to his most recent home, dreading what he knows is probably true. The remains of a charred log are all he can see at first. Clarence searches through the ashes, the gray and black particles coating his pants leg. He searches faster, then frantically, coughing as he inhales some of the ash he's kicking up.

"What are you looking for, Clarence?"

"My knapsack. I don't know, maybe it's wrong to look for your own things and worry about possessions when everyone else is dead or missing, but that knapsack and our suitcase was all I had. All *we* had. It contained the nice souvenirs from my tour around the world. The illustrated book everyone received at the New York banquet. The picture of the Australian cricket grounds that John Tener gave me. That was the first Christmas present I ever got from anyone. I also had a boomerang from Australia and a couple other things in there. I don't think they made it, though."

"What's this?" Gabriel asks, holding up an empty metal picture frame. It's charred around the edges, blackening and tarnishing the formerly silver frame.

"The photograph used to be in that frame. It looks like it's all gone. Everything's gone. Burned up. Destroyed forever. I've got nothing in the whole world now, except you and Mary."

Because he can't see anything else left to do, Clarence calls out to Mary that they're heading for the Milk River, and soon the three sit silently on the bank, just where Gabriel and Clarence were yesterday when the calamity began. Mercifully, the poles and Clarence's knife for cleaning the trout are still there where they left them. Gabriel was smart enough to bring his knife with him yesterday, but in his excitement, Clarence forgot his. In half an hour, they manage to catch two trout, gut them, and start cooking breakfast, but still, no sign of anyone else.

When the fish are gone, but before they can discuss what to do next, everyone hears a dim bugle call in the distance.

# Chapter 8

## Like It Never Happened

"That's a different call than what we heard yesterday, isn't it, Gabriel?" Clarence asks.

"Yeah, I think that bugle call means it's the U.S. cavalry. I recognize the cadence."

"Is that a good thing or a bad thing, Gabriel?"

"Probably bad, but who knows? What do you say we go and check out what they are doing? We'll sneak up on them. I know a way into our camp where we can stay hidden almost the whole way. It's longer, and less direct, but we're in no hurry this time because there's nothing there to go back and rescue."

"Are you sure about this? I don't fancy getting shot again." Then Clarence points to his leg, "And I can't run away if they see us, remember?"

"Don't worry, the whites are blind. They don't know the country the way I do. We'll find out whatever information we can, then leave before they even know we're there. I may not be much of a hunter, but I've been a scout since I was twelve, remember? Besides, I thought you were lucky."

"Well, seeing how I got shot in the leg yesterday, perhaps my luck has run out. Still, I suppose we need all the information we can get right now. I'm in. Lead on."

"Mary," Gabriel says, "we're going to sneak up on the soldiers and see what they are doing. You stay here. We'll be back as soon as we can. There shouldn't be any trouble here, but keep yourself and our horse out of sight over there, down by the water, just in case. You'll hear anyone coming a long time before they see you."

"I don't want to stay by myself," she complains, stomping one foot to emphasize her point.

Gabriel tells her, "The horse is too big to take with us. We won't sneak up on the soldiers because they'll see it or hear it. You'll be okay here. I know it."

Mary folds her arms over her chest and huffs a bit. Apparently, she isn't convinced after yesterday. Eventually, she says, "Fine," and stomps off, sitting down with her legs folded beneath her and turning her back on Clarence and Gabriel.

Gabriel leads Clarence on a path that reaches the village at its north end, instead of the south end where they ran to yesterday. When they've crept within a hundred yards of what's left of the camp, Gabriel says, "All right, Clarence, down on your belly. We'll crawl on our elbows from here. See? They've posted their guards on the other side of the draw because they don't expect anyone to approach from the river side."

Clarence crawls, one elbow at a time, after Gabriel. It hurts a bit, but he hides it and they make no noise. They are near enough to the edge of the draw that they can see most of what is happening. It's a small detachment of cavalry, a dozen men or so. Gabriel and Clarence hunker down behind a couple of large stones and peer through the brown, parched bunchgrass to see what the soldiers are doing. Luckily, the officer giving orders barks out his commands loud and clear, so it is easy to hear him.

"All right, men," he shouts to the dismounted soldiers nearby, "have you gathered all the bodies?"

"Yes, Lieutenant Hamilton," one of them reports in return. "Twenty-one bodies, sir. We've piled them right in front of you. What's left of them, anyway."

"Well done. Now, the rest of our orders go like this, boys. Find some scrap wood left over from some of these charred cabins that is still useable. We're going to burn the bodies. While that happens, you'll dig a trench, so we can bury the bones, and then we cover the trench before we leave, see?"

Most of the men nod, but a handful look around, kick the dirt, stare off with hands on hips, or whistle softly as if they aren't sure what requirement necessitates all that effort.

When Lieutenant Hamilton notices their hesitation, he says to the men, by way of explanation, "What, do you want the damned Eastern press to hear about this? You want all those damn 'friends of the Indian' in Congress to start asking questions? I sure as hell don't."

"But, sir, we didn't kill anyone," one of the enlisted men points out. "Why should we worry about it or have to take responsibility for it?"

"Because, private, either the Indian-loving writers in the Eastern press'll blame the Army anyway, or write that we should have been in control of the situation, or find some fault with us somehow, and no one at the fort wants that to happen. So, we get the job of cleaning up after the vigilantes. Remember now, boys, I want this to look like nothing happened here. All these shacks burned down because of lightning starting a prairie fire, as far as we're concerned. After we've done all that, I want you to sweep the area, all the way to the river, and make sure there aren't any Injuns around."

After the soldiers get their orders, a pair of them walk toward Clarence and Gabriel to grab what wood they can find from the nearest cabin. The soldiers mutter to each other, and they can overhear what the soldiers say.

"Heck of a day, isn't it, Collins?" the first soldier says to the other.

"Ay, that be true," the other replies, with a bit of an Irish brogue. "We spend the waking hours trying to find this place, and on the way, we get in a scrape with a band of armed Indians and have to drive them off."

Gabriel looks over at Clarence. Clarence nods. That must be why no members of the hunting party ever showed up this morning. They met up with the cavalry, and the soldiers drove them away.

"Ya really believe all this rubbish about the Eastern press, Barker?" the Irish soldier asks his companion.

"Maybe, maybe not, but what do I care? Can't read anyway," Barker says with a smile. "Just so long as there's some whiskey in it for us at the end of the day, I'll not complain."

"I hear rumors that the guv'ner wants to kill every Indian in Montana," Collins goes on. "Now, who do ya think is a gonna get that job?"

"You know better than to believe all the rumors, Collins."

"Might as well listen to them," Collins counters as he stoops to pick up a hefty chunk of wood, setting it in the crook of his left arm. "Nothing else to do in a place this remote, is there? I mean, damn, Barker, the nearest town's what, seven hundred miles from here?"

"Nothing to do, you mean, besides drink whiskey?" Barker says with another smile. "Still, you may be right. This is an unusual assignment for us. Perhaps the politicians are planning something, after all. Whatever it is, you can wager your last drop that we'll take all the risks and they'll claim all the credit."

"Right you are, laddie," Collins says, his left arm now half full of chunks of wood. "Let's go on and get it over with. Complainin' about it ain't gonna get us nowhere. Let's go over there and see if there be any wood worth salvagin' at that cabin."

At this point, Gabriel nods to Clarence, and they crawl backward on elbows and knees until they're a safe distance from the camp. Then, they both hurry back to find Mary and tell her what they've learned. The two men find Mary right where they left her, wrapped up in one of the buffalo robes. It's way too big for her, so it spreads out around her on the ground like a fancy ballroom gown. The three are far enough away that they don't have to smell the horrifying stench of burning human flesh when the soldiers set the dead aflame to incinerate what's left of them.

"Why were you gone so long?" she asks plaintively. "I was scared that the soldiers got you!"

"Well, they didn't," Clarence tells her. "But we learned why none of the hunters came back to our camp today. The cavalry met them, and they had another fight. None of the soldiers mentioned killing any more people, though, so hopefully, everyone got away."

Gabriel puts in, "However, we've got to get moving and get away from here. After the troops finish destroying the evidence of what those butchers did yesterday, they're going to sweep the area. We'd best not be here when that happens."

"Do you have any idea of where we should go, Gabriel?" Clarence asks.

"I think we should head toward Havre, but by a cautious route. Maybe, if we're lucky, there will still be a camp of people on the outskirts of town left over from the Wild West Show this summer. We ought to be able to stay with them until we figure out what to do. I have a feeling that at least some members of our camp will head that way, too."

"That sounds like a good idea. I agree it's the best choice we have right now. Let's loop around to the north, so the soldiers will be between us and the fort," Clarence suggests.

"How long will it take us to get there?" poor Mary asks, her voice still sounding forlorn and lonely.

"We'll be there by tomorrow," Gabriel tells her.

"Tomorrow? I'm hungry again."

"I know you are. We all are," Clarence says to her. "But you've got to be brave, okay? All of us have to be brave right now."

"Have I been brave so far?" she asks him.

"Yes, Mary, you've been very brave. You helped me escape when our cabin was on fire, remember?"

"I don't feel very brave. Are you sure?"

"Of course, I'm sure. Your Uncle John will be very proud of you when we finally get to see him, and I can tell him about all the things you've done."

Mary's weary face lights up at the mention of her Uncle John. Even though Mary has never met him, it seems she's latched onto him as a sign of hope for the future.

"When we get to Uncle John's house, will I get to see him play baseball?"

"I hope so, Mary. I hope so. I'm sure he'll be pleased to see you and show you how to play."

"I've got everything packed," Gabriel breaks in. "Are we all ready to ride?"

"I suppose I'm ready," Mary says as Clarence helps her up to her seat on the horse. She rides between Gabriel and Clarence to make sure she doesn't fall off.

They loop to the north, as planned, and later, as they settle down to camp for the night, each person curls up in their warm buffalo robe. It is another cool night, although still above freezing, so even though everyone is hungry, at least they have warm blankets.

# Chapter 9

## Clarence Joins the Cavalry

Clarence has no idea how long he's slept or what time it is in the morning, when he's jolted awake by a kick to his boot heel. "Get up, deserter," a voice growls at him. "You're lucky we don't shoot you right here, you nigger sonofabitch."

It takes a moment for his eyes to clear as Clarence sits up, blinking in the clear morning sunlight. When they do, he realizes half a dozen white men with Winchester rifles surround him and his friends. They're in blue United States cavalry uniforms and, other than the man who just kicked him, all sit atop mounts. In another moment, the dismounted man moves through the tiny camp and kicks Gabriel and Mary so that they're awake, too.

"What did you say?" Clarence manages to stammer while he tries to get his bearings and figure out how to get out of this new pickle. "Did you call me a deserter?" He smells liquor on the man who just kicked him.

"You heard me," the dismounted man snarls angrily as he smacks Clarence's shoulder with his rifle butt. Clarence falls on his back again. "I said, get up!" This time, he kicks Clarence in his ribs. Not hard enough to break them, but hard enough that Clarence coughs for a moment while he struggles to his knees.

"Clarence!" Mary calls and tries to crawl over to him.

"Stay silent, you squaw bitch!" the man growls again as he shoves Mary back, pushing her onto her back side with a shove from his right hand. Two of the mounted men laugh. Then, seeing Mary's terror, the man turns back to Clarence as Clarence wobbles to his feet. Clarence almost falls again when his injured left leg buckles. "Strange company you've chosen to run away with, boy, an Injun and his squaw sister."

"I think there's been a mistake," Clarence tries to protest, holding out his right arm with the index finger raised. His left rests on his knee to provide some balance. "I'm not a deserter. I've never even been in the Army. We're travelers trying to get to Havre, that's all."

"Liar!" the man roars, and then he gets right up into Clarence's face, the bristling brown whiskers of his bushy mustache almost brushing Clarence's cheeks.

*He's at least partly drunk, for sure*, Clarence thinks. *It's possible he's completely drunk.* Clarence can smell the sour whiskey on the man's breath as he shouts. The smell nearly slaps him in the face, the man is so close.

"You're a damned liar, Fred Cooper, and if you try to lie to me again, I just might shoot you right here." The man punctuates his threat by poking Clarence in the chest with the barrel of his rifle, giving him a couple jabs. "You tried to run away from your unit last night, and we've tracked you down. You're coming back to the fort with us, or we're going to shoot you right through the gut and leave you to die, so the coyotes can eat your dead carcass. And good riddance, too."

"You tell him, corporal," one of the mounted men calls down. "When Lieutenant Pershing lost one of his niggers last night and the alarm went up, I was on patrol. I shot someone trying to ride away, and here's this boy with a bullet wound in his leg telling us he's not the deserter. The nerve of some people."

Now things are starting to make sense to Clarence. These soldiers think he's someone who tried to escape from Fort Assiniboine last night. Apparently, the fort has colored soldiers stationed there under the command of someone named Pershing, and these white soldiers got the task of finding the deserter. They probably can't tell one colored soldier from the next, so they just assume he's Fred Cooper, whoever that really is.

Clarence doesn't want them to shoot anyone; even though he doesn't think they will, this man seems angry and inebriated enough that it's not worth the risk. Instantly, he decides to take his chances that, when he gets to the fort, whoever is the officer of the escaped man's unit will realize Clarence is not the fugitive and let him go. It isn't as though he has much choice, seeing that he's surrounded by soldiers with guns who think he *is* the deserter, so he decides to play dumb and play along.

"You'se right, suh," Clarence says to him, faking a Southern accent just like he did at Pacific Junction. "You'se gone and found me, and now I'se got to try to 'splain to the 'tennant why I done it. These two people jus' happen to cross paths wit' me, tha's all. They'se nothin' to bother 'bout."

"Speaking of, what should we do with his friends, corporal?" another of the mounted men asks. "Our orders don't say nothin' about them."

"You two can go wherever you please, although I'd advise you to clear out of these parts," the corporal says to Gabriel and Mary. "Mark my words, the day is coming when we good white folks will have seen the last of you dirty savages." He spits, aiming in their direction. It hits Gabriel's right arm.

Clarence looks over at Mary, and tears roll down her face because she realizes the inevitability of their separation, but she's too scared to say anything. Clarence sees a few drops of blood trickling off her trembling left hand; she must have scraped it when the bastard pushed her down. Gabriel hasn't said anything so far, despite the spit, and even takes the verbal abuse stoically. Clarence supposes his time in the Wild West Show and the Cincinnati Zoo taught him to put on a mask when white people are around. Or, maybe he just thinks better of antagonizing six angry white soldiers with guns.

Before Clarence turns to leave, he mouths to them silently, "See you in Havre." He hopes they understand what he says.

"Okay, Cooper, mount up," the corporal says to Clarence, nodding toward a spare horse the soldiers brought with them and prodding him in the ribs with the butt of his rifle once again. Of course, the horse Clarence and Gabriel rode to this spot doesn't have the brand of the fort, which should make it obvious that it didn't come from Fort Assiniboine and neither did Clarence, but the corporal either doesn't notice or doesn't care. One of his companions notices, however.

"What about the extra horse, sir?"

"What about it? Is it ours?"

"No, it's not branded with our mark."

"This crafty nigger must have traded his for this one, just to fool us," the corporal says. "We'll just hope it turns up. It's our job to recover a deserter, not ride the range to find a horse. Move out!"

The fact that Clarence has no weapon and is not in uniform should have been a giveaway that he's not Fred Cooper as well, but the man's case of intoxication seems to have clouded his judgment there, too. Perhaps the corporal figures Clarence got rid of those to disguise himself, as well. Turning to Clarence, the man says, "If you try to ride off before we get back, you're gonna have six bullet holes in your chest."

"Yes, suh," Clarence says in response as he rides off to some new fate. He looks back once toward Mary and Gabriel. They stand still on the prairie as Clarence rides away, bunchgrass waving around their ankles in the bright light of the morning. Gabriel has his arms around Mary as she buries her face in his side.

# Chapter 10

## Clarence's Punishment

The pain is greater than anything he's felt in his life. Clarence has been sitting on a wooden fence rail all day as his punishment for attempting to desert the 10th U.S. Cavalry, and his genitals, tailbone, and butt burn in agony. He's tied in place, so he can't fall off the rail and get relief, but the rail is just high enough that his feet can't touch the ground, either. That means all Clarence's weight rests on the fence rail, and there is nothing he can do except grit his teeth and hope it all ends at some point.

The officer responsible for his punishment, Second Lieutenant Grimes, leads the troop of the 10th Cavalry to which Clarence supposedly belongs. The troop passes by him several times during the day while it drills and practices cavalry maneuvers from horseback. Clarence supposes this is to use him as an example for the other men. Occasionally, Grimes allows a sergeant to keep the troopers marching while he dismounts and comes over to humiliate Clarence.

"Private Cooper!" he screams in Clarence's face at one point early in the afternoon, "this is what you get for deserting your platoon! You're fortunate we didn't just shoot you dead for desertion, but luckily for you," and here he pauses for a moment, taunting Clarence with the irony of referring to his agonizing pain as lucky, "rumors say we've got an important campaign coming soon, and we need every man we can get, even the likes of you. You're gonna be part of that operation, whether you like it or not. You hear me, Cooper?"

"Yes, Lieutenant," Clarence manages to stammer through the haze of pain.

"Louder, private!"

"Yes, Lieutenant," he tries again while attempting to keep his eyes focused on his tormentor.

"Louder! Like a Buffalo Soldier!"

"Yes, Lieutenant."

Grimes laughs while walking away, his pace brisk and posture upright.

Lieutenant Grimes stops by and scolds Clarence several more times during the afternoon. Clarence would have fallen asleep from fatigue a long time ago, but every time he shifts his body, even slightly, the continuous pain between his legs gets worse. Clarence moans something incoherent every now and again, even though it provides no relief.

The day drags. Forever. Clarence gets no food and no water. There's nothing to do when he needs to relieve himself, either, so now his pants stink of urine, too. Things are so bad, and the pain so great, he can't even feel the bullet wound in his left leg in comparison.

The weather doesn't help. It's cool to begin with because it's October, and around midday a squall passes overhead and rain lashes down. The rain shower is brief but intense, soaking Clarence's uniform, and the day isn't warm enough afterward to dry it out, even though the sun is out most of the time. Therefore, in addition to the pain from the fence rail, Clarence spends the afternoon and evening shivering in soggy clothes even while trying to outlast the burning feeling between his legs. All he can do is stare out at the prairie leading away from the fort in every direction, the golden and brown grass wafting this way and that in the breeze. Clarence tries to follow the landscape with his eyes but loses focus as the grass merges with an indistinct horizon.

Clarence faces west, so the sun is in his eyes while it sets. Whenever he closes them, he can see the light through his eyelids. Clarence runs his tongue over his cracked, bone-dry lips, but it barely helps. He mumbles again. He's not even sure what he's saying by this time. Now, when he looks out at the grass, the golden colors just blur together into a fuzzy haze.

The torment continues. The next time he closes his eyes, Clarence sees a kaleidoscope of colors start swirling, just like he saw last time he passed out, in Colombo. But then the pain jolts him back to full consciousness. Since he can't move his hands, Clarence squeezes his eyes shut, hard, and then blinks them rapidly to try to get out a speck of dust that's irritating one eye. His throat is so dry that even trying to moan again irritates it, so he stops trying.

Clarence is still shivering, however, from his soggy clothing, and every time another spasm of chills wracks his body, it forces him into an even more uncomfortable position on the rail, and he tries to moan again, only to get a quick reminder that moaning makes his throat hurt, too.

Now, as the sun begins to set, Clarence worries that he's stuck here all night as well. Have they forgotten about him, or was everything Grimes said just to keep his hopes up, only so Clarence can freeze to death overnight, suffering the entire time in the icy embrace of his drenched uniform?

In exhaustion, he leans to his left before he realizes what's happening. The rail digs into Clarence's crotch so hard he yelps! Except, he can barely make a sound, so it comes out as a hoarse croak.

It's almost dark now. The sun dropped below the western horizon a few minutes ago, and a haze of gold and orange fills the western skyline. At least, Clarence thinks it's gold and orange in the sky and not just his vision playing tricks on him. Or, maybe it's been longer than a few minutes. He can't tell anymore. The pain is too much to bother with keeping a sense of time.

Every time Clarence leans forward on the verge of passing out, the fence rail digs into his genitals, and his body jerks back up. This only shifts his weight onto his tailbone again, making it ache, too. He thought he'd just go numb at some point, but that never happens. Clarence's eyes water, and when he swallows again, his lower lip cracks open so badly he tastes blood in his mouth. It's warm, salty, and metallic tasting. He'd spit it out if he had the concentration and energy.

Just when he's starting to think he really will be outside all night, a lone figure walks toward Clarence from the barracks. When he gets to Clarence, the man unties the knots holding him in place on the rail and helps Clarence down. Clarence simply flops onto his back and lies on the ground in pain for a long while. He's cold, and the ground is rough, but for the moment Clarence doesn't care.

"Take yo time, Cooper," the man says to Clarence.

While Clarence lies there, his rescuer opens a spare canteen and drips a little water into Clarence's mouth, then a little more. Clarence mouths "thank you." Slowly, he keeps tipping more water between Clarence's lips until Clarence thinks he's drunk half the container.

His throat feeling a little better, through the burning pain Clarence manages to focus enough to tell the man, "I'm not really Fred Cooper."

"I know you ain't Fred Cooper," the private replies. "I knowed the real Fred Cooper, and you ain't him. That don't make no different out here, though. We colored folk all look the same to them white men. But you knowed that yoself, I reckon."

"Yeah," Clarence grunts in response while trying to massage some blood back into his crotch. "I figured that out at my hearing for desertion."

He pauses again, hoping the pain will go down if he just lies motionless. It might be getting better, but still, it hurts so much Clarence can't really tell. The trooper just stands there, waiting patiently in the gathering darkness. Clarence wonders if he's gotten this duty before.

Finally, although still on his back, Clarence manages to focus his thoughts and speak again. His voice is a little stronger. "When they found me, I had no uniform, no weapon, and my horse wasn't from the fort. Plus, I don't know anything about military procedures, but all that didn't matter. One white soldier testifies that he shot a deserter, and here I am with a bullet wound in my leg, and nothing else matters. I suppose the officers holding the hearing didn't want to look bad by having to admit that one of their men ran off, either."

"That Lieutenant Pershing, he a hard man," Clarence's rescuer replies. "But he a fair man. You just go on and do what they tell you from now on, and you be fine."

"But I've got to get out of here and find Mary," Clarence protests.

"Now, don' you go thinkin' no more crazy thoughts 'bout that. They catch you once, you sits here all day. They catch you 'gain, you be dead, sho' as I'm standin' here."

Clarence just stares at the blackening sky for a few moments. It's starting out as a clear night, and he sees the stars grow in brilliance. There are so many, too, each a little pinprick of brightness in the cavernous black of the northern Montana sky. When he lived in Chicago, Clarence never saw so many stars at night. It would be pretty, if he wasn't in such horrible pain.

"What's your name, trooper?" he says to the other man at last.

"Lincoln Washington."

"You don't say." It occurs to Clarence that this man's parents named him after the president who set the slaves free, when they shared their last name with a president who held slaves himself.

"Not my choice," Washington responds. "That jus' what my folks wanted to call me." Probably someone's pointed out the irony to him before, Clarence decides.

"How did you end up all the way out here in northern Montana, Washington?"

"My folks up and died, and I sho' didn't want to pick no cotton or grow no corn all my life, so now I'se here."

"Your parents are dead, too? Well, that's one thing we have in common, I guess. At least, I think mine are dead. I don't even know for certain. You're from the South, then?"

"Yeah, right around Nashville area, down in Tennessee. How 'bout you, Cooper?"

It still sounds weird to Clarence to have someone call him that. He'll have to accept it, though, at least for a while. "I was born in Kentucky, but I lived in Chicago, mostly. Then I've spent the last six years in Butte."

"You work in them mines?"

"No, I'm not a miner. Sometimes I get frightened when I'm underground, and I panic. I do odd jobs around town. Well, I used to."

"I'd ask you what yo real name be," Washington says, "but I don' want them white officers to think I helped you plan yo escape, so I don' wanna know. Don' wanna say it to you on accident, you know?"

"Fair enough," Clarence replies. He considers asking Washington why all the soldiers in the unit are colored men while the officers are white but thinks better of it. He supposes the answer is clear enough. The Army doesn't trust colored soldiers to lead themselves, so the colored troops get white officers. The Army trusts them enough to give them weapons and train colored soldiers how to use them, but not enough to let the soldiers give commands during battle. And the thought of a colored officer telling white troops what to do, well, Clarence thinks he knows what the chances of that ever happening are.

"Say, can you help me with something?" he asks Washington as the pain recedes just a little, and he finally manages to sit up.

"Depends. You ain't thinkin' of tryin' to run again, are you? Ol' Red, the Lieutenant, he don' take no truck with men disobeyin' orders."

"Not today, that's for sure." Clarence hasn't even stood up to try and walk yet, although he supposes he'd better soon. "No, I was going to ask if you'd tell me the basics of what a cavalry trooper does. I've never been a soldier, but the officers are going to think I have, and they'll expect me to know what I'm doing. I don't want to get punished like this again for not following procedures that I don't know."

"Oh, tha's easy 'nough," Washington says with a bit of a smile. "I can tell you 'bout that. Come 'long, now, while we gets some chow."

Clarence gets on his feet, expecting to fall right back down again because of the new pain and his bullet wound, but somehow, he manages to stay up. He takes a couple tiny steps, and then gradually starts limping toward the buildings at the fort. It isn't that far, a quarter of a mile or so, but seems like ten miles with the pace Clarence can manage.

They're about halfway back to the barracks when Washington looks over at Clarence. Clarence limps slowly because a slow limp is all he can do thanks to his wound. Washington looks concerned.

"You betta get tha' wound checked out. If they gonna make you be a trooper, you might as well let them fix you up when you in bad shape."

"You're probably right. Which of these buildings is the hospital?"

Washington points somewhere off in the distance, but it's too dark for Clarence to tell exactly which building it is. He'll figure it out after chow, he decides.

"Say, I jus' thought a somethin'," Washington says to him as they continue. "You talk likes you knows you letters pretty good."

"I do, for all the good it's done me in life."

"Can you teach me some?"

"Be happy to. You tell me how to be a soldier, and I'll show you how to read and write."

"Deal, Cooper."

# Chapter 11

## St. Peter's Mission

Another cool October evening descends on northern Montana. For Mary and Gabriel, the handful of days since their separation from Clarence have seen clear weather, at least, but cool. Winter is in the air. Gabriel Ouellette can smell it in the wind. He can feel it, too, of course. No snow covers the ground yet, but it's only a matter of time. Today is an overcast day. Who knows if tomorrow will bring the low-hanging, iron-gray skies that usually signal snow in this part of the country?

Gabriel and Mary sit on the near-frozen, hard ground, stands of buffalo grass waving stiffly around them, the railroad tracks a stone's throw away, cooking the last of the fish Gabriel caught that morning. Without warning, three horsemen top a nearby hill and ride toward them at a light gallop. Dressed in stiff coats of brown leather, tanned riding chaps, and white cowboy hats, they rein in their horses just a short distance from the bedraggled and beleaguered pair. One of them lifts a glass bottle to his lips, drinks, and then passes it to the man on his left.

"Well, looka here, boys, if it ain't a couple of Injuns campin' out, jus' as if they owned the place," the first man to drink says.

"They ain't no real Injuns. They got no feathers or buckskins or nothin'," says the man on the right while he extracts his own bottle from his coat pocket and takes a swig.

"They look like Injuns, all right," the first man counters. "Wearin' buffalo coats and all. Look at their faces. Yep, they's Injuns all right."

"We aren't Indians. We're Michif," Mary blurts out angrily. "And you're drunk. Go away and leave us alone."

"Why, listen to this saucy little thing," says the man on the left. He takes a final drink, passes the nearly empty bottle back to the man in the center of the trio, and then dismounts clumsily, nearly falling after his foot gets stuck in his stirrup. Hopping a few times, he regains his balance and says, "Here you are, tresspassin' on our ranch, and speakin' like that to a white man. I've a mind to teach you a lesson or two, you mouthy little squaw."

Gabriel steps in between the two. He tries to smile. "It's a misunderstanding. She's a little girl. She didn't mean it. We'll be clearing out. No need to get upset."

The dismounted man clicks his bootheels together, stands up straight, military-style, with his left arm at his side, and raises his right arm, palm outward. Gabriel can smell the stale sweat of a man who hasn't bathed in quite some time. "How, white man. We Injuns speaka English good now. We Injuns smoke the peace pipe. Injuns not take warpath anymore." Then he starts laughing—an annoying, high-pitched whine that goes on for several seconds. He turns to face his companions and then doubles over in laughter again.

His companions crack up, too. "Good one, Will," the man on the right says. "Tha's how you talk to Injuns. We just gots to get our manners right, tha's all."

When the rider in the center finishes guffawing, he reaches for his side. "Damn, where's my gun? Le's jus shoot these Injuns and be done with 'em. Ed, you got your pistol?"

Ed, the man still mounted on the right, says, "Naw, Randall, we was supposed to be drinkin' today, not fightin'. It's back at the bunkhouse."

Will, the dismounted man, says, "Well, I still gots me this knife. I guess that'll have to do." He draws the weapon, turns, showing it to Gabriel and Mary, and then turns back to his friends and flashes it for them to see, grinning stupidly the entire time. Then he starts his whiny laugh again.

Gabriel takes this as his chance to act. While Will faces away from him, waving his knife around without much coordination, Gabriel launches himself at the wiry cowboy, lowering his right shoulder and slamming Will in the small of his back. Taken by surprise, Will goes down, landing hard on his stomach, face down in the crunchy, half-thawed grass, the wind knocked out of him. The knife falls from his grasp and lands a short distance away.

"Damnit, I'm gonna kill you, boy," says Randall, who now dismounts and advances toward Gabriel, his fists up, boxer-style.

Gabriel feints toward him, and Randall lunges, swinging his right arm in a long, clumsy arc. Gabriel ducks the blow easily and then turns and kicks Randall in the back when Randall's momentum leads him past Gabriel. Randall lands face down in the dirt but is back up again in a moment.

Meanwhile, the remaining rider, Ed, spurs his horse toward Mary. She screams and tries to dodge, but Ed grabs her by the collar of her buffalo robe and tries to hoist her up onto his horse. Luckily, her robe is far too large for her to begin with, so the sleeves are very loose. Flailing her arms frantically, Mary wriggles out of the buffalo robe and falls to the ground. She manages to scamper away for the moment. Not prepared for the sudden shift in weight, Ed falls out of his saddle backward and lands on his left side, cursing the entire time.

By now, Randall has picked himself up off the ground, and he's ready for another try at Gabriel. Smack! Wielding one of the pieces of wood from the fire, Gabriel conks Randall on the head with a solid blow, and he's down again, cradling his head in his arms. This time,

Randall does not get up right away. Gabriel considers trying to light the man on fire, but then he hears a growling noise to his right. Will leaps at him and swings his knife downward toward Gabriel's face.

Gabriel raises his right arm, the one with the piece of wood, to ward off the blow. He succeeds in blocking the knife, but while deflecting the attack, the knife runs across his right forearm and draws blood. He then swings the burning piece of wood backhanded and strikes Will in the gut. The blow isn't as solid as the one which felled Randall, but Will has doubled over in pain, so Gabriel backs it up by kicking Will in the face. Then Gabriel spins around to check on Mary.

Once again, she's in trouble. Ed, who doesn't seem to have either a knife or gun, luckily, has her again, by her shirt this time, and drags her toward his horse. Not knowing what else to do, Mary lashes out with her foot and kicks him in the groin. Ed crouches down in pain, and Mary tears away from his grasp as Ed's hands drop to cover his crotch, although some of the back of her shirt rips away in the process, the rest waving in tatters while she runs toward Gabriel.

"Quick, run for our horse," he calls, stooping to pick up his buffalo robe while he follows his own advice. He hoists Mary up into the saddle, mounts up himself, and in a moment, they're galloping southward, away from the drunken cowboys. Several times Gabriel glances back to see if they will follow, but for the first time in days, he and Mary have some good fortune. The three men do not pursue.

At long last, the buildings of St. Peter's Mission come into view. Gabriel and Mary, famished and bedraggled, almost fall off their horse when they reach the compound's courtyard. Gabriel, his right forearm bandaged with a linen strip torn from his shirt and caked with dried blood, can barely hold the reins steady as he dismounts. Mary's shredded shirt flutters out behind her while Gabriel struggles to help her to the ground using only his left arm. The buffalo robe they share drops to the ground between them.

A man in a black robe emerges from a large, three-story building, his shadow dulled because threatening clouds hide the midday sun, while Mary and Gabriel stumble around slowly and aimlessly. The black-robed man walks calmly to meet them at first but then breaks into a run when he sees their condition.

"Welcome to St. Peter's Mission, my children," he says. "How might I be of assistance? It appears you may need some help."

"Is Father Damiani here?" Gabriel croaks to the priest through his parched and cracked lips. "I'd like to speak with him, if he is. Several years ago I was one of his students. I just hope . . ."

With that effort, Gabriel collapses to the ground, semi-conscious, and mutters something indistinct through the haze in his mind. Soon, his eyes close, and he drifts off.

Young Mary looks toward the priest with fear in her bright eyes. "Won't you please help us? We haven't had any food since yesterday, and Gabriel gave me the last of our water to drink this morning."

The priest, a balding, middle-aged man with an alert face and gentle features, takes Mary by her hand. "Come with me, little one, while we find some food for you and some medicine for your friend." The man calls out to one of his associates, who has come outside to see what is happening, "Help us! Friar O'Connell, we have a man down, and he needs medical attention. Hurry, right away."

"Yes, Father," the man says, and then he turns and opens the door he just emerged from, labeled "St. Peter's Mission School" just above the doorway. He calls something to the people within, and momentarily, three young men emerge to help him move Gabriel. They pick Gabriel up, draping one of his arms over the shoulder of each of the largest boys, and carry Gabriel inside and lay him down on a bed inside the priest's quarters. Mary sits inside the priest's office, which is adjacent to his bedroom, while the black-robed man brings her some coffee to drink and offers her some buttered bread and an apple.

"Please eat, little one," the priest says to her. "I sense you and your friend have quite a story to tell me, but first, let's see to your well-being. Eat some food while I minister to your companion."

"His name is Gabriel," Mary says between chomping down hunks of bread. "Gabriel Ouellette."

"Is it now?" the priest says quietly to himself. "Gabriel Ouellette, indeed."

Mary takes little notice of these quiet remarks, but after chewing through another bite exclaims, "Do you know what's wrong with my friend? How can we help him?"

"First, let's get him some water to drink. You said he's had nothing to drink since this morning?"

Mary shakes her head from side to side. "Since yesterday, in the evening."

"I see," the priest says. "Certainly, he needs water, then." He takes a metal dipper from a hook on the wall, walks to a small basin of clear water, and inserts the dipper. He then walks slowly and carefully to Gabriel, gently lowers the utensil to Gabriel's mouth, and pours a few short gulps of water down Gabriel's throat. He also places his right hand on Gabriel's head.

"Don't worry about your friend, young lady," he says to Mary. "I sense he will be fine with a little rest and time to recover his senses. He has a fever, and a rather bad one at that, and it's likely he is dehydrated, but once he awakens and regains his clarity, we can see about cleaning up his wounded arm."

Mary nods as she eyes the priest over the rim of her cup of coffee.

"Would you like another apple?" he asks her.

Mary nods, and when the man places a new apple in front of her, she devours it in no time.

"And now, my little child, why don't you join your companion for a rest? You've had a hard day already. In a few hours, I'll wake the two of you, give you some more food to help you regain your strength, and you can tell me your story. Agreed?"

Mary, her exhausted eyes drooping already, nods as she lies down beside Gabriel. The priest takes their buffalo robe, which one of the students fetched while Mary ate, and drapes it over the two of them. Then he turns to the student with a grave look on his face. "Tell Friar

O'Connell I must speak with him as soon as he concludes his present lesson. I fear we may see more refugees such as these in the days to come."

# Chapter 12

## Winter at Fort Assiniboine

Clarence spends the next four months learning how to be a soldier at Fort Assiniboine, Montana. His life is very structured, to say the least. Every day he wakes up, dresses for duty, makes his bed, and then heads off to drill, eat, and drill some more.

Some days the troopers drill outside, but not all of them, mainly because some days, the snow is too deep, and others, it is just so cold. Clarence hears that on a few days, the temperature is as low as forty degrees below zero and once it hits sixty below. Each soldier receives a buffalo coat as part of his standard issue of supplies at Fort Assiniboine. Clarence's buffalo coat is very warm, but nothing keeps a person warm at that temperature, and on the days when the wind howls across northern Montana, which is most of the days, it feels far worse than that, if worse than forty, or even sixty, below zero is even possible. When Clarence lived on the streets of Chicago, he was cold all the time in the winter, but nothing has prepared him for this much cold. The air is so cold, he can taste the difference when he breathes in. Somedays, Clarence feels like he'll never be warm again.

Many of the other men in Clarence's unit, which is part of Troop D of the 10<sup>th</sup> U.S. Cavalry, are even worse off than he is. Most, like Lincoln Washington, come from the South, and all winter long they constantly wish they were back home. Most of the other enlisted men are young, like Clarence is, and they have the natural ability of young people to look on the bright side of things, but even their morale drops when the thermometer stays below zero Fahrenheit for ten consecutive days.

Occasionally, however, a chinook blows through and thaws things for a bit, and on those days, the troopers drill by marching, practicing obeying commands, testing their marksmanship and horsemanship, and similar activities. The horses are eager to leave their stables and run for a while, too, and these days help restore the spirits of the men.

Clarence even learns the regiment's song:

*We're fighting bulls of the Buffaloes,*

*Git a goin' – git a goin'*

*From Kansas' plains we'll hunt our foes;*

*A trottin' down the line.*

*Our range spreads west to Santa Fe,*

*Git a goin' – git a goin'.*

*From Dakota down the Mexican way;*

*A trottin' down the line.*

*Goin' to drill all day*

*Goin' to drill all night,*

*We got our money on the buffaloes,*

# Winter at Fort Assiniboine

*Somebody bet on the fight.*

*Pack up your saddle and make it light.*

*Git a rollin' – git a rollin'.*

*You are training fast for a hard fight;*

*A rollin' down the line.*

*Untie your horse and boot and gun,*

*Git a goin' – git a goin'.*

*Shake out your feet or you'll miss the fun,*

*A rollin' down the line.*

*Goin' to drill all day*

*Goin' to drill all night,*

*We got our money on the buffaloes,*

*Somebody bet on the fight.*

*It's troops in line for the buffaloes,*

*Git a movin' – git a movin'.*

*Then squadron mass when the bugle blows*

*A movin' into line.*

*Pull in your reins and sit your horse,*

*Git a movin' – git a movin'.*

*If you can't ride you'll be a corpse;*

*A movin' into line.*

*Goin' to drill all day*

*Goin' to drill all night,*

*We got our money on the buffaloes,*

*Somebody bet on the fight.*

Whoever made up those words didn't include Montana, Clarence notices. Perhaps the songwriter knew it gets to forty below zero in Montana, too, and that soldiers don't belong there in the winter. It's also funny listening to the men sing the words. Most are from the rural South, and the variety of accents and pronunciations makes the singing strangely discordant, to describe the matter charitably. More than once Second Lieutenant Grimes curses out the troopers for not singing the words right. Some of the men Grimes curses truly are singing the right words, but their accents are so thick Grimes can't tell.

One day in mid-February, when the weather is merely cold rather than deathly frigid, they're lining up for drill out on the parade ground when First Lieutenant Pershing, the commanding officer for Troop D of the 10th Cavalry, steps in front of the troop and addresses them. He stands shin-deep in the hard, crunchy snow that's frozen across the parade field again and again over the past few months, his riding boots just barely tall enough to prevent the snow from falling inside them. The occasional snowflake drifts down on the men as they hurry to form ranks. The misty vapors of the men's breath billow out in front of their faces while they stand at attention.

He begins to speak, and like most of Pershing's speeches, it is to the point. "Men, the U.S. Army has adopted a new firearm for field action. Immediately, we will cease drilling with the old weapons and begin learning to use our new carbines. Because these new carbines are different than the old, we will double our marksmanship practice until you become more accustomed to them. Now, fall out to turn in your old weapons and receive a new one."

Once the lieutenant stops speaking, an excited murmur spreads among the men. It seems this news takes most of them by surprise. Lincoln Washington and Clarence go through the line, get new carbines, and look them over.

"These sho' is a pretty gun, ain't they?" Washington says to Clarence.

"The label here says they're made at an armory in Springfield, Massachusetts. Never been to Springfield," Clarence tells Washington. To himself, he's a little surprised that Spalding Sporting Goods didn't get the manufacturing contract because six years ago when Clarence worked for him, Al Spalding seemed intent on owning everything else. Maybe he decided to stay with sporting goods and leave firearms to others. Clarence wonders if Spalding ever started the rickshaw business he talked about on their trip.

"Notice a difference with these things?" Washington continues, eyes down the barrel of his new gun.

"They seem a good deal lighter than the old guns."

"Almost a pound, I'd say. Tha's good."

"Yeah, it is." Clarence could care less, although he supposes having less weight in the saddle can't hurt.

After they're issued a cartridge box of bullets to go with the guns, Washington looks those over as well.

"See Fred, loading's gonna be dif'rent wit' these."

By now Clarence has learned to take things in stride when Lincoln calls him Fred. "Does that mean we'll have to learn a new sequence for loading and firing?"

"You bet."

"So, more drilling outside when it's too cold to feel your fingers anyway?"

"You gots it."

"Hurrah for the Buffalo Soldiers!" Clarence says in a mock cheer.

Washington smiles a bit at his weak joke. Sometimes, it's all a soldier can do. Then Washington says, "How long you fig'r it'll take to larn these?"

"Beats me. I was a mediocre shot with the old gun. I suppose I'll be mediocre with this new model, too."

"Now, don't go sellin' yourself short, Fred. You is gettin' better."

"Maybe. Doesn't seem like it most days."

"But you is. When you started, you had troubles even hittin' the target. Now, you hit the center sometimes."

"I suppose that's true. It just doesn't seem that way with Grimes in my face all the time, telling me to shoot straighter. He doesn't like me much."

"He don' like no one much."

"True enough. You know, Lincoln, your English is getting a bit better."

Now it's his turn for denial. "I don' know 'bout that."

"It's like my shooting, I guess. It's hard to tell how much better you've gotten until you look back on where you started. That's how it was for me, too, when I got my first real reading lessons from a newspaper reporter. He knew all about speaking and writing English, and I barely knew anything. Boy, did I feel ignorant. But, it was a start. You have to start somewhere."

Partly, Clarence changes the subject to avoid the conversation dwelling on the finer points of shooting a carbine. That way, he won't have to admit that the only reason he's learned to fire at all is so that he won't attract any more negative attention after his "attempted escape." When it comes to that issue, Clarence figures lying low and staying out of the vision of his officers is the smartest thing he can do. Unfortunately, Washington takes their conversation back to where it started.

"I tell you, Cooper, joinin' the cav'ry the hardest thing a soldier can do."

"Why do you say that?"

"You have to larn to shoot two ways. Standin', and on horseback."

"Good point. I can barely shoot standing still. Mounted, I'm atrocious."

"You ain't practiced as much on horseback," Washington reminds him.

"Because it's twenty-five below zero in Montana in January and I can't feel my fingers."

They both laugh a little, then wander off to look at the new carbines by themselves. The men learn to fire both mounted and dismounted, but firing while mounted is tougher because the soldier's horse is bouncing along while the trooper tries to aim and steady himself. But, it's part of what a cavalry soldier does, so Clarence practices when called to. He'll need years more practice to ever be any good at it, however. When he first started, he barely knew how to fire a gun, and he barely knew how to ride a horse, either, so it was like learning two new things at once.

Not that Clarence cares much about his marksmanship. Officially, the garrison at the fort is there to protect the northern and central parts of Montana against Indian attack, but based on his own experiences, Clarence thinks it should be protecting the Indians rather than guarding against them. All he wants to do is get away from here at the first opportunity, so he can go and find Mary and Gabriel.

The opportunity just won't arise, however. In addition to all the risks of Fred Cooper trying to desert a second time, Clarence knows it would be foolhardy to run away during the winter because it would be so easy to track him with snow on the ground. In northern Montana, however, the winter seems to last forever, and as February merges into March, much of the snow remains. Restlessly, he bides his time. Clarence doesn't have any idea where to look for Mary and Gabriel, anyway. The problem is, he'll never get any idea of where they are if he just stays at the fort.

In early March, Lincoln Washington and Clarence get to talking after drills one day. Washington says to Clarence, "Well, Cooper, you still gots some things to larn 'bout shootin', but you is a good soldier in all the other ways."

"You did a good job teaching me what to do. It isn't that hard to follow orders once you learn the routine."

"I know them officers still gots they eyes on you, but you ain't stepped outta line even once since October. That's how you gots to do it in the Army."

To make small talk, Clarence adds, "Even if it's always cold, at least in the Army I get regular meals, and I won't freeze to death in some log cabin."

Maybe he shouldn't have said that. It only brings his thoughts back to Mary and Gabriel. Clarence wonders where in Montana they are and what they did to stay alive over the winter.

Washington brings him back to the moment. "Still, not all the boys stay out o' trouble, but you does."

"Where would I go to get out of line? There's no place to go, nothing to do, even if I wanted to get in trouble."

Washington smiles a bit. "You gonna join us for a poker game one of these nights? That's somethin' to do."

This comment brings back more memories for Clarence. It's a little sad that many of the men spend their spare time at Fort Assiniboine gambling and drinking. In their defense, a soldier doesn't have much else to do at a fort in northern Montana during the winter, but still, it is a little distressing to Clarence that for some of the men, it's almost all they do. He thinks back on going around the world with the Chicago and All-America baseball teams and how much the ballplayers gambled. He's never liked doing it since.

It's true that Clarence taught the ballplayers on Spalding's tour how to play craps, and that is a type of gambling, but he's very rarely played during the past six years. His craps dice that Tommy gave him are yet another thing Clarence lost in the fire in the Milk River camp. They were in his knapsack along with the handful of other mementos he used to own, and because they were just wooden cubes, they didn't survive the fire.

"You there, Cooper?" Washington's voice startles Clarence out of his memories.

"Sorry, Washington. Just thinking back on better days."

"Well, you is welcome to join us for poker, like I says."

"Will there be whiskey, too?"

"Probly. Some of the men asks me if you gonna be there, sometimes."

"You know I only go to be part of the group, Washington. My heart really isn't into drinking. Or gambling, either."

"Yeah, I thunked that was true. I sees you usually only have but one drink, and you usually leaves before anything rough happens."

"Yeah, that about says it," Clarence tells him. What Clarence doesn't say is that he doesn't want to know too many of the men that well because that way, when he finally has his chance to escape, he'll miss them less.

Instead of saying this to Washington, he says instead, "Maybe we should have another reading lesson rather than gamble. Those are free, you know."

"I won two dollas last time we plays poker."

"Isn't that the first time you won money instead of losing it?"

"Nah, I win some other times, too."

"Really?" Clarence raises his eyebrows and looks Washington in the eye. Usually, Washington is down after poker night because he doesn't do well. Clarence thinks he's a bit too honest to be a good gambler. At least he's smart enough to only wager small amounts. The Army doesn't pay enough to wager large amounts, anyway.

"Well, okay, not very often, but I've won money a couple times."

"Well, it's an open offer if you want more practice at reading, Lincoln. Let me know whenever you want to have more lessons. The library here at the fort isn't much, but I've seen worse."

It's true that the fort does have a small library. It contains a couple books on United States history, a few biographies of famous Army generals, that sort of thing. Clarence hasn't gone in there, though, because it's for white soldiers only, but he got one white private to tell him about it one time. Clarence got lucky when he approached the soldier. The man said he loved reading and didn't understand why more of the soldiers didn't read, and that he'd smuggle Clarence out books if Clarence ever wanted them. Clarence is yet to take him up on his offer, though.

Most of the men don't spend any time at the library because they don't consider reading a very "soldierly" or "manly" thing to do, and many of them can't read at all. Clarence doesn't know if he's the only one in Troop D possessing full literacy, but he knows there aren't many others. No need to flaunt his reading skills in front of them, however. Keeping that quiet is another part of his strategy to try to fit in.

Once again, Washington's voice calls Clarence back to the moment. "I'll think about it," Lincoln tells him.

"Suit yourself. I'm ready to help you out anytime."

Clarence has made the offer to help. Since he's not here at Fort Assiniboine to do his duty to his country, he figures he can at least offer to do his duty toward his fellow colored man.

# Chapter 13

## Gabriel & Mary's Winter

When Gabriel awakes, it is nearly dark outside. The sun has just dropped below the Rocky Mountains to the west, and the last rays of light fade quickly, like they do in Montana in November when fall gives way to winter. The priest has lit an oil lamp and started a fire. Gabriel's stomach growls from want of food, but for the first time in nearly a week, he is warm enough to rest comfortably. Gabriel looks toward the priest—the last person he remembers seeing before the darkness took him. He runs his tongue over his lips. They remain cracked and dry but feel a little better than he remembers from earlier in the day. The small room he's in has the musty smell of the old buffalo robe mixed with the aroma of burning wood in the fireplace.

The priest sitting nearby notices his movement and says, "I am glad to see you awake at last, my son. How is your fever?"

Gabriel grimaces as he shifts his position. "I've certainly felt better," is the best he can come up with. Gabriel's head hurts a bit, and when he touches it, it's still warm from the fever.

"I can imagine. After going without food for so long, and water as well, you may need a few days before feeling yourself again. How does your right arm feel?"

Gabriel looks down and sees that the priest cleaned his wound and dressed it with a new bandage while he was out. "It still hurts a fair deal."

"Also understandable. Lucky for you, the cut was not too deep and struck no major veins. It will heal, given time. Come, wake your young friend and let's get some more food and water in the two of you."

Before getting up, Gabriel asks, "What happened after I blacked out? I remember helping Mary down from our horse, seeing you come toward us, and then things faded. I think I said something to you, but I can't remember what. Then I saw this explosion of color and blinding lights in my eyes. It's the last thing I remember."

"I believe the hunger, blood loss, and lack of water contributed to you fainting," the priest says. "You asked for Father Damiani and then collapsed. We helped bring you inside. You've been asleep for," he pulls out his silver pocket watch and glances at it, "nearly four hours. Come now, drink and take some food."

Gabriel turns and gently touches Mary on her shoulder. "Mary, Mary, wake up now. It's time for some food."

Mary's eyes slowly open, blinking in the dimming light. Then, the memories of the day flood back to her. "Is your arm all right, Gabriel? Are you sure we'll be safe here?"

"I think so, Mary. We made it to the mission, at last. We've been asleep for several hours, and it's nearly night outside now. Are you ready to eat?"

"Yes, I'm very hungry, Gabriel."

"Come, my friends, and eat some potato soup," the priest says. "Then you can tell me how you came to be my guests."

Soon, Gabriel sits in a rough wooden chair at the priest's wooden table. He says, "I was hoping Father Damiani would still be here at the mission. Many years ago, I was his student here, for a little while, at least. I don't know if he'd remember me because I didn't stay that long."

"Father Damiani left the mission some time ago, my child," the man replies. "I am his successor, Father Andreis. I have led St. Peter's for the past six years. Perhaps, in a few minutes, you can tell me your story? Have some bread and coffee for your refreshment."

"Thank you, Father," Gabriel responds. "We are much obliged for your aid."

A little while later, once Gabriel and Mary have had a chance to eat some soup and bread, Father Andreis grows serious. "And now, my friends, what tale can you tell me? Why has God brought you here today?"

Gabriel begins. "Father, my name is Gabriel Ouellette. My family and I were living in the Milk River settlements until a few days ago, when a mob attacked us and destroyed our homes. They were local ranchers, I think."

Father Andreis's face darkens at the news. "Word has reached us of the violence on the Milk River, but the two of you are the first survivors I've spoken to. You were there? Tell me what happened."

"Well, Father, I was fishing with my friend, Clarence, when the posse attacked our homes. As soon as we heard the gunfire, we rushed back to the camp to see what had happened. By the time we arrived, several of our cabins were aflame already, and Clarence and I just managed to rescue young Mary here, find a horse, and get away."

"How many deaths were there?" Father Andreis interrupts to ask. "We have heard only rumors, so I fear the worst."

"It was horrible. Twenty-one died, I believe. All were women, children, and old people. Our hunters, like my father, Pierre, were out looking for game when the attack happened, and it took our village by surprise. Clarence, Mary, and I went back the next day to try to find anything useful that the killers left behind, but we found nothing except the buffalo robe we have with us now. They destroyed our entire village, every single cabin. All burned to the ground. The men stole all our horses, too, and looted the cabins before burning them."

Upon hearing this news, Father Andreis genuflects and says a quick prayer to himself.

"And they shot Clarence, but he didn't die," Mary puts in through a mouthful of brown wheat bread. "He's with the soldiers at the fort now, we think."

"Hold on just a moment, young friends. Your father is Pierre Ouellette, my son?"

Gabriel nods.

"I know Pierre, or, I should say, we know his name here at the mission. When I first arrived here at St. Peter's, Pierre was among those who escorted me and transported my belongings in Red River carts. It is a pleasure to meet one of his progeny, especially the son of a man like your father. He is a man true in the faith, quick to laughter, and steadfast to his friends in time of need. That is his reputation, at any rate."

"Yes, that is my father," Gabriel says. "I tried to find him after the attack, but the cavalry from Fort Assiniboine attacked our hunters as well, and I don't know where he is now. Have you heard any news of him?"

Father Andreis shakes his head slowly and sadly. "No, Gabriel, it has been many months since he visited us at the mission, and that was the last I saw or heard of him. I will pray to God for his safety."

"And Clarence, too. Will you please pray for Clarence?" Mary puts in.

"Indeed, I will pray for your friend," Andreis answers her. "But first, please tell me, who is this Clarence that you speak of? Tell me about him."

"Clarence is my best friend," Mary says quickly. "I miss him. I'm lonely without him."

"Our friend is Clarence Duval," Gabriel adds after gulping down the broth of his soup. "A member of our band, Louis Berger, helped save Mary and Clarence at the Great Northern station at Pacific Junction, and when he learned that they had no money and no transportation to get to St. Louis like they planned, he offered them the chance to live with us in the Milk River Valley until springtime came."

"We were going to see my Uncle John in St. Louis. He's a famous baseball pitcher," Mary interjects. "But then some bad men stole our seats on the train. We spent our last money on those seats, and now we don't have any more money."

"Clarence is colored, you see," Gabriel puts in. "And so, the station conductor just sold his seat to a new person and kicked him off the train. That is how Clarence and Mary came to stay with us. After losing their seats, they hopped another train, and that is where they met Louis."

Father Andreis shifts slightly in his wooden frame chair, turning so he can address Mary. "And how did you and Clarence come to be friends in the first place, Mary?"

"Because Clarence went around the world with my Uncle John once, a long time ago, and Clarence tried to help Uncle John free Ireland. They got to be friends, and they helped each other out. Then, after they got back to America, Clarence came and lived with me and my parents in Butte, and he got to be my friend."

"Where are your parents, Mary?" the priest asks.

"They're dead. My father died in the mines, in a cave-in, and then my mother shot herself," Mary says sadly, her voice trailing off. Then, she sniffles a bit.

Father Andreis crosses himself and says another quick prayer.

"That's why Clarence and Mary were taking the train," Gabriel says. "Clarence was trying to take Mary to live with her Uncle John in St. Louis, before everything went wrong, and they ended up with us, instead."

Father Andreis speaks again. "You say that this Clarence is with the soldiers at the fort? How did that come to pass?"

"After we got away from the killers who destroyed our village, we tried to ride east because we thought the ranchers wouldn't go that way. But then, some soldiers from Fort Assiniboine took us by surprise the next morning. It appears that they were looking for a runaway solider, a deserter, and they thought that Clarence was the person who ran away. They took Clarence back with them. As far as we know, he's still at the fort."

"Ah yes, some of the colored soldiers at Fort Assiniboine are known as the Buffalo Soldiers," Father Andreis says while shaking his head. "Mistaken for a deserter. I am very sorry that all this has happened to you, my friends."

"I just hope," Gabriel begins to speak, then stops short when he sees Mary looking at him, "I just hope that the soldiers are treating Clarence okay over there."

Father Andreis gives a knowing nod to Gabriel, realizing full well that the U.S. Army often shoots deserters to send a message to the other soldiers. Instead of maintaining that line of questioning with Mary present, however, he decides to shift the subject a bit.

"What happened to the two of you after being separated from your friend?" he says to Gabriel.

"We turned around and headed back west, looking for my father, or anyone else from our village we could find."

"From the looks of things, you were unsuccessful."

Gabriel nods and gives a weary sigh. "Instead, we found some drunk cowboys. I don't think they were part of the group who attacked our camp, but two days after we lost Clarence, they found us. They said we were trespassing on the land of someone or other, but I know that isn't true because we were just riding along the tracks of the railroad that goes from Great Falls to Havre when they met us."

"Am I correct to assume they are the source of your present arm injury, and for the state of Mary's clothing, as well?"

"They tried to catch me, and one of them grabbed my buffalo robe, but I got away," Mary says defiantly. "I lost my buffalo robe, though, because I had to wiggle out of it to escape from the bad cowboys. Then they tried to get me and grabbed my shirt, but I got away from that, too."

Father Andreis smiles at this news.

"Then, we rode south as fast as we could to get away from them," Gabriel says, bringing the story to its conclusion. "That was yesterday around noon. We had to leave our gear behind—fishing pole, knife, Mary's buffalo robe, my water canteen, everything—when we got away. We haven't had any food since then because we were afraid to stop in any of the small towns between there and here. The whole state of Montana is out to get us, it seems."

"You have nothing to fear here with us," Father Andreis says to them. "Our mission school serves the people of the *Nehiyaw Pwat* for the most part, so it will be easy enough for you to blend in, on the small chance someone comes here looking for you. You are welcome to stay with us for a time, until you've regained your strength and can decide what to do next."

"Thank you, Father," Gabriel says. "I will be happy to do whatever work you need, so I can earn my keep, as soon as my arm is better and the pain goes down." He glances over at Mary. "And, I'll do whatever I can so that Mary can stay here and go to school for a while."

"Go to school? Me?" Mary says, her face lighting up. "Oh, please, can I? I did love going to school when I lived in Butte. I can even read a little and write my letters." She has on the best smile Gabriel's seen in days.

"You are welcome to start on Monday," Father Andreis tells her. "In a few days, Gabriel, we'll send you out to do some work. The woodcutters can always use an extra ax, and with winter coming on, I believe they'll welcome whatever help you can give them."

"Yes, I gladly agree to help your mission. I need to try to find my own father soon, however. I know he'll be worried about me and wonder where I am, and he'll want to know if I'm safe."

"I will do what I can for the son of Pierre Ouellette, as well," Father Andreis says. "Next time the opportunity arises, I'll send a message to the people at the Boyd Creek School near Lewistown and inquire after Pierre."

"Lewistown has a mission school now, too?"

"Yes, established earlier this year. It serves the Michif people of central Montana as best it can."

"In the morning, may we go into the schoolhouse and look at things, Father?" Gabriel asks after a pause.

"Certainly, my child. Tomorrow, we must also see to the matter of finding the two of you a place to live while you remain here with us. But please, rest tonight. The grace of God be with you." Father Andreis genuflects once more, and then exits, leaving Gabriel and Mary by themselves for a moment.

"I'm worried about Clarence," Mary says. "When will we see him again?"

"If he's in the army, it's impossible to say, Mary. I think when you join the army, you have to stay in the army for a certain length of time."

"But Clarence didn't join the army! Those men made him!"

"I know it, Mary, I know it, but we can't get Clarence out unless we can prove it. We'll never do that. White people just won't listen to us. Every white person in Montana is out to get us, it seems like, and I don't know what we can do. At least we know where Clarence is. I really want to find out about my father, too. I have no idea where in Montana he is now. Hopefully, Father Andreis will help me locate him."

In the morning, Gabriel and Mary go to the schoolhouse and look inside. On the way, Gabriel walks around the grounds and gets his first real look at the mission compound in nearly a dozen years. It's another cold day with a brisk wind. Gabriel and Mary can see their breath as they walk along and survey their temporary home.

Gabriel's memories of the mission have become a little fuzzy over time, but it's clear that many things are different now. The mission is much larger, for one thing, with more buildings. At the northern end of the compound is the chapel. It is a one-story, clapboard wooden frame building whose whitewash is in good shape. The roof of the chapel, however, is another story, being uneven and sagging in spots.

100

The doorway to the chapel faces west, a wooden cross guarding over it from above, and two young pine trees flank the entrance. To the right of the entrance is a wooden three-story bell tower, complete with a brass bell and weathervane on top. The American flag flies alongside, rising a bit higher in the air than the tower.

Just south of the chapel, lying between it and the boys' school and dormitory, are the horse corral and cemetery. A smattering of headstones poke skyward in the rail-fenced, rectangular final resting place of the mission's previous occupants. Some of the headstones are truly stone while others are merely wood. A wooden barn stands adjacent to the corral, in about the same condition as the chapel.

Looking from north to south, the next building, right in the center of the mission compound, is the school and dormitory for boys. It was not there when Gabriel left the mission as a boy. It's almost incongruous to the rest of St. Peter's because it is four stories tall, constructed from stone, and sports a mansard roof and cupola. The residence for Father Andreis where Gabriel and Mary slept the night before abuts the dormitory to the south. Father Andreis's house is three stories, built from wood, and has a steeply-sloping roof. It's surrounded by a white picket fence, which encloses a small vegetable garden.

"Is that the school where I'll go?" Mary asks Gabriel, pointing at the massive stone building.

"No, Mary, that is the school for the boys."

"Boys and girls don't go to school in the same school?"

"Not here they don't."

"Why not, Gabriel?"

"Jesuits founded the mission, and Ursuline nuns run the school. They are both part of the Catholic Church, and they believe boys and girls should be in separate schools."

"Still, can we go inside for a moment, just so I can see it?"

"Sure, Mary, let's take a look."

Gabriel and Mary completely lost track of what day of the week it was because of their adventures, but it turns out to be Saturday, so they are the only ones in the classroom. They can both hear a constant metallic clanking sound, however, as well as hammering, indicating the building also contains the mission's smithy and carpentry shop.

Gabriel leads Mary to the front of the room.

"This isn't where you'll get to go and learn, Mary, but the school for girls doesn't look that much different. Promise me you'll try very hard, okay?"

"I promise, Gabriel, I promise. Is it true you went to school here once when you were my age?"

"I was exactly your age, Mary, ten years old. But I didn't like it here very much, so I left after a while. I shouldn't have done that, though, because now, even though I'm a grownup, I can barely write my name, and I can't read at all. Clarence told me he would try to teach me a bit, but I don't think we'll get the chance now. Promise me you'll do better, okay?"

"I already promised, and I will. I went to school for a few years in Butte, you know. I can write my name, and add the small numbers, and spell some of the easy words."

Gabriel smiles, and then he points to a framed photograph at the front of the small classroom. "Do you know who that is, Mary?"

"No."

"That is Louis Riel, along with his wife, Margaret, the day they were married. The priest with them is Father Damiani. He and Louis Riel were the teachers here at the mission for my short time as a student. But then, Louis got thrown in jail by the Montana territorial government."

"They put your teacher in jail? How come? Was he a bad teacher?"

"No," Gabriel says, smiling and then laughing for the first time in days. "He was a very good teacher. The Montana government put him in jail because he tried to get the right to vote for the Michif people. Louis realized that whenever white people and Michif lived near each other, the whites always took advantage of us, so he wanted the Michif to be able to vote, so the whites wouldn't do that anymore. I left school while he was in jail, and that was the last schooling I've ever had."

"What happened when he got out of jail?"

"After a little while, Louis went north, to Canada, to try to help the Michif people there against the Canadian government. It didn't work, though, and after he surrendered, they strangled him and killed him. But I got to be his scout before the battle. That's when I got to be such a good horseback rider."

"Gabriel," Mary asks thoughtfully, "am I ever going to make it to St. Louis to meet my Uncle John?"

"You will, if I have anything to say about it. I know how much you miss Clarence, but I'm gonna watch out for you."

Gabriel puts his arm around Mary's tiny shoulders. She takes his hand in both of hers. "I'm glad," she tells him.

Stepping outside once again, Gabriel pulls his coat tight against his body. A dirt road, the one he and Mary rode in on, splits the compound in two, although the only significant building south of the road is the Mount Angela Convent which houses both the nuns who teach at St. Peter's and the school for the girls. It hadn't been there, either, when Gabriel stayed at the mission as a boy, but it's almost as impressive as the boys' school. It is three stories, rather than four, but also made of stone. From the smell wafting in their direction, Gabriel guesses that is also the location of the mission's bakery.

One day late in January of 1896, Gabriel approaches Father Andreis. "Father Andreis," he says to the kindly priest, "has there been any word of my father yet?"

Andreis shakes his head sadly. "We've heard nothing. Nothing from the Lewistown area, and nothing from my fellow priests down in Butte or Helena. We just can't seem to find out where he is."

Gabriel's face falls, and he shuffles his feet. "Maybe I should go and look for him."

"Where would you look, young Gabriel? How far could you travel, in the middle of winter, just to try to pick up the trail? Patience, my son. I know it is hard but have patience. God has not forgotten about you, or your father."

Gabriel nods, a mix of disappointment and understanding. Father Andreis puts his hand on Gabriel's shoulder. "I hear you are doing fine work as a woodcutter. The work you do helps heat the schoolhouse for the children, and the logs we float down the river to Great Falls we trade for flour, bacon, and other articles of food. You are earning your keep. Do not fear that you will wear out your welcome here."

"Mary says she likes school very much."

"Friar O'Connell, her teacher, informs me she is a very bright young girl, and would do very well as a student, if she could only stay here long enough to memorize her facts a bit better."

"That is another thing that troubles me," Gabriel says to the older man. "Our goal, Clarence and me, was to send Mary on to St. Louis this spring to be with her Uncle John. We think that's where he lives, but we don't know for sure, so we have no way to mail him a letter and let him know what has happened to us. Is there anything you can do to help us?"

"St. Louis is a very large city, my son. I don't know how many souls reside there now, but several hundreds of thousands, I should think. Finding one man amongst so many, without knowing where to begin the search, is a daunting task indeed. Still, I will send a letter to Archbishop Kain, who is the new head of the diocese in St. Louis and see if he can help us. I think that the Holy Church elevated him to archbishop only recently because Archbishop Kenrick presided over the followers of the true faith in St. Louis for several decades, but perhaps he can find a way to help us. Your young friend's uncle is a Catholic, is he not?"

"So far as I know, yes."

"Well, we have at least a small chance, then. Have faith, Gabriel. God has His own plans for us all and will answer your prayers at His appointed time."

# Chapter 14

## The Cree Deportation Act: Washington, D.C.

Richard Olney, Secretary of State of the United States, unfolds the letter from Governor John Rickards of Montana that lies on his immaculately polished desk in Washington, D.C. Dated January 21, 1896, it reads:

> *Sir,*
>
> *This office has had previous correspondence with the Department of State in relation to the presence of a number of Cree Indians in our State. These Indians as you may know are wards of the British Government. In default of a reservation and the restrictions of the Federal Government, they have been an intolerable nuisance, constantly violating our game laws, foraging upon our herds, and not infrequently looting isolated cabins. The patience of our people has been severely tried, and I have at times feared that bloodshed would result. The police power of the State is not equal to the task of protecting the people from these*

*marauding bands. This condition of affairs cannot be allowed to continue indefinitely.*

*I desire to call your attention to the very serious fact that the number of the Crees in our State is increasing very rapidly through accessions annually from their relatives in Canada. Investigations show that only about 100 of them crossed our borders as refugees at the close of the Riel Rebellion. In a letter bearing date November 1, 1887, from J. D. C. Atkins, Commissioner of Indian Affairs, addressed to the Secretary of the Interior he said, "The fugitives number about 200, men, women, and children." I learn from a conference with their chief "Little White Bear" that they number about 500. Hence we should not only get rid of these now annoying us, but prevent others from coming.*

*The question of supreme importance is the adoption of some plan by which these Indians can be deported across the boundary line to the British Possessions from which they came.*

*Let me indulge the hope that you can in some manner afford us relief in this matter.*


*I have & co.*


*J. E. Rickards*


*Governor of Montana*


Next to this letter from Governor Rickards lies the most recent response of the Canadian government, dated Ottawa, March 26, 1896. Olney runs his right hand through his bushy mustache, wondering what the Canadian response will be. Slowly, he unfolds the light, yellow-tinted paper and then adjusts his necktie while settling deep into his cushioned leather chair. Although the Canadian authorities required nearly two months to decide on a course of action, it reads:

# The Cree Deportation Act: Washington, D.C.

*Sir,*

*I have the honor to acknowledge the receipt of your letter of the 25th ultimo, transmitting return of Indians belonging to the North West Territories, believed to be in the United States, and with reference thereto, and to former correspondences, to inform you that this Government has determined to co-operate with that of the United States to compel the refugees in Montana to leave that State and return to Reserves in the Territories.*

*The Department has requested the Comptroller to instruct the Commissioner of the North West Mounted Police to consult with you and arrange to have a sufficient force take over the refugees and escort them to their respective destinations.*

*No doubt about the middle of May would be the best time, but earlier if possible, so that some gardening might be done.*

*When all arrangements have been completed you will be kind enough to put yourself into communication with the Governor of Montana and arrange time and place at the International Boundary for meeting and taking charge of the Indians.*

*I do not know that there is anything further to add than that the Battleford Crees had better be sent to Onion Lake, where they will probably be more closely looked after and made to exert themselves, and of course the various Agents concerned should be warned to expect the arrival of the Indians.*

*Kindly report to the Department any action on your part.*

*Your obedient servant,*

*Hayter Reed*

*Deputy Superintendent General of Indian Affairs*

Olney breathes a sigh of relief. He'd been confident that the Canadians and their British overlords would cooperate, but still, it is good to have the agreement in front of him. Probably a wise move on their part, he concludes. The British Empire is as large and grand as ever on paper, but its fault lines are showing a bit. Britain's colonial competition, especially with the French, is alive and well, and more importantly, the Germans, under Kaiser Wilhelm II's leadership, are building up a blue water navy that might someday challenge Britain's dominance on the high seas. Britain might need America's help someday, Olney thinks, so why quibble over a couple hundred Indian refugees?

He is aware that the United States is not acting reciprocally here; after all, several hundred Sioux still live in Canada, and the Canadian government has not insisted the United States take them back. Nonetheless, it will be nice to get this little affair over with and get this pesky Montana governor off his back.

Olney has much bigger worries than Cree Indians, after all. The people of Cuba are, once again, in rebellion against Spanish authority, and who knows what might happen on that tropical island? American companies have more investments in Cuba than ever; how long before those companies call on the State Department to protect their investments with military force? And what if the revolutionaries win? Having a second Caribbean nation run by the mixed-race descendants of Europeans, Indians, and African slaves is not an encouraging thought. The fact that one such nation, Haiti, exists is bad enough; if Cuba becomes another Haiti, the United States might have to turn to force to keep the government there in line and American investments safe.

Speaking of the possibility of using the U.S. government to protect foreign investments, the matter of the Hawaiian Islands is also on Olney's mind. The Dole Delegation had come to Washington in 1894 seeking annexation of the islands, but the president, Democrat Grover Cleveland, had opposed the idea. Dole, the missionaries, and the planters of Hawaii still favored annexation, however, and Olney senses they're merely waiting for another opportunity to gain their ends. His party, the Democratic Party, must be ready with a plan, should that possibility transpire.

And what of Japan? Almost exactly one year ago that nation, shaking off its primitive, feudal society, defeated the Chinese in war. Clearly, Japan was a nation on the rise in East Asia and the Pacific; America must take note.

Compared to such weighty questions, the fate of a few Montana Indians, or Canadian Indians, whatever the case might be, is of little concern. Olney debates how he should handle the request of Governor Rickards. Montana had just gained statehood late in 1889, and although political observers considered the state solidly Democratic at the time because of its Irish population, recently the state elected a Republican governor, Rickards, so clearly, party loyalties there are more fluid than political experts anticipated just six years ago. Fluid enough, at least, that Montana Republicans like Rickards needed some diplomatic victories if they were to hold their state in the upcoming national elections. It bothers Olney that, if he helps the governor now, it might advance the interests of Montana Republicans. However, the administration also ran a risk in not helping. If Governor Rickards doesn't get help against the Cree, the Republicans might use that against Montana Democrats in November, claiming that the Democratic Party stands on the side of Indians, and foreign Indians at that, against the forces of civilization and progress.

Olney knows that the Democrats must also consider the wildcard in the upcoming national elections, the Populist Party. He is aware that some of the leaders of his party have already started making overtures to the Populists to join with the Democrats in 1896. If the Democratic Party takes up the issue of the unlimited coinage of silver, it might be enough to lure the Populists into an alliance and win the state of Montana, regardless of what the Republicans did, because mining is so important to the Montana economy. Make no mistake, the Democrats need all the help they can get in 1896, too. With the Panic of 1893 not over yet, Republicans are hammering Democrats nationally with accusations of poor economic policies.

Either way, there are risks, but there are rewards, as well. If the State Department aids Governor Rickards and Montana Republicans, Montana Democrats can also claim credit with the people for ridding Montana of its "Cree menace." They can ride an anti-Indian wave to popularity just as well as the Republicans can if they play their cards right and don't let the Republicans claim all the credit. That, mixed with the silver issue, can catapult the Democrats to victory in Montana in November.

In any case, it is time for a decision. Olney calls in his secretary. "Cable Montana's honorable governor and tell him that I've received a response from the Canadian officials at last. They have agreed to take the Cree."

# Chapter 15

## The Cree Deportation Act: Montana

John E. Rickards, governor of the state of Montana, eyes the cable from Secretary of State Olney with immense satisfaction. At last, Montana will be rid of the marauding Cree and, with his reelection thereby almost assured, his state can get on with economic prosperity. Rickards also holds in his hand a letter from A. E. Forget, Canadian Indian Commissioner at Regina, Saskatchewan, dated April 1, 1896. It reads:

> *Sir,*
>
> *With reference to negotiations which have recently been pending between the United States Federal authorities and the Government of the Dominion of Canada relative to the removal from the State of Montana of certain refugee Cree Indians who entered the territory of that State during and since the Canadian North-West Rebellion of 1885, I have the honour to inform you that the Dominion Government having decided to co-operate with that of Washington in bringing about this end, I have been*

*instructed to place myself in communication with you for this purpose.*

*I should therefore be pleased to learn whether your arrangements for the delivery of these persons at the International Boundary will admit of such being done not later than say 10th of May next and at Coutt's Station on the Great Falls and Canada Railway.*

*I may say that if you can secure their being brought to that point by rail, it will very greatly facilitate the transfer being effectively made, as I would take them on immediately by the same train to Lethbridge, a distance of about 50 miles towards the interior, thus minimizing the chance of straggling parties breaking away from the main body and returning secretly to the South.*

*We are desirous of effecting the transfer at the earliest possible date in order that they may be distributed to their various Reserves in time for agricultural operations.*

*In conclusion I would invite your attention to the fact that not a few of those who passed from this country to your territory as Indians have during the interval changed their status by legal process provided by the laws of the Dominion governing the discharge of halfbreeds from our Indian Treaties.*

*Many of these persons are now therefore not Indians in the eyes of the law, as while residing abroad they applied for, through Attorneys, and received from the Dominion Government certificates of the termination of their disabilities as Treaty Indians.*

*These persons having now resided for 10 years more or less on United States soil (principally in Choteau Country, Montana, I believe) it is assumed that it is not the intention of the United States Government to disturb them.*

*I send under separate cover a map which may be of service to you in this connection.*

*I have the honor to be,*
*Your obedient servant.*

*A. E. Forget*

*Commissioner*

A few paragraphs from this note trouble Governor Rickards, especially the part about some of the halfbreeds changing their legal status and that the Canadian authorities have no plans to accept them. He knows all about the people living in Choteau County that Commissioner Forget referred to, of course. Most live near towns such as Havre and Fort Benton, subsisting on the garbage and leftovers of the good white people of Montana when they aren't stealing cattle, begging the Army for food, or illegally hunting game. The white cattlemen near Havre had done the right thing in attacking their camps the year before, but it hasn't been enough; too many halfbreeds still wander Choteau County, menacing the people of Montana, refusing or unable to adapt to modern civilization. The thought that the Canadians might not accept these degenerates is intolerable.

But the governor has already made up his mind. He is going to send these people north to Canada, whether they are welcome there or not. The Christian voters of Montana are not interested in the technicalities of Canadian law regarding halfbreed Indians; if any stay behind, Montanans will not want to hear about how their governor had only persuaded the Canadian authorities to take some of the desperadoes. No, he can't allow that. All of them must go, Canadian law be damned. If the Canadians do not allow them to enter and some wander back to Montana, Rickards can always place the blame on the Canadians for not holding up their part of the bargain or blame the shiftless nature of Indians, should things come to that.

The governor decides not to mention this in his reply to the commissioner, however. Instead, he dictates a brief response to his secretary for transmission to Regina. It reads:

*Sir,*

*I have the honor to acknowledge the receipt of your communication under date of April 1ˢᵗ, 1896, and to say that the information therein contained has been forwarded to the Department of State, Washington, that the Federal authorities may act upon the suggestions made, the matter being of an international character. I trust the Government will take up this matter at once and that the necessary arrangements for deporting the Cree Indians will be made with as little delay as possible.*

*With respect,*
*Yours very truly,*

*J. E. Rickards*

*Governor of Montana*

His reply note to Secretary of State Olney, of course, also makes no mention of any distinctions of legal status among the potential deportees. Nor is Governor Rickards concerned with when these vermin arrive at their ultimate destination in Canada. The sooner they are out of his state, the better. To him, anything else is an inconvenient triviality.

# Chapter 16

## The Cree Deportation Act: Congress

On April 29, 1896, Montana senator Thomas Carter stands to speak on the floor of the United States Senate. A Republican, Carter rose to the top of Montana politics for the first time in 1888, when he became the territory's delegate in Congress. When the Treasure State achieved statehood the following year, he'd become its representative and followed that with a term as Chairman of the Republican National Committee. Recently, the people of Montana returned him to Congress as a member of the Senate in the 1894 midterm elections. His beard had been several inches shorter back in 1888, and the hair atop his head a little fuller, but Carter has a great deal of pride in himself and the figure he cuts in the Republican Party.

Carter strides to the speaker's podium full of confidence and purpose, his speech memorized and polished. No sheaf of notes on this occasion. This is the United States Senate. He realizes, of course, that many of his fellow senators rank rather below the level of intellectual giant. Many have bought their position through some combination of their own money and party funds. Others, his Southern colleagues especially, are only there because their state elections are noncompetitive, foregone conclusions. Still, Carter feels the need to stand out.

Partly, this is because he represents Montana. It is among the newest states in the nation, and because of its ranching and mining economy, some politicians see the state as somewhat akin to an unruly younger brother. To properly represent his state, Carter needs respect, and he looks for ways to gain respect at every opportunity. Today is one such day.

Despite the gravity of the occasion, Carter feels no fear. Why should he worry? After all, no one had even expected him to win an election in Montana in the first place. For one thing, he is a Republican, and every political expert believed Montana was a Democratic stronghold because of its heavy population of Irish Catholics working in the mines of Butte. What the political experts hadn't counted on, however, was that Carter is also Irish and Catholic, while his Democratic opponent for his first election in 1888, William Clark, was a Scotch-Irish Presbyterian, born in the Ulster County of Tyrone. Clark is not only an elder in the Presbyterian Church but a Grand Master Mason, too. Add to Clark's religious liabilities some healthy spending by Carter's fellow Irishman Marcus Daly, Clark's chief rival in Montana mining, on Carter's behalf, and he had scored a dramatic political upset.

Clark committed his share of gaffes during the 1888 campaign as well, but what did one expect from a political amateur like William Clark? Carter is a member of both the Ancient Order of Hibernians and the Robert Emmet Literary Association and a friend of Irish patriots Michael Davitt and Charles Stewart Parnell. He always keeps the most recent issue of Patrick Ford's *Irish World and American Industrial Liberator* on his desk in Washington, D.C., and his brother-in-law is Thomas Cruse, the man most responsible for Helena's Catholic Cathedral. With all these things working in Carter's favor, he'd won a good share of the Irish vote in 1888, and retaining that vote helped win him his present seat in Congress during the 1894 elections.

Carter, like his fellow Montana politicians Charles Hartman and John Rickards, is a member of the Grand Old Party, and now it is time to use his influence on their behalf and convince the Senate that the time is at hand to remove the detestable Cree from Montana. This will take some work, however. Some senators, especially the soft-hearted Easterners, are all too ready to forget their own removal of Indians earlier in the century while disapproving of Montana's present efforts to do the same. Indeed, a handful have already spoken against the Cree Deportation Act now under discussion.

Particularly disturbing to Carter is that his opponents have produced letters from Army officers and other government officials to bolster their case, notably one written by John Atkins, Commissioner of Indian Affairs, based on information from Colonel E. S. Otis, commander at Fort Assiniboine in 1888. The unfortunate words echo in Carter's memory even as he strides to the Senate podium to speak.

*Colonel Otis thinks that they ought to be placed at some agency and assisted. He speaks in praise of them; says they are workers and eager to have land assigned to them; that they have some knowledge of tillage, and would under favorable conditions raise enough to meet their wants; that they would set a good example to other Indians and be a positive benefit to them; and furthermore, that the agent at Fort Belknap has signified to him his willingness to receive and assist them at his agency.*

*I am aware that these refugees are not native Indians of the United States, nor have they any rights on any of our Indian reservations, but as a simple act of humanity I think they should be given a chance to earn their bread when that is really all they ask. They have been wandering about from place to place now for nearly three years, homeless and hopeless, and but for the little assistance they have received from the military (for which reimbursement has been made by this Department) they would certainly have starved to death long ago.*

*Bad as they may have been at home, they have committed no offense since they have been on our soil, and it is known that some of them have starved to death when they could easily have supplied their wants from the cattle ranges of northern Montana. No complaint has ever been made against them; but, on the contrary, their conduct has called forth the warmest expressions of praise and sympathy from the white people of the Territory.*

*It is not likely that they will ever go back to the British Possessions, and instead of longer treating them as felons and outcasts to be driven away on sight, I think the dignity of the Government requires that they be given a place somewhere, where they can raise food enough to keep them from starvation at least.*

*The fact that the agent at Fort Belknap Agency has expressed his willingness to receive and care for them at his agency would seem to indicate that his own Indians would make no objections to having them in their midst, and I therefore have the honor to recommend that this office be authorized to direct him to allow the refugees (numbering, as it appears, 160 souls) to come to his agency and cultivate as much land as they may require to support themselves, and to render them such assistance as he may be able to give without injury to the welfare of his own Indians.*

It will be difficult, Carter knows, to overcome such effusive praise, coming as it does from a military officer and Indian commissioner, but he's beaten the odds before, and he isn't scared of taking them on again now.

Taking his place and glancing about the Senate chamber, Carter begins speaking slowly and calmly. "Colleagues of the United States Senate, it is my honor to speak to you today regarding a most pressing issue in my home state of Montana. The bill we have before us, for the amendments to House Resolution 8293, is a matter of the greatest concern to the Christian citizens there. We have already heard from some of the opponents of this most important piece of legislation, so I come before you to speak on behalf of the honorable citizens whom I represent.

"The letters read for our consideration so recently, from Indian Commissioner Atkins and Colonel Otis, I fear miss the mark in representing the reality of the situation in Montana in 1896. Even if things were as Commissioner Atkins represented them when he penned his letter of April 1888, I can assure this body that things are not so today. Nor did all the commissioner's contemporaries agree with him. Consider the following communication from Brigadier-General Thomas Ruger, head of the Department of the Dakotas, written the same year, 1888. General Ruger expressed his views that the United States should compel the Cree to move north of the International Boundary, and that in the fall of 1887 the commanding officer at Fort Assiniboine received instructions to do precisely that. That officer's instructions charged him with removing all Cree Indians taking asylum in the United States after the Riel Rebellion of 1885 and permitting no more Cree to come south of the boundary and join them.

"Sadly, this has not happened. Commissioner Atkins mentioned that in 1888, the renegade Cree numbered 160 souls. I have it on good information that this number, today in 1896, exceeds 500 and grows larger yearly. The threat they pose to the settlers and ranchers of Montana grows apace, as any perusal of Montana's excellent daily newspapers will make plain.

"In addition, I would like to make you familiar with additional evidence for the removal of these savage individuals who are so offensive and obnoxious to their white neighbors. I have in my hand a memorandum from James Blaine, United States Secretary of State in 1892, proving that not only were these refugees plundering the farms and ranches of northern Montana, but that their horses carried contagious diseases, since communicated to the animals and livestock of that location. Mr. Blaine sent this missive to the Canadians in January of 1892, and in their reply, of March 29 of that year, the Canadian Governor General expressed a desire to cooperate with the

United States in returning to Canada any Cree Indians guilty of marauding in the United States.

"Fellow senators, this was a great missed opportunity for the United States to end the Cree menace for good. Our present Secretary of State, Mr. Olney, is now in receipt of a second offer from the Canadian government to take these people back to where they belong. Let us not tempt fate and await a third fortuitous offer from our friends to the north. It is unlikely the Canadians will offer such a kindly reception a third time. Just last week, Mr. Olney received a diplomatic note from Mr. Julian Pauncefote, British Ambassador in Washington, informing us that as soon as this body passes the necessary legislation, his Government stands willing to cooperate with the United States. Mr. Olney further states that it would be a great mistake, should we fail to act now.

"Finally, according to Secretary Olney, President Cleveland stands ready to use the Army to carry out the necessary operations. He lacks only the funding to carry out such maneuvers. It is our duty as American citizens to provide President Cleveland with the approval and funds to complete this long-overdue removal of the foreign, Canadian Cree from United States soil. Therefore, I move that we accept the proposed amendments to the House bill, and vote on this legislation, worded as follows:

*Be it enacted by the Senate and House of Representatives of the United States of America in Congress assembled, that there be, and is hereby appropriated, out of any money in the Treasury not otherwise appropriated, the sum of five thousand dollars, or so much thereof as may be necessary, the same to be immediately available, to enable the President, by employment of the Army or otherwise, to deport from the State of Montana and deliver at the international boundary line to the Canadian authorities, all refugee Canadian Cree Indians in said State.*"

# Chapter 17

## Hope at Last

Fort Assiniboine is open—it has no defensive wall. For Clarence, that makes trying to escape even more tempting, and his inability to find a good chance to do so even more frustrating. Many days, while he parades across the snow-pocked ground in March, tufts of green grass starting to emerge, it's all he thinks about while going through the motions of drilling.

Clarence also learns that Fort Assiniboine has about 500 soldiers stationed at it, including officers, although it has enough buildings that it appears as if the place could hold more people. Some of the troops are colored, some white. Clarence supposes he should be thankful for the undermanned status of Fort Assiniboine, however, because it probably saved his life. Most of the barracks, his included, are two-story brick buildings. Clarence's barrack faces one of the flat, treeless parade grounds where the troopers drill and practice.

Drilling is not the only thing soldiers do at a fort, however. The enlisted men also have jobs that they perform to keep the fort in working order. Clarence's job turns out to be baking bricks for use in construction. Wood is scarce in northern Montana, so the Army used bricks when constructing most of the buildings, and the fort always needs a supply on hand for repairs. As a result, Clarence has become a brickmaker. It isn't bad, in his eyes, at least not in the winter, because he's indoor and the heat from the kilns keeps him plenty warm. He's a little scared of how it will feel during the summer months, but then again, he doesn't plan to be around by then, anyway.

One day, as March turns to April, it is warm for a change, and Clarence receives permission to step outside the building with the kilns to take a break from working and cool down. When he steps outside, he sees that several windows are open in the buildings surrounding him; Clarence guesses others are trying to enjoy the day and air out their rooms after the long Montana winter. He wanders around for a little while and then sits down and leans his back against the brick wall of one of the buildings. After working inside making bricks the past few hours, it feels just right to sit down outside. The snow is gone, finally, and while the earth is still damp, especially in the areas that lie in shade part of the day, Clarence doesn't mind.

He closes his eyes for a moment and just breathes in the fresh air. The air would be clean, except for the smells coming from the ovens that the gentle breeze blows in his direction. Then, through the open window above him, Clarence hears two people enter a room; the sound of their booted footsteps and their voices snaps his mind to attention.

Where is he? Clarence was so busy enjoying the nice weather, he didn't even pay attention to where he sat down, but when he opens his eyes, he realizes he's sitting against the back wall of a two-story brick building with six windows on the bottom floor and three on the upper. Each window has an upper and lower half; you can raise the bottom half to open it. Two brick chimneys poke through the shingled roof, and Clarence also notices the aroma of someone smoking a pipe wafting through one of the open windows above. The breeze blows most of the smell away, but just enough lingers that Clarence is aware of it whenever he inhales.

Oh my. Clarence realizes he's sitting outside one of the officers' quarters. He gets confirmation of this when he notices that one of the voices coming through the window belongs to First Lieutenant Pershing, the man the soldiers call "Old Red." It appears he's speaking with another officer who outranks him. Clarence knows he should probably go quietly but decides to stay and listen. He reasons that if he's ever going to get away from here, he needs information about what the officers plan to do, so he decides to risk it. It appears the two men don't even notice that the window is open, or they don't care, because they commence conversing immediately. The other man speaks first.

"How are things in your command, Lieutenant?"

"First rate, sir," Pershing answers crisply.

"Are you sure? I know that having command over colored troops is, shall we say, not a position that most officers aspire to."

"It suits me fine for now, sir. I'm pleased to do my duty wherever the Army sees fit to put me."

"I've never commanded a colored unit myself. How would you describe it? Is it different than leading white soldiers?"

"Well, sir, as you know, I gained this command somewhat by accident. Their regular commander is away recruiting, and that is how I came to lead these men. I suppose I would say it is a rather radical change. Prior to arriving here, I commanded a corps of cadets, the type of citizens from whom the future leaders of our nation arise. These colored men are rather different. They come, by and large, from a group of citizens who have had the most limited advantages in life and who possess the restricted ambitions one would expect of men coming from such circumstances."

"But you've had no problems with the men, correct?" the other voice asks.

"Correct. I've found that Negro troops respond well to the same treatment as other soldiers, for the most part. I have always felt kindly and sympathetic toward them because of their limited circumstances in life, and I believe that fairness and due consideration to their welfare produces the same loyalty and courage in them as those actions do in any other soldiers. We drill outside under difficult conditions at times, but I make sure they're properly supplied with buffalo coats, decent mounts, three square meals a day, and everything else that a cavalryman deserves."

"So, you try to treat them the same as white soldiers, then?"

"For the most part, yes. I've found that men, of whatever race, creed, or color, generally want to do the right thing, and respect officers who live out those principles. I have had no trouble commanding these men. In one respect only have I found them different than the white soldiers stationed here."

"And what is that, Lieutenant?"

"The Negros like to be on display and show off their talents. They like the glamourous side of Army life. I've found that nothing pleases them more than being on parade and marching to the music of military bands."

The other officer gives a quick but friendly laugh. "Well, if that is their greatest flaw as a people, I have seen much worse. At least they avoid the drunken, brawling behavior of the Irish."

"By and large, yes, sir."

"Still, I worry about how they will perform under pressure in the field, should things ever come to that."

"They are well trained, sir. I believe they will give a good account of themselves when the time comes. The 10th Cavalry always has. Most of the men take pride in that fact."

"Well, if anyone can train soldiers, it's you, Lieutenant Pershing. We'll hope these Negros in the 10th Cavalry perform no different from the white cadets you're used to. Now, let's get down to business, shall we?"

"Certainly."

"Some of my friends are well placed in Washington society, and occasionally, I hear news from them regarding the goings on in Congress and the Executive Branch. I have it on good authority that at some point this spring, Congress will take up and pass legislation for the removal of the Cree Indians of Montana."

When Clarence hears the unknown speaker say this, his heart starts beating double time. That means Gabriel and Mary! Even though they are Métis, Clarence has heard people call them Cree before, so he knows that anything about the Cree could also mean them. He's barely breathing as he waits for the speaker to continue.

"I am sure you've heard rumors of this yourself, Lieutenant Pershing?"

"I have, sir, although because they are just rumors, I pay them little heed, choosing instead to wait for evidence and confirmation. Still, I must confess, we had one case this last fall of a deserter who tried to leave my troop. I'd just become the officer of that particular group of men, so it was a bit of a test for me. Although my first inclination was to shoot him after we recaptured him, I chose not to, just for this eventuality."

Clarence swallows hard when he hears this.

The other speaker resumes. "That was probably a wise move because who can tell where these Cree have scattered to over the winter? We'll need every man we have in order to track them down, corral them, and take them to Canada where they belong. Do you know the background to their story, Lieutenant?"

"A bit of it, I think. As I recall, there were some troubles between these Cree and the government of Canada back in 1885, and the troubles culminated in the Riel Rebellion. After the capture and hanging of Riel, most of the participants in the rebellion, fearing retribution from the Canadian authorities, fled to Montana and North Dakota."

"That is correct. They've been a nuisance here ever since '85, especially when it comes to stealing cattle. Our intelligence also indicates that some of the Cree now in Montana might have played a role in the Duck Lake and Frog Lake killings in Canada. Are you familiar with those events, Lieutenant?"

"Not very familiar, I must confess, sir, beyond having heard the names once or twice."

"Early in the rebellion, before the main battle at Batoche, some Cree led by Gabriel Dumont fought with Canada's Mounted Police at Duck Lake. Little Bear and Lucky Man, two Cree who we think are now in Montana, also took part in this battle at Duck Lake. The Cree, being on their home terrain and knowing the lay of the land, defeated the Canadian forces handily."

"Never underestimate the importance of being on familiar ground," Pershing puts in.

"Quite so. In any case, the story of Frog Lake is somewhat more gruesome. There, the savages, led by a man named Wandering Spirit, killed an Indian agent. Quinn, I believe was the man's name. Eight other whites died along with him, murdered by the Cree."

"And the United States has sheltered these men ever since? Haven't the Canadian authorities demanded their extradition?"

"As you know, Lieutenant, several leaders of the Rebellion, the cursed Louis Riel foremost among them, eventually either surrendered to the Canadians, or Canadian forces captured them and rightly hung them for their treason. I believe the Canadian government considered the Cree sufficiently chastised at that point."

"Perhaps that's true," Pershing says after a brief pause. "Although I myself might have taken a more punitive approach. Toward the leaders, at any rate. Still, all the more reason to take strong, aggressive action toward these Cree right now."

"I agree. The United States will be well rid of them. If Congress does approve their deportation, it appears quite likely that Fort Assiniboine will play a major role in the operation. Perhaps the decisive role. The main reason I'm here, other than to conduct a routine inspection of the fort, is to pass on this news to you, so you can train your men accordingly and be ready if this bill passes and the time comes to act. I take it I can count on you and your men, Lieutenant Pershing?"

"Absolutely, sir. You know I stand ready to do my duty, and the men will as well."

"Very good. I'll let you return to your regular duties now."

When Clarence hears this, he knows the time has come to slink away before anyone notices that he's there. His mind swims with possibilities. Maybe he won't have to make another attempt at desertion after all. There's a good chance Gabriel and Mary will be in the group of people this mission tries to capture. Clarence isn't sure what he can do for them, even if their paths cross. But it sounds as though he'll have a bit of time to think of something.

He's almost back to the brick kilns when he sees Washington. By chance, Washington's also assigned to brickmaking. They've become friends and try to watch out for each other. Clarence is still trying to teach him to speak and write better, but although Washington's heart is in it, he's proven to be a slow learner.

"My, you are a fresh one, Cooper," he tells Clarence in a low whisper. "Listnen' in on officers an' all."

"You saw that?" Clarence whispers back. "I didn't even mean to end up there. Just wandered in the fresh air, you know, and that's where I ended up."

"Try tellin' that to them white boys when they catch you. You wanna end up on that rail another day, Cooper?"

"Nope. I'm telling you, it was just an accident. But, if you promise not to mention it to anyone," Clarence pauses while Washington winks his assent and smiles, "I'll tell you what I heard and what we're gonna be doing this spring and summer. It looks like I'll be staying put, after all, so you can stop worrying about what I'm planning to do."

# Chapter 18

## Marching Orders

It is no surprise to Clarence when, on June 11, First Lieutenant Pershing calls Troop D of the 10<sup>th</sup> Cavalry together, so he can brief the men on their orders. They stand at attention on a verdant green parade ground. The grass will turn gold and then brown in a few months, Clarence knows, but it sure is pretty today.

"Men of the 10<sup>th</sup> Cavalry. Finally, I have new orders from the War Department in Washington. In two days, we will take the field."

Normally, murmurs would go through the men at this point, but because they stand at attention on the drill field, no one says a thing. In Clarence's time in the 10<sup>th</sup>, he's learned that, in the past, the regiment often fought against various Indian tribes on the Great Plains, and that is how the regiment earned its nickname, the Buffalo Soldiers. This time, however, he hopes they won't have to do too much fighting, or if they do, that he'll have escaped by that time and won't be around to see it. While Clarence thinks, Lieutenant Pershing continues.

"The situation is as follows. We have, today, in Montana, some five hundred to six hundred renegade Cree Indians. They are, at present, a great nuisance to the law-abiding citizens of the state.

Continually, they have stolen both livestock and other property from the citizens of Montana, in addition to poaching game and generally being disagreeable in their dirty, uncivilized manners. State authorities have tried to rid Montana of these pests, but their efforts have not succeeded, and the Cree remain, their presence a festering sore on the body of the state. Our forces have captured small bands from time to time and marched them back across the border where they belong, but, like lice, these bands squirm back to Montana as soon as our men are out of sight.

"That stops now, here, with us, the 10th Cavalry. Recently, the U.S. Congress has made definitive arrangements with the Canadian government to receive these Cree and keep them in Canada. Our duty in this campaign will be to find the Cree, round them up, and transport them to the Canadian border, where the Mounted Police of Canada will take them into custody and move them along to their final destinations.

"I expect you will carry out this mission with both restraint and efficiency. I do not anticipate much resistance from these savages, but you will, of course, prepare for any eventuality. Our purpose is to round these primitives up and facilitate their transport to the International Boundary. The regiment takes the field in two days, on June 13th. Tomorrow, you will receive details on what portion of Montana our troop will sweep in the roundup. That is all. Dismissed."

After First Lieutenant Pershing finishes his remarks, chatter breaks out among the men. Some are happy to finally stop drilling and take the field. Others seem a bit disappointed that their new assignment seems unlikely to produce any real action.

At first, it seems strange to Clarence why soldiers would want to go into combat. In his experience, life is risky enough without volunteering to take extra chances that could get a person killed. At the next mess, he decides to ask Washington about it.

While the soldiers sit on long wooden benches scarfing food quickly off the simple, unadorned wooden tables, Clarence leans in for a quiet conversation with his friend.

"Lincoln," Clarence says to him, "when we got our marching orders today, why were so many of the men disappointed that we aren't likely to see any shooting? Are they anxious to get themselves killed?"

"I don' know if I'd say anxious, Cooper, but we ain't scared, neither. You don' know much 'bout the history of the 10th, do you?"

"I was hopping trains and living in log cabins when I was supposed to learn that part of the regimental history, I suppose."

Washington smiles. "Well, Cooper, you know well as I do our whole reg'ment is colored soldiers. Do you know why we here?"

"Because the United States' Army is segregated?"

"Yes, tha's true, the Army's segregated, but that ain't really why we here."

"Because being a soldier earns a paycheck, and you get three meals a day?" Clarence tries again. Although, judging by the quality of what he's eating now, Clarence realizes that can't be much of an inducement.

"Tha's true, too, but that ain't why we here 'neither, most of us."

"It's the only place white folks will tolerate seeing colored people with guns?" Clarence ventures, mostly joking.

He looks over at Washington and can see Washington doesn't find this attempt at a joke all that funny. "No, Cooper, we's serious here. Most of us, we here to show white people that the colored soldier is jus' as good as the white soldier. We here to show 'em what the colored people can do, if they only give us a chance. Some of us, we join the cav'ry to stick up for our people. And you a part of that, long as you with us."

"I can see your point, I suppose. A person can serve honorably and stick up for colored people without getting themselves shot in the process, though."

"They can, yes, but we gotta be braver than the white soldiers to make our mark, make people take notice of us, pay attention to us. Show the country what colored people is made of. Don' you ever feel that way, Cooper?"

"I don't know about that," Clarence replies honestly, looking his friend in the eye. "I'm not sure the rest of the country notices, no matter what colored people do. When I went around the world with the ballplayers seven years ago, I made friends with some of them, but that was because I helped them out, not because they suddenly became more tolerant of people who weren't white. You sure this whole idea of proving yourself isn't just another way the whites are using you? Just tricking you into getting shot and taking risks so that they won't have to?"

"How else you expect we gon' get our rights as a people, then?"

"Beats me, Lincoln. Does anyone, even anyone in the Army, notice what our unit does? I have no doubt we have plenty of brave lads in our regiment, most of them braver than me, in fact, but we still have white officers giving us commands, don't we? How brave do we have to be before the Army even trusts us to lead ourselves?"

"You know the 10th has a good reputation, Fred. This unit, we made a name for ourselves fightin' the Injuns in Texas, and Arizona, and all over the Plains. Tha's why we got this job, I'm thinkin'."

"I still don't know how that helps colored people. I just want to find Mary and help her find her family in St. Louis where she belongs."

"You still reckon you gon' find her on this mission?"

"Hopefully. It seems the best chance I have, anyway. I suppose it depends on what part of Montana Troop D ends up covering."

While he speaks, Clarence tries to remember where Gabriel talked about going. He thinks Gabriel said something about a mission at one point but can't seem to remember exactly which one Gabriel mentioned or where in Montana it is located. Then, when they parted, they were heading toward Havre, not to a mission. Clarence doesn't know if Gabriel and Mary ever got to Havre. Too many things were happening to them at the time, and he can't remember all of them for sure because the soldiers put a gun in his chest and made him go with them.

Then Washington jars Clarence out of his thoughts. "You know yous on your own, right? You a good man, Cooper, but I ain't 'bout to get myself in hot water for no little girl. I joined the cav'ry to better my people's lot. You have to do this without my help, got it?"

Clarence nods solemnly.

"You got a plan even if you do find her?" Washington asks.

"I'm working on one."

# Chapter 19

## The Buffalo Soldiers Take the Field

The Buffalo Soldiers have only been in the field a few days when Troop D confronts its first obstacle. That obstacle isn't the Cree; instead, it's the Marias River. The Marias flows into the Missouri River a few miles north of Fort Benton, Montana, and is a bit more than fifty miles from Fort Assiniboine. The river is high, unusually high, filled all the way to its banks with snowmelt from the Rockies.

Clarence rides near Lincoln Washington, like usual, when they approach the water.

Washington asks Clarence, "Cooper, what's the dull murmur I hear? Are those trees I see up ahead?"

"I think it's a river," Clarence replies.

"If it a river, shouldn' it be loud?"

"Only if there's rapids."

"Whadya call this grass again, Cooper?"

"I think it's just called bunchgrass. The buffalo like to eat it, or that's what I'm told, anyway. Back when there were buffalo."

"I ain't yet seen a buffalo since I been in Montana."

"Me, either, Lincoln."

"Funny, huh?"

"Why's that?"

"We the Buffalo Soldiers, and neither of us has ever seen a buffalo."

They both laugh, but for Clarence the laughter comes from realizing the irony of the joke, and it makes him sad. Part of the reason he came to Montana back in 1889 was to try to find a buffalo. He realizes now that was a silly reason, but when a person is only twelve like he was when he got to Montana, sometimes one looks at things differently.

As the Marias comes into view, Clarence says to Washington, "This river just comes up on you all at once. We've been just riding along over these weathered plains for hours. Sometimes they're flat, almost as flat as a baseball field. If it wasn't for the cottonwood trees poking their tops out of the river's valley, you'd never know it was there until you fell in."

"Looks like we's stopping, Cooper. Isn't there a bridge for us to go 'cross?"

"Don't see one."

"Wha's that mean? We gonna swim? I don' wanna swim. The water is fast, and all gray with mud."

Washington's right. The water looks fast, cold, and clouded.

"I don't know," Clarence tells him. "Let's get to the front of the column and see what we can learn."

Cavalrymen ride horses, it's true, but cavalry troops must have other things when in the field for extended campaigns. Wagons to carry food and extra ammunition, for instance. Somehow, the troopers must get these wagons and extra supplies across the Marias River, and no bridge spans the river here. Washington and Clarence get to the head of the column when it stops at the river, so Clarence can just overhear First Lieutenant Pershing while he formulates a plan with one of his subordinates. That subordinate happens to be Second Lieutenant Grimes, Clarence's immediate commanding officer.

Lieutenant Grimes has eased up on Clarence a bit since last October, but Clarence knows they'll never be on friendly terms. He doesn't think any of the men are on friendly terms with Grimes. Unlike Pershing, who isn't afraid to shout at you, berate you, or curse you, but at least has a reason when he does it, Grimes doesn't even wait for people to make mistakes before chewing them out. Clarence has seen him get in the face of men who showed poor marksmanship the day before, hoping to scare them into shooting better, or talk badly about certain soldiers in front of other members of the regiment. If Grimes makes a mistake and one of his superiors finds out, one of the enlisted men always gets the blame. Most in Troop D consider Grimes a lousy officer because of this inconsistency and irresponsibility and because he always finds fault with a soldier's appearance no matter how hard someone tries to have his uniform in perfect trim.

Grimes does try to act the part of an officer, even if his performance doesn't live up to his bearing most of the time. He has no mustache, but instead a long, peppered goatee that drops several inches below his chin. The man has a rounded face that shows the creases of age that all men get when they reach their forties. Grimes stands tall and straight when on duty. Relatively speaking, at least, since he isn't very tall; he and Clarence are about the same height. The other sign that betrays Grimes's true age is his belly. It pushes out his uniform coat several inches more than is good for him.

When at ease, like he is now, Grimes puts his right hand inside his coat by inserting it between two of the buttons in the center of the uniform. Someone told Clarence once that doing that with your hand is an imitation of a famous French general named Napoleon. Clarence has no idea if the story is true.

Clarence listens in as Pershing explains his plans to Grimes. "We'll have to construct a flying ferry to get across the river, Lieutenant. If we are to reach Great Falls within four days as planned, we cannot tarry here. We'll have to get everything across today."

"Yes, sir. Absolutely, sir." Grimes answers sharply.

"I want to turn our wagons into temporary ferries. The horses can swim the river. Once we get a rope strung from one bank of the Marias to the other, you and your men take responsibility for loading the boats, and we'll use the rope to guide the ferries across, so they won't drift with the current."

"Loading the boats, sir? That means the men will have to stand waist-deep in the icy river."

"Then your men will stand waist-deep in the icy river, Lieutenant. Rotate them in and out of the water if you need to, but we must get those supplies loaded and ferried across the Marias, and your men will do so. Step to it, or you can join them."

"Yes, sir," Grimes says again, with somewhat less enthusiasm than the first time.

There's another thing the men dislike about Lieutenant Grimes. He plays favorites. Out of the soldiers Clarence and Washington must work with today loading supplies, Grimes's favorite is a man named Edward Carter. Carter is about Clarence's age, but quite tall, athletic, and muscular. He probably would make quite a ballplayer if Johnny Ward could only work with him for a few months, Clarence believes. Interestingly, it also appears that he has some education. None of the other men know why he decided to join the cavalry because they all resent him and don't want to speak with him if they can help it. Clarence doesn't know how Carter got to be Grimes's favorite, although rumor has it that Carter sometimes buys whiskey for Grimes after a successful night of gambling.

Whatever the reason, Carter can do no wrong whenever Grimes is around, and he's arrogant as hell toward everyone else because of it. When it comes time to load the supplies onto the wagon, he never takes a turn wading into the Marias. Instead, Carter stands on the shore handing boxes full of hardtack to Clarence while Clarence loads them onto the section of the ferry wagon no one can reach from shore. It's Clarence's third time in the water already, and the water is so cold, it's only a matter of minutes until Clarence can't feel his toes. It's a cloudy, overcast day, too, barely fifty degrees, Clarence guesses, so despite the fact it is mid-June, he finds little warmth to console him, even when he gets a moment to rest on shore.

Carter is handing Clarence another box when Grimes approaches to check on the progress of the work. Without warning, Carter purposely tosses the box so that it's just out of Clarence's reach. It glances off Clarence's fingertips, then lands in the river with an audible splash and begins drifting downstream before Clarence can jump forward and recover it. In the process, however, Clarence ends up in the water all the way to his armpits, so now water soaks his entire uniform. It clings to his body, sending chills through his chest.

"Damnit, Cooper!" Carter yells at Clarence. "That's our next meal you just let fall in the water. Get your act together and don't be so clumsy."

Lieutenant Grimes comes closer to see what's happened for himself. "What's the situation here, men?"

Because Clarence is in the water, stammering with cold and shivers, Carter shouts out his answer before Clarence can do anything. "Lieutenant, sir, Private Cooper is an oaf. He just dropped a case of hardtack into the water. May I suggest a suitable punishment for spoiling some of our rations?"

"Permission to leave the river, sir?" Clarence asks Grimes. "I can barely move my legs, Lieutenant; it's mighty cold down here in the water."

"Denied, Cooper. Keep working. You'll have to make up for your mistake with an extra shift in the water. That's your punishment," Grimes exclaims.

"A just decision, sir. That is what I was about to recommend," Carter says loudly.

Because protesting is pointless, Clarence is about to resume working when Lieutenant Pershing himself approaches on his horse. Back when Clarence was a baseball mascot, he used to lead parades and twirl a baton for the crowds. He can catch anything thrown to him, and whatever it might be, he never drops it. He'll never be able to explain that to Pershing, however, because Pershing believes Clarence is Fred Cooper.

Pershing climbs down from his mount, a powerful horse with dark brown coloring, taking off his gray leather riding gloves and holding them in his left hand. "What's the situation here, Lieutenant Grimes?" Pershing asks while running his right hand through his bushy mustache.

Before Grimes can even speak, Carter bursts in. "Private Cooper dropped a case of hardtack into the river, Lieutenant Pershing." He says it with gusto and salutes.

"Private Cooper, out of the water. Now!" Pershing commands.

Clarence obeys as quickly as his numbed body allows, dragging his frozen legs out of the stream and trying to stand tall as best he can in front of Pershing. Clarence salutes Pershing with a trembling right hand and his legs shake and wobble so badly he nearly falls over. It's hard to keep his balance because Clarence can't feel his feet.

Then Pershing turns to Carter. "What's your name, trooper? Private Carter, isn't it?"

"Private Edward Carter, sir!" Carter shouts back with energy as he salutes again.

Lieutenant Pershing curls his right fist into a ball, steps forward with his left leg, and draws his right arm back. Then he unleashes a punch that hits Carter square in the face. Carter falls backward from the blow, into the river, arms and legs thrashing about uselessly. He disappears below the water for a moment before his head and upper body emerge. Then he loses his footing, slips, and goes under again. When Carter resurfaces the next time, he's coughing, spluttering, and gasping from the shock of the sudden cold. An instant later, Clarence can also see his nose bleeding. Probably broken, Clarence thinks to himself.

"Private Carter," Pershing shouts at him from the bank, "I see that until now, your uniform was not wet, although you've been assigned to loading the ferries with supplies. Furthermore, I watched you toss the box of hardtack out of Private Cooper's reach, and now you blame him for it. I won't tolerate it. Do you understand?"

"Yes, sir," Carter splutters between coughs, the icy water still dripping into his eyes and off his face. Then he stands there, awaiting further instructions, while blinking his eyes and trembling. It's hard to say if he's trembling at the cold of the river or in fear of Pershing. Both, probably.

"Salute your officers!" Pershing roars back at him. Carter meekly does so, the blood dripping from his nose and chin.

"Well done, Lieutenant, sir," Grimes says to Pershing. "That's what I've been wanting to do to him all day, the shirk."

At first, Grimes surprises Clarence that he is sucking up to Pershing so blatantly. Then, Clarence remembers it is Lieutenant Grimes, and the surprise fades. Clarence wonders if Pershing can tell that it's all fake.

In the meantime, Pershing says to Grimes, "Next time, do so, Lieutenant. I do not approve of such methods in general, but at times an example becomes necessary. When the usual methods of enforcing discipline are not available, occasionally you must resort to other means." Then Pershing turns back to Carter, who still hasn't moved, other than the shaking and trembling.

"Private Carter," Pershing barks, "when all the supplies are loaded, you will seek medical attention for your nose, but not before. Furthermore, should anything unusual or unfortunate happen to Private Cooper for the rest of this campaign, I will hold you personally responsible. Do you understand?"

"Yes, Lieutenant Pershing," Carter says through gritted teeth. He remembers to salute this time, although his hand still shakes violently when he does.

Clarence has no idea if the lieutenant's warning will be enough to protect him from retaliation, so he decides to be on his guard, just in case.

Be that as it may, Clarence still must take several more turns in the icy Marias to load supplies, and every time is shorter, more chilling, and more miserable than the last, but eventually, they finish. While the men stand watching the last load of supplies cross the river, everyone pats each other on the back for a job well done. Everyone except Carter, that is. He's off to the side sulking. A small roll of gauze protrudes from his left nostril.

One more task remains, however. The men still must swim the horses and mules across the river. That means going in the water one more time, more chills, and more numbness, but after what they've just done, it doesn't seem that daunting. At least the horses will be doing the work this time. Then, Clarence knows, the men can retrieve their spare uniform from their packs, start a fire, and get some warmth back.

Clarence is on his mount as they begin, and things go smoothly when the group wades out toward the deepest part of the Marias River. Because the water is so high, the horses must swim part of the distance. Clarence's does so without incident, and when its hooves touch down on the riverbed once again, Clarence breathes a sigh of relief. The worst of the day should be over. He's soaked once more, water dripping from every part of his uniform from his chest down, but in a few moments, he'll be able to relax, get warmer, and rest.

Suddenly, from a small copse of cottonwoods near the bank a short distance upstream, a brown bear appears, probably startled by all these men and horses invading its hunting grounds. Several soldiers nearby notice the bear.

They should have been swimming the river in single file, but the water is so cold, and the men's desire to get to the far bank as quickly as possible so great, that several of them are in a bunch together, trying to get out of the freezing water as soon as they can. When some of these men see the bear, however, they try to swivel their mounts in the river to take aim. The man next to Clarence, Fredrick Williams, is one of them.

"Look, Cooper, a bar! Shoot 'er!" he cries. Williams tries to pivot his horse to get a clear shot while he says this. It bumps Clarence's horse.

This knocks the horse off balance, and because Clarence's legs are so numb from the frigid water, he can't use them very well to control the horse or stay in the saddle. He topples backward into the Marias. While Clarence struggles to get his footing, the current starts to sweep him downstream. Soon, he's in a part of the river too deep for him to stand.

The last time Clarence was in deep water was when the ballplayers threw him overboard into the Indian Ocean on their trip around the world. Clarence couldn't swim then, and sadly, he still can't. He never thought he had a good reason to learn, so he never did. Now, he wishes he had, because he's kicking around wildly, his head occasionally going below the water, and his legs are already numb, so it's hard to coordinate his movements and figure out how to get to safety.

Clarence gulps down another draught of freezing river water. When he does, he realizes that his limbs are too numb, and he can barely feel his body move. His head goes under again, and Clarence struggles mightily just to surface for another breath of air. He tries to locate the riverbank, but with his vision blurred by all the water in his eyes, he's not sure how far away it is—fifty feet, at least. Clarence tries to move in that direction but soon realizes he'll never get there because his legs just won't kick.

His head goes under again, and try as he might, Clarence can't seem to move fast enough. The light from above the surface grows grayer, bit by bit, as Clarence realizes he's sinking down. He thrashes as violently as he can, but it feels like trying to punch soft sand. The freezing water slows his movements and he can't generate enough force.

Then comes the searing pain in his lungs, and Clarence knows he can't hold his breath much longer. He reaches toward the surface a final time, hoping that a hand will breach the deadly water and help him.

None does.

However, by sheer luck, Clarence manages to grasp a branch of a tree that has fallen into the river. As he grabs the limb, he feels his weight stretch it downstream, but when the branch reaches the limit of its flexibility, it recoils a bit, and this catapults Clarence's head out of the water for a moment. He gulps in air, mouth wide, like a fish out of water.

In his instant gratitude that he can breathe again, however, Clarence forgets one thing. His body dangles out behind him, still tugged by the swift-flowing current, and he's lost almost all feeling in his hands from being underwater too long. In only a moment, Clarence loses his grip on the tree branch and begins drifting downstream once again.

This time, however, help is on the way. Lincoln Washington, Fredrick Williams, and a few of the other men are riding along the bank trying to catch up to Clarence. Williams gets a little ahead, then directs his horse back into the river, grabs Clarence's arm, and drags him to safety.

"Boy, Cooper," he says to Clarence as Clarence lays gasping and shaking uncontrollably on the riverbank, "I done almost drowned you tryin' to shoot that bar. I'se mighty sorry. I should never a done that."

Clarence just stares up at the cloudy, iron-gray sky for a moment, his uniform plastered to his body, trying to think of what to say. He coughs and splutters some more to get the last of the water out of his body.

"You can make it up to me by teaching me to swim someday," Clarence says at last. It's all he can think of.

"Deal," Williams says with a rueful smile, sticking out his hand for a shake. "My pap back in Loosiana teached me to swim real good. I kin show you how."

Clarence's hand is so numb he doesn't even feel Williams' grip when they shake.

# Chapter 20

## The Montana Roundup

"I'se sorry again, Cooper. I be more careful from now on," Frederick Williams tells Clarence.

"Williams, that's about the twentieth time you've apologized to me. I accepted your apology the first time. You can stop now."

"Okay, but that larned me to be more careful."

Clarence rides beside Williams in the column part of the way to Great Falls. Clarence has not spoken to Williams too often over the winter at Fort Assiniboine. He had no particular reason not to; their paths just never crossed much, and Clarence spent most of his time thinking about how to get away and what might be happening to Mary and Gabriel. Clarence realizes he's missed out, however, because speaking with Williams now, he seems the decent sort. He's also young, even younger than Clarence is. Clarence thinks sixteen or seventeen, but his face looks even younger than that.

"Why this place called Great Falls again?" Williams asks.

"Because the Missouri River has waterfalls here. Five of them, I think, spread out over several miles."

"We gonna swim 'cross this river, too?"

"No, I think all our operations are on this side of the river, Williams."

"Tha's good. Altho', if we meet another bar this time . . ." his voice trails off when Clarence gives him a quick glance, and he remembers not to apologize for the twenty-first time.

Clarence offers him a friendly smile. Clarence is also curious, so he finally decides to ask Williams more about himself. "How old are you, Williams, if it's okay for me to ask?"

"Sixteen. I knows I looks younger, tho'. It just how I is."

"Anyone ever give you trouble about it?"

"Sometimes. Some of the boys, they asks me when I'se gonna shave for the first time." They both laugh a little. It doesn't seem like Williams takes the ribbing personally.

Williams continues. "It's okay, tho'. All the boys, they knows I'se the best shot in the reg'ment."

"Yeah, you probably would have hit that bear if it wasn't for . . ." Now it's Clarence's turn to shut up and not mention the Marias again. He changes the subject.

"You're from Louisiana, Williams? Whereabouts?"

"My pap live up Shreveport way, on the Red River there. Tha's how I knows how to swim so good. We swum in the river all the time when I'se growin' up. An' we hunted bars, too. Tha's why I got so 'cited at seein' the bar back there. How 'bout you, Cooper?"

"I used to live in Chicago. I've spent the last few years in Butte, though."

"I thunked you was from up North," Williams tells Clarence. "You don' sound like you'se Southern." Then Williams lowers his voice a bit. "And I knows you ain't Fred Cooper, neither. I'se friends with Fred, the real Fred, 'cause he from Loosiana, too. His pap n' my pap is friends."

"Did you join the cavalry together?"

"Sho did. My pap, he cuts timber, an' he say I weren't no good for timber cuttin', that I weren't no good for nothin', and he wanted me to join the cav'ry. Make a man out of me, he says. An' that I should do somethin' fo' my people. So, when I join, Fred join, too."

Clarence keeps his voice low. "Do you know why the real Fred left the fort?"

"Fred had a temper on him, he sho' did. Didn' take to these white of'cers givn' him commands all the time. 'Specially Lootenant Grimes. Fred never told me why he leaved fo' certain, but tha's what I figur'd."

Before they can say much more, they've reached their destination, Great Falls. Lieutenant Pershing seems pleased when he rides by to check on the condition of the troopers. Now, it's time to set up camp for the night. After the men complete their camp, which is just outside the town, Pershing assembles the troop in the evening to pass along the orders for the next stage of the mission.

"Men of Troop D," Pershing says, his voice firm and even like always, "soon begins the real reason for this campaign. Tomorrow, we ride south until we reach the small town of Cascade. From there, we head west, toward the Rocky Mountains. Earlier today I received telegraphed instructions from General Miles that the first group of renegade Cree we are to round up live a short distance from Cascade, at a place named St. Peter's Mission."

Finally, it comes back to Clarence. St. Peter's Mission! That is where Gabriel talked about going if Havre didn't work out. He may get to see Gabriel and Mary soon! What if Gabriel and Mary never made it there, though? Clarence guesses he'll find out before long. What will he do if they're not there? What should he do if they are? The possibilities send his head spinning, even while he tries his best to listen to the rest of what Lieutenant Pershing says.

Pershing continues. "Our plan is to reach Cascade and, from there, make part of the distance to the mission tomorrow. We will camp at dusk, arise at 3 o'clock, and take the mission by surprise in the early morning. Although our objective consists of a religious house and a school, General Miles informs me of rumors of a camp, or perhaps a small town, populated by Cree in the vicinity, that these Indians may resist, and that they have the means to do so. Therefore, when we set up camp tomorrow evening, all of you must prepare to move out immediately and ready yourselves for combat operations the following day.

"It is my hope that we can take the mission by surprise and there will be no resistance, but we must be ready for anything. Our objective is to round up these Cree and deport them, not to kill them. You may open fire only if you encounter armed resistance. Let us hope that, by moving quickly and decisively, and gaining the element of surprise, we can carry the day without loss of life.

"Once we pacify the mission and neutralize any threats, our troop will return the Cree to Great Falls, where General Miles assures me that rail transportation will move them toward their destination in Canada via the Great Falls & Canada Railroad. I expect each man to do his duty and live up to the proud title of Buffalo Soldier. Dismissed."

While the men eat their grub that evening, hardtack, beans, and black coffee, Clarence ends up sitting with Washington, as usual. He must be doing a poor job of hiding his concern over what's about to happen because Washington gives Clarence a strange look over the rim of his coffee tin.

"You's nervous, Cooper. You don' look yo'self tonight."

Clarence's reply is half true and half false. "I'm just worried about my friends, that's all. I'm still not sure when I'll see them again. They never told me exactly where they might go. I'm getting nervous about what will happen next time I see them."

The morning of their approach, Clarence sits atop his horse as the troop trots over the shortgrass plains leading toward St. Peter's Mission, rays of light just starting to appear behind him. Even though he's focused on his assignment, Clarence can't help but notice the beauty of the country they ride through as the pale light gradually grows stronger. The mountain valleys of Montana are gorgeous in June. The grass maybe isn't quite as beautiful a shade of green as what

Clarence saw as a boy when visiting Ireland, but it's no less beautiful for that. In another month or so, it will turn yellow and brown and then it won't be so pretty, but today it's a healthy green.

Ahead of them, the Rocky Mountains rise like an impenetrable wall, dark, tall, craggy, and forbidding, but also grand and majestic, with snow-capped peaks and alpine forests of pine, aspen, and tamarack. The creek off to the right, where the troopers just watered their horses for the last time before heading into action, is as clear, blue, and swift-flowing as anything Clarence ever dreamed of.

Clarence knows that just to the south, on the other side of the ridge, is St. Peter's Mission, their target. Lieutenant Pershing leads Clarence's troop, Troop D, but he's delegated to Grimes the task of taking a few of the troopers and riding in advance of the rest of the force. The idea is for Grimes to get to the rear of the mission and prevent any Cree from escaping by fleeing into the mountains. So far, they've encountered no resistance. In fact, they've encountered no one at all.

In a moment, the troop's handful of scouts return and confer with Lieutenant Grimes, who rides at the head of the column. He gives the order for a left wheel. This means it's Clarence's time to turn south, over the top of the hill screening the troopers from St. Peter's, and then fan out to cover possible escape routes while the main force advances on the mission and the church. When the men reach the top of the hill, they're screened by a stand of trees, so they have lots of cover. *Hopefully*, Clarence thinks while looking around, *no one will see us up here.*

Clarence is upset that he drew this assignment. Not because he wants to be part of the main engagement—far from it. If the Cree do offer resistance, the troopers with Pershing riding toward the camp from the other side will be the ones who'll do the brunt of the fighting. If the worst happens and a firefight breaks out, Grimes's task is to swoop in and cut down the Cree from behind while the main force engages them. Clarence knows he is likely in the least danger of any of the Buffalo Soldiers. The reason why he's upset is that if Gabriel and Mary do happen to be at the mission, there will be nothing he can do to protect them. If a real battle happens, and Clarence is in the middle of the action, he supposes there won't be too much he can do then, either, but at least it would be possible. From here, however, it's unlikely he'll even be able to spot Mary or Gabriel until it's too late.

He looks up and down the line. All the men are in position now, but strangely, nothing is happening below in St. Peter's Mission. Clarence waits near Lieutenant Grimes. Perhaps he's a better soldier once battle starts than he is on the parade ground, but Clarence would rather not find out. Grimes scans the mission with his field glasses while the rest of the men wait for his orders.

While Clarence waits, he thinks back to all the things he did when he was a baseball mascot to bring his team luck, but who knows if those things make soldiers lucky, too? If he'd have been thinking, he would have gotten himself a lucky rabbit's foot by now, but he doesn't have one. Clarence's horse is brown, rather than white, so that won't help, either. About the best he can think of is to spit over his left shoulder, so he does that. He looks down at his uniform—at least there aren't thirteen buttons on the front. Clarence spits again, straightens his cap, and squints forward to try to see what's going on.

The minutes go by. How many, Clarence has no idea, but it does seem he's been waiting here for quite some time. Some of the horses stamp and champ impatiently. Of course, everyone in the troop worried about being too slow getting into position and ruining the plan, or missing out on the real action, but it appears that isn't the problem at all. Grimes continues looking over the mission, but everything seems normal down there, as if nothing unusual was going to happen today.

"Where is everyone?" Grimes says to the man at his side, the bugler.

"Can't say, sir," the man replies.

"It's quiet down there. Too quiet," Grimes says, still looking through his field glasses.

"Perhaps the lieutenant encountered a delay? Some rough terrain or an unmarked spring stream he had to get his men across?" the bugler replies with uncertainty in his voice.

"Perhaps, but perhaps not." Grimes pauses for a moment and then puts down his field glasses. "It's not like Lieutenant Pershing to be late, obstacles or no obstacles. Unless the Indians set an ambush."

"Wouldn't we hear something, or wouldn't he send a messenger, if a fight started?" the bugler asks Grimes.

"Under ideal conditions, yes, but when in the field conditions are not always ideal."

"Should we send someone back to ascertain the situation and contact the lieutenant?"

"No, we should remain in position. Even if the lieutenant does engage the savages, he has plenty of men and firepower. He'll drive them back in time. Right into our arms. No, we will hold our position here until something develops." Grimes licks his lips in anticipation.

After this, another long pause ensues while they wait for something to develop. As much as Clarence fears getting into a firefight, and the thought frightens him almost to death, just sitting and waiting, wondering if he'll have to fight, is almost as bad. The fact that he may have to switch from sitting calmly to fighting for his life, and do so instantly, scares him. Clarence's guts twist around on themselves as he waits. He notices that he's clenched his jaw, and his left hand shakes a bit. Clarence makes a conscious effort to unclench his jaw, relax his face, and steady himself. When he tries to think about something else for a moment, however, he realizes that he's already clenched his jaw once again. Clarence hasn't vomited yet, but his insides feel like he might at any time. He tries to look forward and find a clue about what is going on at the mission and why nothing has happened yet. Clarence hears a retching sound off to his right.

He can't make out much other than the four main buildings, some posts for tethering horses, a couple woodpiles, some gardens, and other normal things, so Clarence returns his thoughts to finding something that will bring him luck. He scans his surroundings for anything that might be promising, but nothing helpful presents itself. Clarence sighs. Then he crosses himself, like he learned to do when he was in Italy. Clarence doesn't know why he does it. Not being religious, he supposes there's no point. But it can't hurt, either, just in case.

Then, finally, the men hear a bugle call, and they see the main force ride into view, galloping down the road into the center of the mission compound. In a few moments, Clarence sees the tiny forms of startled, faceless people emerge from some of the buildings and run here and there while the main force of soldiers begins taking up position. The frightened cries of some of them, both men and women, are audible even at this distance. Clarence sees many people, most of whom seem to be children, running around and taking shelter inside two of the larger buildings. A group of women, who appear to be nuns although it's difficult to tell at this distance, follow the children, herding them like sheep or lambs. Lieutenant Grimes resumes looking through his field glasses for a few moments to get a closer look. Then, suddenly, he drops the field glasses to his chest and points with his arm toward one of the larger buildings, the four-story one made of stone.

"There!" Grimes says, still pointing. "The tall stone building with the garden! I saw the flash of light on gun barrels. The Indians are waiting to ambush our men in there."

Quickly, he pivots his horse and says to the company's bugler, "Give the call to advance! We must strike them before they spring their trap!"

Instantly, Clarence hears the call to charge, and the troop starts down the hill at a gallop. *This isn't how it's supposed to happen*, he tells himself with a sinking feeling. *I'm not supposed to die here, in Montana, fighting on the wrong side of a battle when all I really want is to find my friends and leave this place.*

Now they've covered half the distance to their target. What appears to be the mission church is on their left as they approach the opposite side of the tall building from where Pershing waits. All

Clarence's muscles have tensed up again, and the strange feeling in his stomach gets worse. Sweat trickles into his eyes, stinging them even as he tries to wipe it away. Even though the men drilled, and drilled, and drilled some more over the winter and spring, Clarence struggles to recall everything he's supposed to do. As they rush onward, their downhill momentum helping speed the charge, he looks toward the building where their enemies lie in wait, just waiting for them to open fire. When he does, from the corner of Clarence's vision he sees a black-robed figure emerge from another building and, with his hands up, wave a white cloth, probably a handkerchief, and approach Pershing and the soldiers waiting in the mission's courtyard.

Clarence thinks that Lieutenant Pershing is the person coming forward to meet the black-robed man, but before he's close enough to tell for sure, he's nearly reached the target, and Lieutenant Grimes gives the order to open fire. The troopers let loose with their carbines. Some of the bullets shatter the windows of the target building while others harmlessly strike its stone facing with a thick, thunking sound, shards of stone splintering in all directions at the impact. At the last instant, Clarence fires, too, but he aims too high on purpose and he's sure his shot clears the roof of the building and hits nothing. Then the men hear the screams of young voices coming from inside. The troopers wheel to the right of the tall building and start to come around for another pass.

Even as they do, Clarence realizes their enemies still haven't returned their fire. That seems strange. He wonders what they're waiting for?

From where he is now, Clarence can see the center of the mission compound, and the black-robed man, who must be the mission's head priest. As soon as the priest realizes what is happening, he runs toward Grimes, waving his arms, yelling at Grimes to hold his fire. Then Clarence sees Lieutenant Pershing and one of his other officers, Second Lieutenant Fleming, do the same from horseback, furiously making the cease-fire symbol with their arms. It takes a few moments, but shortly, things have calmed down enough that Clarence can hear what the priest shouts to Grimes.

"That's the school! Children are inside! Don't shoot them!" he repeats again and again.

One by one, the men of Clarence's troop rein in their mounts and cease firing.

Sadly, it's too late.

Clarence looks toward the school and can see that most of the windows now feature the telltale ragged grin of broken glass, thanks to the gunfire. Before Clarence has time to notice anything else, another man in robes bursts through the schoolhouse door and down its short flight of stone stairs, carrying a young boy in his arms.

The boy looks about seven years old from the size of his body, but Clarence can't tell for sure because one of the troopers shot him through his right eye, and the entire right side of his face is a mess of blood and protruding bone. The spurting blood stains the older man's robes even while he sobs. Following the robed man, nearly fifty weeping, hysterical children run shrieking into the mission courtyard, crowding around the priest.

"Father, help us, our school is on fire and the soldiers are shooting at us!" the first of the children to reach the priest cries out. Soon the others gather around the black-robed man, crying in a similarly terrified way, some pathetically tugging at the sleeves of his black robe.

Then Clarence sees the child is right. Through the open schoolhouse door, an orange light grows. He's positioned just so he can see through one of the windows, and the curtains inside the school are aflame, as is one entire wall. Because the entire building is stone on the outside, Clarence knows it may take some time to burn completely, but there seems little chance to quench the flames in time to save the school.

Finally realizing he is in no danger—that, in fact, there never was any danger from the mission—Clarence takes in the rest of his surroundings in more detail. He remembers to lower his carbine and take his finger off the trigger. Very few adults are anywhere on the grounds of the mission besides the cavalrymen, only the two men in robes and the children. Wherever the nuns who he saw went, they aren't showing their faces now.

While the priest stands talking demonstratively to Lieutenant Pershing, arms waving almost as furiously as a symphony director, the schoolteacher bends over the bloody child. Clarence is close enough to see it is indeed a boy. Or, more accurately, was a boy. The child hasn't moved since the teacher set him on the ground, and Clarence has no doubt the child is dead. Many other children gather around as the teacher kneels next to the corpse, his hands clasped in prayer. Another young boy, who also appears about seven years old, tugs weakly at the dead child's sleeves, muttering through his tears, "Wake up, Johnny, wake up."

As the orange light of the burning schoolhouse grows brighter, and the roar of the flames louder, all the mistakes become plain to Clarence. The people here planned no ambush. There aren't even any adults here to spring an ambush, and these children certainly don't have firearms. Lieutenant Pershing's message from General Miles, stating that the Cree might resist, must have been in error. How could such serious mistakes happen? Why did the troop just rush into action before knowing all the facts of the situation? Now, because of them, a child is dead, and the mission school burns.

It appears Lieutenant Pershing wonders some of these same things because his face has gone from its normal color to a distinctively bright red hue. This must be why some of the men who've been in the 10th Cavalry longer than Clarence call him "Old Red" behind his back. He roars out commands. "Lieutenant Grimes! Now!"

Grimes spurs his horse, and it trots over to where the lieutenant has remounted his own horse. "Yes, Lieutenant Pershing," Grimes barks with a sharp salute.

"Lieutenant Grimes, what is the meaning of this?" Pershing shouts back. Clarence thinks he's shouting both so Grimes can hear him above the burning schoolhouse and because of his anger. "Your orders were to prevent the escape of the Cree and not to fire unless fired upon. Yet, here you are charging a schoolhouse full of children!"

"Lieutenant, sir, I saw the flash of sunlight on metal and took it that there were rifles and that the Cree were waiting to ambush the command. When you were slow in arriving, I assumed they'd tried to ambush you, and that this was part of the trap. Sir."

"Trap?!" We were late arriving because we encountered the main body of the Cree less than one mile down the road, and it took time to get them into custody. Do you think my men and I would just ride straight into the village if they'd already ambushed us once? Lieutenant?"

"We're fighting savages, sir. It seemed wise to assume the worst."

"You were fighting a school full of children, Lieutenant, one of whom is now needlessly dead."

At this point the priest, who is listening to the conversation, decides to speak up. "Lieutenant Pershing, the flashes of sunlight were from windchimes the children made. We attached little triangular pieces of metal to the chimes because the children like the sound."

"Windchimes? How could you mistake windchimes for rifles, Lieutenant Grimes?"

Grimes starts to speak again, but Pershing cuts him off. "No, no more excuses, Lieutenant. Our orders are to round up the Cree, not to kill their children."

"Well, nits will make lice, sir."

Clarence can't believe Grimes is sticking up for himself so forcefully, sniveling coward that he is. Clarence supposes Grimes has decided that he's in deep water no matter what he says at this point, so he might as well throw out some excuses and hope one of them works.

The bright red color still in Pershing's face, along with his furious stare, however, tell Clarence it isn't working. At all.

"Lieutenant Grimes, you will report to the rear and see to the supply train until further orders. When we return to Fort Assiniboine, we will discuss further discipline for your inability to follow orders and poor judgment. Am I understood?"

Grimes salutes weakly and slowly rides away, his head bowed.

Then Pershing turns to the officer mounted next to him. He's losing some of the red in his face and seems a bit calmer. But only a bit because his voice remains very loud and insistent. "Lieutenant Fleming, please lead the men in escorting these children to join their families for transportation back to Great Falls. We will reach Cascade before the day is over, and Great Falls the day after. Then, our orders are to take the field again and head for Fort Missoula. Make arrangements that Lieutenant Grimes stays behind in Great Falls and oversees the supply situation there. I believe we can do without his services for the remainder of this campaign."

As if to punctuate Pershing's command, part of the second floor of the schoolhouse collapses as he says this, sparks and flames bursting through the open door and windows, roaring in destruction. Clarence feels a wave of heat wash over him. When he lifts his head again, he realizes the damage is about to get much worse. From where his horse stands, he can see another building is adjacent to the one the cavalry just attacked. It's the same building the priest ran out of when Pershing first arrived, meaning it's probably the priest's residence.

Grimacing at this realization, Clarence looks over at the priest, who has bowed his head in prayer. He sees a tear glinting on one of the man's cheeks. The other man, the teacher, goes over and speaks with him. Clarence can just barely hear them, so he tries to get a bit closer without seeming too obvious about it.

"I am sorry, Father Andreis. When the shooting began, and the soldiers shot Johnny, one of the other children panicked and knocked over one of the oil lamps in the confusion. While I tried to attend to Johnny, the flames caught the curtains by one of the windows. It wasn't the child's fault. God help us all."

"Yes, my friend, God help us all. Especially Johnny," Father Andreis says. "We can rebuild the schoolhouse in time, and my residence, too, but what of the children?"

At this point, Father Andreis gathers his courage and tries to speak with Pershing again. "Lieutenant Pershing, by what right do you remove these children and their families from our care, taking them from the very house of God?"

"By right of the United States Congress, and the Cree Deportation Act of 1896, and the instructions of my superior officer, General Nelson Miles, commander of the United States Army. Here, Father Andreis, you may peruse the relevant documents, as you desire." Pershing reaches into a uniform pocket and pulls out some papers, which he passes down to the priest. "These Cree will go to Canada, just like our agreement with the Canadian and British authorities stipulate."

Father Andreis takes a minute to study the papers, frowning, his brow furrowed deeply all the while. In the meantime, Clarence continues scanning the mission. He hasn't seen either Mary or Gabriel. Perhaps Pershing and the rest of Troop D captured Gabriel before entering the mission itself, and he's now among those awaiting an escort back to Great Falls. Clarence doubts that, however. If they were here, Mary would have been in the school, most likely, and Clarence doesn't see her anywhere. If Mary were here and hiding somewhere, probably she would have noticed Clarence by now. It seems likely to Clarence they are not here. His eyes drop to the ground in disappointment.

Clarence doesn't know if their absence should make him happy or sad. If Gabriel and Mary aren't here, then at least no one has captured them, and they are not prisoners. However, he still doesn't know where they are. Gabriel said he planned to lead them here, but they aren't here. They could be anywhere in northern Montana. Maybe they went to Havre after all. Or, maybe they're dead.

Clarence then hears Father Andreis speak to Pershing again, startling Clarence out of his thoughts. "Lieutenant, you've made a terrible mistake. This act of the Congress calls for the removal of Cree Indians, but most of these people aren't Cree."

"My orders from General Miles say we must round up the mission Indians at St. Peter's Mission, because they are Cree. We have this on the authority of the Indian Agent at Blackfeet Agency, Mr. Moss. If

General Miles commands it, I'm bound to obey his commands. Tell the Cree, if you must tell them anything, that the Great Mother of Canada has granted them full pardon for all acts done during the Riel Rebellion, and that no punishment awaits them when they reach their destinations."

"But this is not right," Father Andreis protests, raising his arms and shaking his hands. "I have led the mission here for the past six years, and I know these people and their families. These families, whose children are pupils of this school, have been in Montana as long as I can remember, and some of us have been in contact with these families for over twenty years. Our school here dates to 1879. These children are all, as far as I am aware, American-born. Most of them are Michif, and a few are Piegans, which is one group within the Blackfeet Confederacy."

"I know who the Piegans are, and I was warned against such subterfuge," Pershing barks back. "Mr. Moss at Blackfeet Agency informed me you would try to pass off these Cree and half-breed Cree as Piegans. He also wrote that you shelter the parents and children of many of the refugees of the Riel Rebellion, along with a handful of Salteaux."

"These are lies that Satan has put into the heart of the Indian Agent," Andreis counters, a note of desperation entering his tone. "Mr. Moss came here for an inspection last year, but his heart was closed to the truth. He wants to shut down our mission so that these people will go to the Blackfeet reservation and he can control the lives of more people. These people are not Salteaux. The Salteaux are French Ojibwa and, as I told you, all the pupils at our mission are American-born. If any of their parents were followers of Riel, I have no knowledge of it, and I've lived among them for the past six years. These people simply want to farm, raise some cattle, and live upright, godly lives free of the hatred of their neighbors. Can't you allow them that?"

"Orders are orders," Pershing says with finality in his voice.

Then he turns to his second-in-command. "Lieutenant Fleming, you will escort these Cree children, and their families, on foot to Cascade. Give them one hour to gather their belongings for the journey and then burn their homes to the ground. They are going to Canada to stay. No slinking back to Montana this time."

With that, Pershing turns and rides away before Father Andreis can say anything more. The priest has a look on his face that is hard for Clarence to describe, but from the priest's twisted visage, blankly staring eyes, and twitching cheek muscles, it's somewhere between despair and horror.

# Chapter 21

## Tommy's Visit

*"What happened, Clarence?"*

*"I'm sorry, Tommy, but I lost your craps dice. Well, I didn't lose them. They burned up in a fire. It wasn't my fault."*

*"Not to worry, Clarence. You can get more."*

*"I know. But they were all you left me with."*

*"That's not true. You still have the bargain we made."*

*"But, you're dead, Tommy. We can't have a bargain anymore."*

*"Sure, we can. We made a deal. Someday, one of us was going to get off the streets and make something of ourselves. It's up to you now."*

*"I haven't made anything of myself."*

*"You still have a chance. For both of us."*

In his dream, Clarence stands on the streets of Chicago again, and Tommy waits next to him. Except, Clarence is not a boy like he was when he knew Tommy. He's still the grownup Clarence who lives in Montana. Tommy, however, looks the same as he did the day the Chicago police killed him. Clarence supposes Tommy will always look that way to him.

*"You have to go on, Clarence. You promised."*

Before Clarence can answer, gunfire explodes around them. He realizes they're standing back on the Chicago street outside the McCormick Reaper Plant where Tommy died. Clarence looks in the direction of the shooting to see what's happening, and he sees the Chicago police charge again, the huge smokestacks of the factory belching their choking black smoke in the background. When Clarence looks back again at Tommy, instead of seeing Tommy, he sees the mangled face of the boy from St. Peter's Mission today.

"Huhhh!" Clarence bolts upright in his white canvas camp tent, gasping for air. He's panting like he just ran a mile, and even though the night air is cool, he sweats heavily. Clarence just stares down at his hands a moment, trying to calm down, but they shake uncontrollably. Even if he couldn't see his hands in the dim light from the campfires outside, he'd know how bad it was.

A voice whispers, "What's the matter, Cooper?"

Lincoln Washington props his head on one elbow and rubs his eyes a bit. He yawns, too, but he's looking at Clarence expectantly, like he expects an answer in return for Clarence waking him up.

Clarence answers in a quiet voice. "I had a nightmare. I've had them ever since I was a boy and watched my best friend die right beside me."

"Nightmare. That's what I figured. You know you talk in your sleep sometimes, too, Cooper?"

"No, I didn't. Do I do it all the time?"

"No, jus' the other night, after you almost drownded. You seemed mighty scared, though. Jus' like you look now. Your hands is a mess, Cooper."

"I can still see him, Lincoln. The boy from the mission who died today. His face is right in front of me. The image won't go away."

"What do you usually do when you sees the pictures?"

"They only come after something horrible happens to me. But when they do, I can't sleep hardly at all. Sometimes, the images stay for two or three nights."

160

"Well, try to get some rest tonight, right? We gots a tough day tomorrow, I fig'r, and we gonna need all the strength we can find."

"You're right. Sorry for waking you, Lincoln, I didn't mean to."

Clarence lies back down. His breath has slowed a bit, but he needs three tries to grab his blanket with his shaky hands and settle it over his body again.

After he finally does, Clarence can't get back to sleep. He never can when the visions come. He thinks a little about the deal he and Tommy made. Just like in the dream, they promised each other that one of them would be a success someday and that they wouldn't live on the Chicago streets forever. *Have I done the right things?* Clarence thinks to himself while waiting for sleep to come. *I thought that learning to read and write was a big step, but look where it's gotten me.*

The hard, dusty ground digs into his back. Trying to get comfortable outside is almost impossible, and the images of the young boy at the mission keep coming. He's still trying to sleep when he hears a bird chirping. Dawn, and the bugle call to wake up and get moving, will be here any minute.

# Chapter 22

## The Missing Revelers

Gabriel Ouellette and Mary Healy sit on a bench in the modest wooden building while the fiddle music plays on and on. The building isn't much more than a barn, really, except for the wood planks on the floor. The pair had danced one dance after another, late into the June evening.

"Oh Gabriel, this is so much fun! But I'm getting tired. I don't know how many more dances I can do tonight," Mary says.

"How about one more then, little one," Gabriel says as he takes another drink of fresh beer.

"Just give me a moment, please?" she says to him. "How come this music hall is so far away from the rest of the mission, Gabriel?"

He answers with a merry laugh. "The boys wanted somewhere to have a good time but not too close to the mission where the priests could watch everything they did."

"Then how come the priests let them build it?"

"I guess they were smart enough to know that people need a place to blow off some steam and have fun now and then."

"What does it mean to blow off steam, Gabriel? Is that like when you can see your breath when it's cold outside?"

Gabriel just gives her another big smile. "No, Mary, not quite. It's another way to say that people need a chance to have fun sometimes. And dance. Like we're gonna do right now!"

With that, Gabriel picks up Mary and twirls her around twice in the air. He sets her feet back on the ground for a moment, then grabs both her dainty hands and starts to spin himself in a circle. He spins so quickly that Mary's feet leave the ground.

"I'm flying, Gabriel! Like a bird!" she squeals in delight.

He spins around a couple more times, laughing all the while. Then Gabriel slows his spin, lets Mary get her feet back on the ground, and releases her arms. He tries to stand in place, but his balance is all confused, so he topples over and lands on the wooden plank floor of the music hall, giggling as if he were Mary's age again.

"Gabriel!" Mary gasps. "You said you wouldn't get drunk. I don't want you to act like those cowboys did."

"I'm not drunk," he laughs at her from the floor. "Just dizzy. You try spinning around like that and see what happens."

She does, and before long, Mary is lying on the floor next to Gabriel.

"I wish we knew where Clarence is," she says to Gabriel once her head stops spinning. "I wonder if he's far away, off with the soldiers fighting somewhere. I hope they didn't send him all the way to China."

"Why would they send Clarence to China? How do you know about China, anyway?" Gabriel says as he stares up at the brown-gray wooden ceiling.

"We learned about China in our geography lessons at the school. It's a land far away where the people have long hair, and dress funny and talk funny. Our teacher, one of the nuns, told us that the Catholic Church sent missionaries to China a long time ago to try to save the souls of the Chinese, and some of the people in China are Christian now."

"I'm so glad you get to go to school, Mary. Maybe someday I'll be smart like you."

"I'm learning to write, too. We have these little chalkboards at our desks, and every day we practice writing our sentences with the chalk. Sometimes the nuns have us copy our catechisms out of a book, but other times, they let us write whatever we're thinking about. I usually write about how much I miss Clarence. When do you think we'll get to see him again?"

Before Gabriel can answer, one of his friends, Charles Hamelin, walks by and stops. "What're you doin' down there?" he asks, extending his right hand to help Gabriel up while trying not to spill the beer mug he holds in his left.

"What're you doing up there?" Gabriel responds while he regains his feet.

"Might I have a dance with this pretty young lady?" Charles says, winking at Mary.

Setting his beer on a nearby table, Charles helps Mary up next, and while the fiddlers play a slower song, she gracefully spins in circles as they parade back and forth across the hall. Gabriel smiles the contented smile of someone who knows a great day is about to end, but that it will finish with the restful sleep of someone momentarily at peace with the world.

Or who would be at peace, if he could only find Clarence, that is. That thought continually flashes back into Gabriel's mind, disrupting any thoughts of contentment. While he watches Mary dance, so young and innocent, so hopeful, so trusting, so full of a desire to learn and experience life, Gabriel realizes that he's going to have to do something soon. He can't stay at the mission forever. But, if he leaves to take Mary east to St. Louis like Clarence meant to do, how will he find his own father? He's still received no word from Pierre, and that just doesn't seem right. Gabriel's smile fades as he sips the last of his own mug of beer. Tomorrow, he'll speak with Father Andreis about the plans forming in his head.

For tonight, however, why not have a good time while he can? It may well be the last dance he gets to enjoy this summer, and he loves fiddle music. His beer now gone, Gabriel drains what's left from Charles' mug, sallies to the center of the hall, and takes Mary's hands in his. Charles gives her a mock bow and a huge smile and then a little clap to thank her for the dance. Mary beams back a beautiful smile that, Gabriel realizes, in a few years will capture men's hearts. Well, the hearts of men who don't care that she's part Indian, anyway. The music quickening with a new tune, he puts all his energy into one last dance with little Mary, forgetting all his other cares for a few more minutes of innocent pleasure.

In the morning, Gabriel, Mary, and the twenty or so others who'd spent the night at the music hall after their dance walk back toward St. Peter's Mission. The trip is about a mile, and after all the fun last night, they didn't get an early start. However, when they get near to St. Peter's, everyone in the party can see black smoke darkening the sky up ahead.

Gabriel walks at the head of the party when the smoke comes into view, along with Charles and another friend, Bernard Amyotte. They stop walking and stare, speechless, while the others come forward and join them. Bernard speaks first. "Is that the mission? Or our entire town?"

"I don't know. There's so much smoke, it almost looks like both," Charles replies.

Gabriel just stands in place, his face as impassive as stone, while all the young people around him chatter in fear and surprise. Finally, he strengthens his resolve enough to speak. "Quiet, everyone," he calls loudly. In a few moments, most of the other people are looking toward him, apparently glad someone has a plan of what to do.

"Bernard, come with me. We're going to scout out things ahead and see what happened. See if there's still any danger."

165

"Why me?" Bernard says, his voice quavering and hesitant. "I don't know anything about scouting. I want to join the priesthood, not the cavalry. We were at a party last night. None of us are even armed."

"One of us is armed," another young man, Norman Rainville, puts in. "I never go anywhere without my rifle. You shouldn't, either."

"You are the fastest runner, Bernard," Gabriel says. "If something happens to me, you'll have to hurry back here and warn everyone to stay away."

"Take me, then," Norman says angrily. "I'll shoot down any white man who crosses our path. You know I'll do it, too. I'm not scared."

Gabriel takes a moment and looks Norman over. At most, he's fourteen years old. He's also, however, a big, strong lad who's gotten into more than his share of scrapes and fights, causing him to spend about twice as much time in confessional as any other person at St. Peter's Mission. Most of the people like him despite his violent tendencies, however, because he's always sorry and apologizes for fighting afterward, but controlling his temper is not Norman's strength.

"I'm sorry, Norman. I think it's best that Bernard and I go. We don't want to get in a fight. If white people are still around, do you think one rifle will be enough to save us? What if it was a group of soldiers who did this?"

"We'll take some of them with us, at least," Norman protests. "Besides, who made you leader? I wanna make someone pay for this!" Gabriel can see the color rising in Norman's cheeks.

Luckily, Norman's older brother, Joseph, is on hand. "Gabriel's right, Norman," he puts in, laying a soothing hand on his younger brother's shoulder for emphasis and then giving him a couple pats. "You know you have a temper, and we have to keep our composure right now. If it was soldiers, you can't fight them all, even if you think you can. Soldiers are trained to shoot people. You're not."

"But, I can hunt," Norman protests again. "I got a deer last time."

"The first deer you've ever hit," his older brother reminds him. "You know you don't aim very well yet."

Norman's face remains red, and he's set his jaw, too. Gabriel knows he must find a way to defuse this situation quickly.

"Norman, I have an idea," Gabriel says to the young man. "All these other people are going to need protection while we're gone. They need you to watch out for them. Can we trust you to guard everyone else while Bernard and I go check things out? That way, you can protect twenty people instead of just two. The chances of getting to shoot at some white folks are about the same, either way. We don't know for sure where they are, or who they are. Can we trust you to protect all your friends?"

Norman unclenches his fists, and the tension goes out of his face. It worked. "Okay, you're probably right," he says. "But if any soldiers, or any other whites want a fight, I'll give 'em a fight."

Gabriel looks over at Bernard and nods his head. Bernard closes his eyes for a few moments, takes a deep breath, and nods back.

As they trot forward to perform their reconnaissance, Bernard says to Gabriel, "I almost wish the boy was with us. I don't feel good about this. You think soldiers did it? Or more ranchers like those who attacked you last fall?"

"I have no idea what happened. That's what you and I are going to find out."

"What if they are still there?"

"Bernard, just relax. I've done this since I was twelve, remember? We're not going to run straight into the mission without being careful."

"What are we going to do?"

"We're going to find some high ground where we can see the mission but where the soldiers, or whoever set everything on fire, won't be able to see us. I know just the place."

About ten minutes later, Gabriel and Bernard peer around the sides of a large boulder. From this spot, they can indeed see down into the mission without anyone noticing them.

Bernard Amyotte, his voice still shaky, says, "It appears deserted, Gabriel."

"Yeah, it does."

"The schoolhouse got burned down. Father Andreis's house, too. I can see both buildings smoldering still."

"Yeah, they did."

"There's more smoke coming from over there, to the east. That means that our town's gone too, doesn't it?"

"Probably."

"What should we do? How can you stay so calm?"

"I think we should wait here a few more minutes and see what happens. Both of us need to stay calm, so we don't do anything rash. I try to stay calm because that's something my father taught me about scouting. A good scout has to be patient, Bernard."

"But, there's no danger, is there? I don't see any soldiers or other enemies."

"We're probably safe. But let's wait a moment, just to be sure."

While they wait, a lone, black-robed figure emerges from the church. Slowly, he walks past the cemetery, stopping to look at it for a long while. Then, the figure sits down on the stone steps leading to the school's door, which are about all of the building that remains. Then he puts his head in his hands and looks down at the ground.

"Father Andreis!" Bernard exclaims, momentarily forgetting he needs to be quiet. "Shouldn't we go talk to him?"

"Yeah, I suppose it's safe now. I don't think there's any trap here."

After stepping forward for a moment, Gabriel stops and points toward the ground. "Look at this, Bernard."

"I don't see anything. What should I look at?"

"The ground. See the hoof marks from the horses that pock the ground everywhere? The cavalry was here, all right."

A couple minutes later, Bernard and Gabriel walk into the mission. Father Andreis hasn't moved from his spot on the church steps. He finally looks up when he hears the two young men approach.

"My sons," he begins, "thank God you're safe. Where are the others? Are they unharmed?"

"Yes, Father Andreis, everyone who was with us last night is fine," Gabriel says, even as he looks around in despair. "What in Hell happened here at the mission? Where is everyone else?" Then Gabriel blushes at accidentally using such language in front of Father Andreis.

The priest seems to take no notice, however. Father Andreis relates everything that happened during the attack by Pershing's soldiers, including the death of young Johnny and Pershing's decision to burn all the homes in the mission village. Every word comes in a sad monotone. "They've taken them to Cascade for transportation to Great Falls," he concludes. "Men, women, children, everyone. I think we should gather all the people who were with you and escaped the roundup. They must decide whether to turn themselves in to the soldiers and join their families on the way to Canada, or to stay here."

"I'll go and bring everyone to the mission," Bernard says, turning to run back and share the news.

"I've already dispatched Friar O'Connell to Helena, so he can find a lawyer there who will take up our cause and try to block this horrid crime against a peaceful people," Father Andreis says to Gabriel while Bernard hurries away. "I do not know if we have any chance in the legal arena, but it seems the best choice we have."

"You still believe white people will help, after all of this?" Gabriel says with accusation and bitterness in his voice, his right arm sweeping the scene for emphasis. Without any immediate danger to watch out for, he can't hold back his despair any longer. "The law is what white people say it is. This," another sweep of the arm, "this is what white people are," he stammers, not quite finding the words.

"We must put our faith in God," Father Andreis counters. "And, if needs be, the law. We must not lose faith that right and justice will triumph in the end, Gabriel."

Unable to regain his stoic exterior, finally, Gabriel can take the strain no longer. He plops down to the ground, throws his hands up in the air, and begins shouting. "What justice? What justice have I seen in the past year? Vigilantes burned me and my people out of our homes, vigilantes who went completely unpunished by justice and the law. Encouraged by the law, in fact. I haven't seen my father since then. Cowboys tried to kill Mary and me, claiming they were enforcing property rights. The law. White men decided Clarence was an escaped soldier, and now he's a soldier. The white man's law. And now your school is smoldering ashes, your home, too, and your flock is on its way to another country, their homes destroyed, and still you talk of the law!"

"What would you suggest the Church do, then? You know as well as I that violence is not a choice we can make. If all of Christ's teachings against violence are not enough for you, perhaps you remember what happened at Wounded Knee just six years ago, and the carnage that happened there at the merest rumor that Indians might have guns?"

Gabriel continues to stare at Father Andreis intensely, his face flushed and brow furrowed, unpersuaded.

The priest continues. "I read the law, Gabriel, and it calls for deporting Cree Indians. You know that most of the people at our mission are not Cree. They are Michif, just as you are. That is our chance. We will demonstrate that the soldiers from Fort Assiniboine are helping deport the wrong group of people. Our only hope lies in this fact."

The words break through the angry haze in Gabriel's mind. He hops to his feet. "Fort Assiniboine? Did you see Clarence?"

"There were many colored soldiers, my son. All of them, in fact, save the officers. I do not know what Clarence looks like, beyond the short description you and Mary have given me, and even if I did, with the uniforms and hats that soldiers wear, they are difficult to tell apart at times. He may have been here at the mission, but I cannot say with any certainty. Lieutenant Pershing was the only soldier I spoke with, and he is a white officer."

Gabriel stands in thought for a moment. "Even if Clarence was here, I don't see what good that does Mary and me. The army won't let him out, and we still must get her to St. Louis, somehow. If we go to the soldiers to try to find him, they'll catch us, and send us to Canada, and then Mary can never get to St. Louis where she belongs."

"Speaking of St. Louis," Father Andreis puts in, "I've also begun a letter to Archbishop Kain, to let him know what has happened here. I doubt much will come of it, but God can work in mysterious ways."

"Too mysterious for me, I think."

After a momentary pause, Father Andreis looks at Gabriel again. "I just had an idea, Gabriel. I know you will not join the others and go to Canada. You have no reason to go. However, I fear what might happen if you stay here at the mission. The soldiers may make a second sweep to catch stragglers. I don't know if it's likely, but it's possible. From Lieutenant Pershing's words, however, I gather that the soldiers plan to return to Great Falls, then set out again. We must find a way to warn the other camps of Michif in Montana, or the cavalry will capture them and send them away, too. Compassion demands someone undertake this mission. Perhaps you, along with a few others, might go? It's just possible you may find some clues as to your father's whereabouts in the process."

# Chapter 23

## The Grant Family

Father Andreis watches Gabriel, Mary, and two more of his former charges prepare to ride away on a drizzly June Montana day choked with fog. The entire tragic scene seems somehow appropriate. The clinging shrouds of fog will soon obscure his view of the departing riders, just as, it seems, a kind of spiritual fog obscures his ability to discern God's intentions. Although he'd prayed for guidance much of the past two days since Lieutenant Pershing's raid, he still wasn't sure if he was doing right. Of the twenty-three souls the soldiers had not captured the day of the surprise attack, most of them decided to give themselves up to the cavalry because they feared separation from their families. They chose exile together over their personal freedom.

A smaller handful volunteered to stay and help rebuild things at the mission. Once Friar O'Connell returned from Helena, they'd commence work on rebuilding the school and spreading the word that it was still open. Father Andreis had confidence that the philanthropists who contributed money to build the first school would supply some funds to help rebuild it. He'd also dispatched a letter to Archbishop Kain in St. Louis, requesting financial resources and volunteers to restore the mission and allow it to carry on. Andreis lacked confidence in getting too much help, however, from that source, because he'd never received an answer from the archbishop to the query he'd sent about John Healy when Gabriel and Mary first arrived. Perhaps the new archbishop had too many duties to attend to and was unconcerned with affairs in remote Montana, but this seemed a poor sign.

Father Andreis managed to convince three people to ride west, over the Continental Divide, to attempt to warn other camps of Métis of the approaching danger. Gabriel agreed to go, along with his friend Charles Hamelin and one other, Alexander. Gabriel also insisted that Mary go with him, and Andreis had not objected. The young girl was in some peril in going, perhaps, but she'd lost her parents, and then Clarence, in such a brief span that he judged separating Mary from her closest remaining friend might be too much for her. So, despite many reservations, he'd agreed with Gabriel to Mary riding with him.

Now, it was time to say goodbye. Not, he hoped, for good, although who besides God could tell?

"Things may seem dark, my son," he says to Gabriel, "but you have some reason for hope. All of you have plenty of food for your journey, at least."

"Only because we have no more children left at the mission," Charles replies testily. "I'd go hungry for days if it would bring my friends back."

It is clear to Father Andreis that Charles is very nervous about this trip. He's often seen the young man muttering to himself or looking westward towards the mountains apprehensively, but he'd volunteered and seemed determined to see things through, come what may.

"You all have your maps stowed somewhere safe and dry?" the priest asks everyone. They all nod. "Gabriel, I never told you this before, but your father, Pierre, drew the maps you all carry with you. They show you exact locations and directions of how to cross the mountains."

"My father made these maps?" Gabriel queries.

"Ironic, isn't it," Andreis responds, "that you'll be using your own father's maps to try to find him. I told you when you first came here, Gabriel, that your father helped transport me to the mission back in 1890. He also produced these fine maps. Pierre has ridden far and wide across northern Montana and beyond, and he knows almost everything a person can know about its geography."

"Let's just hope we don't encounter any sudden mountain storms," Charles says quietly and without much confidence. "I guess it is June, but still, you never know."

"God will watch over you, my child," Father Andreis tells him. "We do not know for sure where the camps on the other side of the Continental Divide are, but neither do the soldiers, I hope. I believe you have just as good a chance to find them first as the Army does. Go now, my friends, and may the Lord be with you all."

"And also with you," the riders remember to say, although not quite in unison. Kicking their horses into motion, they trot forward into the unknown.

Father Andreis looks one last time at Gabriel and Mary as the fog envelops them. He remains worried about the girl. Mary Healy has spirit, determination, and more toughness than meets the eye, but still, she is but eleven years old, and the journey will not be easy. He'll say an extra prayer for her tonight. No, make that two extra prayers.

After a few moments, he turns his back on the messengers, now invisible through the chilling drizzle and opaque curtains of fog. Father Andreis looks heavenward one final time and blesses them all. His choice made, things are out of his hands, at least for the moment. So many things worry him, however, besides the most obvious task of rebuilding his life's work. His lack of contact with anyone about Pierre Ouellette puzzles and vexes him sorely. It also makes the priest fear the worst.

A few hours after taking their leave of Father Andreis, Gabriel reins in his horse. He doesn't want to do this, but he must. His neck feels like lead while Gabriel slowly raises his head to meet the gaze of his companions and look them in the eyes. Alexander and Charles stop when they see that Gabriel isn't moving anymore.

"I'm sorry, my friends," he says to the group. "But Mary and I must take our leave now. I know that Father Andreis gave us the mission of riding over the Divide, down the Blackfoot River, and on to Horse Plains to try and warn the Michif communities we think are there about the soldiers, but I must find my father. Mary and I will travel a separate route from here."

"What?" Charles says in surprise. "You can't leave us now. You're the most experienced rider we have."

"We were counting on you to help us," the third messenger, Alexander, puts in. "We don't even know for sure where we're going without you."

"You have the maps, so you'll be fine," Gabriel counters. "The route is easy once you find the Blackfoot River." To the looks of crushing disappointment on the faces of his companions, he says, "I know this mission is important, but I haven't seen my father in more than seven months. I've got to look."

"What are you going to do, Gabriel?" Charles asks him. "Just ride around northern Montana until you find him? It'll never work. You don't even know where to start looking."

"No, I've got a better plan than that. Besides, it's not safe for Mary here to ride all over the state, trying to beat the U.S. Cavalry, and being in constant danger. Somehow, I still must get her to St. Louis. I'm surprised Father Andreis even agreed to let her leave the mission with me because I'm sure he knows the risks."

"But I want to go with everyone," Mary puts in. "I don't want to be separated."

"You won't be," Gabriel says in return. "At least, I'm not leaving you. We're just going to a different place than Charles and Alexander are. After we find out where my father is, then we'll get you on your way to St. Louis at last."

"But what about Clarence? We have to get him, too."

"I'm working on that, Mary, I'm working on that." Gabriel hates to lie to her but can't help it this time. He also feels badly for deceiving Father Andreis about his intentions. He hopes the priest will understand.

Charles and Alexander try to argue with Gabriel and persuade him for several more minutes, but after a while, it becomes clear to them he simply won't budge.

"I'm sorry, friends, but I won't change my mind. Your chances of getting through are just as good with two people as with four."

It is true enough. Alexander is about seventeen and a hearty lad. He's cut wood with Gabriel all spring and can work a full day with any grown man.

"Mary and I might even slow you down. The soldiers should move slower than you because of their numbers, and they'll have a supply train to worry about. Besides, both of you have something at stake, right? The two of you both have cousins living in the bands west of the Divide, don't you?"

Alexander and Charles nod.

"You have every reason to make this trip, but I don't. I just want to find some clues about where my father is."

Charles and Alexander look at the ground, trying to resign themselves to traveling on alone. Finally, Charles gets the courage to say, "God be with you, then, Gabriel." Sadly, he adds, "We're never going to see you again, are we?"

"Don't say that," Gabriel replies. "I liked my time at St. Peter's, to be honest. I might come back once all of this is over."

"Goodbye, Mary," Alexander says, sniffling just a bit. "You watch out for Gabriel, okay?"

"I will," she replies. "When I get to St. Louis and live with my Uncle John, I'll send you a letter and tell you all about it."

With that, Gabriel turns his horse northward, and the small company splits in two.

After a few minutes, Mary says, "Where are we going, Gabriel? Do you think you know where your father is?"

"We're going to the town of Augusta, Mary. An old friend lives there. Or, at least, he did, last I knew. I hope he's still there."

"And this friend can help us?"

"I hope so."

By afternoon, the pair nears the town of Augusta, which is less a town than a few buildings huddled together. The Rocky Mountains draw nearer on the left as Gabriel and Mary approach from the south. Before reaching the town's only street, however, Gabriel turns west, heading deeper into the foothills of the Rockies. Most of the peaks still have snow at their tops.

As they ride, Gabriel can't help but stare in wonder at the approach to the mountains. No matter how many times he sees them up close, he's always impressed by their stark beauty. The blue grama grass and other grasses of the plains form a green carpet almost up to the base of the mountains. Then the mountains rise up, like a wall, their stones gray except where covered by snow. It just seems so sudden, like there should be some type of intermediate terrain to separate the horizontal plains from the vertical mountains. The few foothills seem so insignificant.

While he muses on this, he notices that Mary is busy commenting on the wildflowers, birds, and vibrant spring colors.

"Oh, look at the pretty butterfly, Gabriel. Do you know what kind that is?"

"No, I don't know very much about butterflies."

"Will we be there soon? We've been riding for a long time now."

"Mary, we're about to arrive at the ranch of Daniel Grant, an old friend of my father. Did you ever learn anything about the Grant family, either in Butte or at the mission?"

"No, Gabriel, I didn't. Or, I don't remember it, if I did."

"Well, I'm not surprised the teachers in Butte didn't tell you about Daniel or his father, Johnny. The Grant family was the very first family to start a cattle ranch in all of Montana. Johnny started his ranch all the way back in 1845. His plan was to purchase the worn-out cattle for cheap from people traveling overland on the Oregon Trail and then fatten them up on his ranch. Then, when white people found out Montana had gold and started coming out here in the 1860s, he moved his ranch to the Deer Lodge Valley and sold the meat to the miners. He made a pile of money, too, before he moved away."

"How come we don't learn about him in school, then, Gabriel? He sounds important."

"He is important. The mining camps of Montana would have struggled to feed themselves without him. The reason you didn't learn about him in school is that he's Michif, like us, and in white schools you only learn about white people. That's what my father said to me, at least. It's one reason why he never cared if I went to school or not."

"How come he moved away and doesn't ranch anymore? Did he die?"

"I don't know if Johnny is still alive or not, probably not, but that isn't the reason he stopped ranching. After the Civil War ended and people started coming to Montana again, a bunch of them were from Southern states, and they hated Indians and Michif people even more than Northerners did. They threatened Johnny and stole some of his stock. That's when he decided to sell out to one of his distributors, a white rancher named Conrad Kohrs, and go back to the Red River Settlement in the Turtle Mountains."

"How come Daniel didn't go with his dad?"

"He said he liked it here in Montana, that the Dakotas were too flat for him, but he just needed to start a ranch more isolated from white people. So, he came here, to Augusta. Some of the other Michif who used to live next to Johnny Grant did the same thing. They live in tiny towns and ranches all along the eastern edge of the mountains, towns like Augusta, Choteau, Dupuyer, Heart Butte, and Babb. I guess these places are far enough out of the way that the whites don't mind."

"Have you been to this ranch before? I hope we don't get lost."

"Oh, don't worry about that, Mary. I came here a few times with my father before we went up to Canada for the Riel Resistance. I know the way."

Gabriel's memory proves correct. Soon, a farmhouse comes into view, along with a barn, a stable, and a corral. All the buildings are in good repair, although only the house shows any evidence of a paint job, its white coat making it stand out from the weathered gray of the others. A thin whisper of smoke drifts upward from the house's brick chimney. As the two riders approach, an older woman, her long hair a mix of black and gray, comes out the front door of the house to meet them.

Gabriel dismounts and gives a slight bow to the woman. "Ms. Clementine, good to see you. Is Daniel here, by any chance?"

The woman, who appears to be a bit past sixty, stares at Gabriel for just a moment before recognition dawns in her face. She gives a bright, friendly smile. "Gabriel Ouellette! Why, it's been many years since I last saw you. You're all grown up now, and looking so much like Pierre, too. I never expected you'd show up in my front yard today, but then again, we don't get many visitors any time of the year out here. Can I invite you inside for some coffee? And, please tell me, who is your young friend here?"

"I'm Mary," the young girl says excitedly, without waiting for Gabriel to introduce her. "Gabriel takes care of me now that my parents are gone."

Clementine gives a concerned look to Gabriel. "I sense you're not just here on a social call, are you, Gabriel?" She motions them to come inside her home and leads them to wooden frame chairs around her table, which is a thick plank of wood set across two circular sections of timber.

As Gabriel sits, he answers her question. "No, I have several important matters I wanted to discuss with your husband. Is Daniel here?"

"Daniel died two years ago. My sons Samuel and Antoine run the ranch now. You remember them, of course."

"I sure do," Gabriel says with a bit of fond laughter. "When I was a boy and my father brought me here, we'd play hide and seek. They'd always find me, but I could never find them. I'm sorry to hear about Daniel, though."

"Yes," Clementine says with a smile. "You'd play hide and seek, and you'd get frustrated and complain to your father. He'd calm you down, give you some clues about what to do, and then you'd always go and play some more. You were a determined boy, if nothing else. How is Pierre, by the way?" She sets down a tin cup of coffee in front of both Gabriel and Mary.

"Well, that is part of what I wanted to see Daniel about. No one I know has seen or spoken to my father since last year. I don't know where he is, and I can't find him. Part of the reason I came here to visit was in hope that Daniel would know something. They were always good friends. From what you just said, though, I'm guessing that no one here knows anything either, do they?" Gabriel's eyes drop, and he traces his finger over a knot in the wooden table, sighing.

"Well, we'll see what Antoine and Samuel have to say, when they come in from working today. They keep a few things to themselves they don't tell me about, you know?"

A few hours later, while the Grant family and their guests dine, Gabriel and Mary tell everyone their story.

When they finish, Clementine is the first to speak. "The two of you have certainly had a hard time of things. And St. Peter's! It's horrible what the soldiers did. I know Father Andreis just a little, but from all I hear, he's a good man with a true heart."

"Ah, he is," Gabriel puts in. "I know he's sent Friar O'Connell to Helena to try to get legal help for all the Michif people, but he isn't very confident it will work. I think it's a waste of time."

Antoine, who is quite amiable and social, has asked most of the questions during dinner. He is in his later thirties and, although hale and robust in appearance, his hair has started turning gray already. He is also rather tall, over six feet, and has unusually bushy eyebrows.

"You're probably right about that lawyer," he says. "The only reason we can stay here in Augusta is that no one seems to want this land yet. Plus, we raise quality livestock, and we don't bother anybody. It's probably only a matter of time for us, though."

Clementine frowns when she hears this. She appears to have more faith in people's decency than anyone else in the room. Either that, or she's more resigned to whatever happens.

"I don't suppose either of you know anything about my father?" Gabriel finally asks Antoine and Samuel.

Again, it's Antoine who speaks. "I met him in Great Falls last year, but that was before all this trouble began again up along the Milk River. I don't doubt it is John Collins who's behind all this violence and who organized the attack on your homes."

"Who is John Collins?" Mary asks.

"He operates a ranch up in the Milk River region," Antoine answers. "He hates Indians and Michif as much as any white man alive. Collins claims some threatened his wife and children once, but no one's ever proven it."

"Right," Samuel puts in, speaking for once. "I still remember the time, back in the winter of '87 and '88, that Collins had his cowboys poison animal carcasses and then tried trading the meat to the local Michif people during winter when they were starving."

"I've always suspected it was Collins who organized the attack, too," Gabriel says. "But I've been too busy taking care of Mary here, and just trying to survive, to do anything about it or find out anything more."

"As for your father," Antoine resumes, "that was the last I saw or heard of him. I'm tempted to conclude he might have just crossed the Medicine Line into Canada for a while to hide out until the trouble passes."

"No, I don't think he'd do that," Gabriel replies. "He fought in the Riel Resistance, remember? The Canadian authorities might try to catch him if he went there."

"Maybe," Antoine replies, "except the Canadians wouldn't know he was coming, and they'd have no reason to suspect he was in

Canada. Your father's a resourceful man. He could have gone up there without anyone knowing a thing about it."

"It's not like him to just leave me, though. I don't think he'd do that. I'm starting to think he's dead. Maybe one of those vigilantes, or a soldier from the fort, killed him."

"Now, Gabriel," Clementine puts in, "don't worry yourself with what might be. I think he'll turn up somewhere. He's probably trying to find you just as much as you're trying to find him."

"But how come no one, nowhere, has heard anything about him?"

"Montana is a big place."

At this point Samuel, who has barely spoken all through dinner, breaks his silence for a second time. "I think it's time to fight back against the whites."

Gabriel looks him over. He's at least thirty, but he looks as strong as a bear, probably from all the labor he does at the ranch. Samuel is rather stocky, unlike his older brother. Compared with Antoine, Gabriel remembers him as the quieter of the two brothers; when Gabriel visited the ranch as a boy, that had been true. Right up until something upset him badly, that is. One time, when Gabriel was a guest, Antoine teased Samuel just a little too much when Samuel fell off his horse, and then, Samuel was like a stick of dynamite exploding. It was several days before he calmed down completely and spoke to his brother normally again. Gabriel wonders if his temper is still like that.

"Now, son," Samuel's mother says, "I know you're angry, and you've every right to be, but you've got to keep your anger in the right place. You're old enough to know you can't go fighting all those soldiers yourself. Let's not have any more of that talk."

"I'm not saying I'm going to march straight into their camp and just let them have it," Samuel responds. "I haven't lived to be thirty-two because I'm stupid. But I'm tired of those white devils just robbing people. Our family should've been rich, and would have, if it wasn't for white people pushing grandfather around, stealing his cattle, and making him sell off his ranch. It was his idea to start that cattle ranch and feed the white miners, not Conrad Kohrs. But who has all the money, fame, and reputation now? Besides, if they're roundin' up people from the mission, how long until they come up here after us? How long until they clean out every Indian and Michif from the entire county? The entire state? The country, even? We've been here in Montana longer than the whites have, and they're trying to tell us we're the ones who don't belong."

"What's your plan, then?" Antoine asks his brother, eyebrows raised and eyes intent.

"I'm sayin' we should start treatin' them the way they treat us. I'll ride with you, Gabriel, while you search for Pierre, and we'll just see what happens if any more cowboys try to harass you. We've got rifles and ammunition here on the ranch, just in case."

Clementine frowns deeply. "And who will help run our ranch, while the two of you do that?"

"The cows can eat grass without us watching them, mother, and the crops we've sown won't be ready to harvest for a couple weeks yet, at minimum. I think at least one of us should go with Gabriel and Mary."

Clementine just folds her hands on the table and scowls again, saying nothing further. It's clear, however, that this debate is not over.

To relieve the awkwardness, Gabriel says, "I think we'd better head back to St. Peter's in a day or two. Father Andreis won't be pleased that I left Charles and Alexander, but I've got to keep looking for my father somewhere."

# Chapter 24

## John Healy's Letter

Several days after the departure of Gabriel, Mary, Charles, and Alexander, Father Andreis sits at his rough, unpolished, wooden desk. He's relocated his office from the burned-out shell left over after the fire to a corner of the mission's chapel. Bright sunlight streams through the open windows. Then, he hears a rider approach outside. Putting down his quill pen and rising, he steps out to see who it is, hoping to see anyone but another soldier. To his relief, it's Friar O'Connell, back from Helena.

Dismounting from his well-lathered gray horse, O'Connell manages a travel-weary smile. "I have some good news about our situation," he says. "And some mail you'll want to see. A letter from Archbishop Kain arrived at last."

Andreis takes the mail, setting it aside for the moment by tucking the envelope into his priest's robe. "What news from Helena? Will someone help us?"

"Yes. A local lawyer of unusual compassion, named John Hoffman, volunteered to request a writ of *habeas corpus*. He plans to force the Army to show cause for removing our people, the American citizens, from their homes and transporting them to Canada against their will. He is unsure of our success. It depends, he claims, on the political persuasion and attitude regarding Indians of the courts."

"We live in Montana. What are the chances a court will rule in our favor?"

"Slight, most likely, Father. Still, we can always appeal and hope a higher court has more sympathy. Delay the process, at the minimum. Maybe, in time, we'll succeed in persuading someone that our people are not Cree, and that an act to deport the Cree therefore doesn't apply to them."

Father Andreis frowns, then sighs. "I agree. It's probably the best we can hope for at present. You'll be returning to Helena like we discussed, then?"

"With your permission, Father, yes. Do we still agree that someone must be there to speak out for our cause?"

"Yes, and I still think you're the one for this job. In any case, we have no one else to send, other than one of our nuns, so I think it has to be you."

"Thank you, Father. With God's help, I'll do all I can."

"By the way, while you were gone, I sent out three people to warn the Michif of western Montana to be watchful for the soldiers. Well, four people, in fact. Mary and Gabriel went together. We must pray for their success and safety as well."

"Yes, Father. Most certainly," Friar O'Connell says as he stands to take his leave.

"Very well, my friend. Take some rest, so you'll be ready to return to Helena tomorrow."

After Friar O'Connell's departure, Andreis turns his attention to the mail, especially the letter from Archbishop Kain. He goes back inside the mission's wooden chapel and sits down. Breaking the archbishop's seal and opening the letter, another, smaller, sealed envelope falls from the letter when he opens the pages. Bending over to pick up this other letter and then placing it on his desk, Andreis looks over the archbishop's missive. After the usual salutations and blessings, the archbishop apologizes for the delay in his response, citing the duties of his office and the time necessary to look for one person in a city the size of St. Louis. However, near the bottom of the first page, the letter reads:

*Despite these travails, I can inform you that, through the Grace of God, my staff succeeded in locating John Healy and, in accordance with your wishes, shared your communication with him. He lives in this city still and remains true to the Faith. After sharing your letter with him, like you requested, I'm pleased to enclose his response with this missive. It should arrive in its own sealed envelope.*

The archbishop's letter closes with the usual expressions of goodwill, but Father Andreis hardly reads them, reaching instead for John Healy's letter. Again, after skipping over the obligatory introductions and salutations, it reads:

*Thank you, Father Andreis, for informing me of the unfortunate situation afflicting my niece and her temporary guardian. I am, needless to say, saddened greatly by your news of what's befallen Clarence as well. Once I have Mary here with me in this city, we will waste no time in trying to secure his freedom, you may count on that.*

*More than anything, I want to meet Mary and see her delivered safely to me in St. Louis. Although I've never yet met her, she is precious to me because Thomas was my brother. Rest assured I will take good care of her and raise her as my own daughter.*

*I've enclosed sufficient money for two railroad tickets to St. Louis with my letter. Archbishop Kain's representative assures me this money will reach you safely. My intention is for Mary and a guardian to travel to St. Louis as soon as possible. Whether the identity of this guardian is her new friend Gabriel, or a member of your mission, I leave to you to decide the best course of action.*

*Thank you so much for contacting me. If you would be so kind as to send me a letter informing me when Mary and her companion will arrive in St. Louis, I will forever be in your debt.*
*Peace and God's love be with you, Father Andreis.*


*Yours & co.,*

*John Healy*

Peering into the envelope once again, Father Andreis can see the money mentioned in Healy's letter. There it is. Mary's ticket home. Except, just a few days ago, he'd agreed to let her leave the mission. Now, presumably, she is somewhere on the other side of the Rocky Mountains, trying to warn other bands of Métis of their danger while helping Gabriel Ouellette find his missing father.

Just as he's done so often lately, Father Andreis puts his head down while blinking back the tears. Now, this young girl's fate hinges on things outside of his control, and it is his own fault. If only this letter had arrived a week sooner. If only he'd been more insistent that Mary stay at the mission. If only, if only. Silently, he rebukes himself for his weakness, knowing Mary would be preparing to travel to safety with her uncle, had he only been a wiser man.

# Chapter 25

## Charles & Alexander

Clarence rides out in front of his troop, scouting ahead. He's not sure why he's scouting ahead. The cavalry hasn't met any resistance today. It didn't meet any resistance yesterday. For that matter, it hasn't met any resistance on the entire expedition, except for what Sergeant Grimes imagined back at St. Peter's Mission. Clarence doesn't imagine they will meet any resistance tomorrow, either. Lieutenant Pershing is thorough, if nothing else, he supposes, and plays things by the book, so he imagines they'll keep on scouting ahead, just in case.

"Funny, isn't it," he says to Washington, who rides next to him. "For all this talk about marauding Cree making all this trouble in Montana, and the Cree being a dire threat we must remove, we've seen no trouble the entire time we've been in the field. We've seen no stealing, or cattle rustling, or anything. If it wasn't for Sergeant Grimes telling us to charge that schoolhouse, none of us would have even fired our weapons on this whole excursion."

"True enough," Washington responds. "Well, 'cept when we met tha' bear, an tried to shoot it, an you almos' drowned."

They laugh. Everyone's said that so many times, it's become a joke now. Whenever someone almost does something, they would have done it, except then they meet a bear, someone tries to shoot it, and Clarence almost drowns. *It's a little macabre*, Clarence thinks to himself, *but it's all in good fun, so I can take it.*

Still, joke or not, the thought of the ice-cold Marias is enough to make him shiver one more time, even though it's late June now and plenty warm in western Montana.

The troopers have about two days to go before stopping for a brief stay at Fort Missoula to resupply. Then they ride west in search of any Cree living in western Montana. Rumor says they'll face two hundred Cree and that they may be hostile. By now, however, Clarence is quite aware that the people are much more likely to be Métis than Cree, and he's equally aware of which side tends to be the hostile one, but while pretending to be Fred Cooper, he judges it best not to speak about those beliefs too much.

This is his first time viewing the countryside on the western side of the Continental Divide, but this area doesn't seem that much different from the eastern side in terms of the types of trees or grasses. Clarence sees more rolling hills west of the divide, though. On the other side, the plains go almost right up to where the mountains begin. Here, the terrain is not so level.

There are plenty of insects, however, just like in central Montana. Clarence slaps at the flies even while his horse does the same with its tail. He doesn't know why he bothers, though. Two seconds later, they're back. He thinks he's managed to kill three for the entire day. Rather than continue his futile attack, Clarence looks down to try to concentrate on something else for a while.

The grass is still green, for the moment, but the days are getting warmer, and it hasn't rained too often, so Clarence knows that means the grass will probably turn golden, then brown, before their time in the field is up. That also means they'll choke on dust before the roundup is over. Not an encouraging thought. For today, however, things are tolerable.

Instead of dwelling on the future, Clarence asks Washington, "How do these rumors start circulating in the cavalry, anyway? Rumor said the people near Cascade were probably hostile, and they offered no resistance. A few even turned themselves in, voluntarily, afterward just to stay with their families. None of them even had weapons to speak of. And now, rumor has it we're facing two hundred or so more hostiles who are armed and dangerous."

"Oh, you know, tha's what happens when you's a private and you don' hear the real orders, Fred. The officers, they don' tell us much unless it's a order, and they never 'splain to us why we do things, so people, they imaginations get goin', and pretty soon, a man don' know wha's true and wha's not."

"You reckon that's all part of Old Red's plan? If we're all worried something might happen, we'll be on guard and take more precautions?"

"I never thought of it tha' way, Fred, but you might be onta somethin'."

"Well, onto something or not, that still doesn't make this ride any more interesting. Where are we headed, again?"

"Rumor has it the Cree, they at a place called Horse Plains or there 'bouts. We 'sposed to look there first, after we leave Fort M-, M-."

"Missoula."

"Right, Missoula."

"There we go again with the rumors." Clarence rolls his eyes.

They talk for a while longer, but Washington's comments are brief and rote, and so are Clarence's, so mostly they just ride along and scout in silence. Nothing interesting happens, and after a brief stop to water the horses, they're almost ready to ride back to camp and make their report for the day.

First, however, the scouts top one more rolling hill, and up ahead spot two figures to their northwest, the same direction they're headed. The head scout gives the men the command to rein in their horses, and he scans the pair of riders with his field glasses. They appear to be only about a quarter-mile away; only the hill kept the scouts from

190

seeing them until now. The two men sit on the ground, with a small campfire, and they don't stir even while the cavalry watches them, so Clarence doesn't think they know the scouts have spotted them. Nearby, he sees two horses tethered.

"Looks like trouble," the head scout reports. "A pair of Injuns makin' camp. Better git 'em. You two," pointing at Washington and Clarence, "you ride 'round, careful and quiet, on this side of the hill, until you get in front of 'em, so they don't git away. After a few minutes, we'll ride in an' capture 'em."

Washington and Clarence follow orders and move out. They're careful and quiet, but like every other precaution the scouts take today, it turns out to be unnecessary. The scouts capture the two riders with no trouble. Like the supposed Cree the Buffalo Soldiers rounded up at St. Peter's Mission, they have no weapons. Soon, they're riding back to the main force and their evening camp, the two captives in tow.

On the way, Clarence thinks back on some of the things he read about when he learned to read. He remembers reading in civics books about the glories of the American legal system—about how all Americans enjoy precious safeguards to their liberties, like the right to a fair trial, a jury of their peers, how everyone is innocent until proven guilty, and on and on. Yet, here the Buffalo Soldiers are, rounding up people and taking them prisoner, even though they pose no threat to anyone and the troopers have no way of knowing if they are even the Cree Indians they're supposed to be after. But the men have orders to capture any Indians they come across, just in case, and bring them in for questions.

Clarence also knows from reading those books on civics, and from living in Butte for several years, that Indians are not United States citizens, or, at least, most of them aren't, so he supposes that is how the U.S. Army can get away with what it's doing. Maybe some distinction exists there, but it doesn't sit right with Clarence that these people live in the United States and the government of the United States can make decisions about their lives, including where they can live and can't live, yet they aren't citizens and don't have the equal protection of the law. But, already having one strike against him after his so-called desertion, Clarence follows orders and doesn't voice these ideas to anyone else.

That's as far as he gets in his musings by the time the scouts rejoin the main body of soldiers. Washington and Clarence get the task of presenting the captives to Lieutenant Pershing. Not that either gains any glory or any great credit in doing so; all the other scouts are just tired and want to eat and turn in for the evening, so the two of them get this task.

"Well done, men, well done," Pershing says to them. "Have you learned anything from them? Any intelligence as to where the others are?"

Just as they prearranged, Clarence lets Washington reply to Pershing because the less Pershing knows about Clarence, the better. "No, suh, no intel'gince," Washington replies. "They's done plenty o' talkin', but it ain't English, suh. Must be Cree, o' somethin'."

"Well, we'll get them to talk, one way or another," Pershing says. "Put these men under guard tonight. The two of you will stand watch over them. Tomorrow, we'll have someone else from the troop escort them to Fort Missoula. After you two get your rations for the evening, report for duty guarding the prisoners. Carry on, men."

Clarence's hopes jumped when Pershing mentioned taking the prisoners to the fort, but they crashed just as quickly when Pershing said someone else would escort them to Fort Missoula. That might have been the perfect chance to escape and go looking for Mary and Gabriel. Apparently, Pershing remembers how Clarence, as Fred Cooper, tried to desert the 10th Cavalry once already, and he isn't going to give Clarence another chance. In addition to being careful and playing by the book, Pershing also appears to have an excellent memory. While Clarence and Washington walk to the commissary for chow and then back to their new duties as guards, Washington keeps looking at Clarence. Once they're on their own and can talk quietly, Clarence decides to ask him what's on his mind.

Washington beats Clarence to it. "You was thinkin' a runnin' when Ol' Red talked about taking them Indians to Missoula, wasn't you?"

"Yeah, it would have been a great chance to get away. Unfortunately, the lieutenant has a good memory for details. I guess he decided someone else would get that assignment."

"You know you cain't do that, right, Cooper? Go runnin' off right now?"

"Why not?"

"'Cause whoever was ridin' with you would get it hot, fo' sure."

Clarence doesn't admit he hadn't thought much about that. Instead, he says, "Lincoln, how come you spoke that way to Lieutenant Pershing back there? I know you can speak better English than that. We haven't had much time for our lessons lately, but I know you've improved a lot since we started practicing."

"Sho' I kin, I'se kin do betta, Massa Coopa, sho' 'nuf," he says, really pouring it on to tease Clarence. "But, you see, Cooper, if I talks like the 'tennant 'spects colored people to talk, he won't 'spect so much outta me. It's easier to impress him that way, see?"

"Good point, Lincoln. That makes sense. Although, it also makes us look stupid when we aren't. I thought one of the reasons you joined the Buffalo Soldiers was to prove that colored people were just as good as white folks."

"Now you has a point, I 'spose. I wish white people could jus' 'cept us the way we are, and all this provin' stuff wasn't necessary."

"Yeah, that'd be swell. I guess the difference between you and me is that you think that day will come at some point. I'm not sure that I do."

"Well, Cooper, sittin' here talkin' 'bout it won't make it so, anyway. You want first watch on the Indians, or you want me to do it?"

"You take it, Lincoln. Wake me in a few hours."

Clarence lies down and tries to get comfortable on the rocky soil, but soon, his skin's crawling. Ants! Ugh! Unknowingly, he tried sleeping right next to the exit of their tunnels. Clarence hops up and brushes himself off furiously. When he thinks he's gotten them all, he moves about twenty feet away and tries to sleep again.

If a soldier can avoid sleeping by anthills, it isn't hard to sleep while in the field, generally speaking. After a full day of riding, Clarence is always tired, and after adding in the fresh outdoor air, he just slumps down under his blanket and nods off right away. It became easy for him to sleep once he got used to the background noise of the camp and he's been on campaign long enough that Clarence is plenty used to it by now. The only other problem is the flies, mosquitos, and other insects buzzing around because it's summer. Sure, the soldiers have tents, but the insects get inside, anyway. Clarence guesses he's now used to that, too, because he's asleep in no time.

Any sleep is always too short, however, because every morning the troopers must break camp and take the field again, and it takes some time to pack supplies. Because Clarence has also drawn guard duty, he doesn't even get to sleep all through the night. So, when Lincoln prods him awake to take his turn on guard, Clarence is not in a great mood. Even though it's been two hours, he feels like he just closed his eyes two minutes ago.

Clarence stumbles over to his station and, for the first time, takes a close look at the people he helped capture. They are both about his age—in their late teens, he guesses—and from the look of their clothes—dirty, dusty, and getting ragged—they've been traveling for many days. They've been eating well, at least, and had plenty of food in their packs when the scouts discovered them, and not just hardtack and coffee like Clarence has been eating. Although the moon is out, it's just a quarter, so it's still rather dark and Clarence can't see much about their faces.

Given how tired he is, Clarence assumes they are asleep, and he knows that if he doesn't do something to keep awake, he will be, too, before long. He can't afford to fall asleep on guard duty, though, however small the threat might be. That kind of thing gets you in hot water in the cavalry. As a result, Clarence finds himself musing out loud about his situation just to keep awake.

Like they usually do, before long Clarence's thoughts come around to how he can get out of the cavalry and figure out what's happened to Mary and Gabriel, since he didn't find them at St. Peter's like he thought that he would. Absentmindedly, he must have mumbled something about them too loudly because to his surprise he hears one of the captives whisper, with a bit of a French accent, "Did you say Mary and Gabriel?"

Clarence's head jerks over in the direction of the prisoners. One of them, the older of the two, is awake after all, and is looking at him. "Did I hear you say something about Mary and Gabriel?" he repeats.

"I thought you only spoke Cree," Clarence says to the young man in a low voice, trying to avoid attention. Should he be conversing with a prisoner? It can't hurt, he supposes, and maybe he'll learn some intelligence to share with Pershing. Besides, the man hasn't done anything wrong as far as Clarence knows—he just had the misfortune of looking like an Indian when the cavalry was searching for Indians.

"Cree? I don't know any Cree. But I'll speak to you in Michif if you don't want these soldiers to know what I'm saying."

"I can't speak that," Clarence replies. Which is true. Even though he lived among the Métis for a few months, they always spoke English when he was around, so Clarence never learned any Michif. Just getting a decent grasp of English was tough enough. So, he decides to ask, "Who are you?"

"Who are you?" the man whispers in reply.

Clarence sees no reason not to reply honestly, seeing that by tomorrow it won't matter, and these two will be on their way to Fort Missoula and captivity there until the roundup ends. "Clarence. Clarence Duval."

The next thing the captive says almost knocks him over. "I thought so. When you started mumbling, I assumed you were thinking about Gabriel Ouellette and Mary Healy. I can tell you where they are."

He certainly has Clarence's attention. "How do you know that, and how do you know who I am?"

"I know where Gabriel and Mary are because up until about a week ago, I was traveling with them. I wish I still was. If Gabriel had been with us, I don't think you'd have caught us. I'm Charles, by the way. Gabriel is my friend. He told me about you and how these soldiers forced you into the cavalry. I figured there couldn't be another pair of people named Gabriel and Mary traveling together in Montana looking for a colored friend who got stuck in the cavalry."

"I'd shake your hand, but someone might see," Clarence says to Charles quietly. He's relieved to know Gabriel and Mary still worry about him and that they are alive, but distressed that Mary is still in Montana and not in St. Louis. More than ever, that means he must escape so he can help her. "What were you doing when we caught you?"

"Trying to find the Michif communities of western Montana and tell them about you, of course. You, meaning the cavalry, that is. We'd have made it, too, except we had trouble finding the headwaters of the Blackfoot River without Gabriel."

"So, we didn't capture the whole group at St. Peter's, then?"

"Correct. Gabriel, Mary, and I, along with about twenty others, were off at a dance the night before the troops attacked the mission. We didn't come back until late in the morning, and by then, you'd come and gone."

"Well, that explains a few things. Has Gabriel found his father since I last saw him in November?"

"No, and that is the reason he wasn't with us when you caught up with us. He was supposed to be, but instead, he went to Augusta to try to find word about Pierre. He took Mary with him." When Clarence hesitates to respond, Charles adds, "They're safe, as far as I know. Gabriel was supposed to lead us to Horse Plains, but I suppose now we'll never get there."

"Horse Plains is just where we're headed. It appears Lieutenant Pershing has good intelligence on where to look." That triggers another thought for Clarence. "Say, maybe you can help me with something. Do you know what's going to happen to you and your companion?"

"Not for sure. Are the soldiers going to kill us?"

"I don't think so. Tomorrow, or should I say later today when the sun comes up, they're going to take you to Fort Missoula. I assume that after that, you'll go to Canada with the other Michif who we're pretending are Cree. But, Pershing, or maybe someone at the fort, plans to question you to get more details about where to look for the others. They think you know where you're going, or where you were going. If you let me inform Pershing, perhaps I can gain some of his confidence. I'm hoping he'll send me to take you to the fort, and if he does, we just might get a chance to escape together."

"Well, I don't know that it's really my choice now, is it?" Charles says. "I've already told you everything I know. Not that I know very much, anyway. You might as well, if you think it'll help you. If your army is going to Horse Plains anyway, I'm sure they'll find who they're looking for. Alexander and I didn't get there fast enough, and now we're done for, it appears."

In the morning, Clarence goes off in search of Lieutenant Pershing to tell Pershing what he's discovered. Clarence finds Pershing inside his field tent, ink quill in hand, doing paperwork at a portable wooden desk. He gives a crisp salute as he enters. "Lieutenant Pershing, I have news, sir."

"Go on, Private Cooper."

"While I was on guard duty last night, I got one of the prisoners to talk a bit. He said they were on their way to Horse Plains to warn any Mé-, I mean, Cree, in the area about our approach. He seems to think the Cree are at Horse Plains, just as our intelligence predicted."

"Indeed. And how, may I ask, did you get these Indians to talk to you? I thought they only spoke Cree."

"No, sir, they can speak a bit of English, too. As for why they talked to me, I convinced them they were going to Fort Missoula as prisoners no matter what they did and then on to Canada with their tribesmen, so they had nothing to lose. I also convinced them that speaking to me would be less painful than whatever you had in mind for them. You know these Indians, sir; they scare easily. Especially young ones like these."

"Well, if that's true, then you've done well, Private Cooper. We'll follow up with the prisoners, just to make sure they haven't changed their story, but still, good work. I plan for the captives to ride with us today. You'll resume scouting ahead once we break camp."

"Yes, Lieutenant. Of course, sir."

"That will be all, Cooper. Keep up the good work. You might make a Buffalo Soldier yet."

"Thank you, Lieutenant. I try my best, sir."

Clarence marches away in disappointment. Still no chance to escape, slight as this chance might have been. At least the lieutenant seems to have a little confidence in him now. Pershing still remembers when Clarence, or should he say, when Fred Cooper deserted and probably always will, but ever since his capture, Clarence has been a model soldier. Well, maybe not in talent, but in his ability to follow rules and do what he's told, Clarence has toed the line as well as anyone since last November. Not to mention that, all his life, he's had to practice telling white folks what they want to hear, so keeping a low profile comes naturally.

Clarence also hoped to stay on guard duty because even though he doubts by now that the people he's after really are very hostile, still, one never knows. He sure doesn't want to get into any firefights or die here in some mountain valley in Montana, when he still needs to find some way to help Mary get to St. Louis. But every step his horse takes removes him further from his goal. At least he knows Mary and Gabriel are still in Montana, and he has some idea of where to look, if he ever gets a chance and can start looking.

# Chapter 26

## Fort Missoula

Once the sun comes up, the Buffalo Soldiers are on the march again, which Clarence always thinks is a funny thing to call it, since they ride horses. Whatever the proper word, Clarence's scouting takes him through the valley of the Blackfoot River, which is still green and very scenic in late June. The river itself, while not wide or deep in most spots, is a beautiful blue, but still cold as the last of the winter snowmelt heads downstream. Trees shade the slopes of the valley, casting their slanted shadows in the early morning sun.

As usual, Washington rides beside him. "Lincoln, how many people do you reckon live in these parts?" Clarence asks his friend. "We haven't seen more than a rancher or two all day, have we?"

"Nope."

"I don't see anyone here for the Cree to bother. Why do we care what they're up to?"

"Orders, tha's why."

"It doesn't bother you that we're rounding up harmless people?"

"I ain't sayin' it do, and I ain't sayin' it don't. But we got orders, Cooper."

"You still think you're going to earn someone's respect by following orders?"

"Ain't got no choice right now, do we?"

"There's always a choice, Lincoln."

"'Cept when you in the cav'ry and you got orders."

"You said the 10th Cavalry earned its stripes fighting Indians in Texas and other places, right?"

"Tha's right."

"You know we colored people don't get a fair shot in this country. And the Indians don't, either."

"True 'nuf, I 'spose, Cooper. I can only speak for colored folks myself, but I reckon the Indians get treated 'bout the same as we do."

"So why on earth are we helping the whites do awful things to other people who get treated just as badly as we do? Wouldn't it make more sense to work with them instead of against them?"

"Orders, tha's why we doin' it, Cooper. 'Nuf said for today, alright? We the Buffalo Soldiers, and we gonna act like Buffalo Soldiers."

By midday, they've reached the confluence of the Blackfoot with the Clark Fork River, which is deeper and wider than the Blackfoot, and by afternoon, the troopers meander through the canyon leading to Missoula. Someone says its name is Hellgate Canyon, but no one in the party seems to know how it got the name. The sides of the canyon rise steeply, especially on the south side of the river, their gray rock mixing with the browning grass and studded with trees.

As evening sets in, the men arrive at Fort Missoula, which is located a bit to the west of the town of the same name. Clarence is surprised when he learns that Fort Missoula is the home of another regiment of colored soldiers, the 25th Infantry, although as usual, their commander is a white man, Colonel Andrew Burt.

The men have a bit of down time that evening after setting up their tents on the flat, green parade grounds of the fort, so Clarence has the chance to wander around a bit before moving out in the morning. Fort Missoula is a big place, and there appears to be lots of room. He's surprised once again when he finds that not only is the 25$^{th}$ a colored regiment like his, but in one of the buildings he finds colored soldiers with bicycles. Four men tinker with them in the pale gaslight. Curious, he stops in to see what they're doing.

"Evening, private. You men are with the 25$^{th}$?" Clarence asks the nearest soldier.

"We are," the soldier replies. "And you must be with the 10$^{th}$ Cav that just rode in, right?"

"Yeah, my name's Fred, Fred Cooper," Clarence says as he shakes hands with everyone. "I was just curious about your bicycles. I've seen lots of people riding them before, of course, but I didn't know we had them in the Army."

"We do, but just barely," another soldier says to Clarence. "We just got permission to organize a bicycle corps about six weeks back. One of the officers here, Lieutenant Moss, loves bicycles, and he got special permission to organize a bicycle corps as part of the 25$^{th}$."

"What do you use them for?" Clarence asks.

"The lieutenant says he wants to test if they'll make infantry more mobile, especially here in mountainous terrain. The four of us here, plus four others, are the bicycle corps of the 25$^{th}$ Infantry."

"How do you stow all your gear?"

"Well, we're still working out the most efficient places to put everything, but right now we do it like this. You strap your knapsack, bedroll, and shelter to the handlebars, trying to keep the weight balanced, of course. You sling your rifle across your back, although I personally think it might work better if we found a way to strap it to the horizontal bar of the bicycle. The whole thing weighs about sixty pounds once you pack your gear."

"Can I take a closer look at one?"

"Sure, Cooper, give it a look. You can see these units have steel rims, heavy side-forks, and a thick, sturdy frame because we use them in rugged terrain and we need durability."

Clarence is about to ask who manufactures the special bicycles, but now he can see the label on them for himself. He should have known. Clarence just laughs and shakes his head.

"What is it, Cooper? Something wrong?" the first soldier asks.

"No, nothing at all," Clarence says, still smiling while shaking his head one last time. "I'm just laughing because I know the man whose company manufactures these things."

The label, of course, reads "A. G. Spalding Company."

"How would you know Al Spalding?" one of the men says.

"Doesn't he own a baseball team or something?" another asks.

Clarence tries to think of a way to explain without giving away his real identity. Not because he thinks it will really matter in this case but just because he's tired and wants to avoid having to explain everything. He replies, "I was born in Chicago and grew up there, near West Side Park where the White Stockings play ball. Except I guess the team calls itself the Colts now. Anyway, our paths crossed here and there. It would be a stretch to say Spalding and I were ever friends, but I did a few odd jobs for him around the ballpark when I was a kid." It isn't the whole truth, but close enough for Clarence, and, apparently, good enough for the other soldiers because no one presses him for any more information.

He tries to change the subject back to bicycling. "How far have you boys traveled?"

"We've been all the way to Lake McDonald, up past Columbia Falls," one soldier replies. "It was around 150 miles each way."

"But we've got a bigger trip coming up," another man puts in. "Lieutenant Moss has plans for us to ride all the way to Yellowstone Park and back, to show how useful bicycles can be over long distances and varied terrain. We leave in August, assuming you boys don't get all the Indians in Montana too stirred up."

"Moss hopes that we can show the nation how useful and manly bicycles are, unfortunately," the first soldier says.

"Why is that unfortunate?" Clarence asks him. "Your bicycle corps is unique. Isn't that a good thing?"

"Because he thinks we might have to talk to the newspapers and tell them about our glorious trip, Moss makes us take all these reading classes here at the fort, so we'll sound good for the reporters when our time comes. If it ever does."

"You don't like reading?" Clarence asks.

"We've got nothing against reading," the third man of the four puts in. "It's just that we signed on to be soldiers, not to sit in a classroom with a book part of the day."

"Yeah, I guess that must be frustrating," Clarence replies. Secretly, he wouldn't mind trading places with them.

His curiosity satisfied, he takes his leave of the bicycle corps and heads to his tent. It's dark by now, and they'll be on the move again tomorrow, so getting some sleep sounds like a good plan.

Clarence gets yet another surprise when, in the morning, not all the troopers break camp and head northwest to pursue their objective. There's been a change of plans, it seems. Word passes through the ranks that there may be more Cree near Missoula, so some of the men stay behind with the purpose of locating and capturing these small bands. Once again, Clarence learns that Lieutenant Pershing is nothing if not thorough.

He's also pleased to learn that Private Carter is among those remaining at Fort Missoula, while he is not. Ever since the incident at the Marias River, Carter has kept a low profile, especially without Sergeant Grimes to shower favors on him. Oftentimes, however, when Clarence happens to see him, Carter just rides along, silently brooding. Clarence doubts that he's had his last tussle with Carter, but for now, Carter's fear of Pershing seems to outweigh his desire for revenge. Clarence just hopes he can pull his escape before the scales tip in the other direction. Still, for now, another several days out in the field is worth being away from Carter.

# Chapter 27

## Completing the Roundup

After Clarence rides away from Fort Missoula, heading north and northwest, the countryside changes. It's drier. Now that it's July, the grasses start turning gold while the Buffalo Soldiers ride over hills and across lands dedicated to grazing cattle. There's hardly even a fencepost to mar the unending, unbroken fields of knee-high, green-gold bunchgrass.

Most of the time, they follow the route of the Northern Pacific Railroad, which means heading north from Missoula to a place named Ravalli. It has a post office but there is no real town to speak of, most of the so-called townspeople being ranchers. From Ravalli, they turn west, traveling with the hills to their left and the Flathead River to their right. Clarence doesn't relish the thought of crossing another river, but that seems to be his fate.

Besides the increasingly drab hues of the vegetation and the occasional cow, Clarence doesn't see much that is very interesting to him. Above the rim of the river valley, it's mostly high plains bunchgrasses and thin, rocky soil. Clarence sees some trees but not many, mostly cottonwoods where some small stream meanders through the rolling hills toward its rendezvous with the Flathead. Higher up in the hills he notes a few more trees. They look like stands of pines.

Clarence sighs to himself. Still no buffalo. Foolish as it may have been, seeing a majestic buffalo was one reason he came to Montana after the Spalding Tour. He's been here for seven years now, and he's still never seen one. Clarence felt he'd have a good chance of seeing a buffalo on this campaign, given that the Buffalo Soldiers must traverse a good portion of Montana, but nothing so far. Doubt creeps in that he ever will.

Returning his thoughts to his present situation, Clarence knows most of the other men don't relish another river crossing any more than he does. Even the jokes about shooting a bear while Clarence almost drowns have become old by now. Therefore, it's a pleasant surprise when they reach a place named Perma and Lieutenant Pershing calls the men together to speak with them.

"Troopers, I've received new intelligence regarding our mission. The Cree, supposedly at Horse Plains, being the shiftless, nomadic race that they are, have moved their camp. We now believe they've relocated somewhere north of here, on the other side of the range of hills you can see to our north." Pershing points for emphasis, then resumes. "Reports now put the Cree somewhere on Camas Prairie. I feel time is of the essence if we are to surprise the Indians and complete our mission because they may not stay put for long."

"But sir, we still must cross the Flathead River if we're to get the Cree, and that could take a full day," one of the sergeants says.

Pershing glowers at the man for speaking out of turn, his face turning the slightest hint of red. "Yes, you're right, sergeant. It would take an entire day. Had you let me finish, however, I was about to lay out our plan. Here at Perma, such as it is, we'll catch the next Northern Pacific train headed west. One should arrive shortly, so keep your gear packed. In about an hour, we'll unload at Horse Plains, *on the other side of the Flathead River*," he says with sarcastic emphasis, "mount up, and dash eastward to Camas Prairie and attempt to apprehend the hostiles."

After allowing a moment for the men to let these orders sink in, Pershing continues. "That is the good news. The bad news is, after we corral the Cree, we must march them back to Missoula, then over the Continental Divide, and finally north to Great Falls. You men must do all in your power to herd these people without losing any along the way. Because we are deporting them, if the Indians have possessions, we should allow them to bring those possessions so long as they are portable. You must show all due restraint once we've captured and disarmed them. Am I understood?"

The men voice their agreement.

"Good. Now remember, speed and efficiency are essential to our plans. Dismissed."

Just as Pershing told the men, within an hour the Northern Pacific train arrives, and within another hour, they've reached Horse Plains. From there, Troop D remounts and rides east. Before long, they crest a ridge of hills and look down on Camas Prairie from the west. The prairie grass here, like everywhere else in this part of Montana, has begun the transition from green to gold by now.

The colors don't hold Clarence's attention long, however, because soon everyone else in the Buffalo Soldiers begins pointing off to the northeast. Sure enough, there's a camp of people there, probably only a mile or two away. Troop D immediately prepares for action.

Clarence is close enough to Lieutenant Pershing to hear him when he passes orders down the line. "Remember now, men, no unnecessary shooting. Surround the camp quickly, before anyone can try to dash away. Move!"

Before his time in the cavalry, Clarence always thought that it took a long time to travel a mile. When one gallops forward on horseback, however, it takes no time at all. Especially when one doesn't know what will happen at the end of the journey. Just like at St. Peter's Mission, Clarence's stomach churns in circles as he draws near the camp. He crouches down a bit in his saddle, almost like he's trying to present a smaller target for the bullets that might fly at any time. Once again, he resists the urge to vomit, but just barely. An enormous cloud of dust billows out behind the troopers while they advance.

The people in the camp have noticed the cavalry by now, and the camp stirs in chaotic commotion—people running here and there, the screams of women as they scoop young children into their arms, men running for their horses, and a hundred other things. Clarence watches as frantic people knock over two tipis in the confusion.

The Buffalo Soldiers achieve surprise. Although a few of the Métis have mounted their horses, they haven't even left the camp by the time the cavalry surrounds them. A middle-aged man emerges from one tipi, his hands in the air, looking about wildly. Clarence can see the sunlight flashing on something he wears around his neck. A medal. In his right hand the man waves a white handkerchief.

Clarence looks around while reining in his horse. No firing yet, thank goodness. There appear to be about seventy-five people in the camp, including older people and children. They've already realized the cavalry has them surrounded, and things are strangely quiet when Pershing motions the man with the medal over to him. Clarence guesses the people are waiting to see what will happen. He's close enough to the lieutenant to hear the conversation that comes next.

"Who are you?" Pershing asks the man.

"I am Imasees, but you whites call me Little Bear," the man responds.

"And you lead this band of Cree?"

"These people not Cree. We are Michif. No Cree here."

"Enough with the semantics. In the eyes of the United States government that I represent, you are Cree. Under the orders of the United States Army and an act of the United States Congress, I'm charged with taking your people home to Canada."

"Canada?" the man responds, startled. "Canada?" he repeats, frowning in surprise and taking a step back.

"Yes. The Cree Deportation Act recently passed by the U.S. Congress authorizes and commands your removal from the United States. We are taking you back to Canada where you belong."

"But, we are not Canadian. These people here, they are born in United States."

While the man speaks, Clarence takes a closer look at him. Standing erect, Imasees is a very dignified looking man, although he isn't very tall. It seems to Clarence like he's in his late forties or early fifties. He has on a hat made of beaver fur, with several eagle feathers trailing from the back. Besides the medal Imasees wears around his neck, the other thing Clarence finds most unusual is the man's shirt. It is a linen shirt, with buttons, which is common enough, but it's the designs on the shirt that fascinates him. Across the chest Clarence see a sun, and below the sun, a bald eagle with wings outstretched. The eagle's body is an American flag, and it holds a banner in its beak. Clarence is not close enough to read what the banner says, however. Imasees also wears the sash around his waist associated with the Métis people.

Meanwhile, Pershing continues. "Little Bear, you and your people must go to Canada. The legislation passed by Congress leaves no choice in the matter. Your people have one hour to gather all of their portable belongings and such food as they can carry with them."

Imasees starts to protest, but Pershing cuts him off. "As for you, I know you were involved in the Duck Lake Conspiracy, and that's why you've come south to Montana. The Great Mother of Canada has given me Her word that Canadian authorities will not arrest you or harm you once back on Canadian soil. I also give you my word. Now, go and tell your people they must be ready to move within one hour."

Leaving no room for further discussion, Pershing turns and rides off, leaving Imasees standing while trying to explain himself.

When Pershing's hour is up, the company prepares to move south, toward Perma. The sight is, Clarence must admit, a pitiful one. While the group slowly lurches into motion, he tries to keep track of everything he sees people doing. The Métis men walk, carrying whatever personal possessions they can carry. Most of the women and children ride on horseback or in Red River carts. A few of the horses pull travois instead of carts. Nearly everything these people own, although admittedly they don't own much, they've piled in these carts or have their horses towing by travois. Besides the lodge poles and covers for their tipis, it is mostly cooking gear, whatever food they had when captured, and clothing.

When Clarence stayed with the people of the Milk River the previous fall, he saw plenty of Red River carts in their camp, of course, but it's different when dozens of them are in motion at the same time. The Métis build Red River carts completely from wood. No metal, no grease, nothing else. When the carts move, the screeching and squealing is something awful.

At least Clarence has seen them before, and he anticipates the noise. The other troopers, however, have never seen a Red River cart and don't know quite what to make of them. One of the other men of Clarence's troop, Lawrence Smith, starts asking Clarence about them. Like Clarence, Smith is a quiet soldier who mostly keeps his head down and follows orders, so Clarence doesn't know Smith that well, but today it appears he's willing to talk a bit.

"Cooper, you ever hear such a noise before?" he says, almost shouting, so Clarence can hear him.

"No, I don't think I've ever heard anything squeal quite like this. Except maybe when a train comes to a halt. But it's over quickly with the trains. Can you believe we have weeks of this ahead of us?"

"Why are these carts so loud?"

"Because the Michif, I mean, the Cree, construct the carts completely from wood. They use no metal."

"How come they don't use metal, Cooper? Wouldn't it be better than all this noise?"

"I don't know, I guess, except probably metal is scarce in these parts, Smith."

"Those wheels must be as tall as we are."

"Yeah, I'd say about five and a half feet, just like me. The platforms in between the wheels are, what, about eight feet long, would you say?"

"Yeah. The wheels sure seem to work, though. They aren't getting stuck much, anyway."

After nodding his agreement, Clarence says, "It's a good thing for us we captured everyone in our first raid because we'll never sneak up on anyone else with all the noise we're making."

"Yeah," Smith laughs, "they'd hear us coming a mile away. Nah, two miles, at least."

"Well, we're lucky about one thing, you and I."

"What's that, Cooper?"

"We aren't on guard in the rear of the column. Those guys back in the rear are eating dust already."

Smith laughs again. "I guess you're right. This part of Montana sure is a dry one. There's no place like this back in Alabama where my folks are from."

"Well, I'm sure we'll get our turn in the dust cloud before we get back to Fort Missoula. Maybe we'll get lucky and it will rain some before that happens, though."

Early the next morning the cavalcade reaches Perma, but that means crossing the Flathead River, and this time, Clarence sees no train to make things easy. He knows that the horses and Red River carts probably can't handle the railroad bridge, given that the bridge has gaps between the planks of wood that the animals could slip through. Soon, Pershing's orders move through the ranks: The soldiers will man the ferry that takes women, children, and supplies across the river. The Cree men and horses must swim.

Perma, although it has just a handful of houses, has a ferry, which is a surprise to Clarence. The ferry is too small for the horses and carts, however, and doesn't look that sturdy, anyway, so the men swimming must be extra careful, especially since the river remains high with the last of the winter snowmelt. Because Clarence still can't swim, he's overjoyed when he gets his orders: He's supposed to guard the Cree and their supplies on the other side, on the south bank of the river. That means he'll only have to cross once, which is a relief after what happened at the Marias. The boys in charge of running the ferry back and forth, well, he doesn't envy them at all and wouldn't change places with them for anything.

After reaching the south bank, again, Smith is next to Clarence. They don't have that much to do while standing guard because the Métis mostly concern themselves with getting their families and supplies safely across after they swim the river.

Smith says to Clarence, "Look at them Indians, Cooper. All naked while they swim over."

"Better than getting your only set of clothes soaked, isn't it?"

"I suppose it is. Although if it were me doing the swimming, this July heat would tempt me to keep them on anyway, so the wet fabric would cool me down for a while afterward. How long you reckon this will take?"

"Can't say, Smith, but I'd guess most all of today. What do you think?"

"Yeah, I thought about the same. That ferry doesn't look too sturdy."

"Can I ask you something, Smith?"

"Sure, Cooper. You're a good man, and I don't mind talking a bit while we wait here."

"I was wondering why you joined the Buffalo Soldiers? You seem a bit like me, don't talk that much, and I was curious."

At this, Smith puts his head down for a moment. Then he says, more quietly, "Where are you from, Cooper?"

"Chicago, Illinois."

"Well, my folks, they're from northern Alabama. You know anyone there?"

"No."

"Never been to Tuscumbia, Cooper?"

"No."

"Don't ever go there."

"Why not?"

"You promise this stays between us if I level with you?"

"Of course."

"My name isn't Lawrence Smith. It's Thomas Delaney."

"How come you changed it?"

"Same reason I left Tuscumbia two years ago. To get away from my old life."

"How come you needed to get away so badly, Smith?"

"In April of '94, me, my older brothers Emmet and Fayett, and our cousin, Ed Felton, were running a farm just on the outskirts of Tuscumbia. Growing corn, mostly, and a bit of cotton. Had a few hogs, too. We weren't sharecroppers, like most of our neighbors. Owned our own farm. We weren't rich, for sure; most farmers aren't in that part of Alabama, but things were good, all in all. Good enough that I even got to go to school most of the year to get an education. I hoped to go to the Tuskegee Institute someday, maybe have my own business, too."

"What happened, then, that brought you here?"

"We had this neighbor, a white man, who always hated colored people. Well, that ain't sayin' much, I guess, because most white folks in Alabama hate colored people, but this man, he was one of the worst. Hated to see a colored man get ahead. He owned his own farm, like we did, but he was real poor because his wife was always sick, and he had to take care of her and run the farm, too. They had three daughters, but all of them got married and were living somewhere else, so it was just the two of them in this old, run-down shack. It had a stove, two rooms, and that was it."

"What about your house?"

"We weren't kings, but it wasn't bad. It was a frame house with a good, solid, shingled roof and a red coat of paint. We even had some glass windows put in a couple years back and had a front porch. It was as good as most in the neighborhood, I supposed you'd say."

"Was this neighbor the cause of your problems?"

"You got it. You see, one night, our neighbor's barn caught on fire. No one ever found out why it happened, but he liked to drink a lot, so I'll bet he did it himself, somehow. The next day, though, he went to town and got everyone all fired up, blaming us, calling us uppity, and all sorts of other things less polite than that. Well, the town sheriff, he's as mean and ornery as they come, and he hates colored folks even more than this farmer does, if that's possible, so when the farmer told the sheriff we'd threatened him earlier the day before, why, the sheriff, he got together a posse of townsfolk and brought them to our house. They caught my brothers and my cousin and hung them. While they dangled there, struggling to breathe, the farmer and the sheriff set them on fire, as payback for the barn. I don't know if the flames or the noose killed them first."

Clarence doesn't know what to say about this. He just stares at Delaney. Clarence knows what he's saying probably is true, yet it's hard to imagine people being that brutal to their neighbors if a person's never seen it for themselves. Except, Clarence has seen it himself. In San Francisco, when he witnessed a mob murder a Chinese man in cold blood. He wonders if recalling this memory will trigger his nightmares again tonight.

He isn't sure what to say back to Delaney but knows he needs to say something. Finally, he just asks, "How did you get away?"

"Just luck, more than anything else. I was at the post office when the lynching posse formed up. The postman, bless him, was one of the few white folks in town who treated colored people decently. He encouraged me to go to school because he said he never got much schooling but wished he had. Sometimes, he even borrowed a few books from the town library and then loaned them to me. That's why I was there when everything started to happen, to return a book to him. Well, he sees the posse coming and knows I need a place to hide. So, he takes me in the back of the post office and throws canvas bags on top of me, so no one will know I'm there. But, I can still hear what he says when the posse comes, and I know he lied to them about me, saying he didn't know where I was. He also tried to calm them down, but they wouldn't listen."

"And then you ran away before the posse could find you?"

"Yes. I didn't even dare to go home and get any possessions. As soon as the posse left, I jumped on my horse, rode north for a while, then hitched a ride on a railroad car that took me all the way to Indianapolis. I had to read about what happened to my family in the newspapers later. As soon as I could, I joined the Army under my new name. I've been in the cavalry ever since, although the Army only transferred me to Fort Assiniboine out here in Montana in February. Still, compared to what I left in Tuscumbia, Army life suits me just fine. I'm never going back there if I can help it."

"I guess you have some sympathy with these people, then, after the people who stand for law and order forced you from your home with no warning?"

"More than some, Cooper. What we're doing, it isn't good. I know we have orders, but how can anyone feel good about seeing this? How can anyone claim that this is justice?"

"I agree, Smith; you're right. I don't know why the higher-ups in the Army picked us for this mission, but it doesn't sit well with me, either. Half of me wants to help these people, instead of herding them around like we're doing now."

"Yeah, me too. I really could care less about the reputation of the Buffalo Soldiers or anything else. I know this regiment earned its good name fighting Indians in Texas and other places on the Great Plains, but this isn't fighting. There's no glory earned here. It seems to me we're doing someone else's dirty work."

"Maybe that's why they picked us, Smith. Maybe we got this job because the Army command knows it's a lousy assignment, but they know we have a reputation for wanting to prove ourselves, and they're using that against us."

"Wouldn't be the first time this country has used colored soldiers, Cooper. My cousin Ed, his father fought in the Civil War. Enlisted right at the very end, in February of '65. He was ready to fight for the

United States, and look how things are in the South now. Then my uncle lost his right to vote a few years ago because he couldn't pass a literacy test. Cousin Ed went to ride the railroads once, before the mob murdered him, and he and all the other colored passengers had to ride in their own separate car. I wonder if my uncle would enlist again, if he had it to do over? I guess I'll never get the chance to ask him now, though, since I'm never returning to Alabama."

"You might, you never know. I'd say his experiences would sour me on joining the Army if I'd been in his shoes. How come you joined, Smith, after all of that?"

"Oh, I'm plenty sour, even though I'm in the Army myself. I just had to do something to get some pay, so that I can save up and get back to farming somewhere, someday. As soon as I've got enough money saved, I've done my last tour in the Army, that's for sure. What about you, Cooper, how did you get here from Chicago?"

Clarence considers whether he should tell Thomas about what happened to him last fall when, suddenly, he's distracted by what's happening in the Flathead River. One of the horses gets itself tangled in a submerged tree and can't free itself. It throws its rider into the water, and while he floats helplessly downstream trying to swim out of the current and get to shore, the horse goes under. Several of the other Métis swim or try to lead their horses over to help, but it's in vain. They get the poor animal free eventually, but the body of the horse drifts downstream, lifeless.

Smith looks over at Clarence. "Cooper? You're shaking."

"Sorry. Bad memories. Let's go see if we can help."

All Smith and Clarence can do is get to the riverbank and help the poor, exhausted swimmers out of the water. Their frowns and, Clarence presumes, curses in their own language give him pause, though. It's not hard to understand why they are in a surly mood. Clarence decides he'll share his story with Smith some other day because as more and more people start floundering into the makeshift camp on the south side of the river, he's got to be more watchful and make sure everything stays orderly.

Similar things happen several more times during the river crossing. Clarence thinks the group loses five horses in all, but by some miracle, no people. By the end of the day, most of the captives collapse in exhaustion, and no one looks very happy. After being torn from their homes without warning, Clarence can't blame the people if they show a sour disposition. He fears there may be trouble ahead. This is only the second day of the march, too. Ninety more miles back to Fort Missoula, and from there, who knows how many more miles to Great Falls, where they can load the prisoners onto train cars for the last leg of their trip.

# Chapter 28

## Leaving for St. Louis at Last

Inside the mission's dormitory for girls, Mary finishes packing her spare change of clothes into the knapsack that she and Gabriel will share for their trip to St. Louis. Gently, she folds the bright yellow dress one of the nuns gave her that morning. One of the girls captured by the cavalry left it behind, so the woman thought Mary should have it. The knapsack also contains a couple loaves of bread for the trip, some cheese, and a few other scraps of food. At first, Father Andreis wanted to send Friar O'Connell with her instead of Gabriel, but O'Connell is in Helena, and he has no one else. Mary hums a tune, one of the fiddle tunes she learned last fall, while she finishes packing.

Mary feels ecstatic to go meet her Uncle John at last. She has so many adventures to tell him about since leaving Butte last year, and she can't wait to get going. All she and Gabriel must do is ride to Helena, leave their horse with Father O'Connell, and then they can catch the Northern Pacific eastward. All the arrangements are complete, except for buying the ticket itself.

Gabriel comes inside the now-empty dormitory after saddling up their horse. He smacks one brown leather riding glove into his hand.

Then, he goes to help Mary stow their travel supplies. In his pocket, he has the money sent by John Healy. One more horseback ride, and they'll be on their way at last. Then, once he gets back from St. Louis, he can put all his effort toward finding out the fate of his father.

"We're very lucky, aren't we, Gabriel?" Mary says to him, chipper as usual.

"Lucky? After all that's happened to us?"

"Aren't we lucky that we decided to come back here after meeting the Grants and that my Uncle John sent money while we were away, and now we have the money, and we can go? If we had gone with Charles and Alexander, this would never have happened to us."

"Well, I suppose if you look at things that way, yeah, we're lucky."

"And once you take me to St. Louis and then come back, you'll find your papa, right?"

"I hope so."

"I'm so happy, Gabriel. I get to meet my Uncle John, and he even said he'd help Clarence, too."

Gabriel isn't sure if John Healy can do anything to help Clarence, but maybe if a white person gets involved, there is at least half a chance. Instead of saying that to Mary, however, he just smiles and cinches the bright blue ribbon in Mary's hair a little tighter, so it won't come loose.

"You look so pretty," he tells her. Her clothes are new, too; she has on a blue-and-white checkered skirt. Gabriel knows it's another thing left behind when the cavalry took away the girls from the mission, but he and Father Andreis decided to tell Mary it is a present for her, special for the train. Mary has the same battered shoes as always, but other than that, she really does look pretty. "Your Uncle John is going to be so impressed."

She beams at him, a huge smile brightening the room.

Gabriel has a hard time understanding how Mary keeps her spirits up amid so much hardship, but somehow, she does. Mary's already lost both her parents plus Clarence, the three most important people in her life, yet here she is, excited to go on.

Mary speaks again. "And aren't we lucky that Father Andreis forgave you for not going over the mountains?"

Gabriel sighs, hoping that Alexander and Charles found their cousins before the soldiers did. "Maybe God does have a plan in mind for us after all."

"Everyone is ready, Lieutenant. Shall we advance?"

Lieutenant Grimes sits atop his horse, once again looking down into the valley where sits St. Peter's Mission, scene of his big mistake. He is here to redeem himself.

"In a moment."

"Why are we here again, sir?" the bugler at Grimes' side asks.

"Remember when those stragglers came into our camp to join their families? Even though they deny it, I believe we'll find more Cree hiding out here at the mission. We're going to find out if I'm right and capture whatever fugitives are still here."

"Forgive me for asking, Lieutenant Grimes," the bugler says, "but is it really wise to bring in more of the Cree right now? Already, we're short of transportation to get them to Canada, right? I'm no genius, but I know how many people we sent up the line in the first batch, and I know about how much one railroad ticket costs. If First Lieutenant Pershing brings in another batch from west of the Divide, how are we going to pay to move all of them?"

"That's not my problem. We are here to round up the Cree and deport them. That is what we will do."

Grimes hopes this will be enough to restore himself to Pershing's good graces. It is a humiliation—getting orders to stay behind and watch over the supplies and refugees at Great Falls while the rest of the regiment rides down the other Cree hiding and making trouble throughout Montana. Grimes sees no glory in it. None. No distinction, no way to make his name. He comes from a military family in western Kentucky, after all, and he isn't about to see his family's name and honor suffer a black mark on his account. He means to win glory, no matter what it takes. Even if he must do it commanding darkey soldiers like these.

Not that commanding the darkeys is difficult. Because he is from a Kentucky military family, Grimes knows it is in his blood. The Grimes family had held a few slaves until the Thirteenth Amendment ended slavery nationwide in 1865. Even though his grandfather had supported the Confederacy in the War Between the States, he'd adjusted to life without slavery and held no grudges against Northerners. Money was money, after all. It didn't matter if it came from a Northerner or a Southerner, a colored man or a white one. All grandfather had done was turn his slaves into sharecroppers, rent land to them, get them into debt by charging them exorbitant prices at his local store, and rake in the money from the crops the sharecroppers grew for him. It wasn't much different from slavery, really, when one thought about it, except with sharecropping, the plantation owner didn't even need to feed, clothe, or house the people growing crops for him.

Grimes doesn't hate colored people the way many Southerners do. They are inferior to whites, certainly. He, like everyone else he knows in Kentucky, does not doubt that. They tend to be slow mentally and a bit on the lazy side without the presence of whites to keep them working. However, they are good farmers, by and large, and when they stay in their proper place and don't get uppity, they make decent enough neighbors. A few of them even have clever instincts, like a fox does, although they are the exceptions.

Now, he is going to use these colored soldiers to earn back his reputation.

"Give the call, private. It's time to move out."

Grimes rides into the mission at the head of his small column. He's always hated this part of being a soldier. The people riding out front tend to be the first ones shot at, after all. Why can't someone else lead the men into action, instead of him? There are plenty of lives less valuable than his for this sort of thing.

They ride into an empty mission. No one in sight. The charred remains of the schoolhouse stand as a silent, yet glaring, reminder to Grimes of his failure. He wishes he could burn down what remains of the blackened timbers, eradicate all memory of the school's existence, so he won't have any lingering reminders of his mistake.

"What now, sir?" Grimes' corporal, Thomas Banks, asks.

"Search the buildings that remain, Corporal Banks. All of them. I'll interrogate the priest."

Grimes is taking a great risk, and he knows it. If this fails to turn up anything, he could face another reprimand for undertaking this operation without explicit approval.

He doesn't even have to go looking for Father Andreis, as it turns out, because the priest storms out to meet him.

"What is the meaning of this?" Father Andreis demands. "You've already burned our town and our schoolhouse, and now you're back? There's nothing left here, thanks to you. Just leave us alone."

Grimes has no patience for such behavior from civilians. His gentlemanly military upbringing taught him that one does not hope for respect, one demands it, and this priest needs someone to put him back in line. One of Grimes' many weaknesses, however, is an inability to remember the names of people he's met previously. He'll have to cover for this lack of ability somehow.

"Be silent, Father," he barks at the annoying black-robed figure. "We have authority to operate here, and we are rounding up stragglers for deportation to Canada. If you're harboring any more refugee Cree here, we must send them with their people."

"But can't you see there are no Cree left here? You've already taken everyone, or they turned themselves in by their own choice."

Just then Grimes glances over as a few soldiers drag Gabriel and Mary into view, Mary clutching the knapsack while it drags on the ground behind her. Slowly, they walk up the dirt path from the dormitory for girls.

"This is all we found, Lieutenant," one of the men reports. "Just these two Indians. All the other buildings are abandoned except for a few nuns."

"These are *not* Indians," Father Andreis shouts. "Like I've been trying to tell you, these people are not Cree. They are not Indians. They are Michif, mixed-blood people born right here in Montana, and you've no right to take them from here."

"They're Indians, and they're coming with us. We have authority from the U.S. Congress to remove these people to their homeland in Canada, and that is what we'll do. Step back, please." His prize, and hopefully his personal redemption, now in hand, Grimes isn't about to back down.

"We will have our day in court," Father Andreis stammers. He knows it's a weak threat and unlikely to impress the lieutenant, but it is all he can think of while the soldiers lead Mary and Gabriel away. As they go, Mary looks back at him, and he sees tears glistening in her eyes. "We'll bring all the people back here where they belong!"

Grimes already has his back turned as he rides away. He doesn't care what the priest says, and he isn't about to respond. To a quizzical look from Corporal Banks, he merely says, "Carry on, corporal. Escort the two captives back to Cascade. We'll take them to Great Falls tomorrow. The men have done well today."

Because it's a hot July day, the small group of soldiers stops midway to Cascade to water their horses. Lieutenant Grimes walks slowly to Mary and Gabriel as they sit, silent, frowning, heads down, under a tree for shade.

Unaware of protocol, Mary stands and stomps angrily over to Grimes. "Why did you take us away?" she demands to know. "We were going to meet my Uncle John in St. Louis. He's a famous baseball pitcher, and I'm going to tell him about what you did to us!"

Unsure of how to calm down a young girl like Mary, Grimes drops down on one knee to look her in the face. He starts to say, "Now don't you worry, little thing, there's nothing to be afraid of. You're going to Canada where you belong. I . . ."

Before he can go on, Mary shouts at him, "I don't belong in Canada, I belong with my Uncle John. You'd better takes us to Helena, so we can get our train ticket and go there!"

"Now, like I said, you'll like it in Canada with your own people . . ." Grimes attempts to continue.

"Now, Mary, wait a minute," Gabriel begins, but too late.

Mary's faces flushes. "I want to find my Uncle John! You can't take us to Canada!" With that, she gives the lieutenant a quick push, one hand on his right shoulder, the other to his face, and Lieutenant Grimes ends up on his backside in the dirt. A couple of the men chuckle quietly to themselves.

Grimes simply sits back up, then whips his arm around, slapping Mary's face with his gloved hand. She falls backward, her new checkered dress badly smudged with dirt and a bright red mark spreading across her right cheek.

Gabriel reaches behind him for the knife he's taken to carrying while cutting wood; the knife he just realizes he left back inside the dormitory when the soldiers surprised him. Instead of fighting, of stabbing this monstrous cavalryman in the middle of his chest like he deserves, he runs over to Mary and helps her out of the dirt. She's trying not to cry, but she's sniffling as he picks her up.

Gabriel looks up and sees that all the soldiers who are standing nearby watch them because the argument between Mary and the lieutenant drew their attention. Now, their gazes are on him, watching to see what he'll do. A few level their carbines at him, just in case.

Not saying anything, he simply gathers little Mary into a hug and tries to comfort her, brushing some grass and loose dirt off her skirt in the process. At the same time, he gives Lieutenant Grimes the most hateful stare he can.

"Get them out of here" is all Grimes can say. "Take this Cree squaw and her half-breed friend out of my sight. Tie their hands, too."

Gabriel grunts as he's tied. It's all he can do not to fight back, but he knows these are soldiers with guns, not drunk cowboys. Mary is still too dazed to offer any resistance.

Then, just when one of the soldiers begins to follow his orders and lead the pair back to their horse, a thought flashes through Grimes' mind, a memory that pierces the mists clouding his angry consciousness. Something the girl said comes back to him. "Wait a minute, private," he calls.

"Yes, sir?" the man says as he turns back to see what Grimes wants.

Many of the other soldiers, seeing the drama subside, turn back to checking on their horses. Only a couple still watch, and only because they find nothing else interesting to look at. "Private, why don't you check these captives for intelligence," Grimes says.

"Intelligence, sir? On a little girl?"

"Just check."

The soldier does so, and quickly, he locates the envelope where Gabriel had stashed the money for the train tickets. He pulls it from a pocket of Gabriel's leather jacket and hands it to Grimes.

"That's ours . . ." Gabriel tries to protest, but he stops when the soldier spins and smacks his ribs with the butt of his weapon.

"No more talking," the soldier says with a bristling stare.

Gabriel winces in pain. He didn't hear any of his ribs crack, but the blow bruised a couple of them, for sure.

Grimes looks through the envelope, pleased when he sees the money it contains. "Private," he says, extending his hand as the angry soldier turns around. He shakes the man's hand, leaving a folded dollar bill in place as he does so. "Well done, private. Although the captives possessed no intelligence, you've done your job well." He finishes with a little wink. The soldier nods in return and pockets the dollar.

Grimes looks down at the envelope again. Still plenty of money in there for buying alcohol. He is going to look back on this day fondly for years to come.

# Chapter 29

## Imprisoned in Great Falls

"How much longer will we have to stay here, Gabriel?" Mary asks, her face downcast. "I'm really thirsty," she adds in a listless monotone.

Gabriel looks at the water bucket and sees it's empty. He calls out, "Guard, can we please have some water, Mary's thirsty."

A soldier walks in, one Gabriel has never seen before. He's colored, like all the other enlisted men who guard the prisoners.

"Gimme de bucket," the young man says. His face appears neither friendly nor hostile. Gabriel decides to attempt a conversation while he passes the bucket to the soldier through the cell door.

"Soldier, can you tell me what day it is? I've lost track, I'm afraid."

"July de 16th."

"Are you in the cavalry like everyone else?"

"Yep. I'll be back wid de water in a minute."

Gabriel looks around their jail cell, which is located on the second floor of the building next door to the Great Falls courthouse. It's spartan, for sure, but at least they aren't sleeping outside. Lately, the temperatures have been in the upper nineties, and outside, the mosquitos and flies are everywhere. Although, come to think of it, things aren't that much better inside their cell. The windows face west, no shade reaches the second floor, the temperatures are brutal in the evening, and it's hard to sleep at night when it's above eighty degrees on the second floor. Plenty of insects get inside their cell, too. It's that or close the window and bake all day. The weeks of confinement have been difficult, for Mary especially. The food is borderline rotten, and there's never much of it. Gabriel tries to give a little extra to Mary anyway because she is young and thin to begin with and doesn't deserve to starve.

At least it isn't too loud. The other people from the mission have already left for Canada. Other than the drunks who spend the evening in a cell sobering up, Gabriel and Mary have little company in the jail. For the moment.

It's about as boring as can be, however. One of the more sympathetic guards found them a checkers board to pass the time, but a person can only play so many games of checkers.

In a few minutes, the soldier returns and passes a new bucket of water into the cell. Mary immediately takes the wooden dipper and drinks several gulps.

"Careful there, miss," the soldier says. "Take yo' time."

Gabriel tries another question. "Soldier, is Clarence Duval a member of your unit?"

"Never heard o' him."

"But, you're from Fort Assiniboine, aren't you?"

"Yes."

"There should be a soldier in your regiment named Clarence."

"Don't know anyone by that name."

The soldier turns and leaves.

This is discouraging news. Gabriel looks over at Mary, whose eyes droop while she gives a little sigh, followed by a sniffle. Dirt and stains from sweating in the cell have long since tarnished Mary's checkered dress, and Gabriel's clothes look about the same. "We'll find him, Mary," he tells her. Mary just keeps her head down, but the glint of a tear in her eye says she isn't so sure. "I'm trying my best."

When Gabriel looks her over again, however, he sees that Mary looks wan and pale, and her chipper spirit has not been in evidence for several days. Gabriel's also scared that Clarence doesn't seem to be at Fort Assiniboine. Did the soldiers shoot him for deserting after all? Have they spent months thinking about him and ways of trying to free him when he's been dead all along?

To Gabriel's surprise, about an hour later the soldier returns. "Someone asked to see you," he says and then walks downstairs.

Gabriel looks up, and his surprise grows when he sees his visitor's identity. It's a friend, Louis Thomas, who owns a ranch on the north side of the Missouri River, right opposite where the Musselshell River joins the Missouri.

"Louis, what are you doing here? Aren't you ranching over by the Musselshell?"

"I was, yeah. Still am, too, as soon as I can get back there." Taking off his heavy leather riding gloves, Louis reaches through the bars and shakes Gabriel's hand.

"You didn't come all the way to Great Falls just to see us in prison, surely? How did you know we were here?"

"Nope, this isn't a social call. Although it is good to see you, Gabriel. I got caught in the roundup, too, and sent to Canada."

"How did you get back here, then?"

"I had this with me." Louis pulls out a document from his brown leather jacket. "It's a letter signed by Sergeant Wood declaring that I'm an American citizen. I finally got the soldiers to let me come back here where I belong. It also helped get me in to talk with you. I just flashed this for the guard, and he let me come up. Didn't even have to make up any big lies about what I was doing." He says the last line very quietly, smiling.

Gabriel smiles back. "How did they catch you in the first place?"

"I was just minding my own business, cutting wood on my ranch to sell to the riverboats, like I do every year. The cavalry swooped in, captured me at gunpoint, along with my wife and my family, and

227

shipped us to Coutts Station. No trial, no chance to prove my citizenship, nothing. I was lucky to get back."

Gabriel just shakes his head.

Louis speaks again, urgency in his voice. "Listen, Gabriel, we have a bunch of things we need to talk about. You can't go to Canada."

"Why not? It can't be worse than Montana, can it? Wait, are they trying to track down everyone from the Riel Resistance at last? I was only twelve then. Surely that doesn't count. How could they even know about me?"

"One thing at a time. Let me tell you about the trip north to Canada. The cavalry is going to herd you into railroad cars. Like cattle. They'll cram you into a livestock car with as many other people as can fit. Just slats in the walls of the car for air and a bucket so people can relieve themselves. No chairs, no stools, no place to sleep at night. And the insects, Gabriel. Insects everywhere, day and night. Buzzing in your face, biting your neck, crawling in your pants, landing on your eyelids while you try to sleep at night."

Mary looks over at Gabriel. The tears in her eyes are back.

"Your possessions, if you have any, go in another car, a coal car, and when you get to Coutts Station in Canada, they just dump everything on the ground and tell you to find what's yours. If it didn't break along the way when the soldiers crammed it together with what everyone else brought. Then, if you want to go north and west, to Calgary or Edmonton, they corral you in one camp, and if you want to go east, to Battleford or anywhere east of that neighborhood, the Canadian Mounted Police put you in a separate camp."

"Did you see anyone else from St. Peter's Mission while you were there, Louis? I know the cavalry sent a big load of people up the line after their first raid on the mission. Do you know what happened to them?"

"Some of them, yes. It isn't good news, though, Gabriel. You remember Day Bow?"

"Yeah, of course. He knew my father from way back. Plus, he was here at St. Peter's for a while this winter. I last talked with him just a couple months ago."

"Day Bow is dead."

"Dead? What happened?"

"He killed himself. Stabbed himself in the chest with his hunting knife."

Mary, who'd been listening quietly, gasps out, "Why would anyone do that?"

Louis looks over at Mary and then at Gabriel, a quizzical look on his face.

"It's all right, Louis," Gabriel says. "It's a long story, but Mary is with me. I'm taking care of her. Trying to, at least."

Louis nods and goes on. "When they rounded everyone up, the cavalry promised that those who'd been involved in the Riel Resistance would get amnesty from the Canadian authorities. But they lied. I don't think they'd care about you because like you said, you were only a boy and had no part in any of the action, but Day Bow was at Frog Lake, remember?"

"I wasn't at Frog Lake," Gabriel says. "I was just twelve when it happened. But my father told me about it. Some of the people there killed an Indian agent and a handful of other white men."

"Day Bow was with the Cree that April day in 1885. I never heard that he killed anyone himself, but he was there, and the authorities knew it. The Canadian Mounted Police came to arrest him once he got over the Medicine Line. I was close to him when they came to get him. Day Bow said the Canadians were going to kill him anyway, and he wasn't going to give them the satisfaction. So, when the police came to get him, he pulled out his hunting knife and did himself in."

"He had a lot of pride," Gabriel says. "It's sad, but that doesn't surprise me."

"There's more, Gabriel. The people heading east, the authorities sent them all the way to Regina."

"Regina? Why so far? That has to be about four hundred miles away."

"Yes, it is. Closer to five hundred, really. The only way the Mounted Police got the people to get back on the train in the first place was to promise them a meeting with the Commissioner of Indian Affairs, who is in Regina. But then, once the Cree were inside the railroad cars, they locked the cars shut, so no one could get out along the way. You see, the Canadians got worried they might try to jump the train at Maple Creek or somewhere else along the way and sneak back into Montana through the Cypress Hills. So, they locked all the train car doors. The people were prisoners, locked in a cell as surely as you are here."

"They might be right about people wanting to get away," Gabriel says. "But locking people into a cattle car . . ."

"They'll do the same to you."

"How do you know all this?"

"Some of it I've seen myself, and the interpreter at Coutts Station, a man named Hourie, told me the rest after I bought him a couple drinks. He's getting on in years, but he still enjoys a good time now and then."

"I have to ask about one other thing, Louis. Have you seen my father? I haven't seen him since November, when a posse of vigilantes attacked our camp on the Milk River, and no one anywhere has heard from him."

Louis looks Gabriel in the eyes, then puts his head down. "Yeah, I've seen Pierre."

"You have? What news can you tell me? Where is he?"

"He's dead, Gabriel."

Gabriel says nothing for a long time. After several minutes of looking at the floor, he simply says, "How?"

"Pierre told me about what happened at your camp on the Milk River last November and how everything was on fire by the time he and his hunting party got back. Well, in the shootout with the vigilantes, a bullet hit him, and the bullet must have grazed one of his lungs. The pain wasn't too bad at first, but as time went by, it was harder and harder for him to breathe. He spent the winter in Havre, hoping to get better, but he never did. By the time spring came, the pain was so great that he couldn't even ride to go look for you."

"I guess that explains why no one has heard anything about him since November."

"I think so," Louis says sadly, now starting to sniffle a bit himself. "Pierre told me he spent most of the winter at the home of a rancher friend just outside of town, but the pain only got worse. In any case, someone in Havre must have tipped off the soldiers from Fort Assiniboine because they came and got him right quick once they started their roundup. I didn't know it because we were in different cars, but we went to Canada on the same train. I didn't find out until we got out at Coutts Station, and then I saw him. Pierre could hardly even walk by that time. He could only stagger a short distance before he had to lie down because of the pain."

"And no one helped him the entire time?" Gabriel asks through his own tears.

"None of the doctors in Havre would see him, even though his friend offered money. Probably, it was one of the doctors who gave his location away. By the time I found Pierre, it was too late to do anything. He'd just gasp for air and make a gurgling sound in his throat, and with every little step he winced in pain."

"The bastards," Gabriel says. Mary comes over and hugs his arm.

"He never stopped asking me about you," Louis tells Gabriel. "And, he also gave this to me to give to you when I found you."

Louis reaches into the weathered, creased leather saddlebag he'd set down on the floor when he'd first come in. He pulls out an intricately beaded sash. Louis hands it over.

"He apologized he didn't have anything else to share, but you know how much this meant to him."

Gabriel nods and then says, "How can he have had anything else to share? Everything else we had burned up in our Milk River shanty."

"He's buried on a small hill near the railway stop at Coutts Station, along with an old person who didn't survive the railroad journey. I'm sorry, my friend."

"Thanks for coming and looking for me," Gabriel replies.

"Now, we have to find some way to get you out of here. I don't suppose you have any proof that you're an American citizen, do you?"

"Everything I had burned in the fire, too. I hear there's a lawyer trying to contest things in local court? Maybe that will help," Gabriel says, although the flatness in his voice says he really doesn't believe it.

"I doubt it. The local judge, Benton, is known for two things. Being on the side of mining companies and hating Indians. We'll have to come up with some other plan."

Before Gabriel can answer, they hear footsteps coming up to the second floor. Both men turn to see who it is. The young soldier reappears.

"Sorry, but you gots to leave. Jus' got word from de sergeant: no visiting prisoners."

"But what's wrong with talking to someone?" Louis tries to protest.

"Orders, suh, orders. You come wid me now."

"I'll see you again somehow, Gabriel," Louis says as he starts for the door. "Remember what I told you about Canada."

After the pair descend the steps, Gabriel looks over at Mary. She gives him another big hug.

"What do we do now, Gabriel? What are we going to do?"

"I don't know for sure, but I'm trying to figure it out. I think Louis is right, though. We've got to find some way out of here, so we can get to St. Louis. I have no reason to stay here anymore."

# Chapter 30

## The Dearborn River

Clarence collapses in the muddy buffalo grass and looks up at the darkening early evening sky. Or, more accurately, at the massive gray clouds obscuring the sky. It's all one cloud, really, just gray stretching forever in every direction. It's rained, hard, for most of the last three days. No one can believe it—Clarence doesn't remember ever seeing something like this in Montana during all the years he lived in Butte. His blue uniform is muddy, his horse is caked in mud, and all of the prisoners stink from fighting their way through the mud on foot. It wouldn't surprise Clarence if their dinner is hardtack dipped in mud.

Lincoln Washington drops down next to him. "When we gon' get there, Cooper? I'se flat worn out."

"We've got a little way to go still. You know where we are now, right?"

"Yeah, this the Dearborn River again, ain't it?"

"It is. That means we'll be back at Great Falls in a couple more days, and then hopefully we'll take the railroad to wherever it is on the Canadian border we're supposed to bring these poor people."

"And then go back to drillin' an' sittin' around at the fort, twiddlin' our thumbs. It beats this mud, though, sho' 'nuf."

They both laugh a bit, but not for long. Even laughing seems to take more energy than Clarence can muster after today's march. Even if all the drilling and marching they did to practice back in April and May was rather dull, still, he'd prefer drilling and marching around at the fort to this grueling work any day.

Clarence sits up and looks out at the camp. He and Washington have set up their tent at the very southern edge of the group. Only a few other tents are between them and the perimeter of the camp. Besides the cavalry with all its horses and its supply train, the party now includes close to 125 Cree and Métis people. They've got their horses, their dogs, the Red River carts, and all the belongings that they can carry. This evening, mud coats all of it. It's a sight to behold.

He looks at Washington for a moment. "For a while, I wondered what was worse—this mud, or all the dust we choked on while we were riding up the Blackfoot River from Missoula. I'm pretty sure that I know now. I'll eat dust any day compared to trying to push wagons loaded with supplies through mud for three days."

"Yeah, I think you's right, Cooper. My muscles is sore as can be."

"I can barely sit up, and we were only helping with the hard work for a couple hours. We spent a good part of the day making sure none of our guests wandered off while they herded their horses along the trail. Now, my calves are so sore and heavy, I feel it with every step. It's like someone dropped a chunk of lead in them."

"It's too bad that we has to escort the Cree on this ride. It sho' would be pretty if we could just look at nature. The mountain pass was beautiful. Or woulda been, if we coulda took our time and enjoyed it."

"Yeah, Lincoln, a painter could just camp out in the mountains and paint majestic scenes for days, I think. What with the snow-capped peaks, the pine trees, the grassy mountain meadows, the occasional deer, the Blackfoot River, and everything else."

"Did you hear the news, Cooper?"

"What news are you talking about? The news about how someone's coming to relieve us of this assignment tomorrow?"

Washington laughs, but again, it doesn't have much gusto and it dies quickly. "Nah. A baby was born the other day. Right when we camped for the night."

"You don't say. I wouldn't want to try to have a baby on the march like this. I'd guess it's painful enough to have one anytime, let alone now."

"Yeah, I hopes they makes sure the baby gets plenty o' food."

"Does that make up for the old woman who died a few days back? You know Lawrence Smith, Washington?"

"Yeah, quiet guy, don't talk much."

"He was riding guard duty about four or five days ago, when it was still really hot, and he says that this old woman, who must've been seventy-five at least, just fainted. Dropped what she was carrying and fell over. They tried to give her water and revive her, but she never woke up. I guess that's what happens when you march old people with heavy packs through the mountains in the middle of summer."

"Tha's a shame, fo' sure, Cooper. We's probably lucky tha's the only person who died so far, don't you reckon?"

"Yeah, I reckon that's true."

"How many more people is gonna have to die, you think, 'fore we get there?"

"I don't know, Lincoln, but I'm getting awful tired of this whole business. These people hate us, you can see it in their eyes, and I don't blame them. I wouldn't like us either, if I were them. This whole operation wasn't our idea, but we're the ones who must do all the work of herding them around, and so we're the ones they're angry with. I think the only reason we haven't had any big trouble so far is that they seem to have a lot of respect for their leader, Imasees."

"Imasees is the one everyone calls Little Bear, right?"

"Yeah, Lincoln, that's him."

Washington ponders things for a moment and then says, "The people who plan all this, they's miles away, back in Washington.

Maybe they ought to come out to Montana for a while and see what it's like."

"You know what worries me most, Lincoln?" Clarence asks and then answers when Washington shrugs his shoulders, "What happens when one of the captives gets angry, or scared, or whatever, and tries to escape, or fight one of our soldiers, or something? It might take just one little incident to set off a big explosion. Then we might end up killing more people, and it'll all be for no good reason."

"Le's just hope it don't come to that, Cooper. We's made it this far okay."

"So far," Clarence says through a big yawn that he just can't hold back any longer.

"Well, Cooper, we's lucky 'bout one thing. We don't have no duties tonight. We can just rest and git ready for tomorrow's ride. Let's git our chow, and then we can rest up."

After another meager dinner of hardtack, beans, salted pork, and coffee, Clarence staggers back to his tent and collapses next to Washington. He's exhausted, but unsure of how much he'll sleep because another rainstorm just came through and soaked everything. His blanket remains musty and damp as Clarence unrolls it and lies down. There's nothing comforting; he can smell the dampness all around. He gets to sleep finally, but rests uneasily. Despite his exhaustion, Clarence wakes up a few times in the night and comes close to waking several other times.

An hour or so before dawn, Clarence comes wide awake suddenly, and he's soaking wet. Washington is gone. Clarence lies in a puddle of water. No, wait, it's not a puddle. The water is moving. As he comes to, Clarence hears shouts, screams, and commotion outside. While he sits up to get out of the water and take stock of his situation, he manages to hear a clear voice rise above the chaotic babble.

"The river is rising! Everyone get your supplies and move to higher ground!"

Just as Clarence turns and reaches to grab his carbine and pick himself up to leave the tent, he hears a violent splash, and someone comes into the tent from behind him. Before he can even look to see who it is, however, Clarence feels two hands grab his neck from behind and start to squeeze. He knows it's Edward Carter even before he hears Carter's voice. Because he takes Clarence by surprise and Clarence was barely awake to start with, Clarence drops his carbine into the water.

"Now for paybacks, Cooper," Carter hisses. "I've waited a month for this, and now you get it!" While Clarence tries to get his balance and pry at the hands around his neck, suddenly Carter sticks one knee into his back and Clarence topples forward into the rising water.

It isn't high enough to drown him yet, but it's close. Clarence turns his neck to the side and gasps in some air.

"Go ahead and scream," Carter taunts. "No one will hear you with all the noise outside. They'll just think you drowned, if they even find your body."

It's getting terribly hard for Clarence to breathe, even with his mouth out of the water. Then, out of all the things flashing through his mind, Clarence somehow recalls what he learned on the way to Hawaii seven years ago. Some of the wrestling moves William Miller taught him while on board the *Alameda* suddenly come back to him. He's only practiced them a few times since his trip around the world, mostly against Thomas Healy in Butte when Thomas was still alive, so Clarence doesn't know how well they'll work, but it's now or never.

With Carter's knee still pressed in his back, Clarence can't flip him over his head, and Carter's face is too far away for a reverse head butt. So, Clarence uses the one option available. He grabs Carter's right arm with both his hands and rolls to his right with all his strength.

It works! Clarence disrupts Carter's balance, and he rolls off Clarence, splashing into the water beside him.

Clarence takes a moment to gulp in some oxygen. Unfortunately, Carter landed on top of Clarence's carbine. Quickly, Carter gets to his knees, grasps it, and brings it up, leveling the carbine's barrel at Clarence's chest. He pulls the trigger.

Nothing happens. The powder is too wet, and the gun doesn't fire.

Clarence tries to lunge at Carter before Carter can think of what to do next, but his right foot slips in the mud, and instead of leaping at him and toppling Carter backward, Clarence ends up slipping and falling on his chest, arms weakly slapping Carter's torso. Just as Clarence pushes up to his knees again, the butt of the carbine slams into his left shoulder and he half-slides, half-falls to his right.

Carter raises the carbine again, this time intending to bring it down on Clarence's head and crush his skull. He swings downward with a demonic howl of rage. Clarence braces for the impact, curling his arms around his head in a feeble attempt to cushion the blow.

It never comes. Instead, just as Carter starts his swing, someone outside the canvas tent slips and falls in their mad scramble for safety, and their body lands on the tent, bumping Carter in the process. With no way to prepare for this, his killing blow splashes in the water just inches from Clarence's face. Half of the tent collapses on top of them.

Seeing his chance, Clarence uses the best wrestling hold William Miller showed him. Miller said it was his favorite move to get his opponent to give up the match. While Carter and Clarence's unknown savior struggle to disentangle themselves, he grabs Carter's head while positioning his body behind Carter. Clarence's right arm goes in front of Carter's neck, locking it in the crook of his elbow, and his left arm behind the neck, and Clarence grabs and squeezes his arms together with all his strength. Then, Clarence pushes Carter's head down into the water.

Carter thrashes around like a fish, trying to elbow Clarence or break his grip. Clarence puts his head down, near Carter's, closes his eyes so Carter can't rake them with his fingers, and holds on tight. Eventually Carter's struggles slow down and then cease. Clarence holds on longer, just to be sure. It seems to him like it's been forever, even though Clarence doubts it's been even three minutes since Carter jumped him from behind. Finally, he lets go, and Edward Carter's body just floats there in the water, face down. Then, it slowly drifts out the back of the tent into the darkness.

Clarence gasps, pants, and coughs, his breath coming in ragged pieces. Kneeling, hands on his thighs, he just waits there, staring forward into the inky water. The water is probably six or eight inches deep now.

As the shock of the fight slowly leaves him, it's replaced by the shock of the fact that Clarence just killed another person. It was self-defense, and he knows the situation was kill or be killed, but still, it's hard for Clarence to believe he really did it. He can feel his heart thumping, hammering in his chest, and he looks down at his hands, which shake feverishly. Finally, Clarence decides he'd better grab his carbine and see about getting out of the tent. He can try to make sense of the feeling later.

When he stumbles out of the half-collapsed tent, Clarence still sees people running everywhere, shouting and calling to each other. He sees Washington sloshing toward him.

"Lincoln, where have you been?" Clarence says incredulously. It sure would have been nice if he'd shown up a few minutes ago.

"I'se out relievin' myself when this flood start, so I went to check de horses. They fine. I figur'd you'd wake up and see to the tent."

"I was just getting to that, but I had some problems. Someone slipped and fell, and they knocked over half of it." Clarence doesn't think it's the time to mention Carter's attempt to murder him. In fact, if no one else ever learns what just happened in the tent, he'll be grateful beyond words. "Let's grab our packs and move this thing before it washes away."

Although the water is knee-deep now and the current gains strength, Clarence and Washington gather what they can and move to higher ground, dragging their saturated tent behind them. Once everything is safe, Clarence just collapses in the slick grass and looks up at the gray-black night sky. His breath still comes in gasps.

"You okay, Cooper?" Washington says to him. "Tha' was crazy, I know, but you looks like somethin' spooked you."

Clarence tries to make up a convincing cover story. "Sorry, Lincoln, but getting woken up in the middle of the night by flooding water was just too much for me, especially since I can't swim. Whatever else we do on this march, I think I need to stay away from rivers for a while. They've been nothing but bad luck for me. They're my hoodoo, my Jonah."

"What's a Jonah?"

"It means the same as the word hoodoo; it's just an expression for bad luck. Ballplayers like to say that another team is their Jonah if they have bad luck against a team for no clear reason. I think it comes from some story in the Bible, but I've never read the Bible, so I don't know for sure."

"Well Cooper, you's right about these rivers being bad luck for you. Only problem is, we ain't crossed this one yet."

As if Clarence needed someone to remind him of that.


The next morning, the Buffalo Soldiers get their orders and assignments for crossing the Dearborn. Once again, Clarence is supposed to help Smith and several other troopers stand guard over everything on the far side of the river and make sure that the prisoners stay out of trouble once they get across. By now, Clarence's inability to swim is well-known amongst both the other soldiers and the officers; he thinks he gets this assignment out of pity as much as anything else.

Just as he's about to cross the Dearborn and see to his duties, however, Clarence receives a summons to meet with Lieutenant Pershing. He suspected this might happen, and after he and Washington moved their equipment out of danger, Clarence spent most of what remained of the night working on his story. He was too wet and his senses were too on edge to sleep, anyway, so he's had lots of time to think over what to say to the lieutenant. His left shoulder hurts, too, from where Carter walloped him, just one more reason he couldn't go back to sleep.

Clarence finds Pershing looking at some papers inside his tent. Clarence has noticed that the tents where officers sleep are a lot larger than the ones regular soldiers get. "Private Cooper, please enter," Pershing says when Clarence arrives.

"You requested to see me, Lieutenant Pershing?" Clarence says while giving the proper salute.

"Indeed. Have a seat if you'd like." Pershing motions Clarence to a wooden folding chair.

"I'll stand if it's all the same to you, sir. My uniform is still right soggy after the surprise of last night, although today stands to be a warm day at last, it appears. Do you have special instructions for me to carry out, sir? I was told I'd be on guard duty on the far side of the Dearborn today."

"Yes, last night was both a surprise and a practical lesson in one of the oldest axioms of frontier military service: Never camp on the near side of a river that has to be crossed if you can help it. However, we couldn't help it. I've decided, however distasteful I find the delay, that we should wait one day before crossing the Dearborn, due to its swollen condition at present. I've sent messages to notify the men of the change of orders."

"I'll relay your message promptly, sir."

Pershing holds up one arm, index finger extended. "Not just yet, Private Cooper. The messages will get where they need to go through the proper channels. I've something special in mind for you today."

"Of course, sir. What is it?" Clarence does his best not to fidget or appear nervous, but he isn't sure if it's working.

"At roll call this morning, one of our men was missing. Private Edward Carter. You remember him as well as I do, I'm sure."

"I remember the incident at the Marias, yes. I've had little direct contact with Private Carter since that day, sir."

"That's good, considering I forbade him from having anything to do with you. In any case, no one has seen him since last night. It appears he's gone missing."

"And how can I help in this situation, Lieutenant?"

"Well, call it a hunch, Private Cooper, but you seem to have a kind of lucky air about you. Between your dramatic escape from drowning when we crossed the Marias River, to your good fortune in locating those two Cree messengers outside of Missoula, to your success in getting intelligence out of them, you do seem to have a knack for getting things to break your way. I plan to send some men to try and locate Private Carter's trail if possible. Since your orders call for you to cross the stream anyway, I want you to accompany the soldiers who plan to look for Carter on the far side of the Dearborn today. Your mission will be to pick up Carter's trail and find him if possible. Any questions, Private?"

"No, sir, none at all."

"Good. Dismissed, Cooper."

When the day is over, Clarence reports to Lieutenant Pershing that the search party was unsuccessful in picking up any trace of Private Edward Carter.

# Chapter 31

## Reunited

"How hot is it today, you figure, Lincoln?"

"I'm not sure, Cooper. Ninety, at least."

"Remind you of home?"

"Some, but down South it's humid. This is jus' hot. An' with these uniforms, boy, we's in for another warm one today, I'll wager."

Clarence looks over at Washington. The dust clouds are back along with the heat, and the dirt coats everyone's face brown, streaked with rivulets of perspiration.

"You knows your uniform is ripped, right, Cooper?"

Clarence nods and looks down at himself. His formerly blue uniform is nearly brown, too. One elbow is torn from all the work he's done to move the supplies and captives this far, and he's lost a button in the front, too.

"You ever smelled anything like this before, Lincoln?"

"Nope."

"We've been in the field for weeks now, and the weather goes from hellishly hot, like today, to miserably wet like that stretch we just went through a few days back. No one's had anything to bathe in except river water all this time."

Growing up on the streets of Chicago, Clarence met plenty of people who needed to bathe, for sure, but the sheer number of them in the party just overwhelms the senses.

Clarence speaks again. "I wonder how all these people can stand this. If we're miserable, they must be in worse shape than we are."

"Maybe they jus' can't focus on bein' mad because these wagons creak so loud. I ain't yet got over all this noise, even after weeks. Makes me wish I was fishin' a creek back in Tennessee or somethin'."

"Their discipline is amazing. They'd probably make good soldiers if the Army ever decided to give them a chance. Although after something like this, who'd want to enlist?"

"Look up there, Cooper. Up ahead. Is that the town we's lookin' for?"

"Appears so. We must have reached Great Falls. Finally. I think the worst is over."

As soon as Clarence says this, he realizes the irony. For the 10th Cavalry, it's the end of their journey, but not for the people they've escorted all this way. Physically, the tough part might be over for the captives, too, but that doesn't consider that they'll need to start new lives, in new places, and start over from scratch somewhere in Canada. Clarence wonders what they'll do for food when they reach their new homes. It's nearly August now. It'll take at least a week or two more for the prisoners to reach their destinations in Canada. They'll have no chance to grow anything this year. Will they have to build new homes from scratch, too? Many of them brought tipis with them, yes, but some of the covers have been torn, or the poles lost, or both, along the way.

Just then, as Clarence scans the poor, wretched people he helps guard, he sees an old man stumble and fall to his knees barely twenty feet away. The elderly man sits motionless in the dust, and his bony arms are all that prevent him from falling face first to the ground. He does not move for several seconds.

Washington rides over, dismounts, and hands the man his canteen. He, along with several of the people nearby, assist the old man back to his feet, and two of the Métis drape his skeletal arms over their shoulders and continue plodding along.

Washington, Clarence, and Lawrence Smith take turns helping the people when they can. Often, they've shared water or a bit of food with some of the Métis who appear to be at the end of their strength. Clarence has seen a handful of other soldiers do the same, although not all do.

Even with what small help they can offer, however, two more people have died in the past couple days, making for three fatalities so far. The baby who was born on the way is still alive, as far as Clarence knows, but who can say if it's healthy?

Their arrival in Great Falls occurs during the final week of July. Despite his earlier conversation with Washington, the fact that there have been no incidents of note along the way disappoints Clarence sorely. Now that they are back east of the Continental Divide, and Clarence knows that Gabriel and Mary are somewhere in the Augusta area, he thinks this might be his last good chance to get out of the cavalry. Unfortunately for Clarence, however, Imasees seems to hold great respect among the Métis, and nothing has happened to create enough confusion for Clarence to make a final try at escape. He supposes, looking back, that the night at the Dearborn River might have been that chance, but after nearly getting strangled, Clarence didn't have enough composure to think of it at the time.

Soon, Washington rides beside Clarence again.

"Is the old man going to make it?" Clarence asks.

"Can't say for sure, Cooper. He's alive, but he don' look too strong. His eyes was far away. I don' know if he even heard what everyone said to him."

"He's only got to make it another half-mile or so, I think. Then he can rest a bit."

"Are those people linin' the road up ahead, Cooper?"

"I think so, yeah."

"What're they there for?"

"I guess we're an event in these parts."

It's true. When the Buffalo Soldiers approach the town, people come out to look at them. For Clarence, their arrival in Great Falls reminds him of his days as a baseball mascot, in a way. While they march toward the town, many of the residents take up a position on either side of the line of march to watch their approach. If only Clarence had his marching baton and bandleader outfit, it would feel like old times in Chicago. This time, however, he's riding on the right-hand side of the column while it starts moving through the crowd, instead of at the front of the line, and he's not the one calling out, "dress ranks there."

There's another difference between this march and leading parades in Chicago, however. Clarence wasn't sure what kind of reception to expect in Great Falls, but he must admit he is unprepared for what happens next. Perhaps he should have seen it coming. Once the prisoners start trudging through the streets, the onlookers hurl abuse at them. After walking several hundred miles through heat and pouring rain with little more than the shirts on their backs, when the Métis reach the conclusion of their hellish journey, they're greeted by revulsion and scorn.

Not just an occasional taunt, either. Some people scream obscenities, their faces twisted by anger and rage. They lash out verbally at the poor captives with all manner of slurs. Others raise their fists and throw garbage or small rocks while their neighbors cheer. When Clarence rides by, he hears one onlooker ask a young Métis girl if her parents both live in a brothel. The man's face contorts with intense hatred, a snarl stretching across his visage. There's even a pastor of some Protestant denomination warning those around him that the arrival of the captives signals the coming of the Anti-Christ. This man's jumbled utterings would be funny, Clarence decides, except that those around him seem among the most enthusiastically abusive of the whole crowd. Just as Clarence passes out of earshot of this man, he hears the pastor raise his voice to say, "and the day draws nigh when the Lord's righteous shall take up the sword and kill the ungodly . . ."

Nor are the Métis the only ones getting the abuse. While Clarence passes down the street, another onlooker makes a loud comment about "niggers leading red men," while yet another calls out for the soldiers to stay in Canada, too. Clarence looks to his left and sees Smith riding nearby. The look in Smith's eyes is a little uncertain, but all he says is, "Stay steady, Fred. Just take it. It'll only last a few minutes."

No sooner does he say this than a brick flies from Clarence's right. It strikes a middle-aged Métis woman in her right shoulder. She falls to a knee. A cheer goes up on Clarence's side of the street.

A moment later, something splatters on a soldier a few yards ahead of Clarence. Then he catches the smell. Someone emptied a chamber pot while the troopers ride past one of the hotels on the way into town. Washington is only a few feet from the soldier; Clarence sees him say something to the man. The other soldier slowly slides his finger off the trigger of his carbine.

"Steady, men, steady." It's Smith again.

As soon as Smith finishes saying this, a minor commotion breaks out on the other side of the street. A few citizens of Great Falls leave their places on the wooden plank sidewalk and try to attack an elderly Métis man as he passes by. Clarence doesn't know if the old man said anything to them because of all the other noise in the street, but luckily, the soldiers nearby restore order by herding the spectators back to their places at bayonet point. Looking across at the confrontation, for just a moment, Clarence fears the rest of the crowd may join them, and then they'd have a riot on their hands like one he saw in San Francisco in 1888. It appears, however, that most of Great Falls' citizens aren't willing to tangle with armed cavalry, and so they hang back and content themselves with jeering and verbally abusing the soldiers and captives.

Finally, they're through. Clarence hears several sighs of relief when they reach the north side of the town.

The Buffalo Soldiers are lucky that Great Falls is home to only about 10,000 people, or else the ordeal might have lasted longer and ended badly. They make their camp a bit northwest of the city, on the north side of the Sun River. Between all the Métis they've rounded up and those still held here waiting for transportation, about two hundred people are in their custody, either in the camp itself or waiting in the Great Falls jail.

The next morning Lieutenant Pershing calls the soldiers of Troop D together.

"Men of the 10th, thus far you've performed admirably. You've conducted our mission efficiently and professionally, yet with restraint and humanity. Montana, and the United States of America, owes you a debt of gratitude. So, for that matter, does the Canadian government. My hat is off to you for your success to this point."

At this, some of the men cheer, thinking their job complete, but Clarence focuses on why Pershing ended his statement by saying "to this point." The roundup is over, or so the men believe, and the railroad should be taking their charges to Canada from here. Is there a catch?

Meanwhile, Pershing raises his arms and gestures for the men to calm down, so he can continue. "I'm sorry, men, but it's not the time for cheering just yet. We have more work to do."

Clarence hears grumbling, and the soldiers look at each other questioningly. He thinks they're as exhausted and ready to be through with this operation as he is.

Pershing continues after a moment. "Some of you may have heard rumors about a legal challenge to our deportation. A misguided local lawyer named John Hoffman, a longtime friend of the Cree, or at least so he claims, has challenged the legality of our operation. This lawyer," Pershing pauses to expectorate, then continues, "claims that the law passed by Congress merely appropriated money for removing the Cree but did not authorize their removal explicitly."

A few boos ring out at this announcement. Again, Pershing calls for quiet, this time with a mere scowl in the direction of the dissatisfied men. "Do not worry any further about this rumor, for the local magistrate, Judge Benton, assures me the complaint is without merit, and the removal of the Cree will proceed without hindrance."

Pershing never mentions the fact that most of the prisoners are American citizens and are not even Cree. Clarence wonders if the omission is intentional. Well, honestly, he doesn't wonder at all. He's pretty sure he knows the answer.

Pershing continues, projecting his voice a bit more so that everyone hears him clearly. "That brings me, however, to the real reason I've called the troop together this morning. Buffalo Soldiers, we have more work to do. I am sad to report the fact, but the money appropriated by Congress for the deportation is insufficient to secure railroad transport for the remaining Cree. Our company must escort them on foot the final one hundred twenty-five miles to the International Boundary."

Clarence sees many of the men shake their heads. After riding several hundred miles already, crossing the Continental Divide twice, and then slogging most of the last fifty or seventy-five exhausting miles alternating between a mud bog and a furnace, now the lieutenant wants the Buffalo Soldiers to ride north with their captives instead of riding for Fort Assiniboine. This will probably add another two weeks to the campaign, assuming there are no more problems. And, if this trip has shown anything to Clarence, it's that something is always a problem.

While he broods over these facts, Pershing continues. "This is unwelcome news, I know, but we will do our duty, just as all of you have done so far. I expect nothing less from the Buffalo Soldiers. You've all lived up to that proud name on this campaign, and I know that no man here will tarnish his admirable record now by shirking duty. We leave tomorrow morning. In the meantime, while I see to the organization of the supply train and finalize our route for this last leg of our journey, take the rest of the day today to enjoy the pleasures of Great Falls, such as they are. Dismissed."

When evening arrives, Clarence decides to wander the streets of Great Falls for a while. His calves ache, so his walk is more of a limp or a slow trudge, but he knows he needs to plan a way to escape tonight. The city has no paved streets, but they've dried sufficiently from the recent storms that they are not muddy. Dusty, yes, but no one cares about that right now. Everything everyone has is dusty already. Who will notice a little more at this point? Not much consolation for three days of hellish torment pushing Red River carts and travois over the mud and clay roads on the way here, but it's something, Clarence supposes.

To begin with, he walks the streets with some of the other soldiers; after how some of the people jeered and yelled and insulted them when they first arrived, it seems a wise precaution to travel in a group. Only some soldiers go into town. Most, including Clarence's closest friends, are too tired. The troopers get no trouble this time, however, other than a few hostile glances. The crowd that jeered them earlier has dispersed. Clarence guesses that these people in Great Falls are like most of the people he met back East in his days as a baseball mascot—afraid to act on their anger without a group to back them up. The fact that the troopers have carbines probably helps, too.

While they walk, some of the other soldiers point out buildings and other sights. The men try to go in one of the saloons they come across, but the proprietor rudely tells them to leave because he won't serve colored people, even if they're soldiers. After they're thrown out of a second saloon for the same reason, the men give up on the idea of getting drinks and just walk the streets to see what they can see in Great Falls. For someone like Clarence, who grew up in Chicago, and who has seen Cairo, Rome, Paris, and London, it isn't much, but they've been on the trail long enough that it's worth it to see a town.

When the troopers head back to camp, Clarence thinks he's planned his escape route for that night. He knows he's running out of chances to get away, so he decides that, come what may, tonight is the night to risk it.

Then, with just a random glance down one of the streets, Clarence sees a line of people walking parallel to him just one block away.

"What's that, I wonder?" one of his companions says.

"Hey, look, it's Sergeant Grimes on his horse," says another.

"Who be all the people in that line?" asks a third soldier.

"Must be more captives for us to deal with," says the first.

The men keep talking and speculating, but Clarence stops listening when he sees a young girl in a dirty checkered dress holding the hand of a man about his age with long, dark hair.

Mary and Gabriel. Clarence is sure of it. He's found them, at last.

"I'm going to go over there and have a look," he tells the others.

"We ain't on duty now," someone says in response. "You sho' you want extra work? With Grimes over there?"

"I want to check out the new prisoners," Clarence says in return. "You never know, some of them could be trouble. Anyway, I just want to have a look. You all head back to camp, I'll meet you there."

The others all shrug and move off. Clarence believes they think he's a little crazy anyway; it's clear he's a mediocre soldier but a quiet guy who thinks a lot and can read, while most of them are the opposite—quality soldiers who, for one reason or another, have never had the need or the opportunity for much education. Not that they hate Clarence or think badly of him; they just find him strange and believe that his priorities need adjusting.

On his own now, Clarence follows the group of prisoners, but slowly and at a distance. He doesn't want Mary or Gabriel to see him just yet. They still think he's Clarence, and he doesn't want to cause a scene or try to explain what's happened to him in front of everyone. No one around here will believe them that he's not Fred Cooper, anyway. So, Clarence lurks some distance behind the group and follows them to the camp. After seeing where Mary and Gabriel are, he returns to check in with his fellows. Then he heads off to see his friends at last.

They aren't hard to find because they don't even have a tent to sleep under. Mary and Gabriel sit talking, looking toward the setting sun while it falls behind the Rocky Mountains in a scintillating mix of red, orange, and yellow. Clarence walks up behind them as they take in the view.

"Mary, Gabriel," he calls softly.

They turn around. "CLA-rence," Mary starts to shout, but then immediately goes back to a normal voice when she sees Clarence's right index finger over his lips. Then she leaps into his arms and gives him a big hug.

Clarence hugs her back for a moment, then sets her down. "I'm so happy to see you safe," he tells Mary. "But you aren't supposed to know who I am. I'm pretending to be a soldier, remember?" He looks around to see how many people noticed the hug. If anyone did, they aren't giving it much mind. Clarence decides that probably they're just too tired to care.

"I'm so happy to see both of you," he says again, looking at Gabriel as he says it. Gabriel's got a broad smile on his face. "I wasn't sure I'd ever find you again, but fate has brought us together at last," Clarence says while shaking Gabriel's hand. "Your friends Charles and Alexander are here, too. Somewhere in the camp." Gabriel's face brightens again, but then he gives Clarence a quizzical expression.

"Did they make it to Horse Plains in time?" he asks Clarence. "From how many people I see here in the camp, I'm guessing they didn't."

"No. In fact, I was in the group who captured them. They're unhurt, too, as far as I know, but they never made it to their destination."

"How did you catch them? They should have moved a lot faster than you did."

"Charles told me he couldn't find the Blackfoot River without your help."

Gabriel rolls his eyes and gives a rueful smile. "He had a map, and he still couldn't find it? One of my father's maps, too. How could he miss it?"

"Speaking of, I don't suppose you ever found Pierre, did you?" Clarence asks Gabriel.

He looks Clarence in the eyes, but his hesitation to speak and lonely stare tell Clarence the news will be bad. "He didn't make it, Clarence. The day we escaped at the Milk River, one of the vigilantes shot him, and the bullet pierced one of his lungs. He died a slow and painful death. I just found out the news myself about two weeks ago."

"I'm so sorry. I was sure you'd find him again. Are you sure of the news? You've been in prison here for a while."

"Yes. An old friend brought me the news and gave me my father's sash to prove it. There's no doubt that he's dead. He's buried in Canada. I guess it's fitting, since he was born in Canada, even if no one cared about the boundary in those days."

"Clarence, tell us about being a soldier," Mary puts in, although she remembers to use her normal voice. "We've been so worried about you. I thought you might have to go to China or someplace like that. Please, tell us about your adventures!"

"I will, Mary, but first, you have to promise me something."

"What's that?"

"You have to call me Fred for now, okay? Or Cooper. The people in the Army think my name is Fred Cooper. That's who I'm pretending to be. Can you remember that?"

"I think so. But why do you have to be Fred Cooper? Why not Clarence?"

"Because a person named Fred Cooper really escaped from Fort Assiniboine the night before the soldiers captured me. When those soldiers caught me that day, the Army just decided to make me Fred Cooper, so it could pretend that it never lost a person in the first place. I've been going by the name Fred Cooper for almost nine months now."

"That's a nice name, I guess, but I like Clarence better," Mary tells him. "But I promise I'll call you Fred. Now you must tell us about your adventures. Did you fight any dragons?"

"Dragons? No, no dragons. I don't think we have any of those here in Montana. Maybe they live over in China, but I've never been there," he says with a smile.

Clarence proceeds to tell Mary and Gabriel everything that's happened since last November. Which isn't all that much, considering the number of days he spent at Fort Assiniboine just drilling and learning how to be a soldier. But he tells them about some of the things he did to practice soldiering, about nearly drowning in the Marias River, crossing the Continental Divide twice, meeting the bicycle corps at Fort Missoula, and how he was lucky enough to learn their whereabouts from talking to Charles. Clarence does not mention anything about Edward Carter. Then he has Mary and Gabriel tell him about their winter, so they talk about escaping from the drunk cowboys, life at the mission, their visit to the Grant ranch at Augusta, and how Sergeant Grimes caught them and imprisoned them at Great Falls.

"I'm surprised at Sergeant Grimes," Clarence says to Gabriel. "I know I only have experience with one regiment, but he may well be the worst officer in the whole Army."

"Well, he caught us just as we were getting ready to leave St. Peter's. It was bad luck, that's all. Our bag was packed, my riding gear was on, everything was ready. Had we decided to leave thirty minutes sooner, we wouldn't be here right now."

"He stole our money, too," Mary tells Clarence. "We got a letter from Uncle John in St. Louis, and he sent money for a train ticket, and we were about to leave, and then he just came and took it from us."

"This hasn't been our lucky year for riding trains, has it, Mary?" Clarence says to her. "Maybe we should just steal a horse and ride."

"Can we do that?" she asks me. "I'm not very good with horses yet, but Gabriel taught me to ride a little."

"No, that was a joke Mary, sorry. I wish I knew some way to get your money back from Grimes but trying to desert the cavalry is risky enough."

"I think it's gone, anyway," Gabriel tells me. "My guess is he's already spent it on women, alcohol, or gambling, or maybe all three. There are plenty of houses of vice in Great Falls, and they aren't hard to find."

"Where does this leave us, Gabriel?" Clarence asks his friend in a quiet voice. "The cavalry is going to take you and Mary to Canada. I'm stuck at Fort Assiniboine until my enlistment is up, whenever that might be. I have no idea when the real Fred Cooper enlisted and how long it'll be before my time is up. How are we going to get out of here before that? The march to the Canadian border is about 125 miles, which means we won't have much more than a week. That's all the time we have left to get away."

"Well, Fred, I've spent the past couple weeks in a jail cell in Great Falls thinking on that very question. It's going to take a big disturbance to draw everyone's attention, and we'll have to get away when they're all distracted."

"I was thinking the same thing," Clarence tells him. "The problem is that Imasees, who is the leader of the people we've captured, has convinced his people not to resist with any violence. There were no big incidents all the way here from Camas Prairie, except one night a few days back when the Dearborn River rose after all the rain and flooded us out of our camp. But since I almost drowned, and I can't swim, either, I was too busy saving my gear and myself to take advantage."

"When I was at St. Peter's, Father Andreis mentioned trying to get a lawyer to stop the deportation," Gabriel mentions. "Do you know what came from that? Nothing, is my guess, since we're all here and leaving tomorrow morning."

"Nothing came of it," Clarence replies. "The judge wouldn't hear of it."

"I don't want to go to Canada," Mary tells her friends. "Then I'll never see Uncle John, or get to learn more about baseball, or go to school, or see a big city like St. Louis. Won't you please help us get away, Fred?"

The three talk for several more hours, catching up with each other and trying to plan as best they can.

# Chapter 32

## The Final March

Gabriel lies on the sodden ground, coughing and gulping in air. The buffalo grass, which was a beautiful golden color just a few days back, is almost as gray and muddy as everything else around him. Mary sits beside Gabriel, arms around her knees, shivering uncontrollably, teeth chattering, her formerly bright checkered dress long since besmirched with mud and dirt. The beautiful blue ribbon in her hair is long gone, too. The group decides to camp for the night, if camping is what one can call it when one has no tent, or campfire, or even a bedroll. They are just a day or two away from the Canadian border. The rains came back about three days ago and haven't let up since then. Presently, it sheets down on the soaked, exhausted, bedraggled pair.

*Who cares?* Gabriel thinks to himself. With no tent or shelter, it is impossible to get wetter than they already are, so more rain isn't going to matter.

"What's wrong, Gabriel? You really look sick," Mary says in a quiet, monotone voice.

"I feel terrible. My head is on fire, and my brain feels like it's going to burst."

"Why are you so sick? Is it because we don't have a tent, and we've had to sleep on the ground every night, and it won't stop raining?"

"Maybe. I don't know. I'm not a doctor, and we don't have any doctors with us to ask."

"Or is it because we hardly get any food?" Mary goes on, her little voice getting quieter still. "Or did a bad insect or snake get you? There've been so many flies, and mosquitos, and other bugs. They just torture me all night, when the rain stops, and I can barely sleep at all. I have all these little red bites all over my arms." She looks at Gabriel for a moment and then says, "Look, they're on your arms, too."

"Mary, those aren't insect bites. At least, not all of them. I'm afraid I've gone and caught the measles. Word says that they've been going around to some of the people in our camp. You should probably stay away from me when I cough. It seems that's how you spread the illness. Someone probably coughed on me back when we were in the cell in Great Falls, or maybe when we camped outside of town before leaving, and that's how I got it."

"How come I didn't get it, then? I was in the same cell as you."

"I don't know, Mary. Maybe it's one of those diseases where sometimes people catch it and sometimes they don't. I wish I could say for sure. But I think I might have something else, worse than just measles. My chest and my lungs hurt. All the time. I've got a fever, too, and my head has been hurting for a couple days now. I can't seem to drink enough water, no matter what I do. I'm always thirsty."

"How long until you get better?"

"I don't know, Mary. Yesterday I thought I was improving, but I've been getting worse again today."

"How much farther is it to Canada, Gabriel? I'm so tired of walking, and the mean soldiers telling me to hurry up and go faster. It's hard because the trail is always wet and muddy, and I fall down all the time. My shoes wore out, so now I'm in my bare feet. And I'm so hungry and thirsty."

"I think we have two days to go. It isn't much farther. Can you make two more days, do you think?"

"I don't know, Gabriel. I just want to fall down and rest after almost every step. I wish we had a horse to ride on like Clarence does. It would be so much easier."

"Yeah, it would, but we don't. The soldiers stole that from us, too, remember?"

"I remember. We were about to leave to catch the train and go to St. Louis. I'm never going to make it to St. Louis, am I, Gabriel? I'm gonna have to live my whole life in Canada, aren't I?"

"Two days is a long time, Mary. We'll get our chance yet. Just stay close to Clarence while we ride along. And don't forget to keep calling him Cooper. You've been wonderful about that so far. I don't think you've forgotten even once."

"I don't want to let Clarence down. He's my best friend. And you, too. You are both my best friends now."

It's true that Clarence rides near Gabriel and Mary as much as possible each day. He doesn't say much because he's acting like he's doing his job as a soldier and he doesn't want to raise anyone's suspicions. However, many times, Gabriel watched him help people who had fallen in the mud, or noticed Clarence offering a little extra water from his canteen to someone who looked ready to drop from exhaustion. The problem is that the group has way too many Cree and Métis people who need help and not enough soldiers willing to give them a hand. Gabriel has seen a few others helping people, but not all. Not by a long shot. Three people have died in the last week. Three that Gabriel knows about, anyway. Plus, the camp had the measles outbreak, which Gabriel fell victim to himself. He still can't believe Mary hasn't gotten the measles, too, but he's grateful for that. He wasn't sure if she'd make it even two more days if she had.

"Yes, we're lucky to have a friend like Clarence," Gabriel tells her and then turns away so he can cough again. As much as he wants to give her a big hug to help her shivering, he doesn't want Mary to catch the measles. Or to see that, since yesterday evening, he's begun coughing up blood.

Two days later, Clarence rides along listlessly while the pitiful and bedraggled group trudges and shambles along in the late afternoon. It stopped raining about a day and a half ago and became very warm again, so the ground is still soft, but it's better than squishy mud.

The change of weather has not helped the prisoners, Clarence realizes. One child, a boy of about seven, died two days ago, and a young girl died yesterday. Whether from the measles or from something else, he doesn't know. There have been two more adult fatalities, too.

One of the adults was a man of about sixty. He wore buckskins and moccasins, but also a black suit jacket over his white linen shirt. The man was so skinny and emaciated, Clarence worried his bones might break when soldiers carried his body away from the main group. His sash was a brilliant combination of green, gold, and sky-blue beads, arranged in a diamond pattern. He wore a pair of eagle feathers in his long, black hair.

Clarence knows all this because he was among the soldiers assigned to dig the grave. It has no marker to identify the body, just a rudely hacked wooden cross. Clarence never even learned the man's name.

Turning to his right, he says to Washington, "Lincoln, are we almost there? Is that the Boundary up ahead?"

"Huh?" Washington shakes his head and sits upright.

"Were you sleeping in the saddle?"

"Not sure. Was I? I jus' closed my eyes for a moment, I thought. I sure is tired, Cooper. What did you say again?"

"I think that's the International Boundary, our destination, up ahead, right? I think I see some soldiers on horseback."

Washington shades his eyes with his left arm. "I think you's right, Fred. Maybe we's there finally. Amen to that."

"We've been on the trail for about two months, but it seems like two years."

"Hopefully these people will find they's new homes before long."

"You know something, Lincoln?"

"Wha's that?"

"We've been out here two months, and I've barely even thought about what's going to happen to these people when they get to Canada. Should I feel bad about that?"

"Don' know, Cooper. You's just doin' your job, same as the rest of us, I guess."

"Yeah, I'm doing my job, but shouldn't it at least cross my mind now and then?"

"Everyone different. I don' think no ones judgin' you 'cause of that."

"You still think we're doing the right thing here, Lincoln?"

He looks toward the ground and speaks quietly. "Don' know, Cooper. Not my job to decide."

# Chapter 33

## Coutts Station

When they reach the International Boundary, Clarence can see the Canadian Mounted Police in the distance at Coutts Station set to receive them. After he finishes speaking with Washington, he's riding close to Gabriel and Mary, like he usually does, and it appears he and Gabriel will have to try the last option of their escape plan.

Wait a moment. Off to his left, Clarence sees a few soldiers trotting their horses to the front of the column. In their midst ride Imasees and Lucky Man. He hears murmurs from the prisoners. Then Clarence remembers. When they captured Imasees and Lucky Man back at Camas Prairie, Lieutenant Pershing told them that the Canadian government would not prosecute them for their role in the Riel Resistance of 1885. Could it be that he told them a lie to get them to cooperate?

It appears so. Clarence watches intently as the riders approach the Canadian police, and even though he can't make out the words from this distance, he can see some men, including both the Mounted Police and Lucky Man, wave their arms, point fingers, and stomp the ground.

A spirited argument. Then, in the bright light of the setting sun, Clarence sees guns drawn and sunlight flashing on metal.

He's not the only one watching with interest. Just from listening to the hum of voices around him, Clarence can feel the tension rising minute by minute while many of the prisoners watch to see what happens.

Clarence continues staring to see what happens next, and soon, events confirm his suspicions. The Canadian police lead away Imasees and Lucky Man under guard. Suddenly, from the other side of the group, he hears angry shouts. Lots of them. Several of the prisoners surge forward, toward their betrayed leaders. A few knives flash. Another group of prisoners bolts in the other direction, heading south. Some of the soldiers on guard around Clarence decide to ride toward the commotion and help contain the disturbances.

Clarence looks down at Gabriel and nods. Wearily, his eyes struggling to focus, Gabriel nods back. Then, while the action on the other side of the group distracts everyone's attention, Gabriel tugs on Mary's sleeve and they creep, slowly and inconspicuously, into the shadows of the waning day. Clarence doesn't think anyone notices.

He rides over to the nearest soldier to provide a distraction for Gabriel and Mary. Clarence thinks his name is Private Johnson. He says to Johnson, "Shouldn't we go and help keep order? It looks like things are getting crazy over there."

"Don't know, Cooper," he replies. "Aren't we ordered to guard over here?"

"Things look calm over here, don't they, Johnson? Over to the west is where the action is. Come on, let's go make sure no one gets away."

"I don' know if tha's a good idea, Cooper. We's on duty here."

Clarence then recalls that Johnson isn't the brightest man in Troop D. If Captain Anson were here, he'd call Johnson a rube. Although he hates to do it, Clarence knows he's going to have to try and trick him.

"Johnson, do you think Lieutenant Grimes is going to care about orders while prisoners escape? We've got to get moving." Sad to say,

Grimes is back in Pershing's good graces and is in command over Clarence once again. Clarence starts riding toward the commotion. "Let's go, man! We can't let them get away."

"But, orders," Johnson stammers, looking around nervously for someone to give him advice or help him out.

"Perkins and Clark are already there, Johnson. You gonna let them get the credit for helping while you sit here?"

Johnson glances around one last time, as if help will magically appear to save him from making his own decision.

"I guess not. Hee-yah!" he says as he spurs his horse into motion.

They ride to the west side of the field together. There's plenty of chaos, for sure. Clarence even helps Johnson retrieve one young boy, just so Johnson won't feel that Clarence used him too badly. Johnson may not be too bright, but he has a good heart. Clarence knows he is one of the soldiers who shared food and water with some of the captives along the way. As for the little boy, Clarence thinks the confusion of the moment took him by surprise because he looks scared about what's happening. He's probably only five or six years old, so the boy lets Johnson pick him up and set him in front of Johnson on the horse. Clarence also hopes this will keep Johnson out of trouble for disobeying his orders. He can blame Clarence, if he likes. If Clarence's plan works, he won't be here to take the consequences, anyway.

Hoping Gabriel and Mary have had ample time to get out of sight, Clarence next searches out Lieutenant Grimes. It doesn't take long to find Grimes because he's doing the same thing that Clarence is—riding around at the scene, so it looks like he's helping, but in fact he's just trying to stay out of harm's way and avoid having to do anything risky.

"Lieutenant Grimes, sir," Clarence says to him breathlessly, even though Clarence is not tired and merely fakes fatigue to impress Grimes with how much he's supposedly helped, "I think I saw a couple of our captives trying to sneak away on the other side of camp, sir. Permission to pursue?"

"Granted, private," Grimes says immediately, without really thinking. "Don't let these savages get away."

"Yes, sir. I'll report back when I have them," Clarence pretends to pant out while he gallops off.

He heads straight for the landmark he and Gabriel selected when they arrived at the border. The Sweetgrass Hills are off to the east, and Gabriel spent quite a bit of time there when he was a boy. The plan is that, if Gabriel did cross the border, he'd sneak back to this side the first night and meet Clarence at a place he remembered. Gabriel told Clarence about a small cave at the base of a hill with some peculiar rock formations on top of it and said he'd meet Clarence there. Now, however, they've put their plan into motion early, thanks to the dishonest treatment of Imasees and Lucky Man creating a panic among the deportees.

Clarence rides toward the rendezvous. But then, he sees another man from Troop D, Private Tucker, off to his left. He flags Clarence down, and Clarence rides over to him.

"Where are you going, Cooper?" he asks. "No one's over this way."

Lucky for Clarence, Tucker is a lot like Johnson. Tucker works hard, he's a quality soldier, and he always tries to do his best, but he isn't the brightest.

"Lieutenant Grimes gave me permission to pursue any captives possibly fleeing this way."

"But I haven't seen anyone, Cooper. There's no one to go after."

At least he hasn't seen Gabriel and Mary. That's promising.

Clarence says to him, "Still, Grimes wants me to check things out, just in case. You know how he gets those crazy ideas sometimes, Tucker, and how mad he gets if you try to tell him it's a bad idea."

"Yeah, he sure does," Tucker says with a quick little nervous laugh. "He does get a little crazy now and then."

"In fact, you can probably go back to the camp and make sure everything is okay there. If anything is going on over here, I can take care of it."

"By yourself?"

"I've got the gun, remember? The odds will be in my favor."

"I suppose," Tucker says as he turns his horse back toward the camp. "You sure you don't need my help? You know I'm a good shot."

"I'll be fine. Don't worry about me. You just go on, and I'll check things out."

Tucker turns and rides back toward the camp. Clarence turns and trots the other way, toward the meeting spot. He doesn't get far, however, only a few minutes, before he hears Mary's frightened voice call out, "Clarence, help us!"

He rides toward the voice and soon finds Mary, who waves him over behind a large rock. Behind it, Gabriel is on his hands and knees, vomiting blood.

"What's wrong?" Clarence asks as he immediately climbs down from his horse to check on Gabriel. He realizes this explains why they didn't make it very far before Clarence found them. "That doesn't look good. Mary, how long has Gabriel been doing this?"

"He started vomiting a little while ago. I've never seen it before, Clarence. Why's he spitting up blood, too? Is that part of having the measles?"

"No, I don't think so. I heard some people back at camp talking about the outbreak of measles and what the symptoms look like, and vomiting blood isn't one of them."

"I think I'm done for," Gabriel says, the words barely coming out in a croak. He still has a bit of blood trickling down his chin, little droplets splashing in the dirt beneath him. "You two go on without me. I think it's tuberculosis. Back when they first threw us into prison in Great Falls, I heard one of the guards talking about it. I think I got it somehow." He stops, and gasps in a few breaths. "I can barely breathe, Clarence, and my head is ready to explode. I can barely walk any—" then Gabriel turns away from them and lets out a long series of coughs. More blood.

"We aren't leaving you behind now," Clarence tells him. "Come on, let me help you up on the horse. You ride, I'll walk. We should hurry, though. I don't know how much time we have before people will start noticing that I'm gone."

Something doesn't sit right with Lieutenant Grimes. It is right on the edge of his mind, but the tussle with these damned Indians has driven it out. Now that everything is back in order in camp, and the prisoners corralled and subdued, he sits on his horse, thinking. The events of the day already becoming a hazy blur, he's still thinking when Private Tucker, one of the dumbest men in the Buffalo Soldiers, rides toward him. Tucker is, however, good at following orders, which for Grimes is the most important quality a soldier can have. It's funny, then, that he's here, when Grimes is pretty sure Tucker's orders were to guard the camp perimeter.

"Lieutenant Grimes, sir. All quiet to the east, sir," Tucker says.

"Why are you here, instead of at your post, private?"

"Private Cooper said you gave him orders to check for any escapees in that direction, sir. I told him there weren't any, but he wanted to have a look, just in case."

Grimes remembers giving the order, of course, but just then, it all hits him. Cooper is the one who'd tried to desert the regiment way back in November. Cooper is also the one who got him in trouble with Pershing, causing his temporary demotion to rear duty in Great Falls. That's it! It is Cooper who means to escape during the commotion. He isn't looking for any Indians. He is trying to get away himself!

"Private Tucker, do you have your weapon ready?"

"Of course, sir."

"Take me to where you spoke with Private Cooper. We have a deserter, all right, but the deserter isn't a Cree."

Looking around for anyone else nearby, Grimes spots Private Scott and calls him over. "Men," he says, "let's ride. We have a fugitive to catch."

Pershing is going to love him for this.

# Chapter 34

## The Chase

Clarence walks beside his horse as they drop down into a gully. He wants to stay out of sight as much as possible because they aren't moving very fast. As much as he hates to admit it, Gabriel is in awful bad shape. He can't stop coughing, and every breath seems to wrack his body with pain. Gabriel also complains about chills, even though it's August and the sun isn't quite down yet, and the temperature is still about eighty degrees this late in the evening. So, Clarence gives Gabriel his uniform to wear over his own shirt. Still, Gabriel's fever will not relent, and he drifts in and out of consciousness as they plod along.

They finally make it to the cave where they'd planned to meet, and with effort Clarence gets Gabriel down and into a sitting position. He's fully awake now but just flops on his back in the dust. The sun, which was on its way down when they started their escape, is nearly gone now. In another half hour or so, it will drop all the way behind the Rocky Mountains. Clarence thinks about collecting shortgrass, along with whatever wood he can find, to start a fire when he hears a voice that fills him with dread. It's distant and faint but getting louder and coming his way.

"This way, Lieutenant. I see more hoofprints over here. Maybe they've gone this way. There's a ravine in the way, but it looks like they went around it over here."

"Well done, Private Scott," Clarence hears Lieutenant Grimes call out. "Wait for us to come check it out."

He looks at Gabriel and Mary. It's clear they heard Grimes as well. "What do we do now?" Mary whispers.

"We've only got a few minutes," Clarence says. "It took us a while to get around that ravine, but they'll move faster because none of them are walking."

"We can't get away," Gabriel stammers weakly. "Three of us can't ride your horse very well. They'll catch us."

"Hurry," Mary whispers. "They're getting closer!"

"Give me the carbine," Gabriel croaks out. "You two take the horse and go. I'll take care of them."

"But you're not a very good shot," Clarence protests. "You said so yourself once. I've been practicing all winter, and I'm pretty good now." In reality, Clarence remains a mediocre shot, but it's all he can think of to say.

"I know I'm a lousy shot. But I'm not going to make it much farther, anyway. You might. Let me fight. At least this way my death might mean something."

Clarence hears the voices getting closer. He knows Gabriel is right but can't bear to let go of one of the few friends he could ever trust. Gabriel doesn't deserve to die, especially not here in the Montana wilderness, punished for something he never did wrong.

"Come on, Gabriel, you've got to come with us, so you can get better," Mary says to him. She tries to tug him up by his shirt sleeve, digging her heels into the dusty soil while leaning back.

"Not this time, Mary. I don't think there's any medicine for me now. When you finally meet your Uncle John, tell him I wish I could be there to see it."

With that, Gabriel picks up Clarence's carbine and uses its butt to prop himself up to his feet. He staggers forward a few steps before bracing his elbows on a rock that is chest high. He steadies himself and levels the gun, making sure it's ready to fire.

"Go on," he whispers. "I've got good cover."

"Come on, Mary," Clarence manages to say through the tears. "Gabriel is right. We have to go now."

Gabriel coughs again, loudly, then regains his balance and peers into the deepening twilight.

"What was that?" Clarence hears the voice of Lieutenant Grimes. They're closer, much closer. "It came from over there, I think."

Clarence puts Mary on the horse, then mounts up. He hardly knows what to say to Gabriel.

Gabriel must sense the same thing. "You don't have to say anything. Get going while you can."

Clarence turns and starts the horse into motion. "No!" Mary shouts out, unable to hold back her sorrow any longer. "We can't leave Gabriel behind!"

She didn't mean to, Clarence knows, but this alerts their pursuers to their position. Clarence hears someone, Private Tucker, he thinks, shout out, "They's over here, Lieutenant."

With no time to lose, Clarence spurs his horse. They're riding away now, as fast as he can ride when it's nearly dark. Mary wraps her little arms around Clarence's torso and holds on. He doesn't know how long it is, but it seems like it's only a few seconds before the exchange of gunfire begins behind them.

It's a brief exchange. Shortly after the firing begins Clarence hears the screams of men struck by bullets. Two different screams. Even though he knows one of the voices belongs to Gabriel, he rides on through the tears and heart-wrenching sorrow.

Soon, Clarence hears pursuit. He can't get his horse to go as fast as he'd like because he's worried about Mary falling off. Growing up in Butte, she's not used to riding a horse at high speed like Clarence is after spending months in the cavalry. Even after all his training, however, he's still just a middling horseman, at best, and he knows that Grimes and whoever is with him are gaining on them. Clarence looks back. Grimes is not more than a hundred yards or so behind, although in the fading light, the distances are deceptive.

Mary looks back and sees it, too. "What are we going to do, Clarence? We aren't getting away. Don't let the bad men catch us!" she shouts in an unsteady, panicky voice.

If Gabriel were guiding the horse instead of Clarence, they might have a chance. Gabriel knows the Sweetgrass Hills. He'd have found a way to lose the pursuit by now. But Clarence doesn't know where he is at all.

Before he can think of a response for Mary, there's more gunfire. A bullet strikes their horse, causing it to fall to the ground and the two riders to pitch forward. They land face-first in the dust. Clarence picks himself up quickly, rolling to his feet even as he hits the ground. Being a middling horseman has given him plenty of practice at falling off a horse and getting back up. A quick glance shows the horse cannot continue. It hasn't gotten back up, but writhes in the dirt, whinnying in pain. "Come on, Mary, this way!" Clarence shouts as he runs to pick Mary up from the ground.

"I can't, Clarence. My foot. I think it's broken!"

"Quick, climb on my back."

Just when Clarence gets her hoisted up, with her arms around his neck, he realizes they're out of time. Grimes and the other private with him, a man whose name Clarence can't remember, rein in their horses only twenty or thirty feet away.

"End of the road, Cooper!" Grimes shouts. "This is the second time you've tried deserting, and it'll be your last. Now set down the girl, and we'll finish this right quick."

Clarence drops to one knee so that Mary can put her feet on the ground. He looks at her face. She's terrified as she hops a couple hops to his left on her one good leg.

Then she turns and shouts, "His name isn't Cooper! It's Clarence! At least call him by his right name!"

"Insolent little bitch, isn't she?" Grimes says to the trooper at his side. "This is the second time she's spoken like that to me. Apparently, I didn't slap her hard enough to teach her a lesson the first time." He dismounts while the other trooper covers Clarence and Mary with his carbine.

"So, what do you want, Cooper? Should I shoot you first and beat some manners into your little friend second, or do it the other way around, so you can watch before you die? I like the second choice. How about you, Scott?"

Private Scott fidgets nervously in his saddle, looking back and forth between Clarence and the lieutenant. He doesn't answer.

"Not sure? Tongue tied? Well, I think I'll go with the second choice. Private Scott, please shoot Private Cooper if he moves." Then he walks toward Mary.

Pitifully, she tries to hop away from him, bouncing along on her right foot while the left dangles at an angle. Clarence can't take it. He gets up and runs toward Grimes. As he does, two shots pierce the warm Montana twilight.

Immediately, Clarence looks at himself to see where Scott has shot him, just waiting for the pain to cascade through his body. Then, from the corner of his eye, he sees Scott slump down off his horse and fall to the ground, clutching his right shoulder and screaming as he strikes the bare earth. Scott's carbine falls harmlessly to the ground on the other side of his horse.

Then Clarence looks over at Lieutenant Grimes. He's put both his hands to the front of his neck, but that isn't preventing the blood from spurting out the back. Grimes looks around, confusion in his face, then sinks to one knee, both knees, and finally, he falls over and stops moving.

Still disbelieving his eyes, Clarence looks around frantically to see the identity of their saviors.

Walking through the tall grass and stunted bushes about fifty feet away, he sees two men. One is tall, seemingly in his late thirties or early forties, with the tan complexion of an Indian. His companion doesn't look much like him. Although his skin is the same color, the other man is in his early thirties and is quite muscular. They both pump another bullet into the chamber of their rifles as they walk forward. Clarence just looks from one to the other in wonder, unsure of what will happen next.

While he waits, suddenly Mary gives a cry of joy, and starts limping toward the pair. "Antoine! Samuel! You saved us!"

Samuel, the stocky man, runs forward, picks Mary up in a big hug, and kisses her on the cheek. "Mary Healy, how are you, my young friend?"

"You know these men?" Clarence says to Mary incredulously, hardly believing they can be so lucky.

"Clarence, this is Antoine and Samuel Grant! Gabriel and I met them at their house a long time ago before the soldiers captured us. Samuel, this is my friend Clarence, the best friend in the world!"

While Samuel gently sets Mary back on the ground and comes over to shake Clarence's hand, Antoine stops a few feet away from Private Scott where lies on the ground, the wound in his right shoulder bleeding freely. Clarence can see Scott look up hopelessly, waiting for the end. "What's your name, soldier?" Antoine asks.

"Pr-private Scott, suh," he manages to drawl through the pain. Private Scott's accent reminds Clarence of Fred Pfeffer. Maybe he's from Kentucky, too.

"Do you want to die, right here, Private Scott?" the tall man demands sternly, the barrel of his gun pointing at the center of Private Scott's chest.

"N-no, suh."

"Then you'll lie still. In a minute we'll bind your wound, and then you'll walk back to camp and rejoin your friends while leading this wounded horse, soldier. You'll say nothing about anything that just happened here. When someone asks you how you got this wound, it was friendly fire. In the darkness, you thought someone was an escaping Indian, but it turned out to be one of your own men. They

shot your horse, then you, and you shot them in return. Am I clear?"
He prods Private Scott's bleeding shoulder with his toe for emphasis.

"Yes, suh," Scott says, wincing through the pain, tears welling in
his eyes.

Next, Samuel walks over to where Grimes lies motionless in the
dirt and shortgrass. His gun still trained on the dead man, he kicks
Grimes's corpse in the ribs, hard. When Grimes still makes no
movement, Samuel simply says, "Well, he's dead as can be. Good
riddance, too."

Samuel then starts going through Grimes' pockets. He takes out
Grimes' knife and his Colt pistol and then turns all the other pockets
inside out. "Ah, here's what I'm looking for," Samuel says as he
extracts a brown canvas pouch. He opens the pouch and pulls out
several dollar bills, then hands them to Clarence. "Payback for what
happened to Mary and Gabriel at St. Peter's Mission."

"How do you know about that?" Clarence asks him. "And how did
you get here just in time to save us?"

"We followed Gabriel and Mary after they left our house in
Augusta," Antoine tells Clarence. "Ma didn't want us to, but we did
anyway. We followed them to Great Falls, waiting for a chance to
spring Gabriel and Mary free, but that chance never came. We've been
following your army for ten days, still waiting for our chance. It finally
came. Samuel and I hid in the rocks right above you when you gave
your gun to Gabriel, so he could buy time for your escape."

"And the soldiers never caught you in ten whole days?" Mary asks
excitedly.

Samuel simply smiles. "These soldiers, they go through the
country with their heads down, seeing nothing. They wanted to keep
people inside their camp, but they never even dreamed that someone
might be waiting outside. Never underestimate the importance of
being on familiar ground."

"Still," Antoine puts in, "it was quite a chance that you came right
to our hiding place. I imagine that was Gabriel's idea?"

"It was," Clarence says. Then, he gets up his courage and asks, "Gabriel's dead, isn't he?"

"We didn't stop to look," Antoine admits. "You didn't have a weapon anymore, so we figured you'd need our help more than he would."

"We have to go and see him," Mary says. "We can't just leave him where he is."

Everyone nods in agreement. Antoine bandages Private Scott's wound, as promised, and after warning him again, releases him, so he can walk back to the camp. Before Scott leaves, he asks Clarence, "Cooper, why did your friend say your name was Clarence?"

"Because it is Clarence. I was never supposed to be in the cavalry. A guy named Fred Cooper deserted, and some soldiers caught me, and they said I was Fred Cooper, just so they wouldn't have to take the blame for letting a deserter get away."

"I'll be damned," Scott says. "You've been with us for almost a year, and you was never a soldier to begin with? And that's why you was tryin' to get away?"

"That's right."

"Don't worry about me, then. That ain't right, what the cavalry done to you. They won't hear a peep out of me. Ain't no one gonna miss Lieutenant Grimes, anyway. He never was worth nothin'. If anyone asks, I'll say he shot me first, or something. If they ask where his body is, I'll give 'em the wrong directions."

"Thank you, Scott," Clarence tells him. Then, just out of curiosity, Clarence asks, "Would you really have shot me?"

"I'd a thought about it. Orders, you know. I would a been of two minds about it, at least," Scott says with a sheepish smile, and then he turns and walks away, his wounded arm dangling at his side.

In addition to Samuel and Antoine's mounts, Clarence takes Scott's horse because it's not wounded, which along with Lieutenant Grimes' horse gives them four, and then they ride back to where they left Gabriel.

He's still alive when the group gets there, but just barely. Gabriel has a gunshot wound in his left shoulder and chest area, and he's closed his eyes. His body lies slumped against the rock just outside the little cave, right where Clarence and Mary left him. As they approach, everyone can hear how ragged Gabriel's breathing is. "If you're here to finish me off, just get it over with," he croaks without opening his eyes.

The four friends just stand there for a moment, looking at their fallen companion. Gabriel coughs, and blood drips from his mouth even as a bit more spurts from his wound.

Mary gets the courage to speak first. "It's us, Gabriel," she says even as the tears well in her eyes. "We've come back to say goodbye to you."

Gabriel's eyes open for a moment, and after he spends a few seconds focusing and realizes he's surrounded by friends, he tries to give Mary a little smile. When he sees the Grant brothers are there, he manages a whisper through gritted teeth. "I never could hide from you guys," he says to Antoine.

The smallest hint of a smile comes to Antoine's face. "I'm sorry it has to be like this, Gabriel. You were a man today. Your father would be proud."

Then it's Gabriel's turn to smile, as best he can manage. He croaks out, "You two know what to do with me when I die, right?"

Antoine nods while Samuel says, "We'll make sure you're laid to rest next to your father, once all this commotion has died down. You'll be in Canada, but you'll also be able to see Montana, so you can rest in contact with both the homes of our people."

"I told them about Pierre," Clarence says.

Gabriel nods slightly and closes his eyes again. Slowly, he says, "Mary, please be good for your Uncle John. Go to school, so you can be smart and read like Clarence."

Mary nods in silence.

With effort, Gabriel's eyes open, and he looks at Clarence. "I guess you'll never teach me to play baseball, Clarence. I did want to learn awful bad. I hope they'll let you play when you get to St. Louis. Mary, you'll have to learn to play for me."

"I'll learn," she says through her sniffles. "I'll try."

"Here, take this," Gabriel says. Slowly, his hands go to his waist, and he struggles to undo the sash he's wearing. "I want you to have mine, Mary, and Clarence to have my father's. I won't need them anymore, and I don't have anything else to give my friends."

They both mutter a tearful thank you as Gabriel tries to shift his body and pull his sash free. When he does, more blood gurgles out of his mouth, his eyes close again, and he lies still.

# Chapter 35

## St. Louis

Tall and thin, just like the day in 1889 when Clarence last saw him, John Healy sets cups of coffee in front of his two guests. They're sitting in Healy's kitchen in St. Louis, which is already warm this morning because St. Louis is in the midst of a stretch of sweltering August weather.

"Just so I have things straight," Healy says as he sits down with his own tin cup of coffee, daylight streaming through the window behind him before landing on the kitchen's hardwood floor. "Clarence. You rode halfway across the state of Montana rounding up these people, most of whom weren't even Cree Indians, and all that time you weren't even supposed to be in the cavalry."

"That's right."

"And Mary, you and Gabriel were at St. Peter's Mission nearly the whole time, and the only reason you missed seeing Clarence the first time is that you were at a party and slept late."

"Yes, Uncle John."

"Then, by chance, this crafty but otherwise incompetent cavalry officer catches you and steals my money that I sent for a train ticket, and you two come together for this forced march to the Canadian border. There's a disturbance when the Canadian police arrest two leaders to whom our military had promised amnesty, and in the commotion, you escape. But only with the help of the two sons of a rancher who are friends with your companion, Gabriel. They kill the lieutenant, get some of my money back, and then give you some extra money, so you can buy a train ticket here."

"I think they sold the horse that belonged to Lieutenant Grimes to make up the difference for what they gave me," Clarence says. "We, or should I say, they, brand all the horses at the fort, but you can always find a buyer if the buyer thinks the cavalry won't come looking. These two brothers live on a remote ranch way back in the foothills of the Rockies. I suppose they figure it is safe. And that the United States government owes them, anyway, due to their family history and all."

"Did these two brothers ever say why they rode so far, and how they turned up just in time to save you, Clarence?"

"Their family was friends with Gabriel's family. Plus, they were angry with the whites for how the whites treated their grandfather a long time ago. They told me they figured Gabriel and Mary might be in trouble, so the brothers decided to go to St. Peter's and check on them. When Grimes took them away, Samuel and Antoine followed, but they couldn't storm the jail in Great Falls and just bust them out with only two people. So, they followed the cavalry all the way to the Canadian border. They told me they meant to sneak across the border that night and spring Gabriel and Mary free if they could, but then everything started happening, and they ended up saving Mary and me instead."

"Well, Clarence, that's quite a story. It almost makes our attempt to free Ireland tame by comparison. How did you get to St. Louis from the Sweetgrass Hills? You haven't told me that part."

"It wasn't all that dramatic, John. A stream named Willow Creek flows out of the Sweetgrass Hills and joins the Marias River a couple days' ride from Fort Benton, which is a town on the Missouri River a bit north of Great Falls. We passed right over the tracks of the Great

Northern Railroad on the way, but our first attempt at hitching a ride on a train didn't go too well." Mary gives a big smile when Clarence says this. "I also knew that the railroad goes right through Havre and would bring us too close to Fort Assiniboine. So, I got an inspiration. Instead of riding the train at all, I decided we should go to Fort Benton and buy a steamboat ticket to get here. I remembered from my geography lessons with your brother that the Missouri River joins the Mississippi right here at St. Louis, so it was perfect. Sadly, I did have to steal some pants off someone's clothesline because I still had on the trousers I was wearing in the cavalry, and I didn't want to give myself away, but I left them a silver dollar in the pocket of my trousers, so I hope they aren't too sore about it."

At this point John Healy gives a big laugh. "I sure was surprised when I got that telegram from you, out of Fort Benton, saying you'd arrive at the docks this morning. It seems that one part of your journey here finally went as planned. I'm very sorry about your friend Gabriel, though. He sounds like a capital fellow. Both he and his father. Can I see those sashes again? My, that is exquisite beadwork. Too bad this one has some bloodstains on it, but I suppose that Gabriel couldn't help it, given the circumstances."

"He gave up everything for us," Clarence says. "Somehow, he contracted tuberculosis, just like Jimmy Fogarty did, and it was killing him from the inside out. Gabriel didn't deserve any of the things that happened to him, John. He was so dedicated to taking care of Mary because he had a good heart, but it cost him everything."

"You shouldn't blame yourself, Clarence. From what you told me, it sounds like there's a good chance the cavalry would have captured Gabriel and sent him to Canada anyway. You can never tell how these things will turn out."

"Yes, but none of it should have happened in the first place. He never did anything wrong. Gabriel never stole from any rancher or caused any trouble. He was even born in the United States."

"Now you understand why I hate governments so much and want to get rid of them," John says. "They stand for protecting power, not providing justice. Do you want to know what's happened in Montana since you left the cavalry?"

"What do you mean, John? I thought the cavalry was going to just drop the people off at the border and then head back to Fort Assiniboine."

"I've been reading the papers, looking for news of what's happening in Montana because I knew you two were there. I guess you must have left before the big argument took place between our boys and the Canadian officials."

"A dispute? What about?"

"The Canadians wouldn't accept all of the people you brought to the border. They took the Cree Indians and started sending them to various places, but they wouldn't accept the Michif at all. Said they weren't Cree, and they'd only agreed to take the Cree."

"What'd Pershing have to say about that?"

"When the Canadians wouldn't accept the Michif, he and his boys just left them there. Headed back to Fort Assiniboine with the Michif standing at the International Boundary."

"You've got to be kidding, John. We destroyed their homes and marched some of them 400 miles or more to the border, and the Canadians never planned to take them in the first place?"

"That's what the newspaper wrote."

"After all the hard work and suffering of those people? Besides losing their homes and everything they couldn't carry with them, some of them died along the way."

"I know, Clarence."

"And now they're just standing at the border, with no home in Canada and no home in the United States, either? What are they supposed to do? Eat grass like the cattle?"

"I told you it was never about justice, didn't I?"

"Now I wish I could go back and help them, but I've had enough of Montana, John. I don't know that there's much I could do, anyway. Did the papers say what happened to Imasees and Lucky Man?"

"Imasees?"

"Oh yeah, that's his Michif name. The whites call him Little Bear."

"Oh, yes, Little Bear. The papers did mention him, yes. They reported he was in prison in Regina, along with Lucky Man. That's all I know so far, but I thought you might like to hear it."

Clarence just sits there for a few moments, shaking his head while staring into his coffee cup. The poor people.

Mary, who has been listening intently the whole time, says, "Uncle John, do you and Clarence still plan to free Ireland? Clarence said I was old enough that I could help."

John Healy gives Clarence a quizzical look.

"I was only twelve, remember?" Clarence says with a shrug and a laugh.

Healy laughs, too. "True enough, true enough. Yes, Mary, if we ever start a new plan to free Ireland, we'll make sure you get to be in it."

"Yay!" she says, her bright eyes beaming at Clarence and John. Then Mary asks, "When will I get to see you play a game of baseball, Uncle John? Clarence told me about baseball, and I want to watch."

"Well, Mary, my old arm isn't quite what it used to be. I still pitch here and there for the local St. Louis clubs, but ever since I hurt my shoulder back in '92, I just haven't been the same out there in the pitcher's box. And, now that they changed the rules so that the pitcher is sixty feet from the batter, I have a hard time putting the ball in there like I used to. Baseball was good to me, and I'll always love the game, but I'm not the player I once was. Still, next time I suit up, I'll make sure you're there to see it. You and Clarence both. He can tell you about what's happening on the field."

"As long as I get to sit in the stands and just watch," Clarence says.

"Don't worry, Clarence, we don't have parades before our local games. Based on everything you've told me about your adventures, though, I'd say you're just as lucky as ever and would probably still make a great baseball mascot, but I don't think anyone will ask you to lead parades again."

"I've always wondered, John, these past seven years. Do you still have it? My baton?"

"Of course. I told you I'd keep it until Ireland was free, didn't I?"

"I'm afraid everything I had from our trip got destroyed when the vigilantes burned down my cabin on the Milk River, John. I don't have anything left from those days anymore. No more boomerang, no photo of the cricket grounds, no craps dice, no souvenir program from Delmonico's. It's all gone."

"It's the memories that count, Clarence. Now you have a sash, so you can start a new collection of memories."

"Well, I do have one other new memory to start from, I guess."

"Really? What is it?"

"I finally saw a buffalo. When coming down to Fort Benton from the Sweetgrass Hills."

"Your dream. That's why you went to Montana in the first place."

Clarence nods, smiles, and finishes the cup of coffee. "I'm gonna walk around for a bit, John, so you and Mary can talk for a while. If you plan to take care of her and be her father, you'll need to get to know each other."

"What are you going to do in St. Louis, Clarence?" Mary says to him.

"I don't know for certain, Mary. We'll see what my luck brings me next."


*Clarence's adventures continue in book four of the Clarence Duval Series*, Darkness in Dixie.

If you enjoyed this book, you can find other books in this series, as well as my works of historical research in baseball history, at my website:

robbauerbooks.com

You can also sign up for my Readers Club mailing list to receive notifications about future books and promotions. If you enjoyed reading the book, I would be grateful if you'd leave a short review on whatever website you purchased it from. Favorable reader reviews are very important to authors like me. They help tremendously in attracting new readers and spreading the word about existing books you think others will enjoy. Finally, if you like the book, please consider recommending it to fellow readers of new and original historical fiction.

Thank you!

# About the Author

I'm Rob Bauer, author of historical fiction and nonfiction books and owner of Rob Bauer Books. I hold a PhD in American History and was a Distinguished Doctoral Fellow at the University of Arkansas.

My fiction has two purposes—entertaining readers and explaining historical injustice. Although I enjoy adventure and humorous books as much as the next reader, I'd like my books to stand for something a little bigger. All my studies in history put me in a position to do that. Whether I'm writing about how racism damages the individual psyche, the deportation of the Métis people of Montana, the South's prison labor system, or the utter terror of the Belgian Congo, with my books you'll find yourself in powerful historical stories.

I also write nonfiction about baseball history because I've always loved the game, its history, and its lore. I sometimes joke that baseball may be the one thing in life I truly understand. Although I love the statistical side of the game, if you don't, never fear because my histories go light on the statistics and heavy on what baseball was like in the past. They're stories about baseball, but stories with a point.

The history blog on my website offers posts on a variety of interesting historical figures and events. I'd love to have you follow along.

When I'm not working on my next story or writing project, I enjoy spending time at the beach. And, oh yeah, I still read a history book or two. When I'm not watching baseball.

# Acknowledgments

I also want to thank the people who helped make this book possible, especially Jim Soular for his help with editing. Ali Holst gets the credit for the cover art and design. Thank you to E.M. Bosso, Mary Asplund, and Jennifer Johnson for reading and making suggestions on various chapters. Thank you to Kyle Lockwood for helping improve the chapters regarding military life in the late 1800s. But, above all, thanks to Nicolas Vrooman for his help with all parts of this book. Without your teaching and research, I would never have come across this story on my own and would know next to nothing about the history and culture of the Montana Métis. I just hope I've done their story justice.

Made in the USA
Middletown, DE
05 March 2021

34918060R00177